AGAINST THE RUIN

Dana G. Devine

James
Without you
this would
be nothing.
Thank you!

She is his heart....
He is her armor....
—Author Unknown

Dana G. Devine

BOOK ONE
OF THE TRIDENT TEAM TRILOGY

Dedication

In loving memory of my worshipped, loved, and adored late husband, Frank P. Devine, Jr.

I am eternally grateful for every minute you loved me. I know I was not your first love, but I was honored to be your last. I will miss you deeply until the moment I awake beside you again. Thank you for making me a part of this wonderful family. Thank you for the gift of these fantastic sons and phenomenal grandchildren. Thank you for encouraging me to "write the book" when you were alive. I hope I made you proud.

For my beloved late father, Philadelphia Police Lieutenant, Giacomo Giovinetti who created the core tenant of this story over 30 years ago, and for my beautiful warrior mother, Diana Casanova Giovinetti who left me the prologue and asked me three months before her death, "Please, write the St. Michael book when I'm gone..." Mommy, I did it!!!!

This story is dedicated to the men and women who wear a badge every day, working tirelessly to protect and serve us, even the misguided and ungrateful. To every courageous first responder who ceaselessly operates in secret to rescue our missing children, may God and St. Michael constantly guard your mission.

St. Michael the Archangel,

defend us in battle.

Be our defense against the wickedness and snares of the Devil.

May God rebuke him, we humbly pray,

and do thou,

O Prince of the heavenly hosts,

by the power of God,

thrust into hell Satan,

and all the evil spirits,

who prowl about the world

seeking the ruin of souls.

Amen.

Acknowledgments

With my whole soul I thank my dearest, treasured ride-or-die, Christy Lamagna who I could never repay in three or four lifetimes for your friendship, support, love, and impeccable counsel. Thank you for always knowing when I needed the sound of your voice. A million thanks for always being the smartest guy in the room.

Humble thanks to my baby brother, Michael Giovinetti—my anchor –who always knows what to tell me at the one-yard line and his beautiful family, my true sister—Dana Marie Giovinetti, and my niece and nephew Giuliana, and Michael. For everything, all the time, always.

My adoration and big thank you to my kids, Chris & Nicky Devine, and my perfect granddaughter Rowan. For loving and validating me as a Mother/Mother-in-law and a YiaYia. For the calls, texts, and Sunday dinners to remind me that though he is gone, his beautiful memory is held close by all of us. My love for all of you is immense and eternal.

Thank you to the underground advance reading circle who endured every rough version of this story and inspired me to keep going. Your encouragement, suggestions, and nudging helped me get to the finish line. Patty, Debbie, Christy, Lisa, Helen, Sooz, my beloved cousins, Suzanne & Linda. Also my darling godfather, Lou Casanova.

An enormous thank you to those who formed

the vortex of my daily existence when I wrote the first six drafts. You made every generous accommodation to afford me the freedom to write uninterrupted and unfettered; Fran Devine, Rachel Keenan, and my very own Titans of Chaos and true loves of my life; Franky, CJ, Ayden, and Mikayla. Thank you for the many nights you, delivered hot cups of coffee to my home office and the walks for Dash & Chima. For the many times you came to silently hug me and remind me that I do not grieve your legendary father/grandfather alone.

A very personal thank you to the Widows: they called, texted, visited, and encircled me in their solidarity with empathy, compassion, and experience when I first lost my beautiful husband. I'm infinitely grateful for your love, wisdom, and silent understanding. Especially my own "Cat," Debbie Romano.

To the young widows of my past who served as an inspiration of unwavering courage, which kept me from drowning in the oceans of despair, specifically my late mother, Diane, and my adored, deceased godmother, Aurora. Your examples were a life raft to me in the first year. May you now rest in peace and reunion with your treasured husbands.

Thank you to my beloved friend, James Rota for his phenomenal cover design.

A very special thank you to Dr. Jason Bradley and Dr. Ali Keramati for keeping my legitimate broken heart beating.

"....He who learns must suffer. And even in our sleep pain, which cannot forget, falls drop by drop upon the heart, until, in our own despair, against our will, comes wisdom through the awful grace of God."

—*Aeschylus*

Prologue

Mont-Saint-Michel
Normandy, France
Present Time

"I can see a strange light, Brother Joachim. It fills me with warmth. What is it? Is someone there?" Brother Luke said.

The two monks were working in the field, collecting snails in the marshy grasses. One was a blind man who could see only shadows since the day he had climbed to the highest limb of a great oak tree and, in his excitement, tumbled to the Earth. The other was a younger man who was disillusioned and morose about his life and all his duties. The blind man exclaimed again, "The light, it hurts my eyes! What is it? Is someone there?"

"No, Brother Luke, there is nothing. Only the last rays of the sun striking something that's glowing out on the moor, perhaps a bit of metal left from the war. Do not be troubled. It grows late. We must return before dark." Brother Luke strained his poor, rheumy eyes, wiping them roughly with gnarled fists, struggling to peer through the fog he had lived with for so many years.

"No, you are wrong. I see something out there. It seems to take shape I tell you." It was difficult for him to contain his excitement, but he suddenly knew he must hold his tongue. He felt a chill go through his body. Brother Joachim had already started toward the monastery. He grumbled under his breath, "The old fool will make me late for my supper."

Brother Luke stood motionless; his face turned toward the light he saw. His smooth, pink cheeks took on a glow and his mouth opened in an ancient, crooked grin. Silently, he crossed himself and tears of joy began to fall from his poor, dim eyes.

He whispered, "Thank you, Lord. I have waited for so long and now you've answered the prayers of an old, unworthy monk." He saw a shield made of hammered metal that was slashed in the center from a mighty blow and yet with enough smooth surface to cast a strong reflection. He saw a soldier, one knee bent as he prayed; his long, golden-brown hair hung down in burnished waves as he bowed his head. His bare arms were strong and muscled, tapering to large hands clasped in supplication. Then, while Brother Luke watched transfixed, the soldier stood and looked about him. The devout monk gasped at his mighty stance.

I know him! he thought. *I'd know him in a teeming throng of strangers. It is Michael, General of the Armies of God, Prince of the Holy City.*

While the monk watched in awe, he saw the soldier turn and walk toward a mighty sword, which stood blade down in the mud of the marsh.

Beside the sword could be heard an ominous rustling; it was a huge snake, its green scales glistening in the setting sun. It reared up and opened its huge hood, opened its mouth, and terrible fangs tested the air. Suddenly, the snake seemed to sense the presence of a danger more terrible than anything it could have imagined. It trembled, fell to the ground, and slithered away frantically. The soldier reached down and pulled the sword from the mud effortlessly. He took a piece of cloth at his belt and wiped the mud away. The metal seemed almost alive, lights dancing off it in streaks as he carefully rubbed it clean. When he was satisfied he stood perfectly still, kissed the hilt, and his image slowly faded out of sight.

Brother Luke scrambled to the spot where the soldier had been just seconds before but could find no trace of him. Even the grasses of the marsh showed no disturbance, no marks where the sword had penetrated. There was also no flattening in the grass where the snake had slinked away. Nothing to mark the spot where the saintly monk had just been witness to the most incredible scene of his entire life.

He fell to his knees in silent, thankful prayer. *Thank you, dear Lord, for sending him. We need his power and strength to save the world from complete annihilation. Without his help we will be destroyed, brought to nothing.* He wept, then, as darkness fell. Silent, happy tears flowed from his eyes and when he finally traced his steps back to the monastery he had missed his dinner; but it didn't matter, it didn't matter at all.

Chapter One

Summer was the favored season in Autumn Lake; yet fall could easily beat it as the town's most picturesque season. The coastal community was long emptied of its visiting tourists when the burnt orange and crimson foliage made its debut. The entire island took a deep breath and lazily returned to its sleepy, relaxed status. Even the surrounding air had reverted to its crisp, Indian summer smell and feel of its namesake.

The widow who lived at the far end of Gull Cove was walking her dogs along the shoreline. All the homes tucked within the large cul-de-sac were set back from the road, and were stone-fronted, two-story, beach-facing cottages. They were individually nestled behind large, weeping willow trees and low stone fences as if time and maritime marauders had abandoned them centuries ago.

Corrine Gladstone spied out from the window above the sink in her bright apple-décor kitchen. "Poor Aurora," she thought aloud.

Corrine had known Ben and Aurora Delsea only enough to wave politely from time to time during the summer, when activity was at its height in Gull Cove. "So young," she tsked as she admired her neighbor's courage from afar. Corrine shuddered at the thought of something so dreadful suddenly befalling her.

The Delsea's ocean view cottage was brand-new construction in the private development, completed only a year prior to Ben's sudden death. She was pleased to see that Aurora had returned; hopeful that it was a positive sign. Corrine had read all of Aurora's books and was optimistic there would be more to come. Maybe it was time to bring over a package of her famous desserts and pay her respects, she pondered. Normally, Corrine and her husband Glenn weren't inclined to acquaint themselves with their neighbors, but something about Aurora had Corrine unnerved.

The phone hidden in her cabinet rang, and she quickly picked up the call. She listened and replied, "She's back."

Aurora was trying to hide. Her friends and family sought to thwart her frequent efforts at seclusion, yet she had mastered the game for almost a year. She tended to fall between the cracks of other people's busy lives; at first, she had resented it, but the feeling was short-lived.

Since waking up a widow, she was prone to drape herself with the title, anticipating it would function as an invisibility cloak wrapped securely around her so that she would remain unseen. Aurora would have preferred to go on with her life wearing a warning sign as well, requesting that contact with her be made carefully and gently. People could say the most stupid things, and it was usually the ones who should know better. She felt broken in every way, raw to the touch, every nerve exposed, and she hated it. Death from a thousand cuts.

She had compelled herself to return to Autumn Lake; she was under deadline to finish the last novel that she contractually owed to her publisher. Aurora's faithful readers knew who she was and all about her recent personal tragedy. She craved camouflage from all the digital eyes watching her wrestle with this newest devastation in her life. They trolled her blogs and website for a clue as to how her writing would change, and which factual details would be woven into her next work of fiction. She struggled with the mental struggle to either suppress her personal pain or let it bleed directly on to the new pages. Aurora went through her days feeling like a baby sea turtle, hatched into a cold, new world and furiously trying to get to the water, dodging semitrucks and other imagined predators until she could stumble into the safety of the ocean.

She found some peace in her new daily routine of walking the dogs along the beach, stopping at Romano's for her morning coffee, wandering semi-anonymously down the aisles of packed shelves at Cookie's Book Nook, and driving around the quaint island running errands.

Writing was the current cause of her anxiety. Her original outline was a supernatural drama interwoven with an unexpected love affair. The concept now fizzled in her wrinkled and shattered soul. She could not relate to her characters and their blossoming romance. Aurora realized she could only currently generate feelings of melancholy.

It was as if her keyboard, her pen, and her notebooks would only divulge tear-soaked words and utter desolation. She hoped the sea air would ease the weight of her grief and prompt her to finish what she started. For Aurora, the major elements of life without her beloved late husband were difficult enough, but it was, ironically, the small facets that knocked her down from behind like a baseball bat to the knees.

Preparing a lone cup of coffee when it was the habit to stand at the Keurig and brew two. Finding the TV remote controls exactly where she left them. All correspondence addressed to her alone reading "Aurora Delsea" on a piece of mail meant for the two of them. Never matching his clean socks again. Driving alone to all the places they'd been together. Listening to music with lyrics was excruciating—she was forced to switch to only classical arrangements in her car and office. The first time she was asked to update her emergency contact information on a medical form reduced her to a sobbing pile in a corner. Cooking, her passion, was now joyless without him. If not for the pleas of her grandchildren, who granted her a month reprieve from cooking before they begged for her legendary French toast, she would have never cooked again.

Concerning the major things, the Gull Cove home was ground zero. When her first book sold famously, her husband announced it was time for their dream house at the beach. In his painstaking and loving way, he oversaw and conducted a large part of the construction. He directed all details, right down to the Italian ceramic tile backsplash in her fantasy kitchen and the stone fireplace with towel warming cabinets in their bedroom. Being here without him was more painful than being with her kids and grandkids at their home in Pennsylvania.

Their love story was on the walls and whispered from every corner of the rocky hearths. His handprints were everywhere—in every perfect cut of crown molding, each painted run of quarter round, and she could instantly summon the nights and afternoons they had christened each bedroom. The spaces echoed the sounds of their laughter, the muttered curses over the chop saw for a wrong measured cut, disagreements on paint color, and breathless, endless passion.

Aurora felt that the cheery little house was itself grieving the loss of Ben. The cottage seemed inconsolable. The water did not rush merrily from the showerhead as it used to, the oven took its time preheating to temperature. The first night she prepared the logs in her bedroom fireplace, they seemed to catch fire reluctantly.

Her two beloved Cavalier King Charles Spaniels were also experiencing his loss differently here. They ran laps searching for him from room to room and would only sleep on her bed in a nest made of his flannel pajama pants.

His unique scent of sawdust and lemon soap permeated everything, even the clothes still hanging in the closet and folded in bureau drawers. She was sure this was all overly dramatic on her part, but his absence gave her such extreme physical pain for such an extended time that she was certain it would kill her as well. It almost did.

Ten months into her sorrow, she awoke before sunrise and slammed into the reality of his death as she careened through each morning. One day her grief was different, she could now clearly grasp the concept that she would be forced to move forward without him. Time then mercilessly dragged her into each new day. It was on that morning that she got up and dressed, packed the bags and the dogs, and returned to Autumn Lake. She was finished avoiding the inevitable and accepted that it was time to confront the ghosts in her peaceful home. Time had elbowed her into the house to pick up the shattered pieces of her life that were now glistening on the hardwood floors.

Aurora was also facing a deadline four weeks from now to submit the last revision of her manuscript to her publisher, after which she was obliged to complete a press tour. Eight weeks on the road would have her missing Thanksgiving with her family but she'd be able to return home in time for Christmas. This would be the second holiday season without Ben, but somehow it did not seem like it would be easier.

Chapter Two

Aurora wasn't wrong to dread the call with her editor, she knew it was a "come to Jesus meeting." She'd been stalling and Jen was about to call her out. After a good nagging session, Jen arrived at a quiet conclusion.

"Rory, you are so close to finishing and I'm aware it feels very unnatural for you to edit and rewrite a love story right now, but you had an amazing and enviable romance. Those memories can be used for this plot."

As she had been during most of Jen's conversation, Aurora toyed with the loose string unraveling from her sweater, tears immediately rushing to her eyes. The boulder that now lived in her chest rose and fell with her shallow breathing. She refused to cry on the call with Jen.

"Rory, are you still with me? How can I help you?"

Hearing the concern in Jen's voice, she took a deep breath and reminded herself that she was the author.

"Jen, I will have it to you on the morning the bus picks me up for the road trip."

"Deal. Now, can we finalize the schedule?" she asked.

The schedule involved eight weeks of travel aboard a fancy, tricked-out-rock-star tour bus. Aurora had to admit she was a bit excited about not having to go to an airport, board a plane, or spend a lot of time in a hotel room. In a post-COVID-19 world, the scheduled appearances would already be strange and unconventional, but living and working out of a luxury home on wheels would be more adventure than she had experienced in a while. The dogs would be able to travel with her, and according to her editor, the technology on it would allow her to video chat with her grandchildren from anywhere on the road. The fan excitement for the tour was built up during the summer, with her website inspiring followers eager to meet her.

"One last thing, Rory," Jen started as Rory was ready to sign off. "Eli wants you to travel with a security team. In addition to your two drivers, there will be a security crew of three, rotating with you throughout the day."

Aurora sighed deeply, knowing the reason but not willing to admit it. "Really, Jen?"

"Aurora, not that I have to remind you of this, but you have a heart condition. Traveling with an assistant and a publicist isn't enough, they are there solely to manage the store owners and venue producers. Drivers handle the road. I need someone with you who can quickly secure medical attention, if necessary."

"I could have a family member make the trip with me…" she said reluctantly, inwardly shuddering at the idea of more strangers invading her space when she least wanted—or needed—the intrusion.

"Not on your life, literally, Rory! Eli and I discussed this with our insurance company and our legal department. We need you protected. You won't know if your ICD goes off since you could be knocked unconscious, and no one would know what to do next."

Heart condition, Aurora sighed. For months she'd awakened in the morning with what felt like an elephant sitting on her chest. Despair, grief, deep inconsolable sorrow yes, but she assured herself it couldn't be an actual physical heart condition. Until one afternoon when she couldn't catch her breath and the racing of her heart would not slow down.

"Takutsobo cardiomyopathy," explained her physician. The doctor, along with fourteen cardiologists, half of them electrophysiologists, gathered around her ICU bed and explained her unexplainable heart attack. It had not been caused by the 80 percent blockage they stented, but by her out-of-nowhere, erratic ventricular tachycardia.

"Broken heart syndrome," the lead doctor clarified. "You have been telling us your heart was broken; you were right, and now we are going to fix it," he explained. She had coded and flatlined before getting to the hospital and left with an implanted defibrillator in her chest.

"Heart condition," she repeated to herself, "That bastard really did break my heart," she chuckled. *But a security detail?* For the love of God, this was ridiculous.

Although this was the first time she was going out in person to meet her fans since she'd lost Ben, she felt too much fuss was being made. She was unsure of strangers surrounding her, but the concern over her heart condition was over-the-top. It had been months since her heart attack and except for the thin red scar above her left breast, she barely remembered she had an implant.

"Jen, I really wonder if this is necessary, legal and all aside. I haven't had any issues in months, and my doctors have checked me out and approved my travel. I'll be fine," Aurora tried again, using her most persuasive tone.

"No security, no trip," Jen shot back, her "I'm the Boss" tone brooking no argument.

Rory knew when she was beat, although she didn't like it. She grumbled, "Okay, okay. Where are we getting these people?"

"Eli is handling it. If you would like to meet and interview them prior, we can set it up to ensure you're comfortable traveling with them. I'm sure Sammy is going to want to be involved in the vetting."

Aurora choked on a laugh as her oldest stepson's insistence on involvement was an understatement. A former Marine scout sniper currently serving as a police sergeant in their suburban Philadelphia hometown, he had a bit of an overprotective streak and would insist on interrogating everyone traveling with her.

"Rory, Eli will hire them because insurance and

bonding will be through the publishing company. But I'll send the resumes and applications to you, and I'll let you manage Sammy."

"Wow, Jen, really? There is no end to your giving," Aurora snickered. She knew what was coming for those poor guys. Sam would probe them like a first-year lab student and once satisfied, probably buy them a few beers.

Eli Haas and his partner Marty Mendelsohn had been running their small publishing company for twenty years before Aurora came along. In the five years since they had signed her, they made more money on her books than the other twenty authors on contract. If they were forced to carry her by hand to every one of her appearances, they would do so, but they would not manage her somewhat intimidating stepson for her.

Chapter Three

Mackenzie "Mack" Egan was extraordinarily handsome. He was the type of beautiful that would qualify him as a magazine cover model—any one of them, actually—*GQ*, *Vanity Fair*, *Men's Health* or *Farm & Ranch Living Monthly*.

He exuded the impression of being equal parts lumberjack and US Navy SEAL, mostly since he had survived both those paths. Mack was not blatantly sexy, yet he was appealing in an unpolished and slightly abrasive way. He stood over six feet, four inches tall, rugged, and rock solid. His resting expression was a frown of intense thought—unapproachable and unwelcoming.

His mane of burnt umber waves was slightly peppered with silver and a three day's growth of beard framed his square jaw. His eyes were never the same color—one day a smoky gray, another a bright blue aquamarine. Mack's face held the vestiges of a dark past, etched with the shadow of things he should have done and regret for those he survived. No children, no pets, lingering PTSD flashbacks from his Special Ops days in Iraq, and an ex-wife with numerous addictions was how he would sum himself up in a few words.

It was going on a year since he had returned to the States and landed in the quiet shore town of Autumn Lake. The small metropolis was subdued enough for him after the summer tourists departed. The year-round resident community kept to themselves, and the neighbors were friendly but not nosy. Mack, himself, possessed no personal baggage that would invite social drama. His comfortable, ranch-style home was hidden at the tip of the island on a private beach. The panorama from his living room windows was stunning—provided he noticed it.

Ken Torres and Quincy Knight found their leader and best friend sitting in a corner on the floor of his sunken living room, a top-secret file beside him, nursing a clean shot of bourbon in a crystal tumbler. "This can't be good," they whispered simultaneously. Bourbon was for messy assignments—that was an unquestionable truth.

"How horrible is it, Boss?" they asked in unison. Mack stood from his yoga-like position and began to brief them.

Quincy and Ken were the two best and only friends Mack had ever made. The threesome had completed tours that made hell look like a Sandals vacation and would have given mortal men years of nightmares.

From their first meeting in BUD/S (Basic Underwater Demolition/SEAL) Training when they were green twenty-year-old kids, until now—twenty-five years later, they were inseparable. Their flashbacks alone were the stuff that Stephen King could fashion into a bestseller, but the stories they were cleared to repeat kept them from paying a bar tab in almost as long.

The intricate project they were currently planning was one of their trickier and more distasteful Dark Ops. Unbeknownst to Haas & Mendelsohn Publishing, Mack was creating a back story for himself and his team, which would allow them to hitchhike on to author Aurora Delsea's book tour and execute the sealed orders they had received at the beginning of the month. Their handler had designed the Op knowing the author would hit all the places the team needed to be. The men had to seem like her rent-a-cop security team while managing a complicated string of arrests.

Days later the men met again virtually.

"It's set, Mack," announced Quincy from his secure home office. Ken and Mack, also on the Zoom screen, looked up quickly.

"All of it?" asked Mack.

"I have a guy who has worked at one of the publishing partner's homes for ad hoc security details. The usual shit, book launch events, teenage graduations, etc. He got the gig approved. She has a stepson, former Marine scout sniper, who wants to weigh in and she wants to meet us before they will approve the contract."

Mack sighed, "The son going to be an issue?"

Quincy sat back and lit a cigar, "Not that I can see, he's one of us. But the challenge is going to be our show of smoke and mirrors. With our complete credentials he's not going to believe we're only getting paid to babysit his mother, sorry stepmother."

Ken cut in, "We're using fake CVs; he could never review the authentic resumes. The guy's a frigging cop, he'll smell the charade in a hot second."

"Unless you want to read him in, Mack?" asked Quincy.

"Negative, the objective here is her protection. He won't approve of an alternate agenda. This is highly classified, and the targets are high profile—we can't risk a breech in information."

"What exactly are we protecting her from?" asked Ken.

"It's not an outside threat, it's her health. She has a heart arrythmia, which is considered like a seizure. She suffered a heart attack about six months ago and had an ICD/pacemaker installed. She wasn't permitted to drive for three months post-op. The concern from the publisher is this travel—if the hardware cannot pace her heart into sinus rhythm, it will shock her. No one on the staff is a certified EMT, which is where our credentials come into play. Ken, revise the CVs and emphasize the medical coverage we can provide."

"What else do we know about her? She lives in Autumn Lake, right? Have you seen her?" Quincy asked.

After securing the dossier from their handler, Dutch Jenson, Mack had completed a comprehensive information deep dive. He was trying to find anything Dutch had missed.

Two nights and untold pots of coffee fueled his research. He managed to reconstruct her entire digital footprint over the past twenty years.

She was a graduate of the University of Minnesota, holding two master's degrees; English Literature and he couldn't for some reason identify the second one. A former high school English teacher. Published author... great fan following... (her website needed some design work)... devotees and bloggers loved her small opus... (he downloaded them to his kindle). Although he didn't like a few online profiles who commented on her blog posts, there was nothing serious. Her social media documented the progress of building her beach house... (many pictures of her late husband sporting a belt of power tools)... had been married, but tragically lost her husband a year prior. It appeared she met him while working for the high school, he had been the principal. She was Ben's second wife; he had been a widower for two years prior to marrying her.

She loved to cook, had adult stepchildren, grandchildren, two cute dogs, and lived with her kids temporarily in Pennsylvania. Currently, she appeared to be sequestered in her nearby seaside residence on Gull Cove. He found it unusual that while she lived within walking distance of him, he had never noticed her or the house before.

He also learned what he already knew—she was scheduled to embark on a book signing and appearance tour shortly. Famous, beautiful, and broken was never an easy detail. Oddly, it might provide the perfect cover, one she would unknowingly be a part of.

"No, just pictures so far, I don't want to mess up the back story by running into her before the official meeting."

"Copy that, boss, now about the real reason we're going...."

Chapter Four

Mack stood undecided in the center of his walk-in closet. How does one dress to appear less threatening and safe? He rummaged idly through his dresser drawers before settling on something to wear. Today was the official meet day with writer Aurora Delsea. As expected, his so-called friends arranged for ensembles to be sent to him, shipped in unidentifiable packaging. Quincy won with the delivery of a pink rabbit suit like the one in the movie, *A Christmas Story*, which would probably fit him, it was so long. Ken came in a close second with the Paul Bunyan, leather, ass-less chaps, flannel shirt with cut out nipples, and ax. *Funny guys.*

Mack decided on black dress pants and a gray cashmere mock turtleneck. He wore his black and gray herringbone suit jacket on top. His goatee was trimmed and neat, growing in like the rest of his hair, reddish and gray. He eerily resembled Dickens's Ghost of Christmas Present from *A Christmas Carol*.

The offices of Haas & Mendelsohn were quiet on a Saturday morning. Most of the staff worked from their homes, which left only the admin team and Aurora's editor there to facilitate the short meeting. The few women in the office froze in their spots when they saw Mack. Not often in publishing did a girl get to see a cover model in the flesh.

Aurora was occupied signing papers when the men were ushered into the luxurious conference room. Jen Patterson was attempting to make quick introductions as she switched out the papers from in front of Aurora.

Mack could not comprehend what happened to him next. It felt like a wave had crashed into him. His entire body seemed to be having a visceral reaction to Aurora. His mind could not keep up with his instinct. Being in a room with her brought him back to his first days in SEAL training when he lived and breathed underwater. Something about her hauled him to the surface, and he felt for the first time he was breathing cool, clean air.

His body was responding to her with an inexplicable sense of recognition. Adrenaline was pumping into his system. His heart began to race, and he felt his face flush. Beads of sweat were forming across his forehead. *What in the actual fuck!* he thought, searching his pockets for a handkerchief. While most experiences in his life were smudged around the edges and fraught with hard to recollect intricacies, this moment was clear and lucid.

Apart from his sweet mother, women represented hard labor to him, and were enmeshed with feelings and moods that had only resulted in unhappiness. He took what he needed from the unlucky choices he made and went on his way. Nothing ever stuck to him. He looked to Ken and Quincy quickly as if they held an answer to a problem he couldn't solve.

Once alone, Aurora looked up to face them and was immediately surprised by their size and appearance. She wasn't sure what she was expecting, but they were not it. They seemed overqualified and a bit intimidating, except the blond guy, *what was his name again?* She hated having "widow brain," she just could not keep some of the important details she needed stuck in her mind. *Impressive* was the word that suddenly came to her.

"It's really nice to finally meet the three of you," she began, adjusting in her chair and taking the last sip from her cold cup of coffee. "You all come highly recommended, and my son was very impressed with your backgrounds."

The music of her voice brushed over the three of them. It softly blew into their ears, rich and soothing like sipping warm brandy in a log cabin during a snowstorm. These hard-as-stone men reacted to meeting her as if she had just tucked fuzzy blankets around them. Quincy and Ken exchanged covert glances, knowing this was going to be in some ways more dangerous than their overseas expeditions.

Mack Egan never fell into anything, and they were watching him career headfirst into an abyss he might never recover from. This woman's shroud of sadness was palpable. A woman in this kind of pain and distress, coupled with a potentially deadly condition, would be compelling to any one of them. They could see for themselves that Mack was having a legitimate problem. Every emotion he had ever repressed in his life was coming to the surface and scorching his skin. They would have a hard time saving him if she couldn't—or wouldn't—return the sentiments.

None of the photos he had reviewed did her justice, and Mack was swooning from being so near to her, hearing the sound of her voice, taking in her intoxicating scent, mythical beauty, and vulnerability. Knowing what he knew about her, his newly beating heart was also breaking.

He could sense the anguish coming off her in waves; her beautiful eyes glistened with tears that were right on the surface. He forced himself to stay in his seat and be nonchalant. Hands clasped together, he took his breaths slowly to squash his fight or flight reaction. He struggled with the uncomfortable urge to jump out of his chair and carry her off to safety. Mack fought all his impulses to look directly at her for an extended time.

"...I'm really quite mortified about this entire plan," she said, completely unaware of Mack's inner turmoil. "I'm not as frail and weak as Eli would have you believe. It's the arrythmia making everyone overcautious as it's not the type someone usually survives. But with the medication I have been quite normal and of course the ICD is a backup..."

Quincy cleared his throat and spoke very gently as he knew he could appear larger than he was and didn't want to startle her in such a small room. "Ma'am, how would you prefer we address you? Which title or name?"

Aurora was slightly taken aback, first by the tenderness from such a bear of a man, and the question was a new one for her. "My name is Aurora, most people call me that or Rory for short. Really, I'll answer to most anything. If you don't mind, please tell me your names again, and a little about yourselves. Lately, I've been terrible at retaining details on the first introduction."

Quincy and Ken spoke first and spent about five minutes each giving a short guarantee that though they were scary looking, they were there to keep her safe. They did not anticipate any shenanigans on the road from crowds but were keen to oversee the crazed book enthusiasts. They also assured her that in case of a medical emergency they were all extensively field trained.

The room stilled when it came time for Mack to speak. He hadn't uttered a word up to this moment. He took a deep breath, steeled himself, and steadied his gaze upon her. He never broke eye contact with her as he proceeded to recite the short bio he had committed to memory for this purpose. In his melodic, South African accent, the words were husky and genuine.

As she had done with his teammates, Aurora appeared to have focused her full attention on him. However, while she was looking at Mack, she wasn't seeing him. It was as if her eyes were covered in a gauzy veil, one that wholly muted the splendid man before her. There was a deep timbre to his voice and an accent she couldn't quite place. Her gaze settled on his very large hands, which didn't look real, but appeared to have been carved by a renaissance artist, intricate and strong. She thought for a moment that she would never bet against him in a fight. She focused on the diver watch on his left wrist—he was fiddling with it as he spoke and then her eyes caught the black corded bracelet around his right wrist. It was anchored by a silver charm attached to the ends. From her brief glance she determined it to be a silver sea turtle. "Ironic," Aurora mumbled.

Mack had a completely opposite experience. He looked intently at her, to forge all the details to his memory. She wasn't a supermodel, nonetheless she was very beautiful in her effortlessness. She was genuine, a bit clumsy, and absentminded— twice she had misplaced her glasses while he spoke. He saw the flecks of gold and green in her huge brown eyes. Apart from simple eye makeup, her olive-toned skin was scrubbed clean and smooth. He imagined it was velvety to the touch. He noticed a heart-shaped birthmark under her left ear, partially obscured by tiny hoop earrings. Her wavy, wind-blown dark hair was piled atop her head in a messy bun held together with two pencils.

Her perfect smile was framed by naked, plump lips waiting to be passionately kissed. Specifically, by someone who knew how. Her hands were delicate, and the light caught the diamond on her left hand as it sat atop her wedding rings.

He finished reciting his bio when Jen reentered the room.

"How are we doing in here?" she asked nervously. "Can I get anyone a beverage?"

Aurora shook her head as Mack tried to regroup from his fantasy of her mouth being crushed with his own.

"I think we are done," said Aurora amiably. "Gentlemen, you're hired. I can guarantee you will be bored to death on this trip, and I apologize for that. But I'll appreciate you being there if only to make everyone else feel reassured." Aurora stood from her chair and gathered her things. "If there is nothing else, Jen, I'm going home. Cookie has the dogs and I'm anxious to get back to the manuscript."

Jen looked around the room at the men who stood as soon as Aurora did, already appearing as sentinels near her. "Do you have any questions? Mack, Quincy, Ken?"

The men shook their heads and Jen said, "We'll be in touch with the schedules, travel arrangements, contracts, and per diem information."

Mack stepped forward from the pack, cleared his throat, and whispered, "Aurora, can we see you to your car?" He wanted to reach for her hand or place his on the small of her back to guide her to the elevator. Anything to touch her and be sure he could make a perimeter around her to keep her safe, but he fought back the need. He took her bags from her, instead, to carry out to her car.

Chapter Five

They departed together in Quincy's black SUV, which he was currently steering away from the garage. He was the first to speak once they merged onto the highway.

"Oh man, I have never seen you react this way to a WOMAN!!!!! And brother, we have been around some magnificent, uncomplicated women," Quincy belly laughed. "Did you clone her phone or drop a tracker in her handbag?" he asked, trying to breathe through his laughter.

Mack sat in the passenger seat, trying to shake off the gossamer around him. He was besotted and helpless, equipped with no skills to manage it. He turned to look at his friend in disbelief, when Ken answered from the back of the car, "I did, both."

The men burst out in raucous laughter. Of course, the tech guy, the ninja nerd, already had her packed and tracked.

"What the hell, Ken? She isn't a mark!" Quincy yelped.

"We have to know where she is starting now. As soon as the paperwork is signed we should meet with her and check out the house."

"Ken, this isn't a secret service detail, we are going on a road trip where she is signing autographs and doing Q&A sessions about her books. This thing plays mostly like a junket; I assume to drum up excitement on the new book due out next year. *If* she finishes it. Although, I'm not against clearing the house. And oh, by the way, we have currently violated twenty or more of her civil rights, for no reason at all," Mack growled, brows pulled into a severe frown.

"Mack, we are taking this incredibly seriously," Quincy attempted. "We have never seen you like this. Brother, have you ever been this close to losing consciousness? We will enjoy not only the ball-breaking opportunities this will provide us— opportunities, by the way, you have *never* given us. Add in locking up degenerate, fucking skells with watching you blush and fawn over a lady for a few weeks," he paused, "it will be like getting a pizza party after the Little League World Series."

Quincy leaned back in the driver's seat, flexing his coffee-colored arms. Not only did he remind his friends of a taller version of the actor Ving Rhames, but some days his voice sounded almost spot on. He was a grizzly bear, former college defensive end, Mississippi-born African American. His shiny, bald head and tightly trimmed goatee made him resemble either an exceptional killer or a great cop. He was actually both but could confirm neither.

"Mack, if your erection lasts longer than four hours you must consult your physician," Ken snarked. Quincy and Ken coughed with laughter again, while a small smile teased the corners of Mack's stern mouth. Of the team members, Ken was usually subdued and appeared least likely to possess a military background. Born and raised in Chicago, he was muscular and sleekly built, though shorter than his teammates. Under six feet tall, blond-haired, blue-eyed, and wiry, he was the geek of the trio. On the occasion Ken smiled, he had dimples for days.

"Seriously Mack, what the fuck happened back there?" asked Quincy. "You don't blush or sweat, you don't lose your cool, especially around women, ever. Of all the dangerous situations you've come up against, a pretty widow writer is your sweet spot?" Quincy was dumbfounded.

Mack shook his head, chewing on the inside of his cheek absentmindedly. "I have no answer for you, Quince," he said quietly. "This one is different… there's something about her… I'm definitely compromised. I should back out of this job. I can't explain it, this has never happened to me. I feel like a thirteen-year-old." He stared out the window, completely unnerved by the experience. And then he remembered—pretty widow writer—*bella scrittrice vedova*, the description and the divination came barreling into his brain from a long-buried memory.

Ten years was it? Had it been that long? It was in Italy—Rome specifically. He was there on assignment and killing time the morning after a one-night stand. She was a hazel-eyed blonde, one of the very rare ones that he stayed the night with, and he gallantly took her out to breakfast in the Piazza Navona. After they ate, ready to part ways, they idly strolled through the tourist trap of tiny stores. An older gypsy woman was situated at the end of the esplanade, seated before a threadbare, velvet-topped table. The girl had squealed with delight, *Let's do it, get our fortunes read*, she begged him. Mack agreed, rolling his eyes—confident that nothing and no one would convince him of a future hidden in a deck of dog-eared picture cards.

He handed the euros over to the woman as the cute blonde took a seat. The arthritic fingers of the gypsy shuffled the cards slowly, never taking her attention away from Mack. Her eyes were the color of pennies, shiny copper; he was entranced by her compelling stare. She dealt cards out in front of the girl and began to read them, speaking softly in Italian. Mack was barely listening as he stood behind the chair, constantly checking the surroundings.

No less than ten minutes later the reading was over, and the satisfied, giddy blonde jumped up from the table and began to happily recant the predictions. The gypsy woman stood from her seat and grasped Mack's hand. She forced him to look at her again, stepping very close to assure that his companion would not be privy to her conversation. Her expression was dire.

"Trovala! La bella scrittrice vedova. Lei cambierà la tua vita. Lei è la tua forza. Lei ha bisogno di te e tu hai bisogno di lei," the woman whispered urgently to him. *"Find her! The pretty widow writer. She will change your life. She is your strength. She needs you and you need her."* Mack nodded politely, acknowledging her quiet statement and quickly

left the area. It hadn't meant a thing to him then. He remembered thinking it was the oddest statement anyone had ever made to him.

Pretty widow writer, *bella scrittrice vedova*—it was lyrical—and he felt his heart seize. *Could it be?* All these years later and from the invocation of an old gypsy fortune teller? Was Aurora going to change his entire life? Impossible for her to be his strength. Nothing scared him. Why would she need him? For what exactly?

Quincy looked over at him with genuine concern. "Mack, what is it about her? I've seen some of the most splendid women to walk the Earth throw themselves at your feet," Quincy murmured.

"It's her sadness, she practically wears it," explained Ken quietly. "It's the ultimate aphrodisiac for men like us. You know, knights-in-fucking-shining-armor. And you are not backing out of this job—Dutch has been lining up these targets and baiting them for months. I also hate to break it to you, in case you missed it, she doesn't see you that way. We have experienced the reactions of women around you. She is shattered in several hundred places and clearly not looking for romance, so you can be like the rest of us and worship from afar."

Quincy took the exit off the highway, nodding in agreement with Ken's careful assessment of their potential mess. "This bullshit sideshow is going to have to wait a few more days. We have to meet up with Dutch in the morning to map the rest of this trip out," Quincy stated. "You gonna be okay now, Mack?"

Mack stared out the window at Autumn Lake, wondering how he would ever be okay again.

Alone, Mack paced barefoot through his ranch, the enduring image of Aurora still close to him. He attempted to identify what exactly it was about her that seemed to have set him on fire. He could feel parts of him awakening with a new yearning.

He consistently ran through the images in his head. Dark, untamed waves of hair scented with flowers. She was tall, her head came to his chin as she walked in front of him to the elevators. Kaleidoscope-like brown eyes with changing bright flecks of green and gold, olive skin, a beautiful mouth. Her body, or what he could see of it in her loose-fitting clothes, seemed soft and curvy in all the right places. Yet, what he felt was clearly much more than a physical attraction, it was her presence. It was practically mythical— she seemed like a sad, sleeping goddess. The air around her, the scent of her perfume, the lingering of her laundry detergent pulled him in. He was ignorant of how women radiated a light aroma in their wake, which could intoxicate a statue. She was dressed simply, a nondescript black sweater, dark wool pants, simple jewelry. Her speaking voice was a raspy, whisky baritone and soothing, as if she read bedtime stories for a living.

This was a new experience for him, and it was haunting. Never was a distraction put in his path during an operation of this magnitude. Naturally, she would also be the most unavailable woman in the universe.

Twenty-five years prior, Mack was married to Deanna for six months and he spent three of those in Washington State, working a logging camp. They'd been drunk kids who met in a Vegas bar; twelve hours later, soaked in tequila, they stumbled into an Elvis Chapel and bought a cheap, quick wedding. They spent the next half year trying to undo the travesty. He awoke the morning after his drive-thru nuptials, realizing the illusion he had married. In the bar she had been sweet; a freckled face, corn-fed, Kansas-born brunette, with sleepy blue eyes.

In the morning, Deanna was an addict in withdrawal; mean, bitter, and concerned only for her next fix. Realizing Mack wouldn't invest in her lifestyle, she did anything she could to make their short time together dismal.

Once clear of his doomed marriage, he found no need to entangle himself with another woman. His work kept him mostly sequestered and his daily routines and comforts neither required or desired companionship.

There was a personal fallout from his biggest mistake. For self-preservation, Mack was emotionally paralyzed, numb, and kept to his vacuum of isolation. International spies and highly skilled female counterintelligence agents targeted him. Magnificent, dazzling women and some men, with extensive covert training tried to tempt him, seduce him, force him to lay bare his secrets. He was stone-hearted and cold in the face of their onslaught.

Why was it Aurora Delsea? In one glance she had shattered his reason and stole his breath away. She gave him sensations and feelings he had never known he was capable of. Suddenly, he sensed hunger and need, the ache of empty arms, and a cold bed. His mouth wanted to taste, kiss, and keep her to himself. He was overcome with an instinct to shield, comfort, and protect her; from what, though, he could not grasp.

He didn't know where or how to begin, yet he knew he would do anything to have her. "Knights-in-fucking-shining-armor, indeed," he whispered to himself and smiled in the dark room "... *bella scrittrice vedova.*" Raising his glass of bourbon, he tipped his glass to the empty space.

Aurora was cushioned and safely embedded within her cocoon of grief. It was like a concrete bunker—dark, damp, and cold. She sat alone, surrounded by the beautiful memories of her love story with her late husband. She could spend hours sadly looking through their digital photos, reliving the moments and searching for inspiration for her fictional characters. With a hot cup of coffee, all she required at this moment was the sound and smell of the Atlantic Ocean.

She opened the windows to her office to let in the sea breeze and sat at the computer, staring at her half-finished manuscript. Her dogs, Tim, and Sydney, were snoring at her feet. She was gladly interrupted by the Zoom call with her amazing grandchildren, The Titans of Chaos, crashing into her reverie. All of them, one screen after another, tiled onto her monitor.

"YiaYia, when does the bus get there? Is it pimped out like an old Aerosmith tour bus? Are we going to be able to meet you on any part of it? Are you going to bring presents back for us? Can you tell us all the places you are going? Is Bon Jovi going with you? How are you feeling? Are you taking your medicine? Did the box in your chest shock you while we weren't there? What are Tim and Sydney doing? Are they still looking for Poppy? Look at what I drew for you YiaYia..."

The questions came fast, furious, and tumbling on top of each other, as usual. The children ranged in ages from four to thirteen and their awareness of her mild fame was comical. These remarkable kids were the greatest gift from her beloved husband. She was a late bride—forty when she married widower Ben Delsea. Never having any children of her own, he gifted her stepmother status to two unruly adult stepsons. But the best prize of all was their grandchildren. Being a grandmother was like a holy vocation to her. Tragically, none of the kids were born before Ben's first wife passed away, making Aurora the only paternal grandmother they had ever known. She acquired the role with grace, honor, and pure, unconditional love. "Slow down, you punks!" she laughed. "YiaYia can only answer one question at a time."

"Seriously, YiaYia, are you okay down there

alone?" asked her oldest granddaughter. "You make me worry."

"I'm fine, cupcake, it's quiet here and I have to finish my last book or I'm going to be in big trouble," she explained. "Now you guys, one at a time, catch me up," she said happily.

Chapter Six

The Church of St. Michael the Archangel sat unobtrusively on the Upper West Side of Manhattan. After the morning masses, it was a quiet day with confessions scheduled later in the afternoon. The community was recovering from a terrible scandal around the holidays when their longtime pastor was arrested and whisked away on charges of sexual assault of a minor. The small parish felt rudderless. It had taken the remaining priests of the church by surprise and even longer to recover. They welcomed the brotherhood and assistance of their sudden new addition from France, Father Micah, to the small rectory.

Since his descent to Earth, the Archangel Michael secretly resided in the human form of the young priest—Father Micah—a man with shoulder-length, wheat-colored hair, and eyes of golden light. He spent most of his time alone in prayer, strolling the grounds daily and reading his Divine Office. He covered early masses and presided over sacraments to lessen the heavy schedules of his fellow priests. Once in the privacy of his room, he spoke directly to the Almighty, who suddenly appeared to him embodied as an elderly priest.

"Father, the time grows closer," Michael whispered, taking a knee before him. The older man motioned for him to rise and sit across from him in the small room.

"I still don't agree, they have free will and everything that comes with it." The older man replied.

"Father, the children. Can you not hear their cries, their agony, and their relentless invocation of your name and intercession?"

"Michael, are you questioning my plan? This is unnecessary for you," said the older man.

"Never Father, but I know my role in the plan and the time is coming. This has far surpassed the evildoing of men; this has become massive worship and adulation to my fallen brother. We can balance the scales."

The older man sighed in resignation. He began to pace the small office, his hands clasped behind his back.

"Father, I have waited for this day, for this moment in time. She has made her choices, she can always use her free will, but I do not see her wavering. Your armies have trained for it. Please, Father, no more wasted time before saving these children. Too many have been sacrificed already. Should we have let them all suffer these atrocities in vain?"

"Michael, they have chosen their way as all my children do prior to their birth. Their lives, their deaths, and the suffering along the way to their final rest in paradise was agreed upon.. You must consent to their redemption; even the vilest, most unrepentant of my children."

"Father, I know we cannot eradicate the crimes,

but my brother backs the enemy, it's my duty to step in and make this a fair fight, when the time is upon us. Give me the word when you agree?"

"And him? He has found his way back to her—will they fight together?" the older man asked with intrigue. Father Micah grinned confidently.

"He was born for this battle; they will find each other as they always have. Sadness cloaks her, yet I don't doubt him, Father."

"Michael, he'll know once you take over. He will glimpse their future trials, he could waver." The older man warned. "They are still human, my son, and they don't retain their past memories on this plane. At any time, they can take steps in the opposite direction."

"Father, I stood between them when this was first discussed. Together they agreed and chose their army. Free will brought them here, and once they unite, nothing on this Earth can divide them."

"This is only your opinion. Again, never underestimate your brother. He wields temptation the way you strike with your sword." The older man placed his hand on the young priest's shoulder and touched his forehead with a kiss.

"Yes Michael, my beloved general, it is time. Send her the dreams, let her see Roscoe. It's all you can do, the extent of it. You cannot augment her faith, merely reinforce it. "

The older man disappeared and left the Archangel to contemplate his next moves.

Chapter Seven

Dutch Jenson was a salty, old-school leatherneck. Former Marine, former CIA, former college football player, and a current ghost. It was as if he never existed. He was untraceable. Dutch Jenson wasn't even his given name. He towered over six foot, six inches tall and retained his military fitness, considering he was on the short side of sixty. Shaved bald and sporting a perfectly groomed mustache and beard framing his stunning smile, Dutch's luminous, hazel-green eyes could reveal profound sadness, followed by the twinkle of a troublemaker almost instantaneously.

No one could decipher his body language or extensive collection of disguises; he was a highly skilled undercover operative and expert forensic profiler. He was doing what he loved most—hunting and catching exceptionally bad men and women. He trained his entire career for the opportunity to apprehend anyone who hurt children. Coordinated under the aegis of the FBI's New York field office, he had built a private Special Forces company and black ops site. It was an extensive command center to accomplish his life's work.

His home, location confidential, served as headquarters for his company, Trident. The entire basement was a Sensitive Compartmented Information Facility (SCIF) from end to end and a complete wall was covered in forty 56-inch monitor screens with various communications and private data relays. Ten people worked for him full-time, all young adult orphans with phenomenal digital acumen. They were commuted to the location covertly every day. Their non-disclosure agreements read like a State Department dossier. Each one of them had an intricately devised back story and sets of ID's. Their job was largely to scour the internet and dark web for human trafficking leads. Most of his crew were former victims of horrific abuse and had invaluable inroads to back channels. They worked intel gathering and research. Dutch also paid for and vigilantly made sure that they remained in therapy sessions to complete the mental healing from their traumas as young children. A smaller, internal squad were former FBI who focused on identifying local rings of predators. Those men and women posed as children on various apps to lure the spiders directly to the web. Dutch was encouraged by the slow process to get to the head of The Culebra, the snake.

Seated in the secure space of his office were Trident's most trusted partners, Alpha Team: Mack, Quincy, and Ken. The years they had worked together accumulating hundreds of arrests and extensive jail sentences for various international criminals was impressive. After serving their time in the Middle East, they operated privately on kidnapping and ransom extractions for insurers across the globe.

This would be the first time they were wading directly into the dark water of miscreants who targeted children. Even with the ugliness they'd collectively seen, entering this realm was a whole new level of evil and all three of them were cognizant of this fact.

"How did the meet go?" Dutch asked, as the men fidgeted in their chairs. Something was off, their body language seemed less assured than typical. No one was making eye contact, squirming as if they had just returned from knocking up the head cheerleader.

Shifty fuckers, he thought to himself. If Dutch was anything, he was a profiler first. He looked them over carefully, "There is no way you three screwed this up. Aurora Delsea is like a bag of cotton candy, not one hard edge," he growled, annoyed at the potential that this op could go sideways.

"Boss, do you know her?" asked Ken suspiciously.

"With the amount of intel I personally gathered for this job, I know how Mrs. Delsea likes her steak prepared. I would have uncovered an issue way before any of you could have," Dutch responded.

"Boss, no problem. She's a piece of cake. We flew under the radar with the son, the publisher, and her, so we're all clear. Our contracts are signed, and we report to her home in Autumn

Lake next Monday," Mack said, his voice firm and steady.

Dutch watched him closely, noting that Mack avoided his gaze while giving his version of the update. "Somebody give it up, because there is no fucking lying to me, and you should all know better," he spat.

Quincy calmed the older man easily, his deep tenor voice blanketing the room.

"Dutch, no one is lying, pump the brakes. She, well, she's a damsel in distress, you know. It comes off her like smoke, so we all got a rush of the overprotective big brother vibe for her. Nothing to worry about," Quincy soothed, knowing most of what he said was true.

Dutch sat back, slightly mollified and chewed on the edge of an unlit cigar. He watched the trio attempt to suppress their cues.

"I don't have anything to worry about, right? No diversions, distractions? Not even you three can defend her from what she is battling. Take it from me, I'm a widower fifteen years. There is no magic, only time. You guys are about to stand on a whale, so don't go fishing for minnows, stick to the mission."

"Dutch," Mack interjected, "she has a double master's degree from the University of Minnesota. One is in English Lit, which fits her résumé, but I can't find any record of the second degree. I've looked everywhere and it's not listed in the University archives, her résumé, or any of her bio collateral."

"And this is important why?" Dutch asked incredulously.

"It's noticeable in its absence," Mack replied. "Who hides an accomplishment?"

"I'll call the dean of graduate studies in the morning if this minuscule detail will suddenly make you better equipped to perform a security detail for a widowed author," Dutch mocked.

Mack let it go for now, but something about the *minuscule* detail and its concealment rang a bell for him.

Dutch passed each man a thumb drive and brought the contents up on the screen. "Gentlemen, this is Operation Pied Piper. The itinerary should mirror the schedule from Haas & Mendelsohn. Make extra sure it does, because we are up to the exact minute and need any modifications as soon as you get them. You meet the tour bus in a week."

"The rotation requires one of you to always cover Aurora, one sleeping, and the other driving the backup Escalade following the bus. Included on the thumb drives are the backgrounds of the people traveling with you. Two employees with the publishing house, a publicist, and an assistant for Aurora. They handle her timing, touring, interviews, and personal attaché. She grew up with the assistant, knows her extremely well." Dutch strolled the office as he recited the details.

"She hasn't met the publicist yet, but she reads as a fluff job, nothing to her. Keep an eye on her, she's a new contractor for the publisher, so there's no history with them. The two bus drivers will rotate, she knows one—worked with him years ago when she was teaching. The backup driver is a stranger as well, nothing in his background is interesting, and if anything, he's too clean, so be cognizant.

"Several of these stops involve hotel overnight stays. The bus won't hold sleeping accommodations for everyone. When they park overnight, one of you, the scheduled morning driver and Aurora will stay on the bus. Hotel nights are for the overflow or if one of you need a bigger bed for a night or two. All expenses use cash, no paper trail; log and destroy your receipts."

He handed them three thick manila envelopes with the money.

"Whoever pulls the overnight shift stays wherever she does. She doesn't sleep without one of you within spitting distance. As for our takedowns, they are fluid. You will have local backup, US Marshals, and field agents. Regional Child & Family Services will be on-site for the rescued kids. I'm waiting for the last of the warrants, so all the paperwork will be ready. If our timing works, there should be one each week. Arrests will fall on non-travel days and around the scheduled appearances, they will never notice you're missing.

"Again, not all three of you on the pinches, one of you always with Aurora. Of course, any one of these assholes could change up their routine. My kids will keep you up to date on locations."

Dutch rose from his chair and whistled out the door to his lead project manager, Kai Adams.

Kai, a slight, young man with short, spiky ebony hair, Air Pods, oversized glasses forever sliding down his nose, and a pocket protector filled with multicolored styluses, looked every inch the Geek Squad genius he was. Give him a computer and he was instantly the smartest guy in the room.

"Kai, send the file now to their secure phones and we can check the download before they leave the Faraday room," Dutch ordered. "Any questions?" He looked over his men again carefully.

The men looked to each other silently and shook their heads, not a question among them.

"Excellent. Kai will be your direct contact but call me with anything major or if you see a conflict in the timing." He paused for a moment, measuring his words.

"Don't go in hot like medieval knights trying to rescue Aurora. She's a grown woman and appears to have survived life before meeting you clowns, her tricky heart condition notwithstanding. As soft as you've suddenly become, Aurora is not the mission. I can't imagine the book tour is going to encounter any surprises, but what the fuck do I know about Barnes & Noble events," Dutch said dismissively.

Chapter Eight

The collective Delsea grandchildren were enthusiastically examining the tour bus in Aurora's driveway.

"YiaYia, this thing is *sick*!" they declared as they ran from front to back, checking all the cabinets and drawers, undoubtedly pushing every button, and managing to lose the remote controls to the televisions. Her sons were watching their kids enjoy the bus as they carried her bags out to the driver.

"Let's go kids, help me get my stuff to the back bedroom," she asked them.

"Holy balls, YiaYia," her oldest grandson whispered. "This is like a Four Seasons back here!" he puffed proudly to her. "I'm taking some pictures, need to flex on Instagram how cool my grandmother is!" he laughed.

They were inspecting the technology in her private suite. Oversized monitor, desktop, hubs for her laptop and tablets. She could write, use the internet, and Zoom with the kids while she was on the road.

The last of her things were loaded when the kids sent the dogs up into the bus. The Escalade pulled up with her security detail and a rideshare dropped off her assistant. Mack, Quincy, and Ken loaded their bags on to the bus and briefly introduced themselves to the driver and Aurora's stepsons.

Billy Taylor had been a driver for centuries, and a school bus driver back in the day when Aurora was teaching high school. He was a tall, thin man with diminishing gray hair and droopy brown eyes. Billy always reminded Aurora of a loyal basset hound. She was thrilled to see him on the trip. He wrapped her in a hug and kissed her forehead. He wanted to mention Ben but looked sadly into her eyes instead. She nodded in understanding; he suffered a loss as well.

"Come on, old girl, get your ass on board, I have a schedule to keep!" Billy's voice rumbled, and Aurora was transported back to years earlier when Billy's voice kept schoolchildren in line on the buses.

Aurora hugged and kissed all the children and her boys, boarding the bus with two of her three "special" overseers. She winced inwardly.

Sam, always the pragmatist, caught her slight grimace, and commented, "Aurora, it's for your own safety. You'd prefer one of us take leave and tag along?" he joked.

Aurora looked even more pained for after the heart attack, her boys and the kids had practically wrapped her in cotton batting. "No!" she laughed, feigning to elbow him out of the way. "At least with these three, I'll get my way… sometimes!"

Quincy and Mack were taking the first leg of the ride with her. It would be nine and a half hours to Bangor, Maine.

Debbie "Cat" Catanzano, Aurora's oldest

friend and remarkable assistant was the first to begin coordinating supplies in the bus. Since the fateful morning in grade school when they found themselves side by side outside the principal's office, they had been lifelong friends and sisters of the heart. Cat's resemblance to the late actress Natalie Wood, with her short, rich mahogany hair and big brown eyes was startling at first glance. She didn't stand taller than five-foot-six and was so feisty that no one—regardless of size— dared dish out any shit to her. Except, of course, Aurora. Cat was continuously at the center of the whirlwind that Aurora created. She was sure this trip would not be different, and it made her quite content.

Impressed with the luxuries available on the bus's supply list, Cat set up the coffee station on the counter, quickly placing a perfectly executed cup in front of her caffeine-addicted bestie seated at the kitchen/conference table. Rory's publicist for this tour, Eve Marcus, was meeting them in Maine.

The men were getting their bunks in order, as it had been decided that Quincy would take the first shift, while Mack would try to sleep during this stretch. Cat watched the two large men, eyeing the small bunks they would claim as home base.

"Dear God, Aurora, that man is breathtaking," Cat whispered to her as Mack disappeared to the sleeping quarters.

Aurora looked up at her, puzzled. "Who?"

"All three are literally movie star handsome. Do you not see it?" she asked, idly running her fingers through her brown-haired bob. Her warm eyes widened as she wondered aloud, "How exactly are those huge men going to fit in those tiny bunks? They might need a shoehorn, I have one in my purse!" she laughed. Shaking her head in bewilderment, she took a seat across from Aurora at the kitchen table.

Aurora was distracted by the work before her. Cat handed her books to sign that would go to the stores to use if there were any delays in the on-site sale lines. Quincy returned to hang around with them and talk to the driver "Miss Aurora, you will tell us when you need a stop for the dogs?" he asked

"They are good for now Quincy, thank you," Aurora replied. "My grandkids had them running around the lawn for an hour before we left. Billy mentioned he would stop in about three and a half hours for us. Roughly somewhere in New Haven. They will sleep under the table near me until then. Billy, lunch at Havana's near Yale?"

"Will do Rory—great minds think alike," he replied from the driver's seat.

"Aurora, did you see Tina Lupo's haircut?" Cat was idly scrolling Facebook while checking in on Aurora's professional social media sites.

"She cut her hair? She's had the same hair since high school. Has she ever cut it since we've known her?" Aurora asked.

"Yes, she cut it, and no never—it was down past her ass. Now she looks like Liza Minelli after her first stint in rehab," Cat snorted, holding her iPad out for Aurora to see for herself.

Aurora put her glasses back on, "Stop it! Who let her do it?" Aurora stifled a laugh. "That's a sin."

"The sin is, who let her dye her eyebrows? I wonder if they even own mirrors," Cat replied.

Mack lay on the bunk in the cramped sleeping quarters, reviewing the intel on the small town in Maine where their first arrest would occur. Listening to her voice was relaxing, and yet she sounded breathless. He wondered if the excitement of embarking had her heart off its rhythm. He listened more attentively as she continued to gossip with her assistant.

"You feeling okay, Rory? You look flushed." Concern was apparent in Cat's tone.

"Yeah, I'm good. It was a little crazy getting ready," Aurora shrugged her off.

Mack slipped down from the bunk and walked into the community center of the bus. The ladies looked up at him as he assessed her flushed cheeks and watched her short respirations.

Aurora eyed him quizzically, unfamiliar with a man's solicitous hovering since losing Ben.

"Slow breaths, Aurora," he said softly. "In through your nose and out through your mouth." His accent was heavy and musical. He squatted down next to where she was sitting and wrapped his fingers around her wrist. Her heartbeat was fast but normal. She slowed her breathing, doing as he instructed. Being so close and holding her wrist was transferring her rapid heartbeat directly to him.

"It's not Welsh," she said, absentmindedly, "but there's some British, maybe Scottish in there?"

He knew she was referring to his accent and ignored the question for now. "How much coffee do you drink?" he asked, still troubled by her rapid heartbeat.

"Oh no, please—don't you start," she pleaded, taking her hand back from his grip. "I'm not giving up anything else this year!" she exclaimed with stark exasperation. "I've had to sacrifice sex, three months of driving, chewy, delicious bacon, and red meat. There will be no more losses. I'm keeping caffeine and nicotine, regardless of the consequences." The look on her face was more mutinous child than adult woman, which Mack thought adorable.

Everyone laughed; Quincy responded from the front of the bus. "We got you, Miss Aurora, no one will mention it in their reports, and a good steak every now and then—or a strip or two of bacon— won't hurt you."

Still shaking his head from her list of sacrifices, Mack stood and retrieved a cold bottle of water from the mini fridge. "After each cup of coffee, drink a bottle of water; it will help your circulation and dilute the caffeine. Don't worry, I won't take your coffee away," he stated—but Aurora knew from his tone that it was actually an order, no matter how gently said.

"...and it's South African." He smiled, answering her inquiry about his accent. He looked at her longer than he should have, the color in her face was returning to normal as her breathing became more relaxed. Her presence overwhelmed him. Now her problem was his. His heart was beating into his ears; he had to move away from her. Just as quietly as he appeared, he vanished back to the sleeping quarters.

Good Lord, he thought, *how the fuck am I going to be near her for eight weeks without carrying her over my shoulder to my bed?*

Cat watched the interaction curiously. Aurora was entombed in the dark winter of widowhood. She was not seeing or sensing the beauty of anything around her. Cat remembered those days, back when she first lost her own husband almost seven years ago. She knew intimately how a widow constructs layers to live within to protect the fragile remnants of herself. Some days it felt as if you had been skinned alive and every nerve ending had been exposed. The walls of ice or concrete were necessary to keep anything else from getting close enough to brush up against you and inflict further injury. Aurora built a personal bunker of shelter around herself, mentally and physically, which included dressing like a caterpillar with oversized garments that were designed and layered to act as an impenetrable chrysalis.

In Cat's mind, the hot ginger security guard

was going to have a problem. He was already caught up in Aurora's magnetic force field, stacking all his chips along the table and she wasn't anywhere near the roulette wheel. Cat laughed to herself—this was going to be an interesting excursion after all.

Four hours into the trip, Billy pulled the bus into the parking lot of Havana's, an intimate Cuban restaurant on the outskirts of the Yale campus.

"Welcome to New Haven, folks," he announced, as everyone stood to stretch and Aurora leashed Tim and Sydney for a walk. Quincy helped her off the bus with the dogs, and she quickly walked them around the park next to the restaurant. She then left them in Billy's care on the bus while he enjoyed his takeout from Havana's to the droning of the TV news.

The remainder of the awkward group of travelers began to break the ice once seated in one of Aurora's favorite restaurants. With the sultry crooning of Celia Cruz enveloping them, the small restaurant transported them to a scene straight from Old Havana, surrounded by rough, patina-painted walls with wrought iron balconies, wooden bladed ceiling fans, and multicolored linens on the tables.

The floral centerpieces were small and tropical, with tiny blossoms of colorful orchids. The atmosphere was pleasant and inviting. Ken sat across from Cat, where they were casually discussing Aurora's daily routine and schedule.

Quincy and Mack sat across from Aurora and were struggling to find topics to talk about. They seemed new to idle conversation.

"I assume you must both be exceptional snipers, since you utterly suck at social conversation," Aurora commented dryly.

They laughed good-naturedly and Quincy responded, "It shows, huh?" while reciting their orders to the middle-aged server openly attempting to flirt with them.

Quincy admitted, "We're not used to being so close to our Package, we're usually on the perimeter. I can't remember the last time we had a meal with one, can you, Mack?" He turned to his partner to include him, only to find Mack's eyes fixed intently on Aurora.

"I'm a Package for sure," Aurora laughed, her self-deprecating humor rising as she fiddled with her phone, "Hot frigging mess is more like it. Say, can you use HFM in your wrist mic when referring to me?"

The food arrived before anyone could deny her request

"So, what do you do when you're not babysitting a famous celebrity like me?" she asked as she quickly stole a small empanada off Cat's plate. Cat mimed dry heaves in reaction to the celebrity description. Aurora didn't miss it and kicked her under the table.

"Global private security work," Mack replied, finding his voice at last. "We spent a few years working K&R extractions for insurance companies before we came back to the US last year."

"Now, that's cool," she gushed. "I'm sure your stories are epic!" She sipped slowly from her club soda and lime.

Quincy laughed, "None as exciting as Russell Crowe in *Proof of Life*—the movie made us professionals look ridiculous."

Cat looked up from her mojito and, with one raised brow, laughed, "Uh, beg to differ—nothing is ridiculous about Russell Crowe. You should tread lightly, as you're referring to Aurora's second husband," she continued knowingly.

All eyes turned to Aurora just as she bit dreamily into a crab croquette. Mack watched her, captivated. He concentrated on her gorgeous mouth and wondered if she tasted everything with the same intensity. His reverie was disrupted by Quincy's swift and hard kick to his shin beneath the table. The notion running through Mack's imagination was not difficult to decipher.

After swallowing, she smiled, "I used to threaten my husband that should Russell show up at the door, I was running away with him..." She paused for a beat, twinkle in her eyes, "For the sole purpose of coauthoring a cookbook with him titled, *Eating Crowe*."

Mack, even more mesmerized by her sense of humor, led the table in laughter, as the group began to thaw into a more comfortable dynamic.

"I must warn you gentlemen now, I have no

shame when it comes to food. I love to cook, and eating is the last pleasure I have on Earth," Aurora informed them, a tiny scowl escaping. "Red meat and bacon notwithstanding!"

She continued, "If you're uncomfortable sharing what you have, please sit far from me—perhaps at another table. I'm accustomed to pilfering off plates, with prior permission of course."

Cat could no longer contain herself, interrupting with, "What she really means is you were just issued your first—and only—permission request. Hence forward, if you want your entire order, seek cover—she's an unrepentant food thief. You will have to break out your rifles if you want to keep your bagel."

The men were enjoying their banter and ease of conversation. It was mostly at Aurora's expense, but she held her own quite nicely. There was no doubt the women were lifelong friends.

Aurora, used to Cat's outbursts, continued without missing a beat, "As I was saying, I'm quite relaxed about having my dish invaded as well. I'm trying to be on my best behavior right now as we've just met. It won't last long. It's been ages since I've dined out with adults. I'm used to small kids and teenagers and their penchant for what is on my plate tasting infinitely better than what exists on their own."

Mack was instantly accosted with images from the cult classic movie, *9½ Weeks*, with himself in the lead role slowly and erotically hand feeding her everything he had in front of him. To put anything past those lips…. He shifted in his chair, shook off the fantasy, and countered with a modest offer of a piece of his grilled pork chop.

"Oh yes," she accepted happily and transferred a portion of her patatas bravas and crab croquettes to his plate. Quincy surreptitiously served her a small slice of ropa veja with a wink. "Denying a woman red meat is communism," he whispered. Aurora smiled secretly at him. Quincy was quickly becoming her favorite.

Everyone loaded back onto their respective rides and settled in for the next five hours of the trip. According to Billy, they would stop outside of Portland, Maine, if necessary, otherwise he was heading straight into Bangor. Cat called ahead to confirm the hotel rooms and spoke to Aurora's publicist to verify the agenda for the next day.

Quincy helped Aurora open books to sign and packed them into the boxes for delivery to The Bangor Book Barn. Mack tried to nap but knew it was impossible. He returned to the large midsection of the bus to get involved in the production.

"Did you always want to be a writer?" he asked Aurora, as he opened a new carton of her latest bestseller.

She looked at him over her glasses, a shrewd grin spreading over her face. "Well, originally I wanted to be Nancy Drew, beyond her all I ever dreamed of being was a forensic pathologist. I watched too many *Quincy, ME* episodes when

I was a kid. You guys might be too young to remember that show."

"I remember it," Mack said. "They played reruns all through the nineties in Johannesburg— my mum is a huge fan of Jack Klugman."

"When we were young, my brother and I created an entire fake crime lab in our basement. We had test tubes and beakers and used our mom's Tupperware as petri dishes. It got serious when we received matching microscopes for Christmas one year. My brother would often storm through the house dramatically demanding, 'If the lab could get the results back any sooner than Easter, we could solve this homicide!'" she laughed.

"Rory, when is the last time you heard from him?" Cat asked nonchalantly.

Aurora stopped to think, "When Ben died, he was somewhere overseas. We have a rule, usually no longer than a month between calls. Since our parents died, we're all we have. I was kind of groggy, but I remember having a long talk with him when I was in the hospital—that might have been the last time."

Cat's attempt at casual interest didn't fool Aurora. She always wondered if Cat's childhood worship of her older brother had seeped into her middle age, but given her brother's career, a relationship was challenging. Quincy and Mack exchanged looks. This was a potential issue, as no siblings popped up on any of the three background checks on Aurora. Mack texted Dutch and was surprised by the instantaneous answer,

"Nonissue."

The bus groaned into the brightly lit parking lot of the Bangor W Hotel. Billy and the three men helped shift baggage and left to check in. Aurora, after settling the dogs, opened the back door of the rig and sat quietly on the step to have a cigarette. After her second drag, Mack came around the back of the bus, surprised to see her sitting there.

"Not a word," she whispered. "It truly is my last remaining vice and only coping mechanism."

He smiled and leaned against the bus, "Well, could I bum one from you?" he asked, "I've been quitting my whole life, I know the struggle."

Aurora smiled and handed him her pack and lighter. They remained there in silence until they were finished smoking.

"Are you ready for tomorrow?" he asked sincerely.

Aurora sighed, "I guess so, it's been a while since I've done a signing, I'm sure it's like riding a bike" she smirked and stood to walk back into the bus.

Chapter Nine

As darkness settled over Bangor, Aurora puttered around the makeshift bedroom. For a bus, it was quite luxurious; the dogs found their spots easily on the queen-sized bed. She chose the comfortable, overstuffed chair next to the desk. After installing her private internet router and setting up the wireless monitor to her ICD, she sank into the chair and logged on to read email and check in with her family. The sounds of Billy relaxing in his bunk, TV on low, and Mack trying to find a tranquil spot in the far end of the bus, were reassuring, as she had spent so much time alone recently.

Since Ben died, she hadn't slept through the night. Doing anything without him beside her had become a succession of cruel adjustments, sleeping being the worst of them. She would cuddle with the dogs and attempt it, but only capture an hour or two at a time. She woke suddenly at 3:30 a.m., her usual haunting hour. This time, slightly winded from a vivid dream, so she gave up trying to go back to sleep and went looking for something to drink.

Mack was sprawled on a recliner, his face backlit by his iPad. He was startled by her sudden appearance.

"Are you feeling okay?" He rose from the chair with urgency.

"Ignore me, I'm sorry to disturb you. Strange

dream…" she apologized and stopped herself before indulging too much information to him. "I don't really sleep well, so I'm going to rummage for snacks and a 'caffeine-free beverage,'" She mocked him with air quotes.

"I have Reese's Pieces in my overnight bag," he whispered conspiratorially. This was truly his final test for her—if she didn't like a Reese's product, he held no hope for their future.

"Oooooohhh," she whispered, her face lighting up with joy. "You holdout! Give them up!" She stood, tapping her fingernails on the counter in front of the microwave, waiting for the bag of popcorn she placed inside to finish.

He returned from his bunk with the bag of Reese's Pieces, watching as she opened the bag of popcorn and sprinkled the candy on top.

"What kind of mad potion is this?" he asked in awe, catching her excitement as he watched her mix the two things together.

"I call it '*Menopause Miracle Mix.*' Obviously, you'll never find a use for it, but I can promise you, the mood elevating combination of salty and sweet, coupled with the alliterative name, will make this a religious experience for you entirely," she assured him with delight.

Mack dug into a handful of Aurora's delicious invention and quickly became a fan. As he'd begun to notice at the restaurant earlier in the day, he was more and more enthralled by Aurora's "being." He was astonished at how easy it was for him—a lone wolf—to be with her. Aside from the outside package, which had surely captured him, "inside" Aurora was even more amazing—funny, relaxed, self-deprecating, unselfish, mischievous, and unaware. Most women flirted shamelessly with him, trying to impress him or seduce him with phony wiles. He wasn't used to a woman this natural, uninterested, yet real.

She looked adorable and showed no shame in her unmatched sleep wardrobe of pink yoga pants and an oversized University of Minnesota football T-shirt. It seemed to him that everything she wore was oversized, non-revealing, and did nothing to enhance her hidden figure.

Her hair was loosely swept up in a ponytail, with a few rogue waves framing her face. She had removed her eye makeup earlier and her eyes were currently alight over the concoction before her. She might be trying to conceal her charm, but it was obvious to him. He was genuinely doomed, and he was beginning to accept it. He was falling hopelessly and shamelessly in love with her, and she didn't give him a second glance.

"So, University of Minnesota, does that make you a Golden Gopher?" he asked, hiding the intel he had recently gathered on her.

She nodded, "Yep, Golden Gophers," she said as her delicate fingers put popcorn slowly into her mouth. Mack struggled with the urge to feed it to her.

"Did you play for the football team?" he joked, indicating the logo on her shirt.

She was so quick; her wit was sharp as a tack. "I did, I was the tight end," she grinned.

He laughed softly; this was completely new for him. She had no guile. He found himself wanting to banter with her endlessly.

She reached out to his right wrist to examine the black corded bracelet, "May I?" she asked in a low voice. Mack felt his skin tingle at her touch.

"Absolutely." He stretched out his hand toward her. Aurora spun the cord to look at the silver charm clasp.

"Baby sea turtle?" she asked, and he nodded in confirmation and launched into its origin. "I picked it up on Amelia Island when I was there years ago and last minute had the opportunity to watch the hatchlings race to the water," he explained, his voice gentle. "They have such instinct and raw courage." Her hand disappeared in his massive palm as she held it and touched the charm. The way in which Aurora's presence quieted him snuck up on him. He was made of granite and dark, internal storms but felt the calm and gentleness she surrounded him with.

Aurora released his hand and gazed up at him, "Odd… that's how I've been feeling lately. As if I suddenly became a newborn sea turtle, sprinting toward the ocean for protection. Ironic." The word came to her again and barely made it out of her mouth. The meaning was just beyond her reach— why the sense of identification and simpatico she felt with the animal? She only recently drew the parallel with the baby sea turtle and Mack appeared with it cast in sterling silver. There was a connection she couldn't make out—her brain was cloaked in grief.

He watched her closely and when introspection caused her nose to wrinkle, he almost sighed aloud. Silently, he made the internal vow that given the chance one day, he would never stop kissing her. "Would you like to wear it? Maybe it's linked to you. I've never grasped why I wore it—I'm supposed to be a big, bad tough guy." He smiled humbly.

She gushed with embarrassment, returning from her reverie "No, I couldn't, but thank you for the offer. Just so you know, it doesn't take anything away from your intimidation factor," she assured him with a wide-eyed smirk.

Mack took a deep breath and changed the subject "Do you have other secret combinations you would like to share?" he asked, helping her finish the last of the unholy alliance of popcorn and chocolate.

"Why Mack, a nice girl doesn't show all her cards on the first bus ride. I might have to play a little hard-to-get with the genius inventions," she teased lightly. "Someday, remind me to detail for you my most epic mixture. It's a coffee/hot chocolate thing with surprises. It's biblical. Speaking of which, are you going to throw me in the brig if I make a cup of coffee?" she asked, looking at him with what might have been her attempt at a death stare.

"Would you try a cup of chamomile tea? It

helps me sleep and doesn't include caffeine?" he cajoled. She silently contemplated this compromise while making strange and hysterical facial expressions that struck him as so funny he burst out in silly laughter. "That's a yes, then?"

"Okay, you tried my concoction, I'll try yours," she exhaled, heading back to the bedroom. She sent an encrypted email she had started earlier when Mack brought the cup back to her. She removed her eyeglasses and took the tea from him.

"Oh wow, it smells amazing," she said, breathing in the steaming herbs. "Thank you so much, it is truly kind of you to share your contraband. I promise to replenish your stock."

"My pleasure. Do you mind if I stay with you until you get sleepy?" he asked, not willing to walk away from her just yet.

"If you like, you can sit with me while I drink the tea. It's a novelty having someone to talk to other than the dogs, lately," she said wistfully. She relaxed back into the overstuffed chair, pulling her legs up and hugging her knees.

Mack observed her surroundings with curiosity as she quickly made herself at home. Photos of her grandchildren and late husband were displayed around the nook with her laptop and monitor. Her computer mouse was shaped like a ladybug, and there was a very small statue he immediately recognized.

He reached for it and asked her, "Archangel

Michael?" holding it up to see its detail, the sword raised, and the foot of the statue clamped on the head of the serpent.

She nodded, "Yes, my kids and their wives are all first responders. St. Michael is the patron saint of police, paramedics, and the military. As soon as one of them leaves the house, I'm praying and pleading to this guy. I had an uncle on the Philly police force, he taught my brother and me about the power of his intercession."

Mack held the small statue reverently. His own father, who died when Mack was two, left very few personal effects after his death; but a laminated holy card with the archangel's likeness in his wallet was one of them. Mack wondered if his mother still had it.

"My father, he died when I was two. He was a pilot in the British Royal Air Force. He carried his, the archangel's, holy card. I never knew why. Well, I don't know very much about him in general… ironic." Mack said quietly. He placed it back on her desk where she kept it.

"I'm so sorry," Aurora whispered sympathetically. "About your father." She felt a wave of déjà vu when Mack used the same word she mumbled to herself only minutes ago.

He was caught up again in her presence, the tenderness of her voice seeped inside him.

"It was a very long time ago; I don't remember him at all, regrettably. Don't feel sorry for me, I managed to get along," he said with pride. "So, about this problem you have sleeping. Have you always been this way or only since your husband passed away?" he asked, mostly to change the subject.

She let him peek briefly behind the curtain, vocalizing her thoughts. "I'm sure it's the latter; this is the hardest time for me, bedtime. I know from experience that the voice beside you, the whisper in your ear as you lay your head down to rest is either your strength or your weakness. He was my voice of reason, my strength. I know I was his too." The words sounded bled from her, as if she opened a vein to give them a voice. "I don't want to burden my family or friends. I'm sorry to burden you. I'm having a hard time adapting to who I am now and who I'm supposed to be." Tears formed quickly in her eyes.

He sat in silence across from her, calculating how far to push her. "You're not a burden to me. Would you like to talk about him?" he began slowly, with care.

She looked up into his cerulean eyes and shook her head. "Maybe another time," she answered with a crack in her voice. She already said too much and to a complete stranger at that. She sipped at the fragrant tea.

"I'm sorry, you noticed this at lunch—I suck at social banter. If you knew anything about assault rifles, this would go smoother," he attempted. She stared back up at him again, her expression entirely changed. This time she had one eyebrow arched and was flaunting a clever little smirk. It was an extraordinarily sexy glance, and his entire body melted like a marshmallow in reaction to it.

"What makes you think I don't?" she grinned, biting down on her bottom lip. Mack was completely undone.

Chapter Ten

The next morning, Bangor was blanketed in fog. On the list with bubbles, amnesia roses, and ladybugs, fog was one of Aurora's favorite things. She loved its obscuring mystery. New England fog might be a cliché, but it was laden with pristine writing opportunities. She took the dogs out at first light to walk along the marina, listening to the lapping of the water against the small boats tied to their docks.

Back at the hotel, Eve Marcus, her publicist, had arrived. She looked as if she was raised on the Kennedy compound. Blonde hair slicked back into a tight bun, a pink sweater set atop a tight, black pencil skirt, red lipstick, and Louboutin heels as high as her cheekbones. Though her shoes were beautiful, she and Eve were off on the wrong foot immediately. Cat eyed her rare Louis Vuitton handbag enviously.

The group assembled early in the hotel lobby for breakfast when Eve introduced herself. She was visibly impressed when she was introduced to Mack. Completely unfazed by the striking blonde, he quicky grabbed a muffin and small coffee before heading up to Quincy's room to change into his tack gear. Ken took over watch with Aurora.

Declan Barlow, their backup driver, arrived not long after Eve and joined the group. He easily connected with Billy to discuss how to divide and conquer the rest of the trip.

Eve was anxious to command and alter the itinerary, but Aurora was belligerent. Between Cat and herself, they were more than comfortable with the current schedule. Eve's only job was to incorporate interviews with local reporters or radio and podcast hosts. Aurora wasn't going to let her take over, as she apparently wanted to.

"Mrs. Delsea," Eve interrupted again. "These additional stops were suggested by the publisher."

"Eve, I'm going to ask you politely only once more to stop trying to hijack this operation. First, please call me Aurora, and second, where is this so-called schedule of interviews?" Aurora asked, folding her arms across her chest before starting her next argument.

"Cat and I agreed to this timeline ever since Jen Patterson created it. You're here to manage the press, not me. We have the stores and appearances locked, we don't need to add side trips," Aurora continued, exasperated.

"Let's go then, I'm due at The Bangor Book Barn to meet with the owners and do a walk-through for tonight," Aurora ordered, standing from the table. "Eve, I recommend you have everything ready for my first interview. Don't waste my time on this trip, understood?" she asked sternly. Cat stood beside her; arms folded across her chest as if to emphasize her best friend's point.

Declan and Billy stopped talking when hearing the change in tone of Aurora's typically soothing voice. Eve froze to the spot and nodded in agreement. Ken fought the urge to high five Aurora with pride.

Cat whispered as they climbed into the Escalade with Ken, "Can we ditch her, Rory? Of course, after I steal her handbag," she asked her boss.

"I don't think so. But it's going to be enormous fun getting her to quit on her own," she said with a bit of mischievous glee. "Are you with us, Ken?" she asked.

Ken turned to look at his passenger, proud of her spirit and nodded his agreement wholeheartedly. Mack wasn't her only fan. Ken knew instinctively that Aurora was more than the cards she was showing on the table.

Aurora reviewed her driver carefully, his blonde hair and blue eyes made him look more like a former surfer than sniper. He was the shyer one of the three. She could tell that he was the real core of the group. It was always the quiet ones.

"Ken, really, you talk too much. I mean, I can't hear myself think," Aurora teased.

"I'm sorry Aurora, it's just you and Cat are much more interesting to listen to," he chuckled, showing off his many dimples.

The small town of Hamden, outside of Bangor, bragged a population of a little over seven thousand. It was a quiet community with a big secret. Through the morning fog, Mack and Quincy assembled a team of local police officers, US Marshals, two FBI agents, and representatives from regional Child & Family Services to their location. Prior to the opening hours of the day care they surrounded the building.

Though big and strapping, they stepped like trained ballet dancers, light on their feet. Sleek and dressed in their tack gear, they slid silently around the building like a cluster of agile shadows. Mack gave the signal and kicked down the secure rear door of Hannah's Hamden Day Care. Their target was owner Hannah Thompson and her husband. They had evaded law enforcement for years, creating a long history of trafficking children through a network of underground child predators, ones who paid a high price for their proclivities.

They surprised the two gunmen directly inside, who were guarding the first floor offices. Mack and Quincy rapidly muzzle stamped the men with their rifles and disarmed them. Hannah was startled and began to scream, attempting to escape.

Mack sailed over a desk effortlessly and tackled her to the ground, pushing her against the floor to cuff her. She was feisty and belligerent. The team was busy clearing the building and searching for the kids. They went room to room, raiding a secret space of servers, stacks of cash, and ten children under the age of eight bound and gagged in the basement. The Hamden police officers were sickened by the conditions in the day care basement and the fact that it had existed right under their noses.

Once cuffed, Mack pulled her to her feet, but Hannah kept up the fight, screaming for her lawyer and listing her rights. Quincy approached to assist Mack when she kicked wildly at his shins. One of Hamden's female law enforcement officers, and mother of two young children, swiftly knocked Hannah's legs out from under her with her baton, "On the ground, knees together, this is not an audition for Riverdance," she ordered, shackling Hannah's ankles when she finally obeyed.

A hidden door creaked open in the back office; Mack spun around and shouted, "Everybody down!"

Hannah's husband was brandishing a 9mm and came in shooting. Bullets ricocheted off the shelves and desks in the small space. Quincy directed his strobe flashlight in the shooter's direction, momentarily blinding him. Mack crawled quickly toward him and took his legs out from under him. "Drop the gun, motherfucker," he whispered. His massive hands gripped the man's wrists like steel traps.

Two ambulances were staged at the location. The EMTs began to evaluate the children after the team gently rescued them from the basement and removed their ropes and bindings. The group from Child & Family Services started their evaluations as the medics treated their injuries.

The speed and precision of the arrests did nothing to keep Quincy from feeling disgusted. "Fucking animals," he snarled. Mack and Quincy supervised the extraction of the children as they were assessed and brought to safety. Out of all the awful shit he'd seen, this was the worst. He would rather arrest thieves who kidnapped CEOs for ransom than witness firsthand what monsters did to children.

"How you doin'?" Mack asked Quincy, covertly handing him a small flask of bourbon and a bottle of water. Quincy was starting to get the color back in his coffee-colored skin and he took a long swig from the flask and handed it back to his boss. "Get comfortable being uncomfortable, right?" he said humbly.

Mack nodded, "The only easy day was yesterday, my brother," he countered with another of the oft-quoted SEAL mottos.

"Ha!" Quincy laughed, "All in, all the time."

"Quince, you did great," Mack added, handing him a small, wet hand towel.

"Intel was spot on, Mack. I'm glad we got the husband and the assistants. The team from Child & Family Services is keeping someone behind to talk to the parents when they do their routine drop offs. I sent everything over to Dutch. We can close this one out," Quincy replied as he wiped down his forehead and face with the cool rag. They concluded their business with the officers and said their goodbyes.

Mack drove Quincy back to Bangor, "Let's go catch up with Cotton Candy," he smiled with delight, using their package codename for Aurora

Chapter Eleven

The Bangor Book Barn was a charming mom-and-pop bookstore beloved by its residents. As its name suggested, it was housed in a restored rustic barn. It had been owned and operated for years by the same couple, Bunny, and Red Johnson. They were thrilled to meet Aurora and excited for an exceptional turnout to their landmark store.

At the back of the shop Aurora was to be seated at a table draped beautifully in burlap linen, decorated with small, galvanized water cans holding pens and markers. The owners placed a lovely vase of fresh-cut sunflowers on the table near where she would be signing. She looked at the flowers sadly, a memory buried deep in her past stole across her face. She shook it off and set her personal bag under the table near her chair.

Store employees managed the book sales, and the line of fans headed toward her for signatures. Quincy took the storefront as Mack stood behind her, watching the crowd. This time the men wore their earpieces and wrist microphones to Aurora's absolute satisfaction.

"Don't forget my Package codename, HFM, Hot Frigging Mess." She reminded him as she took her seat.

"Sorry, ma'am, we never divulge the nickname of the Package," he teased. He quickly looked her over and saw she was shrouded in oversized clothing again. She couldn't conceal her brilliance, her pretty face, and stunning smile, nor her eyes. They sparkled with mischief.

She signaled over to Bunny and nodded, "Let them come."

Most of the attendees were women, as Aurora knew would be the case. Her novels were inherently love stories, though her passion for true crime and forensic science managed to ironically "bleed" through her fictional storylines. Her secret fans were men, and they were proudly represented throughout the night. She posed for selfies and stopped to answer questions.

The fans communicated tender salutations to her as she autographed their purchases, "We love your books," "So happy to finally meet you," "Can't wait for the next one, please tell me you finished it?" and the innumerable "I am so deeply sorry for your loss." Aurora had predicted there would be personal acknowledgments of her heartbreak and several times the sincerity brought tears to her eyes.

Quite a few women confessed they also were widows and touched her free hand in silent strength and solidarity. Thankfully, Cat was beside her with tissues, water, and a hot cup of coffee. Every time she took a sip, Mack would "tsk-tsk" under his breath at her right shoulder.

"Didn't I fire you hours ago?" she whispered, oblivious to the upheaval he was causing among the crowd. They would stare and smile, some brazenly taking photos of him, and a few of her younger fans tried to catch his eye.

He was painfully handsome, dressed all in black with his striking mane of rich auburn hair brushed back from his beautiful face. The women of various ages filed past Aurora to appreciate the man who stood guard behind her. Despite their impressive attempts to distract him, his eyes never wavered from Aurora, scanning the room for threats.

"Woman, you will never be rid of me," he whispered under his breath, knowing she wouldn't hear him, and if she did, wouldn't understand his true intent.

Toward the end of the appearance an exceptionally attractive gentlemen in his early fifties approached the table tentatively. Six foot, two inches of muscled body and a mane of thick salt-and-pepper hair. Dark, hypnotic eyes and full lips were framed by his black and gray goatee. Dressed in relaxed jeans and a blue flannel shirt, his sleeves were rolled up, exposing intricate tattoos along his corded forearms. The attendees lingering around the author seemed to do a double take as he approached.

Cat saw him first, "Oh shit, Pretty Ricky," she whispered under her breath.

He stood at the table with book in hand, "Still sidekicks, I see." He ribbed Cat when he caught her unwelcome expression. He turned to the distracted Aurora, who was finishing her signature for the patron in front of him.

Mack perked up instantly, something about this guest exuded an intimacy with Aurora. He observed the waiting guests around the table turn their heads in appreciation.

"Long time no see, Sugar Britches. Can I have your autograph?" the gentleman asked as Aurora finally looked up from the table. She felt the hair on the back of her neck stand up at the sound of his scorching voice and the use of a long-forgotten term of endearment.

"Rick?" Aurora's voice fractured. "What in the world are you doing here? This is a surprise, how are you?" She stood and moved around the table to embrace him. He was taller than her and he grabbed her up into his arms joyously. "You still wear Elysium, eh?" he whispered, too familiar in her ear, smelling her perfume.

Aurora laughed with nostalgia and nodded her head. Her signature scent was originally a gift from him many years prior. Mack stiffened and inched closer to Aurora.

Rick noticed the movement of Aurora's security and held on to her longer. He stared down at her and smiled, kissing her forehead tenderly. He didn't release her from his hug and his face was very close to hers. A mile too close for Mack's comfort.

"Rory, look at you, you're timeless and the rest of us are decaying around you. I was so sorry to hear about Ben. I wanted to reach out when it first happened, but I was in the middle of torching my marriage to the ground and moving here to

Maine. I had to come out when I saw you'd be here tonight. You doing okay?" His voice and its affection flustered her. He was a space in time she couldn't return to and yet, she briefly yearned for the woman she was when he had abandoned her.

Aurora's eyes filled again with tears, and she retreated from his embrace. Stepping back inelegantly, only to be stilled by Mack's solid frame, he steadied her by grasping her bent elbows. She exhaled when feeling him behind her.

"Thank you," she mumbled under her breath and clutched the tissue Cat put into her hand. "It's good to see you, Rick. It's terrible this news about you and Lauren. I thought you two would go the distance." She dabbed at the corners of her eyes.

Mack didn't relinquish his position behind Aurora and glowered at her friend. Quincy wordlessly appeared beside him. They eyed Rick together with twin scowls of distrust and he shuffled awkwardly. Cat fake-coughed to get Aurora's attention. Reacting, she turned to address the guys behind her and smiled humbly.

"Stand down guys, this is my ancient, college heartbreak. Richard Shearing. Rick, this is Mack Egan and Quincy Knight. They protect me on the road," she said with pride.

Rick shook their hands courteously. "Ancient college heartbreak? Wow, brutal, Rore. Nice to meet you both; can't be an easy detail, she's more than a handful." He attempted to lighten the mood. Mack wasn't having any of it. Quincy huffed. They flanked her, human pillars of stone, unyielding and intimidating. Cat was enjoying the show; Rick Shearing never looked so uncomfortable, and it was a nice shade of karma on him.

"We're actually finishing up this appearance and have to get her back to the bus for the night." Mack said flatly, his South African accent thick with distaste.

Rick looked at Aurora with a plea in his eyes, "Any chance we can catch up? Cup of coffee, dirty martini? You do still drink them?" He smiled, showing off his perfect teeth. "I live less than a mile from here, we can go to my place," he asked sincerely, trying to take her hand.

Mack palmed her hip and easily backed her out of Rick's reach. Rick was visibly annoyed with the delicate but intentional move and his eyes darted up into Mack's icy glare.

"Unless it's okay with your bodyguards to let me on the bus with you for a chat?" he asked sweetly, smiling at Aurora.

Aurora nodded her head, "Sure, it would be really nice, of course." She glanced back at Mack and Quincy to wordlessly inform them that it was nonnegotiable. Mack felt his heart sink. Aurora summoned Bunny and Red to close out the appearance. She sat back down to finish the remaining autographs, including Rick's. Ken arrived to escort Aurora to the bus with her guest after Quincy convinced Mack to take a quick drive with him.

Once ensconced in the bus, they swapped stories about the event with Billy, Ken, and Eve. The chatter heightened when Quincy and Mack returned with a surprise delivery of White Castle burgers and fries.

Billy and Ken were bullshitting in the front of the bus while Aurora, Rick, and Cat sat at the table catching up on old war stories. Cat could tell Rick wanted time alone with Aurora and she wandered toward the conversations at the front of the bus. Rick related the story of how his marriage imploded while Aurora listened empathetically.

Eve was nosing around awkwardly outside everyone's comradery. She was busy attempting to convince Aurora to add a late-night crime story podcast interview to her evening schedule, guaranteeing she could do it from the bus. Aurora was irritated by Eve's intrusion into her private conversation but agreed to the podcast and took the information from her. She was mostly distracted by her overwhelming dislike of Eve, and the smell of hamburgers.

Rick watched her with wonder as the smell of food took over Aurora's attention. "Nothing really changes does it, sugar?" he said happily.

"Sugar? You really are ancient. What's it been—twenty-five years since I've heard that nickname?" she replied fondly. She stood from the table at Quincy and Mack's appearance.

"Quincy, you win today," Aurora sighed with joy. "Gotta love a guy who hand delivers cheeseburgers to a heart patient. I didn't think

White Castle was still in business," she gushed, her face alight.

"I don't know about being the winner, Miss Aurora; Mack *did* personally buy the milkshakes."

Aurora placed her hands on her hips, "I'm pretty sure he's out of the competition. I'm sorry to say that Mack has been placed on double secret probation, due to his propensity to tally and judge my coffee consumption. It's becoming a personnel problem. He does get a few points for not recording my cigarettes, so there might be a chance yet for him. What flavor did you pick for me?" she asked him in mock consternation.

"Chocolate Peanut Butter," he replied, downplaying his triumph, wishing to keep their private moment in the early hours private. He removed her cup from the large carrier of milkshakes and held it out to her.

"Well played," she smiled slowly. "Well played." Their eyes locked for a split second, and he warmed at her reaction. She approached him with delight, taking the milkshake from him. Her devious smile was endearing.

"I did good, right?" he whispered under his breath. Aurora took a long sip, the straw between her puckered lips and her eyes fixed up into his. She nodded dreamily, her long lashes fluttering as she moaned low with appreciation of the milkshake. She answered his question without doubt. "You did great," she purred.

Mack felt his blood rush to his groin. How

could a woman cause such a physical reaction unintentionally to a man typically impervious to nonverbal innuendo? She turned on her heel and returned to her guest. *Vixen*, he thought to himself. What could she do to him when she awakened her power? Mack's low groan was audible.

Cat missed nothing. Something had transpired during the first overnight shift on the bus. There was a bonding or connection the two had made that she hadn't been privy to. Aurora was being playful, but not sending out any invitations. Mack, on the other hand, had dug himself a deep hole. Cat felt pity for him; Aurora's path back to life would be excruciating. Her love affair with Ben was the stuff of legends and might stand as a once-in-a-lifetime. There was no guarantee Aurora would recover her true self and ever settle for anything less. Notwithstanding the current temptation, which had suddenly appeared from the past.

Eve took the opportunity to slither up beside Mack, "Did you know you're trending on Aurora's Twitter and Instagram?" she flirted, mobile phone in hand, ready to share the posts with him.

Mack was several things at this moment: still flooded with arousal from watching Aurora's erotic sip through a straw and annoyed with the presence of the college crush still among them. She was a pesky bee buzzing in his ear.

"What are you yapping about?" he asked the smarmy blonde.

"You—you're trending on her social media tonight. Didn't you see all the guests snapping photos of you? The hashtags are fantastic! Hashtag whosthehotguy and hashtag roryswingman," she fussed.

"Eish girl! Don't you have a job? You won't skinner about me," he huffed, displeasure strengthening his native accent and slang.

Quincy and Cat caught the interaction, Cat's look clearly requested translation of his words.

"Whoa! It takes a lot for Mack to roll out South African slang. It's how you know you have truly twisted his balls," he whispered to Cat. "If I was you I'd get the gum off his shoe, fast." Cat, eager to mess with Eve, quickly approached the twosome.

Leading Eve aggressively to the door, Cat deadpanned, "Thanks so much for all your help today. We'll see you in Boston." Eve tried to push her way back to the small crowd, when Aurora noticed and joined Cat's fun.

"Really Eve, amazing job, thank you so much! We don't need to take up any more of your time tonight. Take a few burgers to go. Have a safe trip to Boston," Aurora chirped in a dismissive tone, waving the other woman off.

"Aurora, the podcast at 10?" Eve argued.

"I've got what I need, thank you. I'll be there on time, thanks again, really," Aurora's firm tone dismissed her. Once Eve was secured off the bus, Aurora looked at Cat with an expression her friend had not seen since they were teenagers.

"Yikes," Cat grinned, "I just saw the eighties

wake up all over you, Rory."

"Something about her is off. She rubs me wrong," Aurora sneered, yet instinctively she felt there was an issue about the younger woman. "Where did Jen dig her up from?" she wondered aloud.

Aurora brought burgers and a container of fries back to the table for her and Rick. He was shaking his head watching her. "What?" she asked curiously, taking her seat again across from him.

"You—you're still a tsunami. You don't take any shit, do you, sugar? Goddamn, I forgot how fascinating you are and, my God, still so beautiful." He gazed adoringly at her. His face was resting on his right hand, his dark brown eyes glistening at the sight of the vision in front of him. She was his first true love, and he never broke free of the spell she'd cast on him. All his favorite memories were rushing back to him, and he admitted as much to her.

Aurora rolled her eyes dramatically. "Clearly not fascinating enough to keep you away from Lauren as I remember." She fired the shot as she happily bit into a cheeseburger slider.

Rick was unwrapping his burger and lowered his head in shame, "I'm sincerely sorry, Aurora, I know there is far too much water under the bridge but believe me, I understand how big of a mess I made things. Please forgive me?"

She laughed, "Believe it or not, being vindicated doesn't feel as good as you think it will.

Rick, so much time has passed, and oceans of new tears have fallen. Don't take this the wrong way, but you breaking my heart is a wood splinter in comparison to the story arc of my life thus far."

They sat eating and talking for over an hour. She was stealing fries from Rick's plate when he brazenly reached out and fed one to her. Mack thought his brain would blow up. He couldn't take it much longer.

Their conversation was low and muted. Mack watched her body language, and every time Rick touched her hand or reached out to tuck a strand of hair behind her ear, she slightly shifted in her seat. He was pitching something, probably a second act for the two of them, but Mack couldn't tell if Aurora was entertaining the idea or not.

Mack was catching snippets of their conversation; she was now actively avoiding Rick's attempts to touch her across the table. "Sugar, think about it," he said softly. ".....always so good together...no one knows you as well as I do..." Mack overheard bits and pieces, and he tasted bile in his mouth. He couldn't hear Aurora's reply.

At last, Rick stood to leave. He hugged her close again and kissed her cheek. They whispered to each other for a short time before Aurora separated from him. Rick said goodbye to everyone and left.

The air was still and heavy in the bus after his departure. Billy had since retired to his bunk, Ken had returned to the hotel, so it was only the four of them: Aurora, Cat, Mack, and Quincy.

"So? I'll concede he looks great. That jackass aged flawlessly." Cat declared snidely, packing her stuff to head over to the hotel escorted by Quincy. "Did he beguile you back into his bullshit?" Mack and Quincy sat captivated by their exchange. Cat never pulled a punch.

Aurora sighed loudly and reached for a bottle of water from the fridge. "He spun his web, but his bullshit doesn't work on me anymore. Have you forgotten how it ended?" she asked her friend skeptically.

"Pfft, forgot? Are you kidding? Let me see if I can summon the memory—as I recall, this legendary breakup required a half case of Ben & Jerry's ice cream and at least six drives to the Wildwood boardwalk for Curley's fries. I think we both gained ten pounds the summer that shitshow went down," Cat laughed. "I still can't listen to 'Patiently' by Journey without a stomachache."

"Exactly," Aurora said with resignation. "I have no interest in a useless distraction, especially one that left me ten pounds heavier and one of our best friends betraying me. What is it Cookie always says? Oh right, 'I don't play with broken toys,'" Aurora said proudly. "Although, it would serve Lauren right, wouldn't it? After everything she did to turn his head, for him to wind up back in my bed? I'd happily send her the pictures." Aurora laughed, sending Cat into a fit of giggles.

"It's not like she's the brightest bulb in the family chandelier; he convinced her the tattoo with your initials on his shoulder stood for 'asta la vista,'" Cat guffawed. Aurora snorted with laughter. Mack and Quincy couldn't help but stifle their laughter from their seats.

"I forgot about the tattoo; she had no idea they were my initials, right?" Aurora was still giggling.

"Rore, the better part of that story is she thinks "hasta' begins with an 'A,'" Cat chuckled.

"Rore, get him back here, we can stage the pictures and I'll tag them all to her Instagram!" Cat shrieked. She walked toward her friend and hugged her, "My sweet girl, you're still embedded in the widow hurt locker. Not much gets in, but he, the son of a bitch, carries skeleton keys. You're one of the smartest women I know, except when it came to him. He's a magician—he waves his wand, and poof! your clothes and your reason vanish," Cat chuckled, causing Aurora to scoff with shame. She shook off the web of flattery Rick tried to ensnare her in. The men were watching and listening to her closely.

"Cat don't lose any sleep over him. I'm not sloppy seconds, especially not someone Lauren is finished with. It's going to take someone infinitely more magical than 'Pretty Ricky' to convince me to come back to the living. The next time, if there is one, will be the last time and it will require someone supernatural," she mumbled under her breath. Not one of them missed the declaration.

Aurora headed toward the back door of the bus to smoke and watched Rick drive away slowly. He beeped the horn and she waved.

"Pretty Ricky, no shit," she said, shaking her head, exhaling smoke. He did unnerve her by showing up because something about his appearance felt staged or intentional. He had poured it on, and she found it all disingenuous, something Rick had never been, and she couldn't figure out why. He reminded of her of the serpent in the Garden of Eden. She wasn't biting into his apple, not again. She was glad, for once, that grief was padding her impulses.

With Aurora out of sight, Mack dropped his head to his chest in relief. His large hands gripped the headrest of the seat in front of him. All the air left his body. What the hell was he doing? He took pains to regain his composure. Of course, she had lived a life before him, he didn't need to feel this way. If all his past conquests suddenly appeared, they would need a small amphitheater to introduce themselves. Quincy slapped him on the back. "You good, Romeo?" he asked, feeling the unrest coming off his best friend.

Mack looked up at him with defeat. "This woman…" His voice drifted off.

Quincy nodded his head sadly, "Yeah buddy, cheap and easy doesn't work for you anymore, does it? Say it Mack, say it out loud, the end of the Frogmen Ballad," he urged.

He laughed quietly and found the words for the mantra. *"Anything in life worth doing is worth overdoing. Moderation is for cowards. I'm a lover, I'm a fighter, I'm a UDT/Navy SEAL diver. I'll wine, dine, intertwine, and then sneak out the back door when the revealing is done...*" They bumped fists and laughed together.

Cat clutched her bag and jacket, prepared to leave with Quincy. She patted Mack on the shoulder, "He's not going to give up this easily, he's a snake. Don't back down, Mack, my money is on you across the board. You are supernatural." Mack was surprised by her statement, it felt like a big sister cheer on the sidelines of a championship game. He grinned up at her from the seat, glad to know he had an ally.

Eve Marcus returned to her hotel room, planning to check out in the morning to make her way to Boston. She placed a call to her direct report who was unhappy with her lack of progress. She'd managed to execute one of her duties but was unable to complete her mission— unacceptable in her eyes. "Step it up, we are running out of time," she barked, before her phone clicked off.

Chapter Twelve

The flowers began appearing at the very next stop on the tour. The two locations in New Hampshire and one stop in Vermont found deliveries to each of the book venues. Dozens of long-stemmed roses: pale pink, white, lavender and burnt orange. Incredibly beautiful and fragrant, each arrangement was magnificent. They arrived in every shade but the right one, Cat pointed out.

"He can't remember, which is ironic since he should know better than anyone it's amnesia roses you love—he is suffering from exactly this affliction." Cat laughed, as she watched Aurora rip up and discard yet another small card with the affections of Rick Shearing poured out in tight script.

Aurora sat at the table preparing for the crowd and asked the store owner to take the vases away. "Cat, figure out if we can donate them to a hospital or nursing home. He is spending a fortune, I'd hate for them not to be appreciated," Aurora whispered with guilt.

Cat got on her phone to arrange for the disposition of the flowers. Mack watched Aurora with interest. She was being showered with affection from an old paramour and there was little impact on her. She was a mystery to him. *Didn't women love flowers?*

Once the event was over, the owners brought

her another delivery that had recently arrived to the store in her name. "Ugh," Cat whispered. "This will be the chocolates, right? He has no shame." Cat sighed, shrill with agitation.

"Hold on," Aurora said with a bit of excitement. "If there are moon pies in here, he's at least getting a thank you text." She laughed as they made their way out of the bookstore toward the SUV with Ken and Mack.

Settled in for the night, Aurora opened the box to exactly what she expected—moon pies and individually wrapped, miniature peppermint patties. She laughed to herself; he did know her weaknesses. This time the card was more insistent. *Sugar, I have always loved you. I know every sensual inch of you, remember? Give me another chance to prove it. People our age don't get another try. Love, Rick.*

She handed it to Cat who read it with dramatic eye rolls. "He's such an asshole. People our age aren't dead yet, who says there can't be another try? It's not ever going to be him. He ruined his chance. What are you going to do Rore?" Cat asked, her voice genuinely concerned now. Aurora was still too shattered. The one-year anniversary of Ben's death was approaching, and she didn't want her friend conned into a band-aid relationship.

Mack and Ken were occupying themselves so that it would appear as if they weren't listening. Aurora was fixing herself a cup of coffee and feeding the dogs. She was quietly thinking about her answer.

"Well, I'm having a moon pie with my coffee, for sure. I told you Cat; he doesn't stand a chance. I'm not in that headspace and I can't imagine the first person to touch me after Ben would be Rick. The idea makes my skin crawl. Not to mention, I'm getting this cringy feeling about him showing up out of the blue. He is trying to turn my head, take my focus off something, and my Spidey-sense is sluggish lately but I'm trying to see the real picture."

Mack observed her curiously, she didn't think like a writer. She read between the lines, and he wondered why she would use such a style of cognitive dissemination for mere romantic gestures. She truly fascinated him.

The appearances in Boston brought more of the same—flowers, cards, and Rick accelerated his game with imported chocolate truffles from Spain. Cat took care of the flowers and Aurora gifted the candy to the store owners with her gratitude even though she knew how difficult they were to procure and were her absolute favorite. She was uncharacteristically quiet when they returned to the bus. She changed in her room and never returned to the common area.

Cat left for the hotel and whispered to Mack, "Those truffles were from Seville—she loves them. I can't believe she gave them away and now, she's on the phone with him. I don't know how to sabotage this, maybe you can think of something?" she fretted, worried Aurora was caving.

Mack smiled at Cat. "I'll see what I can do." They exchanged an accomplices' nod of their heads.

Once alone, he walked quietly to Aurora's closed door. He could barely hear her words but knew by her tone that it wasn't going well for Rick.

He knocked softly and she opened the door, phone still at her ear.

"*Yellowstone* will be on in ten minutes, I know you don't want to miss it," he whispered. Almost from their first day on duty he was deputized to remind her when her favorite show was to air because she could often lose track of the days and times. She exhaled and gave him the five more minutes signal, covered the phone, and whispered, "Would you make the popcorn, please?" before closing the door again.

Hours later, Mack could hear noises from Aurora's room. She had retired for the night after they watched the latest episode of *Yellowstone* together in the bus recliners, sharing a bowl of popcorn. He never did ask her about the phone call and could sense she might have brought things to an end. Mack didn't want to do or say anything to disturb the ambience of their TV "date." He enjoyed their mock hand wrestling in the bowl over the popcorn. It all felt sibling-like, but then, he'd do anything for the sound of her laugh. Currently, those were not the sounds she was making from her bed. Something was troubling her.

"Aurora?" Mack tapped on her door. She was restless, agitated, and crying out in her sleep. There was no response. Mack didn't like to invade her private sanctum, but he was worried about her heart. He took a breath and opened the door. She was at the far edge of the bed, curled up in the fetal position, yelping low in her sleep.

He sat on the bed and tried to wake her gently. "Aurora?" he whispered, grazing his hand over her flushed forehead. She fell onto her back and gasped loudly upon waking. She was surprised and disoriented. He reached for her wrist to check her pulse, "Aurora, are you okay?" he whispered.

She noticed his presence and flung herself into his arms. Her hair and oversized T-shirt were damp from perspiration. He wrapped his arms securely around her. "You're safe, I'm right here," he murmured, comforting her. She was trembling in his embrace. "Tell me, tell me what you dreamed about while you can still remember," he encouraged, strumming his hand down her back.

She was shaking and clutching his strong arms. "Shadows, knives, dark, long hallways, a man in a wheelchair—he… he helped me. Blood, so much blood. Golden light, a sculpture. I can't make any sense of it. It's every night lately," she said, exasperated. Realizing she was blatantly clinging onto Mack, she retreated with embarrassment.

"I… I'm so sorry," she said, her modesty returning, and she slid off the bed away from him. Her movement woke the dogs who now expected to go out.

"Sorry for what?" he asked, standing from the bed, and reaching for the pair of leashes she kept hanging from her tiny closet door.

"Sorry for, you know, all of it…" She pointed to the bed. "I didn't mean to throw myself at you… I… was just, I don't know, scared, and lost for a minute."

Mack was listening to her while he harnessed both dogs and opened the back door of the bus. "Aurora don't apologize. Any time you'd like to throw yourself at me you have an open invitation. Scared, lost, you don't need a reason," he said with a sneaky smirk.

She found her sweatshirt jacket and slipped on her shoes to take the dogs out with him. His offer and invitation thudded up against her dully. Once outside, he lit a cigarette and took a drag before handing it to her. She led Sydney around the grassy island behind the bus while Mack guided Tim.

"This has been happening every night this week?" Mack asked, breaking the silence.

She nodded her head. She was still trying to put the images together. Taking another drag from the cigarette, she handed it back to him. He did the same and passed it back. The ease and comfort between them wasn't completely lost on Aurora. She couldn't refute the safe feelings she had when Mack was close.

"So, since College Crush appeared?" he asked, trying to fit the timeline.

"It's not about him," she murmured, dismissing Rick as a contributor to her nightmares.

Mack walked closer to her as the night had grown cold, and he wanted to wrap his arms around her again but resisted. "He's putting on an impressive show. I haven't seen so many flowers or candy since Valentine's Day in grade school," he teased.

Still in the haze of her dreams, she looked up at Mack quizzically. "You think I'm playing hard-to-get?" she asked innocently. Not waiting for his response, she continued to defend her position. "I'm frozen inside, I have nothing left to give and certainly not to a dead end. And he is. Buried within me is a jungle cat in a coma. It's the best way to describe it. He would have to set fire to me to release me from the igloo I've built around myself. He can't even light a match," she said with indignation.

Mack stared down into her eyes; he was standing too close, but she didn't seem uncomfortable with his proximity. Her sorrow was an art exhibition—multicolored canvases with depth and texture. He thought to himself how he could and would create an inferno visible from space to bring her back to life. His depth of passion for her was inexpressible.

"How did your call with him go tonight?" Mack asked nonchalantly. Aurora sighed with resignation.

"I told him to save his money. I can't love anything anymore," she said, embarrassed and awkward to be admitting this to him. Mack didn't believe her, not about her ending the possibility with her college boyfriend, but her ability to love again. He was convinced she was the love of his life and confident that it wouldn't be one-sided forever.

He stayed close to her, in her personal space. "And the dreams? What's causing them?" He wondered if she could decipher them.

She sighed and stepped away from him. "It's me—at certain points in my life I've suffered from night terrors. Usually when I'm trying to put a puzzle together. Or it happened in college or grad school, prior to submitting exams and papers. It's how my brain works out a mystery, but I can't figure this one out at all. So many different symbols and allegories, I don't know where to start."

"There are that many unanswered questions in English Literature?" he asked with mock curiosity. Aurora was a true enigma, and it was dawning on Mack quickly that there was a great deal more to her than he currently knew. He was willing to bet that her hidden master's degree was something completely opposite of her English Lit major.

Aurora laughed humbly, "Why yes, Mr. Darcy, there are a great deal of obscure messages left by the eighteenth-century masters."

Mack led them back to the bus, "Ugh, anybody but Darcy. That guy—what a pussy. Elizabeth would have fallen in love with him from the beginning if he offered his true self. George

Wickham is the star of *Pride & Prejudice*. Granted, I'm not used to revering officers in the army, but he was transparent and knew what an asshole he could be. And assholes are the most reliable people alive—they always act true to form."

Aurora froze to the spot, completely thunderstruck by this fierce former Navy SEAL sniper who was assessing Jane Austen in a parking lot with her at three in the morning.

"What's wrong?" he asked, realizing she had fallen out of step behind him. He studied her strange expression and started to laugh, "Damn, you caught me. Okay yes, I'm a fan of Jane Austen—can it be our secret?" He fidgeted from her look of disbelief.

"Mack," she whispered with skepticism and a gush of awe, "you've read Austen?" she was flabbergasted. He walked toward her, switching to his pristine British accent, and recited with humility, *"There is a stubbornness about me that never can bear to be frightened at the will of others. My courage always rises at every attempt to intimidate me."*

She gasped aloud and her hand jumped to cover her open mouth. She remained rooted to where she was, unable to move. Her late husband was a high school principal and former professor who absolutely wooed her with his recall and recitation of great lines from the classics. But never were they delivered in a crisp, perfect British intonation. Aurora was unable to fully absorb this moment. Between her nightmares and this glint of light in the darkness, she was overcome with chaotic emotions. Something about Mack was incredibly familiar to her all of a sudden.

He knew precisely what he had done. Mack had easily determined that Aurora was a woman who required mental seduction foremost and was prepared to aim for her weaknesses. By the look on her face, he knew that as usual, he had hit the target. For the first time in his existence, his striking good looks were not going to be his best weapon.

Mack took her hand, "C'mon Aurora, it's cold and your shirt is still wet. We have to get back so you can change. I'll make you a cup of tea." She held on to his hand, letting him lead her and the dogs back to the warmth of the bus. She was still speechless.

He convinced her to change into dry clothes and drink a cup of hot tea while they debated the attributes and shortcomings of Darcy and Wickham. He was boldly sitting up on the bed beside her, enjoying the conversation when she fell asleep against his leg, clutching a pillow to her chest. Tim and Sydney were tucked behind her legs, curled in tight mounds.

He sat there an extra minute to watch her, stroking her hair and covering her with a blanket before leaving the room. Mack felt his body ache with intense withdrawal when he removed himself from the spot beside her. "There will come a day, Aurora, when I'll never get out of a bed you are in." he whispered solemnly into the quiet room.

Chapter Thirteen

With six book appearances between Maine, Boston, New Hampshire, Vermont, and Connecticut completed, the Trident team had concurrently executed six quiet arrests and now the bus headed west to Syracuse, NY. The atmosphere during the five-hour trip was somber. This travel-only day fell on the one-year anniversary of Ben's death, and no one knew how to manage Aurora.

Quincy, Ken, and Mack had each individually formed a profound connection with her. They enjoyed being in Aurora's company and treasured their own private conversations and inside jokes during their time together. More than ever, their desire to protect her was strengthened. Today was one of those days they wished to shield her from her own pain.

Cat took the dogs out early, giving Aurora time to spend the morning in her room, video chatting with her sons and grandchildren. Occasionally, Cat would tap on the door and hand her a fresh cup of coffee. They could hear her blowing her nose, so they knew there were many tears.

Conspiring with Billy and Quincy, Cat organized their lunch stop to be close to a local catholic church so that Aurora could light candles and get some air. Billy reset the GPS for their route while Cat searched for a suitable restaurant near the church.

Quincy whispered admiringly to her, "You really know how to take care of her, Miss Cat"

She blushed and thanked him, "We've been together since we were kids, I lost my husband seven years ago, so I can see the IEDs in the field ahead of her."

"I'm so sorry for your loss," he whispered gently.

"Yeah, so am I," she smiled, patting him on the shoulder.

Mack finally fell asleep in the back bunk as he had spent the night before enduring the sounds of her muffled sobs, floor pacing, and all-night keystrokes on her laptop. She never once came out to the common area, even when he knocked and offered her tea. She was ripping his heart out; he couldn't take the anguish she was suffering while being helpless to alleviate any of it.

The one sound from her room that genuinely surprised him was the distinct ring of a satellite phone. He wasn't aware that she carried one, and for what reason? He could only hear the murmur of her voice, not the conversation she was having with the mystery caller. He reached out to Kai—no response. He thought he might mention it to Dutch as he fell into a troubled sleep.

In Albany, Billy parked outside the Cathedral of the Immaculate Conception. Aurora emerged and slipped out of the bus. Her hair was pulled away from her face in a tight bun, her face partially covered by her Jackie Onassis-style sunglasses.

Once outside, Cat looked her friend over; black wool turtleneck, black pants, one string of pearls and the sunglasses. "You know, after today you are required to advance to the shade of purple right?" she mocked. "Seriously, I'm sure there is a law somewhere that after the one-year anniversary you are expected to retire the Widow 101 uniform. Could be that the memo has evaded you since you're traveling. Just saying."

Using American Sign Language, Aurora gestured perfectly, "fuck you" and headed toward the church.

"Hold up, Miss Children of a Lesser God. I'm coming with you," Cat laughed.

The inside of the cathedral was magnificent and serene. The lingering smell of incense hung in the cool air. Aurora made her way to the nave and found a beautiful grotto with the statue of the Blessed Mother surrounded by intention candles. She slipped the money into the donation box and lit the candles for those who had gone before her: her precious Ben, her parents, and her baby sister, Tieghan. She knelt for a time before the statue, silently praying that they were sharing a magnificent paradise. Tears fell like raindrops from her tired eyes.

Silently, into the pew behind her filed Mack, Quincy, Ken, Billy, and Cat. They sat quietly waiting for her to be ready to leave. When she finally stood up, she was shocked to see them there.

With her hand on her heart, she whispered,

"Thank you," and walked away from them. Before leaving the cathedral, she made one last stop—a small cove honoring the statue of St. Michael, the archangel. She knelt and whispered another solemn prayer. A strange feeling came over her, like an inspiration. She looked up at the statue curiously. Something about it resonated as if she had knelt before hundreds of the archangel's likenesses in her lifetime. She touched the base of it and a tremor went through her, pictures flashing through her mind. *Tieghan?* she wondered quietly. *What do you want to tell me, baby sister?* Aurora sensed her presence intensely. She could almost smell the chlorine; Tieghan was in a swimming pool from before she could walk. Still confused, Aurora stood and made her way from the statue.

As she walked away, she caught sight of a veteran, an older black man in a wheelchair at the front of the church, watching her. She felt a connection—he was so recognizable to her for some reason, and she bowed her head at him before turning to leave. Their spirits, the veteran, and her sister, gave her a surge of courage. Aurora couldn't explain it, but the feeling raced into her blood. She then straightened her hunched shoulders and left the church.

In honor of Ben, the group lunched at a small Italian restaurant appropriately named Legendary Ben's Bistro. "Nice find, Cat," the men acknowledged.

Billy recanted some of the funny stories about

Ben during his years as a high school principal. Aurora smiled warmly when he divulged the epic tale of the day Ben was first introduced to the young teacher. It was during the high school's annual family day picnic. "Rory, when Ben told the story he blamed it all on your dress. What was it? A short sundress with ladybugs printed on it?" Billy asked, struggling for the details.

Aurora nodded in confirmation. A sad smile washed over her face.

"He was struck by a thunderbolt, and he knew it," Billy smiled warmly. "None of us thought we'd ever see him happy again, Rory. You truly saved the man. God love you. He was good people." Billy said gently. Mack watched Aurora in silence. Her grief was dense and wrapped around her securely. He ached to hold her and comfort her. Was it in his power to perform the same transformation in her that she had clearly managed for her once grieving husband? There was no way to tell, but Mack would never give up trying.

Quincy asked warmly, "What are we drinking in his memory, Miss Aurora?"

Aurora looked up from her menu, her eyes tired and swollen. She smiled, "Dewar's White Label scotch, on the rocks."

"Definitely my kind of guy, To Ben!" Quincy raised his glass with the rest of the team.

Chapter Fourteen

The enigmatic and tragic events that had surrounded Aurora's baby sister Tieghan's death were her family's best kept secrets. She had been a happy accident for her parents as Aurora and her brother were both in their late teens when she was born. Her exceptional beauty was difficult to hide, and strangers consistently and brazenly approached their parents with offers to manage a photo portfolio, modeling career, or advertising contracts. As she grew into a luminous toddler with golden curls and opalescent green eyes, the offers came relentlessly.

A Latin American company based out of Cancun was the most dogged. After returning from a cruise in Mexico, the family was tormented with calls and visits to recruit her for their talent and modeling agency. It often puzzled her family—why would they be so laser-focused on a blonde-haired, light-eyed little girl in a dark-haired, dark-eyed market?

Aurora and her older brother instinctively knew that they alone were chosen to protect her. No one ever thought to teach them that Tieghan was incredibly special and by that fact alone, drew all the wrong elements to herself.

For years, the blame went around the table. Her mother for being ridiculously starstruck by the promise of rubbing elbows with celebrities, her father for only seeing endless dollar signs.

Aurora and her brother circled the wagons. They could read the true intentions from the very beginning. They spent most of their adult lives unwinding the sequence of events that led to the ultimate suspect who had kidnapped, viciously abused, and ultimately killed their sister. Alejandro Vasquez, the owner, and CEO of Jovencita Modeling & Talent Agency. He was a vile snake who had slithered around the center of her family and squeezed the life out it.

Tieghan's disappearance at three years old and her ultimate death was a horrific trauma to her family. Her parents could never recover and died within eight months of each other from alcohol and drug abuse.

Aurora and her brother did what they could, digitally recreating their makeshift crime lab, collecting breadcrumbs like grains of sand, putting together the puzzle one tiny piece at a time with one purpose—to bring justice to their sister.

They knew it would be a lifelong pursuit, but on a pinky swear at their parents' grave, they vowed to never let it go.

Together and apart, separated by their lives and sometimes oceans between them, they worked and communicated in secret. Their clandestine efforts and the astonishing amount of accumulated evidence was their private project, shared with no one.

During that time, proof of Tieghan's existence had been completely erased. The only visible acknowledgment of her was a small blue trident wrapped around her first initial, tattooed on each of their left shoulders. Her brother's wife, Lily, went to her own early grave without ever knowing of Tieghan's existence, as did Aurora's beloved Ben.

When her big brother had called the night of Ben's death anniversary, she spoke to him for hours, sitting on the floor in her small bedroom closet. He consoled her through her heart-wrenching tears as she marked the first twelve months without her husband. His deep voice was her only sentinel in an upbringing that was wondrous, right up until their tragic losses.

"It's okay, Tink," he whispered his childhood nickname for her. "We're getting close to him, and you've done amazing work. You have to be ready for what comes next. It's time to see him in cuffs, I promise you. We may finally let our baby sister rest in peace. You are now and always have been the strongest woman I know; I'm so proud of you—you amaze me every day with your grit. I love you and will catch up with you as we get closer."

Chapter Fifteen

The first of three scheduled appearances in the city of Syracuse ended and the whole team gathered for dinner together at Lou's Steak House. The restaurant was dark and masculine with thick leather banquettes and starched white tablecloths. It had been almost a year since Aurora had permitted herself a steak dinner and she was looking forward to it more than Christmas. Though she rarely followed her cardiologist's instructions, she did greatly limit her red meat consumption, which hadn't made her happy.

Nursing a dirty vodka martini, Aurora was bristling beside Cat. She was observing her publicist Eve and her incessant flirty attention toward Mack. She was acting coy and touching him gratuitously. Watching her toss back her straight blonde hair and emit fake giggles, Aurora could feel her long anticipated dinner souring in her stomach. She had not experienced these reactions in a very long time. She hardly recognized them.

Mack watched Aurora pick at her dinner. She was uncomfortable, and he couldn't pinpoint what was causing it. She enjoyed eating and was usually fun to be around during a meal. Seated beside him was Eve, chattering in his ear and trying to flirt with both him and Ken.

Aurora spoke in a low voice to Cat and Quincy, making them laugh. Mack couldn't hear what she was saying, and it was frustrating him.

"So, is it annoying you that she's hovering over the redheaded member of Mount Olympus?" Cat whispered sweetly.

Aurora looked up at her in disbelief. "No! Why would you think that? He's a single man—at least I think he is, I don't even know. Cat, why would it bother me?" She fidgeted in her chair and tried to taste another forkful of her dinner. Her appetite had disappeared.

"Rory, everywhere we go women flirt with him and try to get his attention. Not just her and not only now. You've never noticed before and now, suddenly, it's bothering you. Don't you see he only ever looks at you. And I get that you don't see it. When you snap out of it you won't believe how impressive he is." Cat snickered. "Not to mention, all you've been talking about is having a New York Strip and you only took two bites. Who are you right now?" Cat laughed.

Aurora huffed with annoyance. "Cat, there's something about this girl. I'm telling you—all my alarm bells go off around her, she's a sneak."

"Mmmm, and now she's trying to seduce your number one bodyguard. How dare she?" Cat smiled.

"Pfft," Aurora blew off the conversation and summoned their server for the bill.

The evening prior, as they were parked outside of the hotel, Declan had reported a problem with the electrical system on the bus. Aurora realized it when the Wi-Fi signal in her room suddenly disappeared.

Accommodations were quickly made at the Middlegate Hotel & Suites. Aurora settled into Cat's room with the dogs to watch a movie.

Mack texted Cat around 1:30 a.m.

Mack: *She okay?*

Cat: *Yep, half asleep, movie is almost over.*

Mack: *Text me when she is heading back down here. Copy?*

Cat: *Copy*

Around 2 a.m. Aurora got up to leave. Cat was fast asleep. She rustled the pups to go out for a walk. She brought them outside the hotel, and they quickly did their business, anxious to get back to bed.

She stepped off the elevator and headed down the hall toward her room. Suddenly, she saw a woman slip out from Mack's room. The hallway was dark, but as the woman made it to the service stairwell her face was illuminated. *Eve.*

Aurora's heart sank. *Mack slept with her? Ugh. What was he thinking?*

She walked softly with Tim and Sydney and went into her room. She quietly locked the connecting door between her and Mack's room. She was disgusted and deflated. What a disappointment. She imagined he was smarter and more discerning than to sleep with her—that vacuous girl.

Aurora couldn't sleep; she tossed and turned and finally got up to open her laptop. She read emails and scrolled through her social media before finally feeling her eyes get heavy.

Mack held his ear to the door. She was back and for some reason had locked the internal door between them. Cat had never texted him. He had taken a walk around the outside of the hotel and recently returned to his room. He could hear her fingernails pounding on laptop keys. She must have found some inspiration to work on her manuscript.

Aurora arrived late to breakfast the next morning and sat with Billy to ask about the status of the bus. They discussed the scheduled repairs. Mack took the seat beside her to eat and felt her bristle next to him.

"When do you want to leave for your interviews?" he asked, fixing a cup of coffee for her.

"Ken is going with me," she said, her voice cold and flat. She stood when she saw Ken approaching the table. She made her own cup of coffee at the buffet and left with Ken.

"What the fuck?" Mack mumbled. He looked at Cat with confusion. She shook her head and shrugged her shoulders. "Who knows?" she chuckled. But she did. Mack was toying with a tornado, one who hadn't collected all her wind yet. Cat was truly hoping that Mack knew how to navigate a storm front. She was rooting for him.

The rest of the day went the same. Aurora barely spoke to Mack and purposely sat far from him during their team dinner. He managed to escort her back to the hotel, but she was silent in the elevator and the stroll down the hallway toward their rooms.

"Aurora, did I do something wrong? You haven't said a word to me all day. I was scheduled to drive you around today, why would you ask Ken?" he asked, still confused and almost hurt by her demeanor.

"Nothing is wrong, see you tomorrow." She went into her room and leashed up the dogs.

He waited for her at the doorway and moved to escort her outside.

"I'm good, you don't have to come with me," she said coldly.

"You don't go outside at night without one of us with you, it's not even my order and I follow the ones given to me by my bosses. You want to ignore me… fine," he mumbled with resignation.

She was stoic and cold. He could not for the life of him figure out what he had done. But this was not going to continue the way it was going. He couldn't take another day of it. Mack let her stew and saw her back to her room.

They were on their third day in the hotel when Aurora left with Quincy for the advance meeting at the bookstore. Quincy glanced over at her as she was wordlessly sipping at her coffee.

"So, how long are you fixin' to make him suffer?" he asked, his voice clearly demanding an answer. He'd had enough of the silence himself.

She looked up blankly. "Make who suffer?" Quincy smiled and shook his finger at her.

"You know what you're doing, Miss Aurora. You got him hog-tied in cleat hitch knots. What did he do?" Quincy wondered what could have possibly caused Aurora to shut him down so effectively.

"I don't know what you're referring to," she said self-righteously.

"Miss Aurora, I've interrogated war criminals. You think I don't recognize a woman's battle tactics?" He laughed softly. Quincy could see it happening. Mack was getting under her skin, and she couldn't admit it or wouldn't accept it.

She sighed with resignation. "It's silly and stupid. Just ignore me."

Quincy sat back in the seat and turned the SUV into the driveway of the bookstore.

"I'm gonna let you in on a secret, the man is indestructible. The only thing he is incapable of, is ignoring you. Play nice with your prey before you take it down, baby girl," he said in a brotherly tone. She looked at him strangely as he helped her out of the car.

They met with the owners and walked to the store when the secret satellite phone Aurora carried buzzed in her purse. "Excuse me a minute, please?" she asked the owners of the Campus Book Emporium. Quincy made a motion to follow her, but she shook her head, and he backed off deferentially.

"Tink? Are you alone?" The comforting sound of her brother's voice echoed on the line.

"Quincy is close. You never call in the middle of the day, what's wrong?" Adrenaline spiked inside Aurora.

"Get back to the hotel as soon as you can. Mack was injured during the arrest, and I need you to take care of him. Tink, we've confirmed that they've been tracking you; they know where you are so be ready," he said, concern thick in his voice.

"Let them know who I really am?" she asked him, her voice a weak whisper.

"My guys already suspect something; they'll protect you. Read them in carefully, they don't need the whole story yet. No mention of Tieghan. I'll back you up. This must come to a head when you're in Manhattan. He's there, back in the US for a week, and I'm worried our window is going to close."

Her heart began to race, she knew it was coming. *But Mack? What the hell?* Aurora's anger, envy, and whatever else she discovered churning in her gut about him dissipated suddenly with the knowledge he was injured.

Quincy was on the phone when she made her way back to him, he looked at her with a bewildered glance as he ended the conversation with the caller. "Who are you, Miss Aurora?" he whispered.

"No time now," she said, "We have to help Mack, please get me back to the hotel, quickly."

"Yes Ma'am."

The rooms at the Middlegate assigned to Aurora and Mack were side by side with a connecting door. It was a natural choice to Cat who knew he always took the overnight shift to cover her. Quincy sent Cat back to the book venue to finalize the evening's appearance, as Aurora raced to Mack's room.

Ken only just arrived and directed Mack to the bed. He was bleeding from a gash on his forehead and a knife wound to his left side. Aurora brought her travel bag into the bedroom. With Ken's assistance, she removed his bullet proof vest, and she cut his shirt off him. Ken handed her the towels he fetched from the bathroom.

Mack looked startled at Quincy and Ken, "What the...?" he said. No one wanted to ask her, as they labored to put the pieces together.

"Aurora," Ken asked calmly, "Start talking."

She glanced over at him swiftly, "When he's cleaned up, I'll answer your questions."

Aurora washed and sanitized the gash at Mack's forehead and bandaged it. The knife wound, though superficial, was being more difficult. "You might need stitches here if I can't close it up," she spoke only to him. She was swabbing the oozing blood with a cloth wet with antiseptic. He stared at her with sheer adoration. She hadn't spoken to him in almost three days. He couldn't comprehend her new role in this show, but he was grateful for her gentle hands on his body and the sound of her honeyed voice.

With Mack's shirt removed, the small tattoo on his left shoulder was visible, the rare blue trident wrapped around the letter "T". She now knew without question who they were, amazed how clever her brother operated. She reached into her bag for surgical adhesive glue and carefully closed the wound.

She wrapped him in fresh bandages, cleaned the rest of the blood off him, and handed him a bag of ice to hold against the bandage on his head. Then she stood up before them and lowered the neckline of her sweater, exposing her left shoulder. When they saw the tattoo, which matched all three of theirs, it confirmed what they had begun to suspect. Aurora was Dutch Jenson's sister.

"I knew he knew you!" blurted Ken. "Telling us to not fish for minnows, what an asshole!"

Aurora cleared her throat and spoke gently, "I can't tell you everything, but I might be able to answer your immediate questions." A knock on the door interrupted them. Cat returned with a takeout bag of lunch and a round of hot cups of coffee. Ken thanked her from the door in Aurora's room to draw her away.

Mack struggled to sit up on the bed, "Dutch Jenson? He's your brother?" *Terrific*, thought Mack to himself. *He was in love with his boss's sister?* Mack couldn't buy a break.

She nodded her head. "It's, well... not his real name, but yes, he's my older brother. Please, eat something," she urged. "You need to replace fluids as well." She handed him a bottle of CORE water and a sandwich from the bag.

"How much do you know?" Quincy asked, intrigued, his image of Aurora abruptly evolving.

"More than you do," she replied. "This entire campaign is the culmination of a twenty-year plan that Dutch and I have meticulously pieced together. Within the last five years we established Trident and teamed up with the FBI New York field office. My identity was never to be revealed. However, the real reason you three are traveling with me is, Dutch is zeroing in on the head of the snake, and the snake knows...."

"Jesus bloody Christ!" Mack sat up. "You're the fucking bait!"

Aurora nodded. "He's coming for me and if our timing is right, it should happen when we arrive in Manhattan during my scheduled appearances there. Your pinches have gotten messier lately, haven't they? As if there were tip-offs prior? You took the earlier ones by surprise?"

Quincy shook his head in disbelief. "Cotton Candy, my balls..." he mumbled. "And he insisted you were not the mission. Why all the mystery? All of it could have been easier with this information."

"Hold on!" Ken blurted. "Walk this back. Why does anyone know who you are, and what would the head of one of the world's foremost child and human trafficking rings want with you? You're a former high school teacher and an author. What did you do to him?"

"Dutch and I have cost him millions of dollars and rescued or detoured from his path hundreds of kids he would have destroyed. We have systematically eradicated the layers of networks leading to him. The closest we have come is your recent string of arrests. We are in arm's reach of him, and he's finally traced all his trouble back to us."

"The target," Mack interjected. "What's his plan? Do either of you know?"

Aurora nodded again, taking a sip of hot coffee, her voice shaky "His plan is to kidnap me, torture me, and send the pictures to Dutch before he kills me. For his finale he will send my severed head back to my brother in my empty handbag." She attempted to shrug off the horrible possibility. "It's not even creative, not for him anyway."

Mack struggled to get off the bed, angry and sore from his wounds. "Absolutely no fucking way will I agree to this!" he stormed.

Aurora grabbed his hand in a determined effort to calm him. "Mack, please?" she whispered, using the power of her comforting voice. "We have worked for so many years to take this piece of shit down. Please, you must get a hold of your emotions. I need you… Dutch needs you," she pleaded.

He couldn't look at her, she weakened his knees. He would not be convinced by anyone to put her in harm's way.

"There is more to this story, right Aurora?" asked Ken. There had to be, for them to take this kind of risk. This reeked with the feeling of a personal vendetta, which was always more dangerous.

"Yes, but not now. The backstory doesn't matter right now. The important thing is to stick to the mission. It's about to be slightly adapted. Kai is working on the remaining scheduled warrants and connecting with our confidential informants to see if they have been compromised. We can't let a thing go wrong or he'll disappear forever." She sat on the edge of the bed, still holding the bloody rags in her hand.

Aurora stood to gather up the towels and packaging from the dressings. Mack paced the floor, his head pounding and his heart about to blow out of his chest. He felt the sting still from his wounds but looked down at his side to see the bandages were still dry.

Quincy signaled to Ken—it was time to leave the two of them alone. "Miss Aurora, you two take a minute to talk this through. Ken and I will go smooth out the rest of the day and hopefully get a status on the bus repairs. We'll also report to Trident. I'll be back to pick you up for the appearance."

"Yes, fine. Thank you, Quincy," she nodded, absentmindedly. She watched Mack stalk the small suite like a caged animal.

He was infuriated and battling to get a grip on it. She sat quietly on the edge of the bed, waiting for him to absorb everything she had just dumped on them.

"What do I know about you that's true?" he seethed, glaring down at her position on the edge of his bed.

"Mack," she replied, her voice calm. She tried again to reach for his hand, but he resisted. "Everything you know is true—who I am, all I've suffered. Only Dutch and our life's work has been kept from you. I had no idea who you were until recently and no reason to trust you."

"You didn't know all this time? When your son interviewed us? When *you* met us?"

"No, I didn't know you three were partners with Trident. The identity of most of the team is a secret to me. I was only just informed that you were executing arrests simultaneously while traveling with me. I was briefed the night before we arrived in Albany."

Mack stood at the windows to the suite breathing slowly, attempting to control his fury. Then the tiny bell ringing in the back of his head concerning Aurora turned up its volume. He turned to face her again.

"Your dual master's degrees—English Lit and what was the other major? It's hidden from your complete personal history," he asked, knowing as he did all along that it was the cornerstone to who she really was.

She took a hesitant breath; she was being pressed to trust him. Knowing that her brother did, Aurora quietly answered his question. "Criminal Justice and Forensic Psychology," she whispered.

There it was. The "minuscule detail" that Dutch tried to derail him from uncovering. It would have made all the difference to Mack and his men. Dutch was Special Forces, CIA, a Marine. With her education, Aurora was a formidable partner and the brains shoulder-to-shoulder with her brother. *It was all making crazy sense now, but what was still missing?*

Why would siblings go to these lengths for criminal apprehension? Scrubbing pieces of their pasts as they went along. The night terrors, the mysteries she subconsciously fought to unravel throughout her life, those made sense to Mack now as well.

"I have a real conflict, Aurora," he said doubtfully. She stood from the bed to stand next to him, puzzled by his comment.

She was standing too close to him, the smell of her hair and the touch of her clothing brushing against his bare chest was too much. She was vulnerable and in danger, beautiful and brilliant, unreachable, and so fucking broken that it was making him dizzy. She looked carefully into his eyes but couldn't decipher what he meant.

"What is it?" she pleaded. "Tell me what would keep you from helping us?"

What happened next seemed to take place in slow motion. He cupped her face with his hands, drew her closer and kissed her. Caught entirely off guard and shocked by his actions, she sympathetically allowed it to continue. His mouth softly pressed against hers, and he inhaled her floral essence into his brain. He was savoring the suppleness of her perfect lips and felt his mind and heart quiet. It was the most wonderful thing he had ever done; her mouth was a luscious piece of a candy puzzle that fit him undeniably and he never wanted to stop.

Aurora had not been kissed in over a year. She was sure she never wanted another man to touch her, ever again. Without her consent, a tiny emotion stirred slightly inside of her, and it left her terrified. She pulled away, startled by a shiver, a sense of recognition buzzing at the base of her sternum. She placed her hand firmly on his bare chest to establish distance.

"No, Mack... I'm not abandoning the confinement of my grief. I will never survive another heartbreak and I won't be added to the string of your one-night stands."

He nodded in understanding and took her hand in his, raising it to his lips. His eyes pooled with affection as he easily and willingly declared himself to her.

"This is my secret; I'm in love with you. No, it's bigger than that. I have never in my life felt this way for anyone—I'm out of my bloody fucking mind in love with you. There is no persuading me otherwise. I can and will wait for you until the end of days if it's what you need. I won't hurry you along to a place you can't see in your current stage of anguish." He stood close to her, longing to kiss her again.

He continued, "You would never be a one-night stand, I want you all the days and nights I have left. Now, about you placing your life in danger, on my watch, that's not fucking happening!"

Aurora was dumbstruck. She backed away from him. She didn't know how to answer him. Her heart was so utterly broken, and her soul damaged. The mere idea of a new... *anything* and its potential for crushing loss, again? *No. Never. Never again.* More frightening in her mind was the likelihood that she could inflict a similar despair on someone else. She trembled at the thought. She did her best to communicate those thoughts to him, but was swiftly met with his stubborn dismissals of her "What ifs?"

"Mack," she sighed in resignation. "This debate has to be postponed. We are on a timeline tighter than my brother's security clearance. I'm flattered and surprised. I'm sorry I haven't noticed; I guess I *have* been walking around in a haze. If you are distracted this greatly, you can get us both killed. We need to get you past it."

"Get me past it?" he laughed. "Easily done, Aurora. Let me kiss you again, slap me across the face, and quash this enormous, goddamned crush I'm carrying? What kind of piece of shit do you think I am? I've revealed my only weakness: you. You have all the power, Aurora," he declared honorably. Mack closed the space between them again.

She touched his cheek cautiously. "On the back burner, for now. I need you present and at full strength for me and my brother. This opportunity will never come again, and it's all we have worked toward for twenty years. It is an ancient secret, one never shared with anyone, including our spouses when they were alive, precisely to avoid this situation," she emphasized.

"Bloody hell, Aurora," he mumbled, raking his hands furiously through his auburn waves of hair. "I cannot let him take you! There has to be another way, we are special forces warfare operatives, you are not!" he exclaimed with frustration.

"You must let him take me, Mack! It's the only way we grab him. This asshole is like Teflon, not a charge has ever stuck to him. The huge number of paid off judges and crooked District Attorneys we have campaigned against have covered and protected him. The cartons of evidence and signed affidavits we put in front of the latest judge to write these warrants were delivered in a U-Haul truck. Mack we have been trying for years. Dutch…he lost an entire team of men the last time, almost ten years ago. Horrible tragedy." She stopped talking abruptly.

Aurora's tears rushed to the surface; she was bowing from the weight of so many atrocious secrets. The pure agony it caused her for years to never confide in her husband was soul crushing. She was not once permitted to lay her head on someone stronger than herself.

Mack took her into his arms; her tears were most certainly his Kryptonite. He understood the enormity of her sharing this information with him for the first time. She felt amazing in his embrace, like she belonged there, and he wanted to wrap her up and never let her out of his arms. Her face against his bare chest, his nose in her sweet hair—he was at peace in her presence. Aurora had performed a transformation he still hadn't adjusted to, the internal turmoil he consistently lived with was stilled in her embrace.

She sobbed and whispered into his chest. "Mack, the things he did to our baby sister before he killed her…" She choked on the words but was relieved to hear them finally out of her mouth, knowing even as she shared them that she was treading ever more dangerous waters.

He exhaled knowingly, "The fourth candle." She wiped her eyes and looked up at him in surprise.

"At the grotto on Ben's anniversary, you lit four candles. I counted Ben and your parents, but the fourth candle was a mystery to me. I'm going to guess her name starts with 'T'?"

Now Mack saw the entire picture.

"Tieghan," Aurora whispered, with great hesitation. "I haven't said her name aloud for what feels like centuries. Mack, Dutch asked me not to divulge the rest of the story, the information has only passed between us all this time. We can't take any chances." He wrapped her up in his arms again, mostly because she was allowing it and felt his soul lift when she rested her head on his shoulder.

"Okay, Cotton Candy, I'm going to play nice," he conceded. "I will gather myself together and remain beside you this entire job. While I have breath, nothing ever will hurt you. Ever, do you understand me?" he kissed the top of her head. "When this danger has passed, I will court you like a proper gentleman, wearing your resistance down to a nub."

"Cotton Candy?" She wrinkled her nose in fake distaste. "Don't tell me it's my secret Package codename?" She looked up at him in mock disbelief.

He laughed and said, "Blame your brother. You are quite appropriately named Aurora, a luminous light glow."

"He's only ever called me Tinker Bell. He has since we were kids."

"Well, it's how he described you, 'a bag of cotton candy, not one hard edge.'"

Aurora laughed. "Poor guy, you fell for more than one disinformation campaign."

Chapter Sixteen

Aurora sat back against the bed's cushioned headrest, legs outstretched, watching Mack sleep. He lay sprawled across the bottom of the king-sized mattress, Tim and Syd curled up beside him. "Little traitors," she thought. Since Aurora had arrived in Mack's room to dress his wounds, they jumped on his bed and never left his side.

She didn't know how to navigate his amorous pronouncements. She was preoccupied by the gathering storm on the horizon, with no bandwidth left to process his feelings. Yet here she sat, letting him grip her ankle while he slept. She checked her watch and knew it was time for her to prepare for the appearance. She slid carefully out from his hold, but it wasn't clever enough. He awoke suddenly and clutched her foot.

"Don't go yet, stay here with me a little longer," he whispered, his voice tender and sweet. Smelling her floral scent and touching her bare foot made him hungry for the rest of her. He wanted to slide her down to him and cover her body with his.

"Why me? I thought it was Eve you wanted," she said with a tired bite to her voice, removing her foot from his grasp.

Her remark smashed his brief fantasy like a rifle round through a light bulb. "What would make you think that?" he huffed impatiently. "Wait, is this why you haven't spoken to me in the last few days?"

"I saw her leaving your room in the middle of the night. I thought...well you can imagine what I thought," Aurora whispered sadly. She stood up from the bed and the feeling she experienced on that night swooped over her again, deflating her. Seeing Eve slip out of Mack's room had disappointed Aurora, and she couldn't understand why. Today he confessed his love for her, and it was giving her a brain freeze.

Mack sat up on the bed and looked at her with disbelief. "That I wanted Eve? Wanted Eve for what exactly? And do you think she was in here with me? This is why you've been giving me the cold shoulder? There has been no woman in my room but you, and you don't stay long enough for your perfume to linger."

"Two nights ago, Cat and I were in her room watching a movie. The night we ate at Lou's, when Eve was doing the dance of the seven veils around you. After the movie I brought the dogs out and when I came back up I saw Eve slink out of here, carrying her shoes," she claimed indignantly. He stood to follow her, forgetting his injuries—his blood raging.

"Eve could do cartwheels in a plunging neckline polka dot dress, and I wouldn't notice," he sneered. "Listen to me carefully, Aurora. I can find an easy piece of ass anywhere on the planet, and I wouldn't fuck that girl with Kenny's dick!" Mack bellowed.

He realized when she cringed slightly that he wasn't on the deck of a ship. "Excuse me," he whispered. "I'm not used to being around intelligent women, cursing like a sailor is a real thing. Occasionally, I fucking drink like one too."

Aurora blew him off and was heading toward the connecting door to her room. She didn't know why she even cared. He was free to do whomever he wanted. She was lifeless inside so what difference did it make?

He marched toward her, closing the distance, and invading her space. Reaching over her head, he closed the connecting door in front of her. She was backed against it now, nowhere else to go, when he placed his palms on the door at each side of her head.

"Allow me to list out the things I do want, so you'll never make this mistake again." His voice, thick with his accent, was a smoky, hot caress. Aurora was frozen to the spot, never seeing him like this—anger and reckless desire igniting from him like a lit box of explosives.

He continued, "The 'string of one-night stands' as you call it ended the moment, the bloody second, I set my eyes on you. I don't want an easy lay, not ever again." He paused, exasperated with his lack of eloquence. These beliefs were new to him, therefore hard for him to communicate.

"Aurora," he exhaled, whispering her name like a prayer hidden inside his memory. He traced her jaw with his finger. "I'm crazy for you...I want to make slow, deliberate love to you and root myself so deep inside, a winch and hoist will be needed to bring me out. I want to make you scream with pleasure so loud that the neighbors a block away will know my name. And I'm quite capable of doing it. I want to hear this whiskey baritone you have for a voice, breathless in my ear, moaning my name and begging me for more." He smiled confidently.

He brought his face closer to hers, his dark blue eyes ablaze. "I want you in my bed every single night for the rest of my life. I want to sleep beside you, wake up next to you, and spend my days worshipping you and keeping you safe. I have endured a life of deprivation, hard-hearted and frozen for too many years. You light every match inside of me, ring every bell. Understood?" His voice was low and gravely. Aurora was holding her breath. The things he was saying, the depth and insinuation in his voice pulsed inside her and pounded on the soundproof doors of her wounded, guarded heart.

He ran his hands through his hair, exasperated. He settled them back on the door, caging her in and forcing her to focus on him.

"Aurora, it takes every ounce of my self-control not to pick you up in my arms and run away with you, tossing your shredded clothing over my shoulder. I don't know what's restraining me. I want to kiss you constantly, and not like you have ever been kissed before, but so you taste me in your mouth for hours later. Kisses so fucking deep you won't know whose air you're breathing. I want to run my hands all over you, chasing them with my tongue—and for the love of God—fuck you so efficiently that all you'll ever crave is me."

He paused and took a breath, staring down into her eyes, knowing he was banging his head against a concrete bunker of her construction. The tone of his voice, though deep, sweetened.

"Aurora, there will always be women like Eve. All they see is a pretty boy in uniform. Some fucking piece of meat they think they desire. They don't see past my looks, to the man I truly am. All I see is you and I want you to believe everything I've just told you. I want, what I truly want—is for you to really see me." He ran his thumb across her soft cheek. She was wide-eyed and struck mute by his diatribe. The urge to kiss her was painful to resist, but he didn't want to overwhelm her further.

Instead, he traced his finger across her full bottom lip. "I think it's very sexy you got pissed off thinking I slept with that marshmallow. I've never seen you jealous. I have to say, it's adorable. Maybe you feel a certain kind of way for me and you're not willing to face it?" His smile was perfect and for the first time, Aurora could see the slight gap between his front teeth and for a second, thought how incredibly attractive it was.

Standing still in the moment, flush with embarrassment and unintentional arousal, Aurora thought, *this can't be happening.* She was so downtrodden and sad, how could he like her? Why would he even want her? And why were parts of her body responding to him? He made a good argument, so why did it make her so mad? Why was envy the first emotion to rise up in her?

Aurora knew that when Ben was alive her sexual appetite had been inexhaustible, but now she couldn't muster any desire. She had abandoned it, locked it up and ignored its existence. Aurora didn't want to start over, she wanted to stay frozen in time, tucked in with the beautiful memories she clung to desperately. She was sleeping, but the sound of his South African accent and his lusty assertions were invading her comfortable dreamscape. She was the one who wrote in her novels that a man could give a certain look to the woman he loved, and it could stop time. She wasn't ready to admit it, or concede it, but Mack was doing just that. The way he looked at her, the way he spoke to her, she could faintly hear the gears of Earth groaning to a stop.

"Mack, why me? I'm dead inside. I'm so shattered." Tears filled her big brown eyes. He stared down into her mesmerizing gaze, hypnotized by her beauty. He wanted to kiss her desperately and blow his cravings like wind into her lungs. He ran his thumbs under her eyes to wipe her tears. He kissed her lovingly on the forehead.

"Aurora, I will wake you up. Believe me. I get it, you're not ready yet—I know you have yourself hidden and insulated. When you resurface it will be me who will make your body tremble, your soul shiver, and every granite wall you have built will crumble into dust. Do you know what Navy SEALs say? *No sky too high, no sea too rough, no muff too tough*," he teased. "I will ruin you for any other man." She dropped her head with shame and indecision.

He lifted her chin to look at him, "Beautiful girl, you take my breath away. And I look forward to the nights I will take away yours. Do not agonize over women who think I notice them—they don't exist. You're the only one for me, and I will not stand down until you are convinced of it."

She stared back into his hungry eyes, still unable to see his allure. Her vision was thickly clouded by grief and sorrow. His voice, his accent lulled her for some reason. He smelled good, like cut grass after a thunderstorm. But he wasn't Ben, and he never would be. Somehow, knowing that nothing happened between him, and Eve gave her a profound sense of satisfaction. Aurora was blindsided by her own reaction. She bit down on her bottom lip.

Mack moaned into her ear, "Don't bite your bottom lip Aurora, please...bite mine," he whispered longingly. She summoned her reason back, absorbing all the things he had confessed, and it occurred to her they hadn't solved the true issue.

"Mack, if Eve was in here, where were you?" she asked suddenly.

"This was Thursday night?" he asked, shaking off his desire and following her lead.

"Yes, about two in the morning," she answered.

"And you went out with the dogs on your own? You never called or texted me? Do not do that again, I don't give a shit what you think I'm doing. My mission, *my job* is to protect you. Don't make it difficult for me," he ordered. "I was outside, walking the perimeter of the property. I never saw you or her for that matter," he said quietly.

He stepped back and gently stroked his goatee. Aurora and Cat had bunked in together for a few hours. Mack, knowing she was safe, had taken a walk around the hotel property.

He touched his index finger to his mouth to indicate—*no talking*. He grabbed a flashlight from his bag and began to search the room. He searched under the bed, inside the lamp shades, and inside the closet. He ran his fingers under and atop furniture and fixtures. When he was done, he uncovered two small listening devices. He went to flush them down the toilet.

"Seems like we found our mole. I'm calling Trident." He went for his phone as Aurora left to get dressed. An hour later, Quincy tapped lightly on her door. "How's our boy?" he asked, entering her room.

Mack emerged from his room, "Wait for me, I'm coming to the venue."

"Ken and I had an extended conversation with Dutch this afternoon. He wants to catch up with you later, Mack. He's concerned the heat will be turned up. Now we know who Eve really is and Aurora's location is not secure. He wants all three of us at the remaining appearances; he thinks they'll try to smoke Aurora out and away from us. At the very least, Eve's been trying to get you away from her. We are DEFCON 1 going forward."

"Copy that," he mumbled as he retreated to finish dressing.

It was the typical crowd at the Campus Book Emporium in downtown Syracuse. Mack, Quincy, and Ken were on high alert, but they also weren't sure what they were looking for.

Prior to the appearance, Aurora attempted to elaborate on the possibilities. "The chances are high it will be a woman, with one or more small children with her. She will appear nonthreatening and even familiar. She may cause a small distraction or disturbance. Their objective is for you to take your attention off me, or for her to divert or disable you. Look for the children, even any young adults, that have a gaze, a vacant stare, a camouflaged air of fear. He will use them as bait because he knows I'm unable to resist a child in the sphere of peril he creates. Once you see it, you will never unsee it."

The men listened intently and nodded their heads. Not their first rodeo but they were captivated by her knowledge.

"Miss Aurora, you are never, and I mean this, never ever to take a step without one of us. Not to the restroom, to sneak a cigarette, or to privately pull the panties out of your ass, nothing," said Quincy. She laughed along with Ken and Mack.

"Remember this, he's sneaky and cunning. His resources are unlimited. He will use your weakness, your blind spot against you first." She looked quickly at Mack.

"Someone vulnerable or helpless could approach you for a favor, for example to lift something heavy in the storeroom. Don't eat anything or drink anything someone other than me or Cat hands to you. A tray of cookies from the store owner, a brownie a child offers you. Don't let anyone get close enough to you to administer a needle. Look out for anything that resembles a gnat or fly—it's a micro-drone—it can land and dispense a sedative." She stopped to gather her thoughts again.

"I'm reasonably sure he is going to send a warning shot. If I know him the way I do, he wants me in the city. He wants home field advantage. Manhattan has its history, and he won't resist the urge to repeat it," she informed them. It was the last place she had ever seen Tieghan alive.

Aurora was not bashful as she held up her sweater, allowing Mack to wire her. She was in fight mode, not considering the effect she was having on him. He was messily taping a receiver pack to her back and fishing the tiny microphone up through the center of her bra. He wanted to kiss the thin pink scar over her heart and everywhere else. It made for a clumsy, floundering process. The impact it was having on him was not lost on anyone in the room.

"You about done?' she asked him, rolling her eyes as he finished taping down the small mic to her chest. The edge of his right pinky brushed against the top her of ample bosom. She covered herself again with her long sweater.

"Sorry," he mumbled "I wasn't trying to cop a feel; it's my job to take it slow." They all laughed together at his quick recovery.

The event transpired without a hitch for most of the evening. Adrenaline spiked when Aurora spotted her neighbor from Gull Cove, Corrine Gladstone, strolling through the store with two little boys around the ages of 5 or 6 in tow. She whispered under her breath, "Ten o' clock, a neighbor from Autumn Lake."

Mack spotted the woman and headed toward her when he noticed an elderly man approach her and block their path. They weren't more than one hundred feet from them when Corrine seemed agitated and spun suddenly. She quickly walked to the front of the store, the children following alongside. The elderly man seemed to be ushering her out to the street. Quincy caught the reflection of patrol lights from outside the store and walked over to the windows to see what was happening.

"What was all that?" mumbled Ken into their earpieces.

After about thirty minutes, the same elderly man returned to the store. He ambled around and joined the end of the line to have Aurora sign the book he purchased. The event was ending, so the owners locked the door behind the last of their customers.

The senior gentleman was their last guest. His extended height was extremely hunched over, and he depended heavily on the cane as he slowly shuffled toward the table where Aurora sat.

She started to laugh, tears streaming from her eyes. The men could not understand why she would react this way to the poor old guy. She stood quickly from the table to walk around to greet him.

The team instantly sprang up, when he spoke, "Could you assholes back off so I can hug my sister?" Dutch snapped, grabbing her up into a ferocious embrace. Once he let her go, he removed his baseball cap and peeled back the expensive latex and foam mask that had covered his entire head to create the appearance of a man in his eighties.

"This has got to be one of your worst incarnations yet," she laughed. "You had to know you looked like the ghost of Uncle Lenny coming at me," Aurora said, still chuckling.

"Precisely who I was trying to be! Nice job on the ID. You're sharper than these half-wits. How are you?" He rubbed her back, feeling the tape and receiver. "Which hack did this job?" He looked at his men. "Jesus Christ, you should have tucked the micro-unit into her bra."

"Yeah boss, nobody was touching there," Quincy laughed and elbowed Mack at the same time.

"She could have done the tucking, you Strappers!" he shook his head in disbelief. Aurora giggled at her brothers use of an old South Philadelphia slang insult.

Dutch followed them onto the bus, which was eerily empty. "I sent Billy and Cat to the hotel; we need to talk alone," he said as they began to sit around the table.

Dutch couldn't contain his joy to be with his younger sister. He wrapped her up into his arms again for a good squeeze. "You look good, kid." He grabbed her chin with his hand and inspected her face. "Too many sleepless nights and more tears than necessary, but good, nonetheless. Benny wouldn't approve of all this sadness, Tink, you know how much he hated to see you cry." She nodded in unhappy agreement.

Dutch strode through the bus, back to front, checking under surfaces and using an electronic scanner for bugs that might have been planted. "I swept through here once when you were all out, but since I saw Corrine fucking Gladstone, I wanted to check again."

"What the hell was she doing here?" asked Aurora in disbelief. She moved to make herself a cup of coffee when Mack handed her a hot cup he had prepared for her. "Thank you," she whispered, smiling sweetly up at him. Dutch watched the interaction curiously.

"She's a player in the network, but high level, Tink," Dutch explained. His men were confused but trying to keep up.

"In addition to their small bakery on Autumn Lake, Gladstone's Famous Desserts, she, and her husband Glenn, own a profitable dance academy outside of Atlantic City. Hundreds of little girls and boys under the age of twelve cycle through there a year. One of their previous victims found their way to Trident."

"For Christ's sake she baked me a pie, came to the house, and extended her condolences," Aurora said with disbelief.

"You didn't eat it, right? Or feed any to the grandchildren?" Dutch froze to his spot.

"No, I hate pie, and it was strawberry rhubarb or something wretched like that," she answered. "Good Lord, Dutch! Is she slipping mickeys into her 'famous desserts'?" Aurora gasped.

"Tink, have you ever fed your grandchildren anything a strange adult has given them? Without tasting it yourself first? Whether teachers, coaches, parents, cheerleading chaperones?"

"Never!" she replied, "We learned our lesson the hard way."

Suddenly her face blanched. "Dutch! My weakness...." she whispered, frantic.

"Breathe, I just spent the last two days with Sammy and Robert. Everyone is at Gull Cove and on lock down. Sam dug out rifles I didn't even know he had. Robbie has his volunteer firefighters watching the roads in and out of the town," he assured her.

He sat down beside her. His voice changed to pure delight, "I tell you this, little sister, you should have seen the reactions from your sons when they were informed you have been a covert criminal investigator most of your life." Dutch laughed with pride.

"Sammy about swallowed his tongue. I promised them after I saw you tonight you would reach out directly. They might have a few questions; it took a little convincing."

"So, about the sweet baker/dance instructor, Corrine Gladstone. It's how she indoctrinates them. She prepares and gifts the most delicious sweets for the parents and irresistible cupcakes for her students. All of them dosed. She hosts incredible sleepovers and Disney movie nights for her dance students and then the abuse starts. However, there is no reason to think that she tried to poison you as she couldn't have known who you were then; but it's a foregone conclusion she knows who you are now."

"Where did she go?' Aurora asked.

"With the US Marshals. We have enough on her and Glenn to keep them for a while. They both will see serious time. My guys raided their house and both businesses yesterday. The Gladstone's managed to slip away from us, but we scooped them both up tonight. I had a good hunch she was tailing you. We rescued over a hundred children in various unsavory modes of confinement in the basement of the dance studio." He shook his head with disgust.

"And the boys she had with her?" Aurora asked, concerned.

"They went with the local Child & Family Services; they had been reported missing over a week ago," he assured her.

"She isn't our mole, though?" Aurora asked. "I barely know her."

"Indirectly. Your moles, plural, would be your fluff job publicist Eve Marcus in cahoots with our young driver Declan. They are siblings, Corrine and Glenn's niece and nephew," he revealed dramatically.

Aurora exclaimed, "Declan was no blip on the radar, but I smelled her a mile down the road." Sitting back with genuine satisfaction, she was glad she had been right—Eve was a problem.

"I can't find any buffer between Corrine and the top; they came on direct orders from Alejandro."

Mack looked to them both, "We spent the least amount of time on this trip with the two of them."

Dutch sat across from him at the table, "Enough time for Declan to plant a tracker on the bus and Eve to bug Aurora's bus bedroom and your hotel room. The devil is always in the details."

"Hence the bus's electrical problem," sighed Quincy.

"Where are they now, Dutch?" asked Ken.

"Sitting in FBI black op interrogation rooms, singing like sweet canaries. I'm not confident they have anything we can use. Culebra, a.k.a Alejandro Vasquez, has built many layers between himself and the team on the street. No telling if the siblings will give up Corrine."

Mack, along with his brothers, recognized the

Spanish word for snake immediately.

Dutch continued, "It's too much of a coincidence—those two showing up and Corrine Gladstone in the same area with them. Kai only just found out the family connection. Don't blame yourselves. In retrospect, Aurora and I should have brought you three into this circle a long time ago. You must forgive us; it has been just us for decades. Mack, I apologize for blowing off your catch on Aurora's secondary master's degree. We've tried to keep it invisible for years. I was sure you wouldn't stumble on it, but I had to distract you from it once you did."

Mack tilted his chin in acknowledgment. Quincy and Ken looked at him in silent inquiry.

"Criminal Justice and Forensic Psychology," Aurora whispered to the two of them.

The light brightened in their eyes as their profile of Aurora was coming into focus.

"Without too much detail, I promise when this is all over, I will tell you anything you want to know." Dutch cleared his throat. He took an erratic breath; for the first time his reasons for everything would be revealed to his team and he would have to say them aloud. He gently reached for and held onto Aurora's hand.

"Alejandro Vasquez, Culebra, the snake. This fucking monster kidnapped, raped, tortured, and murdered our baby sister. She was sold to the highest bidders for the majority of her life. While doing so, he took explicit photos of each phase of the nightmare and sent them monthly to our parents. This horror story started when she was five years old. After he killed her, he mailed her severed head, wrapped in her favorite little sunflower print dress, to our parents for fun."

Dutch's voice cracked with emotion. "It was all we had to bury; the rest of her body has never been found." Quincy, Ken, and Mack were frozen still. The surge of anger, disgust, pain, and rage came over them simultaneously. The men battled to keep their fury contained.

"That's why," Mack whispered to Aurora. She looked up quizzically.

"The bookstore in Maine, you flinched when you saw the sunflowers in the vase," he explained. She nodded her head sadly. Aurora was sure it was a slight, involuntary response, and was surprised he'd caught it.

"One more thing, your families are in protective custody. Mack, your mother and stepdad; Quincy, your fiancé and grandmother; Ken, your dad. I rounded everyone up when I found out about the moles. He leads with your weakness," Dutch assured.

The men fidgeted in their seats and looked to their boss gratefully. Mack's eyes fell back on Aurora. He silently wished he could send her to one of the safe houses.

Dutch watched the implicit declaration of Mack's blind spot and shook his head. Here was a new wrinkle. He looked at his sister to determine where she was emotionally. She sat quietly in her own thoughts, shrouded in her sadness, and nursing her cup of coffee. Dutch wasn't sure if Mack's feelings would be an asset or an obstacle to their quest. He would leave it alone for now and trust Aurora to handle it, until she couldn't or wouldn't.

They strategized for another hour before he dismissed the group and they headed into the hotel lobby together. "I'll be on the rest of the trip. I have a room upstairs." He checked his watch. "I'm going to bring Cat up to speed, it's time to bring her into the alliance, and we'll all meet in the morning," he reported, stifling a scandalous grin.

Aurora eyed her brother suspiciously, "What?" He smirked, his hazel eyes gleaming. Even with his repertoire of diversionary tactics, he rarely could get something past Aurora and had resigned himself from a young age to the reality of it. The same was true for her—they knew each other too well.

"I grew up with her, too, and I'm not dead yet, Tinker Bell. A concept that should be dawning on you quicker than you planned. Local patrol will watch the bus; it's secure now and the electrical problem has been repaired. We are keeping the schedule as is we have four days before we arrive in New York, everybody needs to get some rest. We're going to slay an old snake—I need you all on your A game."

Chapter Seventeen

Mack accompanied Aurora to their adjacent rooms, and as she made the dogs comfortable, he opened the internal connecting door to check on her.

"I'd like to change those bandages if you'll let me?" she asked, following behind him.

"Can you take them off now? I'm keen on a shower."

She nodded in agreement and went back to her room for scissors. He sat on the bed to be eye level with her as she carefully removed the packing around the laceration on his forehead. His face was so close to her chest that he wanted to bury it there.

As if she could read his mind, she murmured, "Be a good boy."

He emitted a low, wolf-like growl, "Aurora, you can't imagine how good I can be.... Excuse my honesty but the first time you try to sit down after I've gotten a hold of you, it will be uncomfortable."

She snorted awkwardly, glad he didn't know how he instantly made her wet.

He stood and removed his shirt carefully for her to cut off the wrap she had affixed to his flank. Her hands on his midsection as she gingerly reached under the wrapping to cut it off him raised gooseflesh everywhere and sent blood racing to his cock. He was sure she would see it straining against his pants.

"Join me in the shower, let's both get wet." He nuzzled into her hair close to her ear. "I'm going to have a tough time washing anything vital with these injuries."

Aurora blushed with discomfort, "Is something wrong with you?" she laughed uneasily. *How did he know he made her wet?* The offer and the husky growl with which it was delivered caused another rush of blood to her most secret parts. She admonished herself for the involuntary reaction.

"I might remind you that I professed earlier to being out of my bloody mind in love, any suggestions should be accepted knowing I've laid my cards on the table," he reiterated.

"Let me know when you are clean. I'll redress the wounds," she snipped, as she moved to her side of the fortification, gently clicking the door behind her.

While Mack showered, Aurora placed a secure video call to her sons. Along with their wives and the children, everyone was safely tucked in at Gull Cove. The sounds of the kids noisily pattering around behind them brought on a bout of homesickness.

She smiled happily at her handsome stepsons as they appeared on the screen. Neither one of them was Ben's carbon copy, but slight changes in their facial expressions flashed their father's genes clearly across each face.

Sam, most like him in personality was a

bull—stubborn, arrogant, and more often than his father, easily confrontational. All his emotion lived immediately under his skin. He kept his head shaved clean, and currently his face was mostly obscured with a dark beard. Sam only grew one when he was out of work from an injury. Currently, he was recovering from an accident where a drunk driver had hit his patrol car and luckily only caused broken ribs. His eyes were a spellbinding pale green, and not remotely like his dad's deep, ocean blue gaze.

Robert, who strongly resembled his late mother, was the teddy bear. Blessed with thick waves of brown hair and soft, chestnut-colored eyes, he was tender, warm, introspective, and slow to burn. If Sammy was the fire, Robert was the calm. Both men in their mid-thirties took after their father most in their strength, loyalty, incredible work ethic, and devotion to family. Although their smiles were infrequent, when they appeared, she could see the shadows of their parents clearly.

"Well, well, well," jeered Sammy. "If it isn't Black Widow," he said, referencing the Marvel Avengers character. Robbie, the expert in all comic book characters chimed in, "Black Widow killed her ex-husbands; it's not like she actually lost one she loved to a heart attack."

"Boys," she interrupted. Despite their ages, their sibling rivalry never waned. "Anyone have a question?" she asked timidly.

"Nothing comes to mind," teased Sammy.

Robbie jumped in, "Aurora, we have a million—but first, are you okay?" he asked.

"I'm fine. I'm surrounded, and my brother just arrived," she assured them.

Robbie took a breath and whispered, "Aurora, Holy Christ... your sister." He couldn't complete the sentiment, the rawness of the story clearly still haunted the boys.

Sammy nodded his head in agreement. "We are so sorry, Aurora. How is it possible our dad never knew any of this?"

"It would have put his life and all of you in grave danger. Can you imagine how he would be reacting now?" she asked.

"Oh yeah, I can see it. He would be dressed in cheap tack gear, black strips painted under his eyes, cigarette hanging from his mouth, pretending he knew how to load a clip into an AR-15 while simultaneously trying to grab your ass," Sammy described perfectly.

They burst into laughter with the uncanny accuracy of the description.

"Exactly, Sammy," she giggled. "Dear God, how I miss that man," she sighed longingly.

Robbie interrupted, "Rory, what else can we do? We both feel helpless here and you out there with three rent-a-cops and Dutch."

Sammy responded to his brother, "Oh those are not rent-a-cops, they might have smoked me with fake resumes, but you know exactly what they are when you look at them."

"This is hard for us Aurora, I'm a trained Marine, a cop. Robbie is a girl, but we don't hold it against him..." Sammy stated as Robert elbowed his older brother.

"Sam, leave him alone," she sighed.

"How did you fool us all this time?" he asked sincerely.

"It was never my intention to fool you. You would never be suspicious of it, and you didn't look for it. I have hid this for twenty years. I was compelled to keep it confidential. All the hours I did researching was covered by the writing. You weren't watching me for signs of anything remotely like this."

Sam and Robert were still trying to absorb all the information they had taken in over the past twenty-four hours, not to mention their fears of the all the unknowns.

"How is it you spent your secret life in front of a laptop, but now you are in the crosshairs, preparing to confront him on your own? You're surrounded by legitimate, confirmed, fucking killers. I tried to convince Dutch to let me come. I can take a position on any rooftop and pick this maggot off a horse's ear."

"Sam, first off, your ribs are still broken, you cannot lie on your stomach to line up a shot." Aurora said quietly. Sam looked at her proudly. She knew just enough to be dangerous.

"It has to be this way, and I knew you two would not be happy with any of this. Sam, your reactions are the reason I never confided in your father. I wanted to tell him, allow my burden to be shared with the man I loved. But just your questions and the look on Robert's face confirms I did the right thing. You can't unsee it now, and my nightmare has seeped into yours. I'm sorry we had to tell you both. If not for the risk you all faced being in the dark, I would never have agreed to bring you both into the circle."

She had argued with Dutch during their phone call most of the night of Ben's anniversary. She resisted bringing the boys in. Her brother knew that if he convinced her the grandkids were in danger she would relent, and it was exactly what she did.

She tried to explain to her sons, "This specific monster initiates his cruelty against the people most precious to his target. You both must stay safe and not take your eyes off those kids. You're all I have left of your father; you are my family and mean everything to me. I can't have any one of you in danger. I promised him I would always take care of you all; even as he took his last breath."

Sammy's face went blank, "Holy shit Aurora! The kid's soccer coach a few years ago, that was you? You never liked him. No one could ever trace where the intel came from." He said, amazed.

She nodded humbly. "Some of them are easy to pick out, it's the ones who hide in the darkest places I search for. You should know, when it came to my grandchildren, I was merciless. Not only their coaches or questionable teachers, but every one of their babysitters and most of their friend's parents went through brutal background checks," she assured.

"Aurora," Robbie voice dropped, "You're all we have left as well. You're the only YiaYia our kids know. Please, please take care of yourself. What kind of toll is this taking on your heart?" he wondered aloud.

Sammy iterated, "No kidding, Aurora, don't make us have to break any more bad news to these kids—they worship you. Oh, and when you get back, I have a box of cold cases that will be assigned to you. All these years I could have had a secret weapon," he shook his head dramatically. She laughed and nodded in agreement.

"I love you guys very much, and please be extra vigilant with those kids."

She blew kisses to her grandchildren who were demonstrating their TikTok moves and photobombing behind her sons as they wrapped up the call.

During their weeks of travel, Mack had never fallen asleep during overnight watch with Aurora. The combination of being injured on the arrest, a long hot shower, and her tender touch on his wounds compounded his exhaustion. The emotional day caused him to pass out on the soft, king-sized bed.

Somewhere in the middle of the night, the dreams came; it had been a long time since one of his PTSD flashbacks assaulted him so vividly. He was dressed in heavy desert gear, patrolling a dust tunnel in Iraq. He was stacked with his men, nuts to butts, clearing the maze they were in. They were taking fire overhead and he was frantically searching for Aurora. He carefully went from room to room, in the direction of her screams, holding his rifle tight to his chest. Someone was hurting her, and he was overwhelmed with angst to get to her in time, "Aurora!" he shouted out, hoping she would hear him and lead him to where she was...

She was there quicky in the dark, flooding the room with light. She reached for his arms as he flailed awake, but he quickly overpowered her. Clasping her by the neck he flipped her onto her back.

"Mack," she tried to whisper, rubbing his arm softly with her hand. "Mack, it's me." He awoke suddenly and realized immediately that he was hurting her.

"Oh no! For fuck's sake! Aurora, I'm so sorry!" He helped her up off her back and ran his hands over her throat to be sure he hadn't wounded her.

"Oh my God!" He slumped back on to the bed, taking her with him in his arms. "Are you okay? Did I hurt you? Did I scare you?" He brushed her hair out of her eyes with his finger.

Trapped in his strong grip, she looked up at him, her face at his shoulder. "I'm okay, you can release me now," she joked.

"You *are* safe, you're in my bed; ready to bargain your way out?" he teased, releasing his hold on her, and allowing her to shift position.

"Shit!" he exclaimed. "What in the ever-loving fuck was that?" he said mainly to himself, running his hands over his face. She scooched up to sit against the headrest.

"Flashbacks? Do you get them often?" she asked, concerned.

"They've never starred you, Aurora. I was searching for you; I could hear you screaming." He lowered his head to her lap, ashamed as emotions closed his throat. "I couldn't find you" he choked, and she wrapped her arms around him, letting him rest against her. She rubbed his back as he composed himself.

"Until I see you away from this danger, I'm not closing my eyes," he mumbled.

She sat quietly, his arms draped around her midsection, his head resting on her abdomen. She idly ran her fingers through his thick, rust-colored hair. He was listening to her steady heartbeat. She was far away in her mind. The sound of him shouting her name had brought her running into the room. She knew enough about combat night terrors from sharing travel accommodations with her brother and was confident she could wake him gently. She wasn't prepared for the comfort she felt, being on his bed and holding him in her arms.

It was the middle of the night, but she didn't want to move—she wanted to stay there, reassuring him, and siphoning the sense of shelter his closeness gave her.

In one swift turn he skillfully positioned her beside him, her head cradled on his arm. Aurora's expression of surprise and anticipation fueled his confidence. He hesitated, taking a second for her to resist but it didn't come. His slightly open mouth delicately met hers. He traced his tongue between her lips. She met it shyly with her own. Their mouths together were a perfect fit. The kiss quickly turned ravenous, and he could taste the wanton need she kept repressed, battling to awaken. It was sensual, soft, and hard, hot, wet, and hungry. Mack's body was ablaze with arousal, her kiss—it was extraordinary, and he couldn't get enough. Her hand crept up to touch his chest. He reached for it and held it against his prominent erection. She gasped into his mouth. Then, she suddenly pulled away.

"I... I can't... I won't... I'm sorry," she cried, forcing herself away and off the bed. She felt it again, the strange vibration in her sternum. *What was it? Familiarity, yearning?*

"Aurora, I can't help myself. What I wouldn't give for you to want me back. I know you're not interested," he said sadly, slumping back on to the bed.

"Did I appear uninterested?" she asked while rummaging through the mini bar for bourbon and a small bottle of vodka.

"Well then, get your sweet ass back here and let me implement the rest of the plan," he urged.

He was looking at her adorable outfit. She was in soft, black yoga pants and an oversized, burgundy-colored *Seaside Heights High School* T-shirt. He also knew she was currently braless, though the large shirt concealed everything.

"In no world am I anywhere close to ready for this," she said plainly. "The willing and able have clearly reared their shallow heads. So in the equation of ready, willing, and able; the ready is locked down," she clarified, handing him the glass of bourbon neat and pouring the vodka over ice for herself.

"I tried to explain this to you earlier. I'm safe where I am. I'm deep in a concrete basement of sorrow, where nothing else can hurt me. I live among the ruins. There is nothing out here for me, nothing could come close to what I lost. To take another chance, I would have to sacrifice the protection grief affords me. I know it's an illusion, but it's my only defense against loving something, anything else that death can steal away from me." She dropped her head, hoping it would stop the tears, but they came fast and furious.

"I swore. I swore when he died I would never be in this situation again. There was no possibility. I would never seek it out, therefore I could never find myself here ever again. I don't want to love anything, anyone anymore; it will kill me. I can't risk it; I won't survive a comparable devastation. My heart is like crushed glass, it's not fit to offer to anyone." Her tears quickly turned into hopeless sobs.

He scrambled off the bed to kneel before her. He raised her chin to look at him. Her melancholy, her beauty was all entangled, and she held his heart in her hands.

"I will do anything for you," he whispered, running his thumbs under her eyes to catch her tears. "Celibacy or monkhood for the rest of my days if you asked it of me. I know I'm rough and salty, but you, you take my goddamn breath from me and then you are all the air on the planet. I've never known true love and romance—I want all of it with you."

She sat quietly on the sofa, sipping the vodka, swabbing her face with tissues. The splinter cracks in her willpower were barely audible, but she could hear them.

"Mack, you're a very nice guy. You would make any woman happy, I'm sure of it. I'm damaged, broken and don't know if I can ever put the pieces back. He was it for me. I don't think I'm capable of ever loving that way again. It's not fair to you. Why would you settle for anything less?" she asked sadly.

"Aurora, let me worry about what I will or will not settle for. You're not expected to love like that again. I'm asking you to consider a new love. Your husband's life is over, not yours. He suffered the loss of his first wife and took the chance again with you. Did you feel like you settled for less with him?" he asked quietly.

It was a question no one had asked her to consider. Ben was afraid when they first fell in love—scared that Aurora could suddenly die, and he'd be put through the awful grief again. He often asked her to promise him that he could die first. He never wanted to suffer the death of a spouse for a second time and now she truly understood his request. Aurora was sure she had taken every precaution to avoid being in this sphere of risk. Where in the world did Mack come from and why her? Widows really should be issued a sign to wear around their necks, she thought to herself.

"Aurora," he whispered, still on his knees before her. "Promise me this, don't rule it out completely. I'm so fucking in love with you, I can see you so clearly. A sleeping goddess in her self-built emptiness. You may bury yourself as deep as you want, but your kiss told me it's not as far down as you imagine. You won't stay there forever, and I can wait," he vowed gently.

She was forced to acknowledge that her anesthetized senses were attempting resuscitation. She was bombarded by the timbre of his voice, the clean scent of his skin, his declarations of lust and desire. The feel of his strong body. His kiss, its perfection, its need, the faint taste of cinnamon from his toothpaste still lingered on her tender mouth. Mack was right— she had never been kissed this way. She was anxious to change the subject.

"Tell me a story," she said. "Tell me how you came to have such a lyrical South African accent." She sat back on the sofa and tucked her legs under herself.

"Hmmm," he mumbled, sitting on the sofa beside her. "Changing the subject? Diverting my imagination from the idea you are in danger? All I do is look at you and want to make wine from your tears."

"Very nice INXS reference," she smiled, impressed, lifting her glass in a mock toast.

"Shit like that sinks me further into the lovesick quicksand you have created. Women do not exist who can name an INXS song from just five words."

"I do know I'm a fascinating woman, Mack." she replied, rolling her eyes dramatically. "You did mention you would wait until the end of time, so have the clocks stopped suddenly?"

He laughed and replied, "As the lady requests, the journey from South Africa it is..."

Mack finished the last of his drink and sat back against the cushions of the couch.

"I was born in England, as you know my Pop died when I was two years old. Mum took me back to Johannesburg where she was born and raised. I was a normal kid, played cricket, rugby, always bringing home a stray cat for Mum to care for and save. When I was twelve, it was her turn to drag home a feral animal, she remarried. My stepdad was a wanker from the first day, always out of work, drunk most of the time, and for entertainment liked to swat us around. Typical shit to piss off a pre-teen. I just turned seventeen when he lit her up quite nicely. Broke her jaw, a few ribs, and the like. I packed our bags, and we made our escape. We hid with one neighbor after another, spent time with Mum's relatives, as we headed north."

"Once there, we migrated to Southern Spain. It was there while my underaged ass was bartending that I met a suspicious Marine on leave who saved our lives."

"No!" she gasped.

"Yes ma'am, your crazy brother rescued us both. He became my mentor, guardian, and ultimately steered me to my life in the military. I'm not sure he has forgiven me for choosing the SEALs over the Corps, but he has been a watershed presence."

"My mum lives in San Diego now, still teaching kindergarten children part-time. She remarried, finally picked a great guy, and they travel up and down the West Coast in a beat-to-hell mobile home. Gratefully, they have given up asking me for grandchildren," he paused, gauging Aurora's reactions. He saw tenderness on her face, and he ached to kiss and hold her.

Aurora stretched her arms over her head and yawned. "There are a great many holes in your story," she replied.

"I was a logger in Washington State for a spell, but the rest is all confidential, ma'am." He smiled.

"No children, never married, no girlfriend home waiting?" she asked idly.

"No children, one ex-wife. Total time married:

six months. No girlfriend home waiting, but I'm working on it." He smiled jokingly.

"Oh wow, I'm so sorry," she tsked, completely missing his last remark.

"Nothing to waste your compassion on; it was a bad decision inspired by tequila. Haven't touched it since. If you don't mind, I have a question for you?" He waited for her go ahead. She nodded.

"The tattoos, the company name, why the trident, what is the significance for you and Dutch?" he asked. Aurora looked up at the ceiling, trying to quell the tide of old emotion she kept hidden about Tieghan.

"Mermaids. She wanted to be a mermaid. She could swim before she could walk. Always in a pool or the ocean. Tieghan and the water, she loved it. I watched hours of the Ariel movie with her. As a SEAL you know, the trident is a symbol of King Neptune, the weapon of Poseidon and the protection he provides under the sea. The safety that we couldn't give her during her life." Aurora dropped her head again to her chest. Tears she thought she had exhausted over the years came silently now.

Mack reached for her hand, resting at the top of the sofa. He longed to pull her on to his lap and kiss and caress her tears away.

"It's the main symbol in the gold pin that the Navy SEALs wear. We call it the "Budweiser" or the bird. We work incredibly hard toward the gold pin. They don't come easy. For us it represents honor, integrity, and discipline. When one of our comrades has fallen, one by one we remove the pin from our breast and pound it onto the lid of their coffin. They are buried with our pins."

"Are you issued a new one?" she asked.

"Yes, only after our brother is buried."

"It must be so beautiful to see," she whispered with reverence.

Aurora could listen to him talk for days. She found it peculiar how the tone and cadence of his voice hadn't resonated with her until recently. Suddenly, it was comforting, calming, or... heart quickening, depending on his words. *What was going on?* Maybe it was the fact that she could talk to him about Tieghan. Not once had she shared her memories, thoughts, or devastation with anyone other than Dutch.

Mack's strength was a rock for her to fall upon and it could be her ultimate downfall. Sharing Tieghan was unraveling her, but Aurora was exhausted from carrying it alone for so long. Suddenly, an old quote popped into her mind, *"You may conquer with a sword, but you are conquered by a kiss."*

A few hours later, Aurora went looking for Tim and Sydney since they were not asleep in their usual spots beside her when she awoke. She found her precious, traitorous dogs curled up around Mack's blanketed legs on his bed.

He was sitting up changing stations on the TV, looking for news.

"Good morning, have you decided to join team Mack in the 'bed of bad intentions'?" he snarked.

"What is happening here?" she asked in feigned outrage. Both dogs looked up at her and swiftly lay back down to finish their naps.

"The boys and I held a secret meeting about you, we decided whether you insist on sleeping alone, us gents would nap together," he teased.

"Oh really?" she declared. "Well, since you have formed this little club, I'd suggest you all take your bathroom business outside together and bring me a very large, hot cup of coffee back after your ablutions." Her snark showed her displeasure in the pups' defection.

"All that madness is already taken care of. I had them out ten minutes ago and your coffee is on the counter near my mini bar." Self-satisfaction was written on his face.

She smiled and bowed to him. "How sweet of you," she gushed. He smirked from his spot on the bed. "Taste it first before you thank me."

Aurora took a sip and almost burst into tears. *How did he know?*

"Mack!!!" she shrieked. She was drinking bliss. It was the very thing she had dreamed up on her own, another one of her mad cap combinations of equal parts coffee and hot chocolate with a shot of peppermint syrup topped with whipped cream.

He snickered with delight. "You did promise to tell me about this invention, and not to expose my informant, but Cat gave up the recipe. And it seems you can request any combination in a cup over at Java Jim's down the street. I did okay? You won't ask Cat to donate it to a rest home?" He looked over at her as she took another sip and moaned with appreciation.

She smacked her lips and laughed at his joke, "Yes, you did better than okay. There will be no sending this back." Her voice softened, "You remembered me talking about this? That was weeks ago."

He smiled shyly. "I'm in love with you, Aurora, I don't know many more ways to convince you, with my clothes on, but I won't stop trying."

Aurora was speechless. She was touched and moved by the act. She was embarrassed that she couldn't return the sentiment. "Thank you, Mack, this was very nice of you—all of it. You didn't have to take care of Tim and Syd. I'm your job, not them..." She headed to her room quickly before she started to stumble over the comments that were randomly forming in her mind.

"Aurora, when you love what you do, it's never a job." He stated before she left the room.

She wanted to say something to him, but out of her peripheral vision she saw the FedEx envelope that had been slid under her door as she headed to the bathroom. She wondered if she'd forgotten something that Jen said to expect. Leaving the cup on the dresser, she reached down for the package.

She pulled the tab on the envelope as she

turned the water on in the shower. She slid out the one photo enclosed inside. It was a recent 5x6 color photo of her grandchildren, sitting around the firepit in the backyard at Gull Cove. Each child had a red circle around their head with an "X" drawn through it.

She fell to the floor in a dead faint.

Chapter Eighteen

Alejandro Vasquez was a beautiful child. Stunning, deep olive coloring, huge brown puppy dog eyes and a soft mouth of full lips. His looks and disposition contributed to his utter destruction growing up. His parents worked on the most exclusive resorts in Mexico, where he was groomed by them to be a successful and sought-after catamite. Though the idealistic-sounding title had its origins in Ancient Greece and Rome, it still meant the unnatural use of a young boy.

They proffered him to the older, white businessmen who traveled alone and crossed the border to Mexico to feed their fetishes. It started slow, his small hands ending a massage for a guest his mother had booked for extra money. When his parents realized his money-making potential, they positioned him to provide many other services for resort guests. They turned him into a star recruiter of other children when they managed the resort's day care and child activity center.

Most traveling parents were happy to hand over their small kids to a luxury babysitting service. For a day of adult-only relaxation, they were easily inclined to trust the resort, never thinking to consider what lurked inside. Some parents wondered years later why their children came home with nightmares and turned to alcohol and drugs. They never suspected it was the adorable, kid-only fun center at the Mexican resort.

As he grew into a handsome man, he knew there was no limit to the strange and nontraditional acts people were willing to pay for, mostly from young children. He built an empire underneath his empire with the help of a mysterious benefactor.

Lucius had approached Alejandro when he was struggling to finance his vision. The handsome, hypnotic stranger entered his office offering a service of his own. Riches beyond his dreams and access to anything he needed. All the resources available to feed the demand for children to indoctrinate into the ruin Alejandro had endured as a child.

With his signature and a flash of his pen, Alejandro could have anything.

Lucius was merely an investor, he explained to Alejandro in his rented corner office. "Look out there." He swept his hand at the view from atop the skyscraper Alejandro had been hungering to own.

"Anything, Alejandro. Immortality, riches, access to anyone you desire and immunity from the law. Sign here," he requested.

"What's in this for you?" Alejandro asked, not overly concerned.

"Not much," he assured, "only your immortal soul." He smiled, collecting the signed documents.

Alejandro shrugged his shoulders, "I lost it

when I was five years old beating off old men on massage tables, so there's not much left of it, but it's yours."

Alejandro's path changed almost instantly. He established a world-renowned modeling and talent agency which promoted the pretty children he signed. In the meantime, he could easily snap up the odd, disfigured, deaf/mute, and special needs children that his client base continued to demand. He was successful in part due to the disturbing hubris of most parents. None of them thought their children were ugly or untalented. Everyone had their price. For some, it was the fame they could never attain in their lives and suddenly they could live vicariously through their kids. For others, it was the money and opportunities to be around the famous celebrities they worshipped. It didn't matter what their reason, Alejandro handed over the Faustian contract for their signature, and no one thought to challenge him.

When Tieghan Velarde came into his sphere, he was masterminding the Mermaid Magic Cruise for young families. Leaving out of Cancun, the five-day excursion traveled the Caribbean around Isla Mujeres down to Playa Del Carmen and past Cozumel. Families of young girls and boys rushed to dress as Ariel or other mermaids, King Neptune or Aquaman for the trip. Tieghan was a star during the week and her parents were encouraged to enter her into the toddler fashion show, where she was the clear winner.

Her golden hair of endless curls framed her sparkling blue/seafoam green eyes. He was entranced by her ethereal allure, her spunk and fire. Typically, he preferred boys, but something about her drew him greedily to her.

He knew she would make rain for his company. He would have her as his own toy, but he had to get past her siblings. He showered her family with special amenities and tempting riches. They spent the entire cruise as VIP guests to woo them and gain their confidence.

Tieghan's parents were easy targets. Money and famous people were their weakness. He quickly set up special encounters and loaded the scale with gold coins. They signed her over to him with only two hours of negotiations. Seated in his Manhattan office, their names inked on the contract, Tieghan was whisked away toward her guaranteed fame.

She did photo shoots; thousands of pictures taken in countless costumes and poses. Most were loaded to dark websites, with prices attached. The bidding took off quickly. She was only three when Alejandro grabbed her, so he had years to groom her until she entered puberty and her career would be over. It would have been perfect, if not for the older Velarde siblings. Aurora and her brother were a thorn in Alejandro's side from the very beginning.

Alejandro's team of lawyers worked tirelessly against them, finally gaining injunctions to keep them away from their sister and her contractual obligations.

Now they appeared again in his rearview mirror, causing disruptions across his organization, taking a billion-dollar operation apart one nickel at a time. The voices of the martyrs were reaching his lofty height. The time had come to settle with the two of them. The Culebra was preparing to strike.

Chapter Nineteen

Roscoe Williams rolled his antiquated wheelchair to the usual corner at 9th Avenue and West 34th Street. Close enough to the Skylight Diner to catch folks coming out who would be willing to share their leftovers and far enough from St. Michael the Archangel's Church for him to keep watch for any potential vandals.

His simple life had begun in Brooklyn, but Manhattan was always the destination. He grew up dreaming about the magnificent skyline and its manifestations—he wanted to do so much. He thought about being a preacher for a large congregation or singing in a Broadway show. But the draft changed the course of his life. He was wounded during Operation Harvest Moon in Vietnam, after he had served three tours. He returned home in a wheelchair after trading in both his legs for the new transportation.

Becoming chronically homeless almost immediately after his return stateside, he spent the ensuing fifty-five years being a part of the city. He knew every shelter, soup kitchen, Salvation Army, veterans group, church, and generous food truck. It had been an interesting life of fighting for space to sleep, haggling over a blanket from a dumpster, and the ingenuity that came from putting the chair in places it wasn't designed to go.

Roscoe always had been a man of deep faith.

He felt God had a plan for him. His mother had raised him on the Bible, his grandmother took him to choir practice in their tight-knit Brooklyn neighborhood during the early sixties. The day he stepped on the land mine at the edge of Que Son Valley he had landed on his ass but could still feel the small Bible he carried, tucked in his back pocket. He couldn't tell you what drew him to St. Michael's on 34th Street, but it was his destination every morning for the past six months. God wanted him nearby, and while he didn't know the reason yet, deep inside his heart he understood he was a part of it.

He'd be humbled if God chose an old, broken, black man like himself, folded into a wheelchair, to serve him. "Blessed are the pure in heart, for they shall see God." He knew he had one war left in him.

Roscoe observed the newest priest to come and go from the small rectory. Even his old, tired eyes could see the good in the man. He hadn't known enough decent Catholic priests; his experience was with Baptist ministers. Something about Father Micah shone like the sun off a chrome bumper.

This day, Father Micah walked in his direction. He had never made his way this far down the street. Roscoe sat humbly in his spot; his worn military flak jacket frayed around him. As the young priest approached, Roscoe was filled with an unusual surge of inspiration, power, and vitality. He removed his ball cap in deference.

"Good morning, Gunnery Sergeant," the priest greeted him and placed a strong hand on his shoulder.

Roscoe took a deep breath and looked up into the man's eyes, seeing who he truly was in all his magnificent glory.

"He knows you are on Earth, General. They are awakening everywhere, awaiting your signal."

"They are all in place, Gunny. It won't be long now," replied the young priest.

"The girl? I think she might be ready," Roscoe asked, concerned. "Do you need me to go back to her?"

Father Micah nodded, "No, I need you here. The dreams and your one appearance were enough of an intervention. She can always summon you and if she does you should go. You have done a great job with her through this. We can do no more without crossing a line. Be ready, she also might change her mind, but he is beside her now. We shall see." The young priest grinned, confidently.

Chapter Twenty

Aurora regained consciousness suddenly and attempted to orient herself. She found herself lying on the bed, her head cradled on Mack's lap as he held a cool cloth across her forehead. The rest of her group surrounded her.

She sat up with a shriek, "Oh my God, the kids!"

"Easy Tink," Dutch assured her as he sat on the bed next to her. "It's a warning shot, you know how Alejandro plays. Sammy and Robbie haven't left Gull Cove, and the children are secure."

"You didn't take your medicine yet this morning, did you?" asked Cat, her arms akimbo, using her Mother Superior tone of voice.

Aurora shook her head, "I was heading into the shower, I don't usually take it until after I'm dressed." Cat handed her the box of a.m. pills and a bottle of water.

Aurora tried to shift position but felt herself getting dizzy again. Mack guided her as she found a spot to lean against. Dutch reached for her hand, "Little sister, your heart can't take what comes next and you know it. If you are fainting over a photo, you won't last through the hard part of this."

Aurora shook her head defiantly, "Oh hell no, you are not benching me now! We are so close, and I *know* we are by his little stunt this morning."

Dutch looked up at his men for support. None

of them were willing to put her in the path of danger but remained silent in support of her wishes. He sighed and responded, "Tink, your heart is not strong enough. You're still recovering from surgery; a few hours off your medicine, you get this photo, and you collapse."

"M-uh...Dutch..." She almost slipped and said his true name in her desperation. "Dutch, it was a picture of my grandchildren, I couldn't help myself. You know if the focus is on me, he's fighting someone his own size, not my weakness, my strength."

"I cannot lose you too," he mumbled weakly.

"Never going to happen, big brother, you're stuck with me," she assured.

"Okay, well we have to execute on the new plan," Dutch announced. "First, we are vacating the hotel and getting out of Syracuse. We'll send Billy back home with the bus. Next stop is a secure location."

"You can't cancel the appearances; you know he's watching. If he thinks I'm running he'll adjust his plan, maybe go under and we'll lose the opportunity," Aurora stated calmly.

"No, we won't cancel the appearances, but we can transport you to and from them out of the location I have in mind." Dutch assured her.

"Can I take my shower now?" she asked.

"From now on, Tink, you do nothing alone except shower," he replied sternly.

"Cat, come with me and help me pack her out

of the bus. Mack, stay with her until she's ready to come down. Quincy, Ken, see Billy off when we're done and bring the cars around front. We'll use the SUVs to get to the next location. I'll have Kai arrange to have your personal vehicles brought there this week."

Mack waited for the room to clear before he spoke. "How are you feeling now?" he asked and handed her the cup after he warmed it in the microwave.

She lay her head back against the plush backboard of the bed and took a sip. "I'm okay, it shook me up and before I knew it, I was down," she sighed. "You found me?"

"I heard the thump and ran in here to see if something fell. When I saw the something was you, well, I was hoping to perform mouth to mouth," he grinned wickedly, stood up from the bed, and went to run the water in the shower.

"You never did tell me what you named this concoction," Mack said, pointing to her cup. Aurora laughed, taking another sip.

"I make it around the holidays, it's called, 'Santa has a Secret.'"

He laughed with her. "I bet it goes good with the Menopause Miracle Mix," he said, raising his brows at her.

She flashed him a wide-eyed glance. "I'll bet you're right, what a great idea!"

"I have another great idea. The invitation is still open, Aurora. I can join you in there to ensure you stay steady on your feet," he offered, pointing toward the bathroom.

"Somehow, keeping me upright does not feel like your ultimate intention," she replied calmly, sipping from her cup.

He smiled and returned to his room, "Now you're starting to see the whole picture."

Chapter Twenty-One

The three-hour drive to Echo Lake, PA was done mostly in silence. Dutch drove the lead car with Cat and Quincy. Ken took the Escalade with Mack, Aurora, and the dogs. She had fallen asleep across the back seat with Tim and Syd nestled around her.

Mack and Ken chatted intermittently about the recent turn of events. Dutch had pulled the plug on the remaining arrests and began concentrating on a strategy around Aurora's potential abduction. Ken was concerned for his boss and best friend. He had been witnessing the feelings that Mack harbored for Aurora deepen and asked him if it would make more sense to back off for now.

"Mack, I get it; she is smart, funny, and beautiful. What's not to love about her? Quincy and I are both crushing on her too. She is entertaining to be around, but the shit she's carrying, Mack, it's a lot. All I'm saying is, maybe give her some space," Ken whispered.

Mack looked back at Aurora's sleeping form; his heart melted seeing her safe and comfortable for the moment.

"Not possible," he whispered to his friend. "Kenny, she's the one. I can't fucking breathe without her. I could die and still find a way back to her," he replied. Mack exchanged glances with Ken as he shook his head in bewilderment.

The concealed lakeside log cabin in the Pocono Mountains was an ideal location. The fall colors had peaked, and the quiet spot was posing for its last Pennsylvania postcard pictures. High electric gates were hidden and surrounded the property. The cars were parked in the double garage as the men brought the luggage and provisions into the house.

Dutch coordinated the assignment of bedrooms, with Aurora getting the second-floor master in the rear of the cabin facing the lake. The entire second floor was wrapped with a balcony accessible by the two rooms located up there. Mack carried their bags up and occupied the small room beside hers. Dutch entered the bedroom Mack had chosen and closed the door behind him.

"Is this unrequited teenage love thing going to be a challenge for you?" Dutch asked him, frankly. Mack squared his shoulders to his boss, who only had about two inches on him.

"Nonissue," he clipped, ironically.. Using the same response Dutch had when questioned about Aurora having a brother.

"Mack, she's my sister, the only one I have left. I have worked my entire life to protect her from harm. Right now, she is a puzzle box of one thousand broken pieces. What are you thinking?" Dutch asked with genuine concern.

"Dutch, I'm sorry, this was information you left out when you sent me to meet her. I don't want this to damage our friendship or affect the relationship you and I have in any way. But boss,

I'm in love with her," he whispered with humility.

"Mack, I consider you like my own son, you know it. I don't know which one to safeguard from getting hurt, you or Aurora. She won't survive another hit. Losing Ben legitimately broke her heart, it's physically damaged. How can you guarantee you will never injure her? Even by no fault of your own?"

"Dutch, I can't stay away from her; I don't understand it myself. Since the moment I met her, something I can't comprehend drew me to her and it won't release its hold on me. I feel like my entire life has led me to this moment in time. You've known me since I was seventeen years old, have you ever seen me like this about a woman?"

Dutch stood quietly thinking about it. Mack was right; since his brief, unsuccessful marriage he was never distracted by any other woman. He had taken great pains to protect himself from any diversions. *Why Aurora?* Was the attraction in the impossibility of it? There was a chance she could decide to never emerge from her mourning over Ben.

"Are you prepared for the likelihood that she won't get over her husband? Mack, you didn't see it, it was a love story some people go their entire lives without experiencing. I can't imagine her coming back from this loss and I lived through a similar one. It's taken me fifteen years to even be with someone else." Dutch shook his head, knowing how relentless Mack could be when he actually wanted something.

He continued, "You're going to need a big and I mean, huge, dramatic gesture to even grab her attention. She's in a trench. And my sister doesn't do anything until she is good and goddamn ready."

"Dutch, I will protect her with my life; I would die to keep her safe. Even adoring her from afar is enough for me now. Let me just have that?" Mack asked with humility.

"Well son, dying is not currently the way to win Aurora over. I trust she's had enough death for one woman. Swear this to me—don't push her, let her come to you. Do not hurt her or cause her any pain, not even the anguish of indecision. I will scatter your bones across the globe if that should ever happen, and my methods of retrieving them will not be pleasant," he assured.

"I swear, Dutch." Mack bowed his head solemnly in acceptance.

Ecstatic to have access to a kitchen, Aurora engrossed herself in her first true passion— cooking for others. She was delighted to find her desire to cook again reemerging. The amazing scents emanating from simmering pots and meats roasting in the oven permeated the cabin's air.

"Oh shit," Dutch sang, coming down the circular staircase from the second floor. "Tink, I could swear Nana was in the kitchen with you, it smells fantastic down here," he declared, kissing the top of his sister's head. He marveled as she did her waltz between the range, stove, and countertops.

Cat sat at the counter, prepping vegetables. "I remember your Nana," Cat said dreamily. "She made the best Christmas cookies. And pretty much everything else."

Dutch caught himself looking at Cat and felt a deep love bloom in his heart. He surprised himself with the feelings being resurrected from his busted psyche.

Aurora stood with her hands on her hips in the middle of the room, teasing her brother, "How do you not have a coffeepot in this hideout?"

Quincy came in from the garage carrying the box he packed with the Keurig, along with all the accoutrements from their brewing station in the bus. "Here I come to save the day!" he sang in his deep tenor voice.

"Whew, thank God for you, Mighty Mouse," declared Aurora, "Almost had to halt the entire deployment for an unreliable quartermaster."

Mack lit a magnificent fire in the great room's hearth as Aurora and Cat started to put dinner on the table. The serving platters shimmered with the colors and smells of roasted chicken thighs with orange and pomegranate glaze, creamy spaghetti carbonara, roasted mushrooms, carrots and zucchini, and a baby arugula salad with beets and goat cheese. A basket of fresh-baked focaccia bread was being passed along with whipped herb butter to spread on it.

The group ate languorously, enjoying the food and the intimate company. Mack sat at Aurora's left side and groaned with pleasure from each bite. "Is there anything you can't do?" he asked in wonder.

"Well," she said slyly. "I am forbidden to move frozen precipitation." She touched the spot where her ICD was implanted, "I'm not complaining. It's nice to see people enjoy my cooking again," her voice was heavy with melancholy.

"If this is how you cook, I'll shovel your snow forever," he promised, hand over heart. "Anything you need me to plow, just a wink and a come hither will do it." He laughed quietly.

Aurora watched him enjoy his dinner and felt the absence of her husband fiercely. Ben had been a fussy eater, except when Aurora cooked. She learned quickly what he liked and made it her quest to spoil him. He made every meal they shared together an adventure. He liked to steal from her plate. He also liked to feed her something from his, something she hadn't ever tried. He'd hover around her at the stove, asking to taste what simmered in her magical cauldrons. They could sit at a table for hours after a meal, laughing and talking, flirting, and teasing. His death had taken the joy from most everything, even her culinary prowess. But she stole some of that back tonight, treating the team.

Quincy and Ken were amazed and thrilled to enjoy a home-cooked meal. "Miss Aurora, I haven't eaten this good in a long time, thank you so much!" Quincy sighed with contentment. Ken still had his mouth full but nodded his head in agreement.

They sat around the table for a long time, enjoying what they knew to be the calm before the storm. Their intimate circle was able to relax for a moment. The men were nursing glasses of scotch while Aurora and Cat were finishing a bottle of decent cabernet.

"Aurora, do you have any embarrassing stories about Dutch growing up?" asked Ken.

She was cozy and a little buzzed down at her end of the table. The wine was taking the right amount of edge off her normal unease. "Nah, he was born into military readiness; nothing really comes to mind... except his insistence to never change out of his Power Rangers underwear. Our mom was forced to bribe him to allow her to wash them. She finally got smart and bought six more pairs so she could have a rotation."

The group laughed in unison as Dutch flushed slightly with the memory. "I still have them," he chuckled. "I try to wear them as headbands occasionally."

"It's a shame no one asked me about Aurora's childhood stories," he mumbled. "Cause if we get her to finish a second bottle of wine she performs a mean Sonny and Cher duet on karaoke," Dutch announced.

Cat and Aurora began to snicker and simultaneously picked up their butter knives, using them as microphones, singing, "All I ever need is you..."

"Or the time she dressed up as Billy Idol for Halloween, or..."

"Okay, enough sharing." She held up her hand, mortified. "Time for sharing KP," she announced. "Kitchen Patrol in case you military types forgot what it means."

"I do have one more question," said Ken. "Why Tinker Bell? How did you come up with that nickname for her?" A nostalgic smile came over both of them. Tears suddenly glistened in Dutch's eyes.

Aurora spoke quietly, her voice filled with a dull ache. "Dutch and I loved the movie *Peter Pan* as kids, we watched it constantly. I was given an official Tinker Bell wand for an early childhood birthday. It lit up and made the sounds of a swish and the sprinkling of fairy dust. I kept it forever. Tieghan confessed to us once that she never wanted to grow up. So, she would ask to use my wand and sprinkle her with fairy dust so she could fly to Neverland and live with the lost boys, and they would take care of each other. When she had trouble sleeping I'd wave the wand around her and off to sleep she would go."

"... second star to the right and straight on till morning," Dutch whispered sadly.

Everyone was quiet at the table, powerless to ease the enormous amount of guilt and sadness the siblings carried.

"It just occurred to me; we haven't properly thanked you all. Dutch and I have held these memories, wrapped up in deep shame and remorse, for such a long time. It is an enormous reprieve to finally share it with people we trust."

Chapter Twenty-One

She sat up in her chair and leaned forward at the table.

"We are incredibly lucky to have you all willingly take up the cause with us. We advanced as far as we could alone, and we are beholden to each of you for your support," Aurora said, with great humility.

They each nodded proudly in response.

The men stood together to clear the table and began the cleanup of the kitchen. The sounds of the back-and-forth ball breaking and intermittent snapping of the dish towel among them caused occasional eruptions of laughter. The women opened another bottle of wine and sank into the overstuffed seats around the fireplace. Tim and Sydney jumped onto the ottoman at Aurora's feet and settled into the evening.

"Rory," Cat began quietly. "I'm flabbergasted about Tieghan. It's all so heartbreaking; I can't stop thinking about it. You did know the story we all got after your family moved away was that she died of leukemia. How in the world have you both been shouldering this all alone?"

Aurora nodded and looked at her friend sadly, "I'm sorry I never confided in you, we kept it to ourselves for self-preservation and extreme caution."

"I remember her so plainly—she was such a beautiful baby. You used to walk her around the block in her adorable mermaid stroller, clinging to her favorite stuffed animal," Cat recalled wistfully.

Aurora sat up. "Oh my God! Cat! I forgot, the stuffed animal!" Together they finished the sentence, "… the baby sea turtle." All the air left Aurora's body. The irony was now insurmountable. Cat looked at Aurora with complete confusion. "What is it, Rore?" she whispered with fright.

"Tieghan," Aurora whispered back. "She's been trying to tell me something." She looked over her shoulder at the men in the kitchen and her eyes fell on Mack, busting chops with his men and her brother. It blindsided her… Mack. *But what about him?*

"Talk to me, baby sister," she asked inwardly. "What do I need to know?"

"Cat, the baby sea turtle. It keeps showing up in my life. I felt like one heading back to Autumn Lake—it was the only image in my mind. I was scrambling back to the ocean for protection. Then, along came Mack, and when I met him all I could see was the bracelet he wears with the silver charm," Aurora said in hushed and confidential tones.

Cat glanced over at the men in the kitchen, "You think Tieghan is trying to tell you something about Mack? I've never really looked at his charm—it's a baby sea turtle?" she gasped. "Jesus, Aurora it must mean something, Tieghan would never let that little toy go. She always held on to it for dear life. I remember you had to walk over to the pediatrician's office to retrieve it, she left it there at one of her visits. She wouldn't sleep without it."

Of course, the baby sea turtle. How could she have missed it? She knew it meant something but could not gather her memories through the web of widowhood and its opaque windows.

They sat mute when Aurora glanced back over at Mack. He caught her eye and cocked his head in silent inquiry; she practically heard him ask if she needed anything. She shook her head to confirm she was okay. Aurora didn't notice how they were able to communicate without using words. *When did that become a thing?* Satisfied she was all right, he smiled sweetly in her direction and was drawn back into conversation with her brother. There was something about him, something Tieghan wanted her to know.

"Cat how was Dutch when he divulged all of this to you?" she asked in a low voice, still trying to figure out the message from her baby sister. Cat looked over her shoulder to the kitchen to be sure they were out of earshot.

"A mess," she admitted. "He paced the floor in the room, broke down, and sobbed. He finished off a fifth of Southern Comfort and then well..." she stopped, suddenly embarrassed.

Aurora grabbed her friend's hand, "Cat, you don't have to be uncomfortable with me ever. Besides, you've loved him your whole life, don't deny it."

Her friend nodded her head, as tears stole their way down her face.

Everyone made their way to their rooms. Ken

would take the first watch of the night and made camp in the great room; his weapons close by.

The remaining bedrooms were on the first floor behind the kitchen. Quincy had been asleep for an hour as he would take the second watch at four a.m. Dutch headed to his room and signaled for Cat to follow him. She looked around, then snuck into the bedroom with him.

Upstairs, Aurora was trying to make sense of her luggage. Apparently, her brother didn't pack with military precision. She was looking for her ICD monitor. Every morning between two and four a.m. the machine-made contact over WI-FI with her defibrillator to check for errant arrythmias and sent a report to her electro-physiologist's office. She couldn't imagine where it could be.

Mack tapped on her door and entered, bringing with him a hot cup of chamomile tea, "What are you looking for?" he asked. When she explained it to him, it dawned on Mack why it was missing.

"This must be how they are tracking you, Aurora. With the removal of all other devices from the bus and the bedroom our phones jammed, the only way they can locate you is from the ICD. Dutch must have figured it out and disabled the machine for now."

"Ah, smart move," she said slurring her words from a bit too much wine. She sat on the bed, adjusting the blankets for the dogs. Mack handed her the box of her nighttime medication.

"*Et tu, Brute?*" she said with a smile, taking them quickly with a gulp of the warm tea.

Mack could see she was struggling with her coordination. "Do you need help, Aurora? I didn't think this was possible, but you are even more charming walking two lines," he teased.

"You say the nicest things, Sailor," she replied with a slight hiccup. She stood unsteadily and presented her back to him. "Can you help me with this zipper?" she asked, indicating the one at the back of her knit dress.

She lifted her hair up off her neck for him and he grabbed the slider between his fingers and began to unzip. The scent of her warm skin bloomed around him as her back was laid bare. The zipper ended at the very base of her spine.

He could not resist the temptation and reached into the dress to splay his hands around her uncovered midriff, pulling her close and burying his face in her neck. The feeling of her exposed skin at long last consumed him with passion.

"Mack," she sighed—resignation, desire, and frustration mixing together. "You're not being a gentleman." Another slight hiccup escaped from her.

"You're right, Aurora, I'm a hungry fucking wolf," he growled hot into her ear. He spun her around to face him. Her eyes were glazed from the wine, giving her a dreamy appearance. As he gazed into her face, he saw yearning flash across it. He seized the moment, kissing her with a reckless abandon, as he sought to thaw her very soul and forge it to his. He wanted desperately to claim her as his own, take her here and now and bind her to him for eternity.

Aurora was awash in a maelstrom of delicious memory; the taste of scotch on his tender mouth, the rough brush of his mustache and goatee across her chin transported her back into Ben's arms. She reciprocated, swooning with pleasure into his perfect kiss; she matched his insatiability and need. But it wasn't Ben. Mack's body was larger, his skin smelled different, his hands at her cheeks felt unfamiliar and she plummeted back to the present. She ran her fingers into his waves of hair, grabbing both hands full of it, yanking his head back and his face away from hers.

"No," she said breathlessly, "no more." Aurora found herself equally devastated that it wasn't her husband and her powerlessness at being drawn madly to this man.

Mack was stunned and stepped away. "I'm sorry," he stammered. "I can't help myself and it's not your problem. I won't bother you again," he said unhappily and made his way to the bedroom door.

"Mack," she whispered, as his hand touched the doorknob. He stopped and turned to look back at her. "I'm the one who's sorry. I'm not ready. I'm afraid to let go of him completely… and me, the woman I was with him… I have to let her go too… Please…. don't give up…." She wished aloud.

Aurora could not sleep, so she paced about

the bedroom and tried to occupy herself. She was up and then down. Seated, standing, trying to find a comfortable position on the bed. Nothing was working.

She opened the sliding door to the second-floor balcony and made her way to a pair of large Adirondack chairs to smoke a cigarette. She could hear the lapping of the lake water and the sounds of crickets in the quiet woods.

Mack found his way out there for all the same reasons. He sat unobtrusively in the matching chair beside her. She handed him the pack of cigarettes and lighter without a word.

Downstairs on the main floor, Dutch was awakened by his satellite phone. Quickly alert, he answered and began to assess the horror story the caller was regaling.

"Mother of God," he murmured. "Is anyone hurt?" He waited for his nephew to complete his situation report. "You are all moving *right now*. Pack as fast as you can, I'll have transportation there in fifteen minutes. Not a word to anyone where you're going. Gather up all your tablets and cell phones and leave them with the team I send. Keep only the sat phone with you. I'll go up and wake her now." He hung up abruptly and quickly dialed another number.

"Kai, send Delta team to the shore location. Get everyone out and over to the safe house at 107. They are going to be detained to give statements to the fire marshal, so give Jimmy Batista a call, it's his jurisdiction. We need someone other than the local PD to secure the scene and our people to be a part of the investigation. Take all their phones, tablets, Apple watches, anything with tracking, and lock them in the lead box. Have the Delta leader call me when the packages are secure."

Cat was stirring beside him, "What is it?" she asked sleepily.

"I have to go break my sister's heart, again," he said with disgust, as he stood and dressed quickly.

Dutch slipped up to the second floor to find Mack and Aurora's rooms empty. Confused for a moment, he saw the glint off the tips of their cigarettes on the darkened balcony. He slid the door open, causing them both to jump.

"Jesus, Dutch, you scared me," she snapped, extinguishing her cigarette.

"Aurora, honey," he began. Nothing good ever came after his use of her real name.

"No, no what? Tell me fast Dutch!" she stood quickly from her chair.

"Everyone is safe and unharmed," he tried. She covered her face with her hands, knowing whatever came next would be awful.

"Aurora, there was a fire at the Gull Cove house tonight. The boys responded quickly but there is extensive damage. Your bedroom, the kitchen, the laundry room, and most of the back of the house is gutted. The front has smoke and water damage..."

"The kids?" she yelped with fright.

"They are fine. All fine—a little spooked—but

no one hurt. My team is on the way to move them to a secure location attached to a military base. They will be untouchable there."

Aurora lit another cigarette and let the tears fall. Precisely as it occurred on the night Ben died, she felt the silent, overwhelming, and inexpressible scream gather in intensity inside her, ricocheting within her ribcage, eager to be let free. It promised to be loud and long to shatter the hushed surroundings. Her body leaned heavily against the deck banister, her back turned to the men. She dropped her head to her chest, the inventory of all she owned in the world in her mind's eye.

Their dream house, her husband's exquisite craftmanship. Their sanctuary, ruined. His clothes, their things, memories, books, pictures. His favorite gray cable knit sweater, the one she wore around her shoulders writing at her desk, the handmade coffee cups their grandchildren made for them when they were younger. The Italian ceramic tile from Florence that Ben shipped in as surprise for her to line the stove backsplash. The pillowcases she saved that Ben last slept on, the only ones that still invoked his scent when she held her nose to them.

Her body shook with anger and more loss. The carnage was piling up in her mind. She felt breached, torn wide open again, and dangerously enraged. Worst of all, she knew all that physically remained of her husband was slipping through her fingers like shifting sand.

Dutch and Mack held their breath, waiting for her to speak. She turned around to face her brother.

"Dutch," her voice was tinged with ice. "This son-of-a-bitch isn't going to die good enough for me." The words came through her clenched teeth. Dutch nodded in agreement, unable to comprehend how she could still be standing. He was certain this would be her tipping point.

"I'm going down to the great room to wait for confirmation on the transfer. Join me when you're ready, and we can call the boys from the Faraday room in the cabin shed," Dutch reassured her. She finished the cigarette and snuffed it under her shoe on the deck floor.

Mack, still seated, offered her his hand; she accepted it meekly and he tugged her gently toward him. Aurora's body buckled on to his lap and began keening against his shoulder. She morphed into a rushing wall of water, disintegrating entirely, sobs racking through her. He held her tight, running his hand down her back as her wails of lament were muffled into his neck. Her body was paralyzed with unbridled agony, and he kept her wrapped closely and rocked her in his strong arms.

"Break on me, my beautiful girl. Set it all free, don't keep anything else inside. For the rest of my life, I'll put you back together... every shattered piece... if you let me," he whispered, his lips soft against her cheek. She couldn't answer through the grueling layers of tears raging through her, but she nodded her head in submission. Wrapping her arms around his neck, she clung to him as if her very life depended on it, and broke wide open.

Chapter Twenty-Two

Long, dark hours passed before Aurora reluctantly rose from the protection of Mack's embrace. Sunlight was sneaking over the mountains; a new day was beginning. She remained curled on his lap, tucked into his arms all night. He asked her questions about her husband, their life together, how they met, what he was like. In doing so, she had wrung the last of her perpetual tears until there were none left, and the fount was replaced with the hardened steel of determination.

Mack rose from the chair after she did, stretching his arms. She stood in front of him, staring deeply into his eyes. "Thank you," she said humbly.

"Tell me, what do you see when you look at me, Aurora?" he asked, wondering if her purge in any way changed the optics of her heart. The dawn fully broke on the horizon and sunlight seemed to illuminate him. She gazed up into his exquisite face. "Unfathomable strength, courage, regret, frustration," her hoarse voice caught on the next words, "and unspeakable beauty." She touched his face reverently with the tips of her fingers.

The force of the man he was broadsided her. She could see all of him: his heart, loyalty, compassion, and humility. He'd been a shadow in her orbit until now; she could genuinely see who and what he was, and the clarity was so brilliant she almost covered her eyes.

Mack smiled, "Want to know what I see?" He palmed her cheek. "I see the love of my fucking life." His eyes glimmered, the bluest of blues she'd ever seen. Aurora's vision had shifted impressively overnight.

He took her into his embrace again, if only to reassure her that he would always be an arm's length away. Before he let her go, there was something he needed to know. "Aurora," he whispered. "How did you convince Ben, a sad widower, to take a chance again, to love someone else so completely when he understood the terrible possibility?"

She shocked him when she lifted her head off his shoulder and raised her face to kiss him. It was one of gratitude, innocent and gentle, her lips soft and inviting. He did not push against the serene touch of her mouth, but his heart swelled with hope.

"Like that, that's exactly how I convinced him," she said matter-of-factly, walking away toward her room.

It took him a few seconds to remember what he was doing next.

After showering and getting dressed, she brought the dogs down to let them run across the backyard of the fenced-in cabin. Her head was throbbing from the hours of crying in the night. She hadn't spoken with her boys last night; she wasn't ready for the confirmation that the life she knew was now lost forever in the fire. Yes, the memories remained, but the comfort of her beautiful, Ben-built castle, she knew, was gone. Aurora let Dutch handle everything and the transition for her family.

It was eerie how her feelings mirrored those she experienced the morning after Ben passed away. Her insides were hollowed out and she could hear echoes of her heartbeat within her chest. She had to pull herself back together. There were two days left until they arrived in Manhattan, and with any luck she might exact vengeance. "Please God, let me see him and this time stand beside me?" she whispered.

The time for tears was over for her. She let them all soak into the warm flannel jacket Mack allowed her to bury her head within.

The remnants of who she was yesterday left her soul in a deluge from her body. Once again, she was caught in the ambiguity of her identity just as she'd been when she'd lost Ben. At the hands of so much evil she was compelled to let go of the only things she had managed to cling to for so long. Aurora was beginning to rise from her own scorched ashes. The road back to life appeared to her as flights of long, steep staircases winding in front of her, and she was taking the first step.

She whispered aloud into the peaceful lakeview setting. "Ben Delsea, I will love you forever. I know it's time to let you go. Thank you for our beautiful life together. Rest, honey. I'll take it from here." A breeze came softly from the water and rustled the leaves at her feet. She felt it whisper across her face gently, drying the last of her tears.

The smell of breakfast greeted her as she returned inside the cabin. Dutch knew food was the one way to comfort her. She easily identified the aroma of his famous lump crabmeat eggs Benedict with Old Bay hollandaise sauce and homemade cinnamon buns.

They were gathered around the counter making their plates when she came in from outside. Their voices were soft and muted—unsure of her mood.

Cat handed her a cup of coffee and kissed her cheek. "I'm trying not to be a smart-ass, but remember when your Uncle Jack would tell us, 'By the time you get married it will be all better'? I'm feeling like that might apply to you right now," Cat recalled. Aurora laughed out loud. She always knew what to say—fearless in the face of uncertainty. What a great memory from her favorite uncle. She kissed her friend on her cheek and thanked her.

She fixed her dish and sat with the rest of the group. Aurora was due at two appearances today, one early afternoon and the other this evening. They were working out the details when Mack came down from his room.

Aurora was unexpectedly distracted by his arrival. She watched him descend the steps and move around the kitchen. His walk was an impressive, wide-shouldered swagger. He appeared deep in thought, yet always cognizant of where she was. Since he had asked her to look at him on the deck, she could now plainly see his exceptionally attractive… well, everything. It was as if she previously considered him through a murky lens of fog and smoke. This morning all the veils were lifted, and she fully grasped how astonishingly handsome he was. Strong, naturally sexy, and yet a gentle, tender giant.

Cat, who had been eyeing Aurora carefully since she first sat down, saw the difference in her immediately. She was noticing Mack for the first time. "Welcome back, Aurora—close your mouth," Cat snickered happily. She still never took her eyes off him but did as her friend instructed.

"Cat…?" Aurora muttered in disbelief, her voice cracking.

"I know Aurora—everyone with a uterus knows. I'm sure even those without one can see. He walked right off Mount Olympus," Cat murmured, enjoying her friend's long overdue reaction to Mack.

Aurora surreptitiously watched his every step. He moved like a panther, his muscled back and arms strained against his thin, black shirt. His hair was still wet from the shower and drying in soft, auburn waves. It appeared he had shaved and neatly trimmed his gray-streaked, dark red goatee. He was wearing close-fitting black tactical pants with his handgun tucked up against his lower back. She let her eyes follow the line of his thickly muscled legs. Sunlight was streaming into the kitchen and caught the twinkle of his indigo-hued eyes.

He squatted to adoringly pet the dogs and

handed them both a treat; the poor pets were still waiting patiently next to the counter for one since they had returned from their run outside. They'd already defected to Mack's camp. Seeing him crouching, his body flexed, caused a flutter in her solar plexus. Aurora couldn't imagine how she was blind to him all this time.

How much did she miss while in her frozen tundra of despair? Cat's declaration from their first day on the bus came back to haunt her: *My God, that man is breathtaking.*

She noticed he checked to ensure she had a cup of coffee before he poured his own. He then took his seat beside her to have breakfast. He tilted his head at her in silent inquiry; she smiled and touched his hand, "I'm okay," she whispered, her face lit with enchantment.

He took her hand and sweetly kissed the inside of her palm. Holding it between both of his, he looked into her eyes to assess for himself. She met his hypnotic gaze, seeing him more clearly than ever. He was spellbinding and beautiful, from the inside out. She wanted to recreate him on paper, using all the descriptions now rushing at her. He was magnificent in every way. Her readers were in for a treasure if her prose was strong enough to capture the exquisite human in front of her. Beyond his Greek god-like presence, at this moment he embodied a remarkable crocus that bravely blooms in the middle of a blizzard.

Mack saw the shift in her, in the way she looked at him—he knew she could see him now.

It was in the focus of her pretty eyes, the light finding its way back to her face. In her touch and affection when she reached for his hand. She had wept in his arms most of the overnight hours, held tight to him as he carried her through the darkest parts of the storm. Somewhere in the choking blackness she had struck down her own barricades and surrendered.

He was afraid he might sneeze and change her mind, so he remained still and let her take the baby steps she was initiating in his direction. Mack knew he would never love this way ever again. It dawned on him unexpectedly that this was exactly the intensity of devotion she had tragically lost and was struggling to recover from. He held her hand up to his mouth, kissing it softly. They were lost in each other's stare.

"Tink? Tinker bell? Aurora!" Dutch broke her from the trance formed between them.

"What? I'm sorry, what did I miss?" She shook off the gossamer wrapped around her.

"Are you two okay down there?" Dutch teased. "We can leave you both alone if you need to finish up any business."

Not releasing her hand from Mack's hold, she tossed her half empty plastic water bottle in Dutch's direction, and he caught it behind his back.

"Not sure how many times you're going to throw that pitch, Tink. I'm still a Marine," he chuckled. Aurora shook her head, noticing it never landed. He was too quick but one day she'd clip him.

"The appearances today are in North Jersey," Ken reported. "We have Basking Ridge from twelve to three p.m. and then Paramus from six to nine p.m."

Quincy checked his notes. "Travel time into Basking Ridge is about an hour and half. But only forty minutes to Paramus from Basking Ridge. With a three-hour layover."

Dutch reviewed his paperwork and said, "What do you want to do, Tink, stay in Basking Ridge or go somewhere else before leaving for Paramus?"

"Let's stay in Basking Ridge. Find us a hotel with day rates or something, we'll be out by five."

Cat interrupted, "Your ladyship, we could have tea at The Bernards Inn. You know, act like aristocrats," Cat mocked, holding her coffee cup with pinky extended, nose in the air, cracking the table up.

"Great idea!" Aurora grinned, knowing her brother was going to hate it.

"Negative. No public outings except the ones already scheduled. We don't have enough coverage for another location. You two, no funny shit like escaping to go antiquing," Dutch huffed.

Cat rolled her eyes. "He acts like he knows our profiles—antiquing? As if? You know we're strictly flea market hags."

Aurora shook her head, laughing.

"I'm chipping you today," Dutch announced

to Aurora. "I'm not waiting until we get into Manhattan. I want to be able to track you and you know he'll check you for wires when he gets a hold of you."

Mack felt a wave of disgust come over him.

"You don't think he's going to wait until then, do you?" she asked quietly.

"You're the expert on him, little sister, what do you think?"

The rest of their eyes fell upon her. She didn't have to think about it, her gut knew Alejandro's patience was ending.

"He's done waiting. He's going to grab me up when he can. He has our schedule, it's on my website. It's okay Dutch, I'm done waiting too," she said coldly.

"I need one of you to stay here to watch the place and monitor the comms," Dutch ordered.

"On it, boss," Ken mumbled, the only choice as the tech nerd.

"Kenny, I'm gonna send you some backup to patrol the perimeter. You stay in the shed and track Aurora and all the communications. Check in hourly with Kai to see if he's picked up any chatter from the CI's," Dutch instructed. "With any luck we'll be back here tonight intact."

"Okay Tink, where do you want the chip?" he asked. Dutch opened a black leather case he carried in from his travel bag.

"Well, if he binds my wrists and ankles, it'll interfere with the signal. He'll strip search me for a wire or a weapon. They'll cover my head for transport, check my hair, might even cut it off. But he won't look at the back of my neck. Make sure it's a strong one—you know he has catacombs under his place." Aurora took a sip from her tepid cup of coffee, she seemed unbothered by the conversation. She was ready to confront her nemesis of twenty years, but started to feel the adrenaline burn in her throat

Mack rose quietly from the table and disappeared into the first-floor restroom. He needed a minute and cold water on his face, to wait for the wrath to pass. *What the fuck?* he thought to himself. Nothing ever rattled him; but this woman was inside of him, changing his chemistry. In his career never was an adult female sent in to do the work of trained killers. Unless she was one herself. Mack could not rationalize putting Aurora in the direct line of fire.

Cat slipped in behind him and handed him a small hand towel.

"Thank you, I'm good," he mumbled.

"Welcome to the family," she whispered. "Of all the gin joints, in all the towns, in all the world, you had to fall in love with this one?" She shook her head in pity.

He laughed as he dried his face. "Right back at you, kid," he teased.

"Like you, I know how to pick 'em. She's anxious to get this over with and she's angry. She wants to settle the score, and when she's like this, she's invincible. She has no fear for herself—just for the lives of those she loves. Please don't get yourself hurt—she won't survive it. She can't lose even a fingernail of someone she loves right now, it will literally kill her."

"No worries, Cat. I'm only about keeping her safe. I have plans for her when this is all over," he grinned wickedly.

"How bad was she last night?" she asked him.

"Pretty fucking bad," he replied. "Dawn always comes, something my mum has said forever. She seems okay this morning."

"Okay? Is that what you think 'okay' looks like? You are so smitten it's a sin. Aurora, our Aurora, came back today. Mack, can't you see it? Whatever transpired last night propelled her back from her hidden, protective world and her teeth are showing. If you're smart, you would locate your own Power Ranger underwear and soon, my friend. I realize you have never really met her. You have no concept of the tiger that was awakened this morning."

Mack laughed and moved toward the door. They returned to the great room just in time to see Dutch inject something under the skin at the base of Aurora's neck.

"Oh good," Cat chuckled. "We'll be able to find Mittens if she breaks her leash."

Chapter Twenty-Three

Station Books of Basking Ridge was situated in a beautiful, restored Victorian home. All the floors creaked, and its original residential rooms were now fashioned with delicately arranged shelves and tables filled with books, stationery, and other assorted, high-priced sundries.

"It smells like potpourri and grandma talcum powder in here," Cat whispered.

"You're a snob," chuckled Aurora.

"Snob? Did you count the number of BMWs and Mercedes parked out there in the lot? Um no, I couldn't afford *a candle* in this place," Cat laughed.

Aurora met with the owners, a married couple, Maria, and Linda Lowell. They were great fans of her work and excited about the line queuing up outside of the store.

They showed Aurora to the room in the back of the store where they would direct guests for the signing. It was the first time they were holding a lunchtime appearance and were congratulating themselves on the success it currently promised to be.

Mack shadowed her as Dutch and Quincy took the perimeter. Dutch was in disguise and neither Cat nor Aurora could look at him without flaking out in uncontrollable laughter. He resembled a bad version of the late actor Jerry Orbach, and they couldn't take it. Cat kept singing, "Be Our Guest,"

Lumiere's solo from *Beauty and the Beast*, and it sent Aurora into a fit of laughter.

She settled into a wingback chair behind a lace-covered Queen Anne table in the corner of the room. She could tell the women had cleared everything but the fireplace out to make space for the crowd.

The guests proclaimed themselves to be avid readers and were respectful of her time and generous with their compliments. Most of the women graciously paid their deep condolences to her on the loss of her husband. Aurora also saw for the first time the impact Mack was having on them. Old, young, and in between, they flirted and smiled, all trying to sneak a selfie with him. She laughed to herself, "Widow fog was no joke."

Toward the end of the appearance, the line started to dwindle. The room was half full of the last of their attendees. Suddenly, a young girl, waifish and pale, approached the table. Dressed simply in knit leggings, an oversized army jacket, and brown wool hat, she was wringing her hands, no book in sight for signing. Aurora looked up and into her furtive eyes and knew. She felt her heart still. Mack noticed Aurora's body language and stepped closer to the back of her chair.

"I have a message for you," the girl said in a low voice. "He wants you to know he has your grandchildren and there is nothing you can do now."

Mack whispered into his wrist as Aurora steeled her back, and replied calmly, "I have a message you can bring back to him. You let him know I'm calling the fury of God's own thunder down on his entire empire and there is nothing he can do to stop it." The young girl turned and slipped quickly out of the store.

Dutch and Quincy followed her to see where she would lead them as Mack escorted Aurora and Cat to the hotel to wait out the layover for the next appearance.

"Are you okay?" he asked, reaching for her hand once they were in the car. She laced her fingers between his; Mack grinned with delight through his concern and brought her hand up to his lips to kiss.

"I'll be fine when I know the kids are safe," she said trembling, trying to dial Sammy on her cell phone with her free hand. She heard him pick up and the sound of his voice immediately reassured her. "We're all good Aurora." Sam seemed agitated. "Dutch already checked in on us. We are more than safe, don't worry. Please get yourself away from this danger and don't play into this bastard's hands," he begged.

"I'm perfectly fine," she assured him. If no one can get to you guys, it's the cover I need. I love you all," she whispered.

"We love you too, Rory," Sam replied, "I don't think we tell you enough."

"Sam, we had a rough start you and I, but we have come a long way together, and I'm happy we did. Hug those kids for me, tell them how much I love them, and I'll see them soon."

Mack, Aurora, and Cat checked into the presidential suite of the Archer Hotel in Florham Park, forty-five minutes away from their scheduled evening stop in Paramus. Dutch and Quincy were on their way back, the young girl seemed like a dead end.

Cat was entertaining herself, ordering the crew a generous room service dinner. Sprawled on the room's plush chaise longue, phone at her ear, and flipping through the menu pages. "Mack, how do you like your steak done?" she asked.

"Medium rare," Mack and Aurora answered simultaneously; facing each other, they burst out laughing.

"How did you know?" he asked, his mouth watering to kiss her over and over again, without a care who saw him.

"I didn't know, I guessed," she replied puzzled. "It's how I like mine, so maybe I assumed?" He adored the way she wrinkled her nose when she was thinking.

He cupped her chin and winked. "You—are precisely how I like mine." The tone of his voice was hoarse and hungry.

"Really? How do you like yours?" she flirted back, her expression provocative, which caught him off guard.

He closed the space between them, blocking Cat's view. "I like mine delicious, juicy, and dripping off my chin," he murmured, stroking his goatee for emphasis.

Aurora flushed and stepped closer to him, her hand touching his chest, her eyes glinting mischievously, "I hear you can breathe underwater, Sailor. I hope this is true—it's been a very long time for me." Her voice was mink and the finest bourbon. He could feel all his senses on fire.

Mack's laugh was dirty. "I'm an expertly trained Navy diver, beautiful girl, breathing underwater is what I do best." He stared her down, encircling her neck with his hands, tilting her face close to his. "I'll drain every drop from you till I'm sure I've tasted your soul."

Her breath caught in her throat, and she backed away from him, her heart racing. Mack smiled at her retreat; the protective bunker of ice was melting.

"Oh yes," Cat spoke into her phone. "We'll take the grilled South African baby lobster tails as an upgrade on each dinner." She pointed to Mack. "That's for you, Mackenzie." He chuckled and blew her a kiss.

Mack tried to convince Aurora to get some rest. She was too keyed up and anxious for her brother to return. It started to worry her as they left the bookstore, the young girl seemed like bait and whoever followed her was probably walking into the trap.

She almost passed out from relief when they entered the room. Before she knew it, she was flinging herself into Dutch's arms. "Come on Tink, did you think I would fall for his little fishing expedition?" he assured, holding her tight in his embrace. He whispered in her ear when he noticed Cat, "What is she doing?"

Aurora chuckled, "Burning up your Amex black card."

Dutch released his sister with a guffaw. "She can keep it if she promises that she's finished singing that annoying goddamn song—it's stuck in my head." He walked over to where Cat was sitting, the phone still at her ear, reciting items to the room service manager. He leaned down and kissed her in greeting, publicly, to the complete shock of everyone in the room.

Since he had finally removed his Jerry Orbach disguise, Cat was happy to accommodate his public display of affection.

"What?" he asked, facing their stunned expressions when he turned around. "She was busy, and I wanted to make sure she ordered my steak right." Unable to hide his smirk.

Mack and Quincy turned to smile at Cat, who did blush when she saw them looking at her. Aurora shook her head in amazement, who didn't see this coming? Her heart was filled for her friend and her lovelorn brother.

Ignoring the teenagers in the room, Dutch directed Aurora to the suite's dining table. "Tinker Bell, talk to me. Plans are percolating in your head—I can hear them." He opened his laptop onto the table and was searching for a nearby outlet to plug it into. Mack and Quincy sat at the table next to Dutch.

"Dutch, I want to take the fight to him," she stated calmly. She stood firmly in the center of the room, her arms folded across her chest in determination.

Quincy and Mack's head snapped up at her as if she was announcing her appearance this evening as a lion tamer. "I'm listening," her brother replied seriously. Aurora proceeded to pace around the table, trying to diagram it out in her head.

"Let's postpone the appearance tonight and head to his corporate office on the Upper West Side," she said, matter-of-factly.

"Just walk the fuck in and ask to see him?" blurted Quincy. "I'm sorry, Miss Aurora," he demurred.

"Quincy don't be sorry; if I get close to this bastard, the words I'll use might make you blush." said Aurora, feeling her spine fuse with anger and determination.

Cat finished the extensive dinner order and joined the crew at the table. Aurora quickly glanced over at her, about to say something when she held up her hand, "Three fresh pots on their way up first," her friend assured.

Aurora stood behind the remaining chair at the table, still forming a plan in her mind. "To answer your question Quincy, yes, just walk the fuck in and demand to see him. I would like our sister's remains returned to us and I'm not leaving without them." She spoke directly at Dutch.

"Do you think he still has them—Tieghan's remains?" Dutch asked, his voice softening; he never considered it a possibility. Suddenly, his wounded younger sister was looking like a Marvel superhero to him. She was casting aside sadness for anger and retribution. She stood brilliant, confident, and ferocious in the center of the room. He worried her pendulum was swinging too far to the other side.

"Of course, he still has them. I'm convinced there's a room containing an entire collection. Maybe it's a vault, where a box with her name engraved on the outside sits on a shelf surrounded by untold hundreds of others. He is a classic sociopath and serial killer; he loves his trophies. I'm sure he visits the room to commune with and count his conquests. Not to mention the potential leverage they provide. Families of victims need closure, and to get it they must have something to bury, for both the dead and the living to rest," she explained.

She sat, finally, across the long table from her brother.

"Dutch, I'm tired of playing defense, let's switch the game on him," she urged. "If we can catch him out in public, at dinner, or even walking back to his office, I can challenge him, and he *will* drag me into the lair. He can't help himself. You know he's been plotting as he waits for me. He'll have life-sized photos of Tieghan lining the walls on his flat screen monitors, manipulated pictures of my grandkids, his usual mental library of torment. Short of that, I'm walking in like a fucking boss. No guarantee they'll let me get far enough to face him, but he won't resist the urge to make an appearance. He's dying to degrade me in some way, not to mention the opportunity to utilize his collection of handheld Damascus steel."

Mack was literally spellbound. In the short time he had known her, she had transformed from a broken, sad, sweet woman to a rebel soldier. *Or had she always been in there?* Cat's private conversation with him this morning was becoming more and more accurate. Aurora's teeth were showing.

Dutch sat quietly in thought. She made a significant argument; they were currently running around playing Whack-a-Mole. He checked his watch; they had an hour before sunset. It would take him two hours minimum to put the players in place. Between himself and the FBI field office they would have to call in NYPD, Emergency Management Services, and possibly SWAT and Special Victims.

"Okay, I want some time to work this out with Kai, and we'll get Ken on the line as the rest of us organize, but I agree with you Tink, time to bring the fight to him," he said resolutely.

Aurora stood again, looking for her purse. The coffee had been delivered and Cat was fixing a cup for them both.

"Aurora," the tone of Dutch's voice halted her in her tracks. The rest of the room quieted to listen to him.

"I don't like any part of this. I'm man enough to admit it that I'm scared out of my fucking mind to let you anywhere near him. What he did to our baby sister was enough, and I lost good, strong, well-trained soldiers the last time….and now—now I'm handing over my only sister, my adored and loved remaining sibling." He looked at her intently, his voice thick with dread. He ran his hands over his bald head, hoping to summon a different way from his tired brain.

He walked over to her and put his hands on her shoulders. "Aurora we have been over this hundreds of times, and as much as I hate it, because of his obsession with you this is the only way we can draw him out and potentially bring him down. In no way do I relish the idea that you are going to suffer greatly before we grab the prize. He is going to hurt you, Tinker Bell, and it'll be bad. I don't know any other way, but if you hesitate for a moment, we will come up with something else."

She hugged him and stood back to look at him. His bright, hazel eyes were filled with fright and concern.

"Dutch, he can never hurt me the way he did Tieghan. I'm an adult, and he is disgusted by grown women. He will tell me how fat, ugly, and sickening I am, but so what? It's all he has ever said to me. But I can be scary, too, big brother. I will have you all behind me, and no matter which way this goes, I'm not leaving without justice for our sister." She assured him, leaning up to kiss his cheek.

Dutch nodded his head in acceptance. The rest of the room were collectively still unhappy about the plan. Mack was fighting his own internal struggle over the danger she was heading into. His instinct had been to protect her since the first moment he laid eyes on her.

Quincy shook his head, murmuring under his breath to Dutch. "A bag of cotton candy, right boss?" Dutch sighed with defeat. They were right, it might have been the worst description he'd ever used to describe her.

Aurora was impatient for a cigarette. Mack easily read her need, "There is an outside balcony off the bedroom," he confided.

"Perfect," she sighed, and grabbing the pack and lighter from her handbag, headed out to the private outside deck. Seconds later, Mack joined her. "Did you want one?" she asked, as he stepped outside.

He strode toward her the way a cheetah takes a gazelle. "You—I want you," he growled. His voice was dense with carnal need. Her cigarettes and lighter fell from her hand to the ground. He backed her up against the glass wall and kissed her as if she were the last bottle of Coke in the desert. Aurora let him. She was stirring from a hundred-year slumber. "…. *There were thirst and hunger, and you were the fruit…*" The quote from Pablo Neruda's *Song of Despair*, reverberated through her mind.

"I am so fucking in love with you," his voice was rough, his mouth at her ear. He fisted her hair and tilted her head back to access her neck. He lavished it with his tongue and bit down on her tender skin, inspired by her husky groans. "Is this what you like? Does this turn you on?" he whispered, tightening his grip in her hair. She moaned in confirmation, finding his mouth again with her own.

His head swam in her intoxicating scent. The kiss was heady, and they were breathless as they ran their fingers through each other's hair and trying to get inside each other. He fought back the urge to remove her clothes. "I want to taste you everywhere," he said as his hands roamed her body.

"Mack. I want you. I can't stop..." She confessed between kisses. "I feel guilty and ashamed, and I should, but I just can't stop..." She gasped. His mouth was soft and harsh, and his tongue danced deliciously between her lips. She couldn't get enough. His kiss was perfect, lips luscious and made for her. She was lost in it; it was moving her in ways she had ignored for far too long. Aurora held her arms around him, her hands running down his muscled back, pulling him closer to her. She did something to him he had only wished for since he first saw her, she took his bottom lip into her mouth and bit it gently.

"Fuck me, you know my weakness," he sighed, kissing her ravenously again, surfacing for air occasionally. "Aurora what is it about you? I want to devour you. Let's do this right here, right now," he begged, his ache for her was taking control of him. His hands wandered down her back onto her ass, and he held his erection up against her thigh.

She encircled his rugged, handsome face with her hands and ordered, "Right here, right now—you will stop talking and continue to kiss me." Aurora was starving, kissing was by far what she had missed the most as a widow. Mack had spent the past weeks resisting the scorching temptation to kiss her—it had been long enough. They broke open a dam and there was no way back for either of them.

He crushed her body to his, his mouth overtaking hers again. If a kiss could ignite, they were triggering fireworks over the roof of the hotel, its heat and electricity seemed to encircle them both. Coming up for breath, he held her face in his hands and smiled down into her sweet expression. "Woman, I will own you," he teased, biting her lower lip, and kissing her again. She chuckled into his mouth. "Be careful what you wish for, Sailor, you're rattling my cage. This means big trouble… huge."

Mack laughed aloud and stared joyfully into her eyes. "Baby, give it your best shot."

Aurora dissolved into him, every sense awakening. She pressed her body up against his granite form. This kiss was born from fairy tale legend. A stunning prince bringing a sleeping Aurora back to life.

For a moment, they stopped to gaze at each other in disbelief. Swapping awkward grins briefly, they tilted in again at the same time, moaning in unison with an appetite for more.

The knock on the window surprised them and they pulled apart. Cat opened the balcony door, "Hey Archie and Veronica, the food is here, unless you two are good with feeding off each other."

Chapter Twenty-Four

The PTSD peer support group met Wednesday night in the Veterans Center basement. Roscoe Williams wheeled himself down the ramp and into the room to greet his brothers, as he did every week.

Blaise Turner, one of their youngest members, had seen recent action in Iraq. The older men had taken him into the fold and under their broken wings. They were a mix of armed services: Army, Navy, Air Force, Marines and even a few Coast Guard members, along with current first responders who worked in the neighborhood. Tonight, there were almost thirty of them in attendance. The room was abuzz with excitement, as if they were all in a holding room ready to ship out to an unknown location.

Roscoe started to get a handle on the gossip. Seems there had been some unexplainable things going on the neighborhood. Lots of first responders reporting exceptional recent good luck.

Blaise was going on about it to Roscoe and his small circle of friends. As the story was told to him, a patrolman walked in on an armed robbery at the Diaz Bodega around the corner from the Skylight Diner. Two victims were wounded on the floor, bleeding out when the young rookie, who didn't wait for backup, walked into the trajectory of a speeding bullet. Hand to God, he should have wound up dead, but the bullet froze in front of his forehead and dropped to the floor.

Several comparable stories were circulating the room. Firemen, medics, and EMTs, even transit cops, were sharing the miraculous tales with the seasoned vets. The counselor for the evening hadn't called the room to order yet, so the chatter continued. Most remarkable, in a room of men and women typically haunted by night terrors, they now were giddy from the sightings of unexplainable light.

Roscoe made his rounds to hear them all. Something was brewing in Hell's Kitchen and Roscoe was sure "it" was about to come to a head. He knew St. Michael's would be integral. He circled back around the room, recruiting his brothers for a scouting mission.

For Dutch and his team, the planning continued during and after their early dinner. Dutch looked at his sister as he walked around the room. She was sitting at the head of the table, taking in the information. Her mind was laser-focused on getting the jump on Alejandro.

"Tink, this is your call; we can send the marshals in to lock him up, we have the warrants. If you go in alone we can play his ego, force his hand, and make the charges stick. Not to mention, finally get a judge to sign off on the warrants to his den of perdition. I'd bet my life there are several hundred kids locked in there."

"Dutch, if she goes in, we skate dangerously close to entrapment," said Quincy. "If she baits him, his lawyers can use it against us."

"But if he takes her and she's held against her will, it's kidnapping. Then, we search the whole fucking place looking for her and whatever stumbles out in front of us, evidence wise goes to court," Mack replied with frustration.

"No, then we get jammed up under the 'fruit from the poisonous tree' doctrine, and none of the evidence we gather will be admissible in court. We've been there before," Aurora interrupted, and her voice cooled Mack immediately. "Locate me, and then get the judge to sign off on the warrants to search the rest of the place, everything strictly by the book. I'm going at him alone," she said firmly, then headed into the bedroom to change her clothes.

Ken spoke from the video screen, from his post at the Echo Lake cabin. "We did catch a break, Dutch. A CI reported that Alejandro's scheduled for a private dinner tonight at 1900 hours, a small restaurant in Hell's Kitchen. Meeting with a couple to sign their six-year-old twins to a talent and modeling contract."

"We can do it, Dutch," said Quincy. "We're ready, Mack and I have been on the phone charting the perimeters and the command post with the Manhattan Borough commander.

"Ken, help with the backup, send whatever they need over to NYPD. I'm due on the phone with the precinct night commander; we are going to request SWAT and Special Victims on scene as well. Everybody treads lightly, you never know where he has ears. Double check with the informants. How far is this restaurant from his office?"

"It's practically across the street, he doesn't like to stick his neck out too far," Ken replied.

Mack was not prepared for the vision of Aurora dressed like one of them. She came out of the bedroom in black tack pants and a tight black turtleneck. She was putting her arms through an outerwear vest. The motion arched her back and thrust her breasts forward. Her hair was pulled up into a soft ponytail, making her appear younger and vulnerable.

Mack had never seen her in anything close-fitting. She was always shrouded in an oversized tunic or sweater with soft wool or stretchy pants. Even the occasional dress she'd switched into for an appearance was an A-line knit and two sizes too big for her. Her body reminded him of the high elevation roads across the Pyrenees Mountains between France and Spain. The sharpest curves he had ever driven. There was no mystery as to why she concealed them; a man could lose his life taking a wrong turn. He couldn't help the low wolf whistle, which escaped involuntarily from his mouth.

Everyone looked up suddenly to see what caused it. Quincy shook his head in laughter. *Oh man was his boy done; cooked and fork-stuck deep.*

"Rein it in, Romeo," Dutch rolled his eyes. He laughed to himself as he was forced to endure Mack's appreciation of his sister. His expression mimicked a puppy eyeing an ice cream cone. "Where is your body armor?" he asked Aurora.

"I'm not wearing that thing," she replied in a huff. "He isn't using a gun when he loves a knife so much more."

Mack muttered with amazement under his breath, "Your ass is a work of genius." She laughed quietly and whispered, "So is yours."

"Okay everybody, take a beat, we are going over the plan again. Abuela's Cantina is the location. I want you to study the schematics of the office as well; he is a fucking snake and will slither back there if the temperature is too hot."

"Did Ken say the restaurant is across the street from Jovencita Corporate?" she asked.

"Affirmative," Ken replied.

"Ken, please pull up any blueprints of the old New York subway system. We're convinced there are tunnels under his office. I wonder if they extend across the street to access the restaurant," Aurora asked.

"Copy that," Ken replied.

They reviewed all the maps of the locations and acquainted themselves with nearby landmarks and access points. Quincy, Ken, and Mack had confirmation of the command center and the perimeters with the NYPD. Four unmarked cars were already detailed for pre-op surveillance. Dutch and Mack were waiting on confirmation that undercover officers were detailed to the restaurant prior to the meet. The place was small, and they would be assigned one to the kitchen and one to the hostess stand.

Aurora pointed on the map to the church, St. Michael the Archangel at West 34th and 9th Ave. It was at the very border of the exterior perimeter. She felt something lurch in her gut, the church was critical. "Here, make this the extraction zone if any of us are separated, comms go down, or shit hits the fan. Dutch, you need a medic here."

"Oh, thank you little sister, I've never done this before," he replied, exasperated. Even with all the action he had seen in his military career, he knew Aurora was practically an equal when it came to gut instinct. He never underestimated it.

"Tink, did you test the wire?" Aurora attached the unit into her bra, burying it under her breast and wove the mic up into her hair. She was sure it would be useless as Alejandro would strip her of everything if he got her alone. On a last-minute impulse, she attached a second microphone inside the lace on the strap of her bra.

"Checked," she assured.

"Bravo team will be on location with us. Delta guys are still with my nephews and Aurora's grandkids on the base." He looked around, "Okay, let's move, we have to be at the command post at 1800 hours."

Cat returned from the bedroom after packing up Aurora's things. "I'm coming with you," she asserted.

"The hell you are!" Dutch stormed. "I have a

Marine coming for you and the bags. You're going back to Echo Lake. I need you safe." He softened suddenly. They stood toe to toe, all of Cat's five-foot, six inches, as she strained her neck to glare up at him.

"Please, Cat? We cannot take our eyes off Aurora. I won't risk you, honey," he coaxed.

She backed down and hugged him. He effortlessly lifted her into his arms and kissed her. "We'll be back tonight, one way or another. Take care of the dogs, because I will be exiled out of the country if anything happens to those two on our watch."

Mack wanted a minute alone with Aurora. He squinted back at Dutch, who gestured in acknowledgment. "We'll meet you two in the lobby. Cat, walk us down."

As soon as the room was empty, he pulled her into his arms. "It's not too late to back out, we have the warrants to take him into custody."

"He'll be out before we hit the entrance to the Pocono cabin. It has to happen this way." She lifted her head to kiss him.

Surprised that she made the first move, he gladly reciprocated, while gently sliding his hands down over her ass. "Who carved this? Michelangelo?" he whispered into her ear. She chuckled with modesty.

"Aurora, swear to me you won't do something so brave that I can't undo it? Remember, you're a baby sea turtle—instinct and raw courage. Do you need to wear my bracelet?" Her expression changed to a stern focus.

"Mackenzie Egan, you guarantee me right this second that you will not get hurt; do not blindly rush in to save me without logic and forethought. I won't survive another loss of any kind."

He placed his hand on his heart in solemn oath. "My beautiful girl, I vow to live a day longer than you, you can count on it. And don't take this the wrong way, but could you not muck up this outfit? I have a thorough SEAL/ bad girl thing envisioned for some day down the road. Did it come with handcuffs? Or should I just bring my own?"

She laughed out loud and grabbed her small go bag as they left the room. "I guess you forgot I'm wired, my brother is going to love your last request," she snickered as they made their way to the elevators.

He shook his head in amusement, "I'm already dead, might as well go all in. Aurora, you always smell so goddamn good. What do you wear? It has me half crazy."

The entered the elevator together as she answered him, "Mimosa, the flower, not the cocktail. The perfume is called Elysium. I have it in everything, bath soap, shampoo, hand lotion." He backed her up to the wall of the elevator to kiss her again before they got to the lobby. With her neck in his hands, he moaned into her mouth with desire, parting her thighs with his knee and resting his erection against her.

Chapter Twenty-Four

Through his clenched teeth he whispered, "Jesus Christ—I need to fu..."

"Ssssh," she placed her finger over his lips. "Wired, remember? When this is all over, I promise," she whispered with delight. He kissed her again, hard, and hungry. She reached in her pocket for her phone and turned off the wireless microphones. Once Mack saw they were not being heard or recorded, he looked into her eyes and licked his lips.

"Promise me—when this is over, three days straight in bed with you. No coming up for air. No clothes, all our meals picnic style in front of a raging fireplace; long, soapy showers together; nap dates in each other's arms—rinse and repeat. Three straight days and nights of you and me crying each other's names out in fucking ecstasy," his voice raspy with need. She nodded in agreement and kissed him again.

"Where do I sign?" she sighed, resting her head on his muscled shoulder. He tilted her head back to look at him, his face close to hers.

"I'm not kidding, Aurora. I want pillow talk with you between cardio sessions. Whisper in my ear every dirty thing you've ever wanted to say and do; I want you filthy and unbridled with me. You want me to quote Jane Austen while I'm making you come, I'll do it. Anything you desire, you are mine. You're my every fantasy, let me be yours," he whispered, sultry and hot.

Aurora giggled, "Well, can you quote dirty Austen? Guaranteed it's one way to rev up an

English Lit major." She couldn't control her laughter.

Mack smiled proudly, "Do you mean Mr. Woodhouse's riddle about '*Kitty a fair but frozen maid*'?"

She gasped, "Mack! Do you know it? I can't believe it!" She gently brushed her hand over his erection, and he almost jumped out of his shoes with her slow caress of his arousal. He covered her hand with his, trapping it up against his hard-on.

"Bad girl, think you can handle this weapon? It's loaded." He chuckled with her. Mack nearly orgasmed from her light touch and the eager gleam in her eyes.

She kissed him gently and whispered, "You sexy bastard, you knew, didn't you? You've had a background profile on me and think you figured me out?" she said, biting down on her lower lip.

Mack leaned into her touch, his voice husky and deep, "Figured out you need a mind fuck first? You bet your sweet ass I figured it out. Whatever it requires to take down my target, I'm a sniper baby, I-never-miss." He slid his hands down to fondle her ass cheeks and bent his head to kiss her neck.

He murmured between his kisses, "I want to hear you moan my name, Aurora. Over and over again. Let me love you the way you deserve to be loved, worshipped, and fucking adored." She stared up at him and smiled, reaching to grab onto his lower lip and bit it playfully.

She stroked his mustache and goatee gently

with her finger. "Where did you come from? How did you find me?" she asked, mystified. This man, he could have his choice of any woman. It occurred to Aurora that it was impossible for anyone to ever refuse his advances. *What compelled him to chase her?*

"I've been here all along, waiting for you to notice me. Nice of you to show up." He sighed.

The elevator doors opened on the lobby level as he tenderly kissed her forehead. She turned the mics back on as they headed toward the car.

Chapter Twenty-Five

They stepped into the back of the SUV with Dutch and Quincy in the front seat. Dutch turned to look at them both. "I had to shut the receiver off, the two of you almost bored me to death. Handcuffs and shower soap, try to remember going forward someone can hear you."

"I hope so," said Aurora. On the hour ride into Manhattan they reviewed the plan, anticipating every angle. So much rested-on Alejandro's reaction to Aurora, and where anything could go sideways.

Dutch handed her a small box. "Find a place to keep this with you," he instructed.

She opened it to find an old silver, badge-shaped medal depicting St. Michael the Archangel on the end of a long silver chain. "Dutch! Where did this come from?" she asked, shocked.

"It's Uncle Jack's," he said with deference.

"I thought this was gone forever," she whispered with reverence. Holding the sacred artifact in her hand she explained the story to Mack and Quincy,

"Our dad's brother, Jack, served as a Philly police lieutenant while we were growing up. He was our favorite, always made us laugh, told the greatest police stories, and spoiled us rotten. It was the only jewelry he ever wore, and he almost never walked out the door without it around his neck. He taught us about the patron saint and the protection he provides to soldiers, police, and first responders; he had a fervent devotion to him. The night he was killed in the line of duty was the one time he had forgotten to put it on when he dressed for work. Our aunt, in her utter devastation, blamed it on the one time he overlooked the protection of this medal. Dutch, I can't risk it, Alejandro is going to strip me down. I left my wedding rings with Cat for that reason."

Dutch shrugged and said, "I think we could use his intercession tonight, St. Michael and Uncle Jack, wherever they are. I'm sure they are together in paradise."

Aurora took the chain and placed it around Mack's neck, tucking the medal under his shirt.

"Keep this safe for me," she whispered like a prayer. No one in the car was certain to whom the request was made. Mack reached for her hand to hold until they pulled up at the NYPD tent.

After the briefing, the team at the command post readied Aurora to go. Dutch hugged her closely and whispered in her ear. "Aurora Louise, I love you big as the world, please be careful."

Quincy, adorned in his full paraphernalia, grabbed her up in a hug. "We'll be right behind you, Miss Aurora, don't you worry."

She took a minute to soak in the extraordinary image of Mack in his full gear. He was adorned with a Kevlar vest, ballistic helmet with headset, NVG's (night vision goggles), and his rifle. His pants were encircled with a tactical belt. Its pouches and holsters filled with additional magazines, cuffs, flashlight, and expandable baton.

"Look at you," she sighed. "A glorious soldier, a champion. And you want *me*?" she whispered humbly, resting her hand in the middle of his vest. He beamed at her, bringing her hand up to his lips.

"You and only you, forever." His smile spread across his face. Ignoring the stares of the full squad of uniformed men and women assembled around them, he raised her chin and kissed her. "We have a deal, on the other side of this, you, and me—three straight days. You come back to me, Aurora." His tone was serious and compelling. She nodded her head in agreement.

As she stepped out of the tent, Mack whispered, "I love you."

She laughed to herself; the millions of times she'd murmured the affection to Ben, occasionally he would tease and give her the Han Solo response. She turned around and smiled at him, "I know," she smiled confidently.

It would be a long two block walk alone for Aurora to reach Abuela's Cantina. The temperature had dropped with the sun, and she was already regretting her clothing choices. The street was quiet and closed to traffic, some stores had already begun their Christmas decorating with Thanksgiving only a week away. The streets were wet from an earlier rain, and it amazed her how New York in the evening always mirrored

Gotham City from the movies.

She was focusing on her breathing, trying to foresee dialogue in her head and keep her heartrate as steady as she could. The NYPD commanding officer placed a tiny, neutral-colored earpiece into her ear for her to be able to hear the radio communications. He guaranteed it wouldn't be discovered. She could hear Dutch, Mack, and Quincy positioning themselves along with the undercovers already on the scene.

The young couple arrived at the restaurant and were seated with Alejandro for almost thirty minutes. She passed the four unmarked cars along the route. She suddenly noticed along the way that there were small clusters of homeless veterans in their worn military fatigues, flak jackets, and hats decorated with multiple patches signifying their regiments. They were scattered in abandoned storefronts, some huddled on the subway vents wrapped in blankets for warmth.

She caught a glimpse of one man in a wheelchair with countless others set back from the corners. They seemed to be watching over her, lining the route as if they knew where she was headed and were assembled for her protection. Something about the handicapped veteran was familiar. She turned her head to look back at him again; he was watching her and nodded his head with encouragement. *Could it be the same one from her dreams? From the church in Albany?* She glanced back at him again as she neared the entrance to the restaurant. She heard his voice in her head, "Keep walking, we're right behind you." Aurora was inspired and filled with a new sense of purpose.

She hesitated for a moment at the door, took a deep breath, and entered. She could hear the team in her earpiece. "She's inside, everyone in position."

The lovely young undercover female police officer at the hostess desk asked if she was picking up an order for dinner.

She saw him sitting with his back to the wall at the far corner of the tiny room. He had aged since the last time she saw him. His thick black hair was streaked with gray, and his raccoon eyes were now showing crow's feet. What hadn't changed was the taste of poison in her mouth near him. There was no one else dining in the small establishment. Her heart began to race in her ears.

"Easy Tink," she could hear Dutch whisper, "one inch at a time, and breathe."

She stood before his table; the young couple looked up—perplexed by her arrival. Aurora returned their glance and instructed them, "You should leave now, and get as far away from this fucking monster as you can. Your children are in danger."

They were shocked by her statement and seemed to freeze in their chairs.

"Aurora," Alejandro purred, drawing out the r's in her name. "How genuinely nice to see you again after all these years, would you like to join us? Although, I must say, my dear, you don't look hungry. It seems you have been eating your feelings since the last time I saw you. Tsk, tsk, so much weight cannot be healthy for you, chica. And why are you dressed like this? Were you scaling buildings for a spare donut?" He laughed at his own humor.

She leaned down and whispered into the young woman's ear, "Get out now, he is a fucking predator." That was enough for the woman; she stood quickly, and her husband instantly followed her out the door.

Alejandro tossed the napkin from his lap on to the table. "Why did you come here, Aurora? Haven't you and your cabrón brother taken enough from me?"

"I've come for Tieghan's remains. You have them and we want them," she said icily.

Alejandro stood and smiled like the Cheshire Cat. "Remains? Remains of what? Tieghan is alive and well. There is nothing to give to you, except maybe a little sisterly reunion. She is across the street in the office if you would like to see her for yourself? Aurora, you cannot blame me—she wanted to be a star. You and your brother were so jealous and kept trying to take it away from her. We had to arrange something dramatic for you all to back off and let her live her dream." His smarmy smile and silky tone were the same as she'd remembered.

"It can't be true, Tink," Dutch whispered in her earpiece. "I had the skull tested for her DNA; Tieghan cannot be alive."

"Take me to my sister, Alejandro," she ordered, her teeth clenched with anger.

Two of Alejandro's men came from the kitchen and grabbed Aurora's arms, tying her hands behind her back as they ran their hands over her body, checking for the wire or any weapons. She held her breath as they missed the mic hidden in her bra strap. They forced her into the kitchen toward a broom closet when she saw the body of the undercover kitchen employee lying on the floor with a stab wound to his abdomen.

"*No puedo encontrar, hefe*," the younger man said, as he explained to Alejandro there was no wire. Alejandro pulled her by her ponytail and ran his fingers through it to find the wireless microphone. He slid a Damascus steel switchblade from his pocket and sliced her ponytail cleanly off her head.

Then he and his men pushed her into the broom closet where a secret door led to stairs. They dragged her down into a cramped cellar and through a dimly lit tunnel.

"It amazes me when the trash takes itself out, Aurora. I've known where you are the whole time and I enjoyed hunting you like a prize elephant, and you deliver yourself to me like a lamb to slaughter?" he cackled with glee.

"You don't scare me, Alejandro, there are dicks bigger than yours on chihuahuas," she spit at him. He punched her hard across the face, breaking her nose.

Upstairs, the team breached the restaurant and took the injured undercover agent quickly and quietly to the EMTs. Directed by the undercover hostess, Mack and Quincy found the closet and began their descent to the tunnel with four SWAT team members stacked behind them.

Alejandro and his men had a head start and knew where they were going, but Mack and Quincy had only just reviewed the subterranean tunnel designs and were navigating the dark maze slowly. Underneath Alejandro's headquarters, Aurora saw exactly what her disturbed imagination conjured. Tunnels and hallways, dimly lit, wet, and airless, stretched out in every direction.

She knew it would take hours to search it and she may never be found. These were the hallways from her nightmares. There were children crying behind those doors.

They dragged her down one of the corridors and into a room where they sliced her clothes off with their gleaming knives. She remained in her underwear as they threw her into a chair and tied her against it. She whispered close to her bra strap. "Four clicks to the right, seventh star, straight on till morning."

Dutch caught the clue quickly. "Mack, Quincy did you get it? Fourth tunnel to the right, seventh door from the end of the hallway."

They were struggling in the dark maze underneath the street. They hadn't found the entrance to the headquarters yet, and Mack was seething with dread; too much time had passed between her disappearance and their arrival. Dutch was directing his men as he viewed their location in proximity to hers, but her chip signal was shorting in and out because they were so far underground.

Aurora was freezing and her eyes started to swell from her smashed nose; but she could see the blonde woman in her thirties approaching her. She looked about the age Tieghan would be now, but something wasn't right.

"See, Aurora," Alejandro jeered at her. "I told you your sister was alive—you've been wasting your life playing amateur Federales."

The young woman came close to Aurora, and though her vision was blurry she could see the haunted green eyes and beautiful, curly blonde hair. Into her earpiece she could only hear her brother's voice breaking up, the signal blocked by their deep location underground.

"Ask... the question, Aurora!" he roared.

"You are so beautiful," Aurora whispered to the woman. "You've grown into an exceptional woman, and we've missed you terribly."

The young lady answered, "I'm sorry you've had to think I was dead all this time, but I wanted to live out my dreams and my family tried to keep me from them." Her words were rehearsed, her voice flat, her eyes vacant.

"Do you remember us at all Tieghan?" Aurora asked. "Do you remember growing up with us?"

"Oh yes," she said with a smile. "I remember you taking me swimming, because all I wanted was to be a mermaid."

Alejandro was stalking the two of them, waiting to pounce on Aurora.

"Take a good look at her, Aurora, and then kiss her the fuck goodbye. You never understood my concept and you have made it your life's work to destroy my vision for Tieghan."

"Tieghan, do you remember the nights you couldn't sleep, baby? Do you remember what I did to help you?"

The young woman squatted in front of her chair to look at her. "Yes, I do. You would sing the song from *The Little Mermaid*, 'Under the Sea,' the one Sebastian always sang."

Aurora started to laugh, and tears fell from her eyes. It was brief, but the idea her baby sister might have lived took root instantly. He led with Aurora's weakness and for a moment she fell for it. The young woman, realizing her answer was the wrong one, disappeared from the room.

Mack and Quincy found the first hallway by searching door-to-door.

"Dutch!" Mack yelled. "Where is she?" he shouted into the radio.

Dutch was searching through the mazes for her signal; it would blink on his screen and disappear.

Alejandro taunted her, illuminating the screens in the room with heinous pictures of her sister. The fear and horror on her baby sister's little face. Aurora wanted this fucking snake dead, stuffed, and mounted above her fireplace. Her faith glowed from her like steel in the darkened room. She murmured the prayer quietly. "God, I need you. Please don't let him win, help me take him down this time."

"*Mira!* Look Aurora, look at your beautiful baby sister. She made me millions of dollars. She was sought after by every rich elite in the world. She was taken by all the highest bidders, and she enjoyed it. You confuse this for a crime; this is a lifestyle choice, a sexual orientation. We are forced in secret to love this way, and Tieghan wanted to please everyone. She became a master pupil, knowing how to satisfy her company," he sniped into her ear.

"Look at the fucking pictures, you bloated cow!" he screamed. He held back Aurora's head and roughly taped her eyes open with an office shipping tape dispenser. "You could never satisfy anyone—you are a drooping hag, the child was a superstar," he declared dramatically.

"Keep him talking, Aurora, we're going to hang him in Times Square," Dutch murmured.

"Unlike you, Alejandro, you couldn't jerk off a horny rabbit, you cockless animal." She laughed.

He took a heavy pipe and smashed it into her side, breaking three of her ribs. She screamed in agony.

Mack could hear her cries, and the taste of

bitter adrenaline filled his mouth. They were moving in circles, knocking doors down one after the other, revealing rooms filled with young, half-dressed, imprisoned children. Each room had a cheaply decorated playroom with beds, and some contained adults preparing to violate them.

"Dutch, there are kids down here, room after room of them. Call the judge, I can hear more of them pounding on the walls." Quincy radioed, his voice laden with disgust.

"Keep knocking down doors, we have to find her—he is going to kill her. Hurry!" Dutch cried.

"Did you think you could bring me down, Aurora?" Alejandro laughed. "Do you know who I am? Your idle threat of God's own thunder, I'm still laughing with the irony. You are nothing—you, and your oaf of a brother." Using his shiny knife, he cut her skin, carving into her. She stifled her screams.

Aurora could feel her heart racing, hoping her pacemaker was earning its money. "Alejandro, you're a joke. Did you think you could pass off a cheap version of Tieghan to me? You really are a fucking moron." She laughed again. No matter how painful it was, she would extract vengeance on this wretched excuse of a human. No, not human: beast, demon, pure evil.

"And you are a fat, lazy, ugly *puta!*" he spit at her. "Look at those hideous udders you think are breasts—you could feed calves. You will never be as beautiful as your sister; she was like the sun."

Blood gushed from all over her body; she couldn't take a deep breath from the pain in her ribs. But her anger was so intense, she could not resist cutting him back with her tongue.

"I'm surprised you even noticed Tieghan, Alejandro. I thought you only liked them with tiny little pingas like yours for you to play with. You could never pleasure a woman, you piece of shit!"

He reached for a second switchblade and continued to cut her across her chest, her arms, her legs. This time he sliced deeper and almost nicked an artery near her neck. She cried out in pain.

"What's this, Aurora?" he pointed the tip of the blade at her scar. "We don't want to take this out, right, puta? Will your heart stop I wonder?" he taunted, running the blade lightly across her healed incision line.

"You want to cut my heart out, Alejandro? Go ahead. You can't do it—you don't have one hair on your balls. All you can do is defile children. Tiny, weak, unwilling innocents. I am a fucking warrior! My face will be the last thing you see before God himself smites you down, I promise. I'll be here long after you. Every time I light a match in the future, I'll think of your burning, vile soul in the deepest parts of hell," she growled.

"Warrior?" he laughed. "You can't even make a dick hard, you sloppy twat. I'm going to make you suffer worse than your darkest dreams. Then I'm going for your precious grandchildren. When I'm bored, I will saw your head off your body, slowly while you can still feel it, the very same way I did to Tieghan." He spit with anger at her.

Aurora's heart almost seized when he mentioned the kids, and her blind rage fueled vigor back into her beaten body. She could taste blood and metal in her mouth. She clenched her teeth and warned him, "You will never get to my family, you cocksucking pussy. You can cut me into ribbons before then, but I'll never let you get to them," she seethed.

The photos kept flashing in rotation in the room. A slideshow of her worst nightmares. She was surrounded. She couldn't look anywhere without color confirmation of the horrors that had plagued her since Tieghan disappeared. Aurora's darkest imagination hadn't ever conceived what her sister truly endured. As a baby… she was just a baby.

Mack stopped after the final hallway and froze in his spot. "Wait," he held up his hand and stilled the men, sniffing the air. "Mimosa," he whispered. Her signature scent floated past him. "This way." He pointed as the men followed him into the next hallway to the seventh door.

Alejandro took out a long-bladed machete and held it up before her.

"I'm going to do you a favor in killing you, Aurora, you can't pleasure a man or a woman. You're a disgusting beast, you are unlovable," Alejandro spat the words at her, completely insane in his hatred.

Mack and Quincy finally crashed through the door. "On the ground, hands behind your back!" they ordered.

Mack's eyes fixed on Aurora; he wanted to cover her and get her to safety. She was badly wounded and losing blood. He took his eyes off the target for a split second when the lights went out. Before he could switch on his NVG's— Alejandro spun under Mack and his rifle. He slid up under him and sunk two blades under the gaps of his vest and into his lungs. He managed to slip out of the room through a trap door to escape. The SWAT team followed him. Quincy turned his helmet light on, illuminating the three of them.

Quincy saw the blood start to stream from Mack's sides and radioed to command.

"Aurora, let's get you out of here." They cut her loose from the chair, and she saw the blood.

"Mack?" she looked at him in horror, yanking the tape off her eyes.

"No time Aurora, I'm fine, let's go."

The hallway filled with the homeless vets from the street, and several went after Alejandro while the rest helped Quincy support Aurora and Mack as they quickly led them up to the street outside the restaurant. Pulling up in front of them was a beat-up old Chevy pickup truck containing more military vets, some of the men she had seen on her walk to Abuela's.

The first man out of the cab of the truck threw a long, ragged blanket around Aurora, and the rest helped Quincy and his fellow brothers load Mack into the back.

"Hang on, Soldier, we're taking you to safety."

Aurora was lifted into the tailgate with Mack and the men. Quincy quickly stripped him of his heavy gear and vest to assist in his breathing. It was done.

Chapter Twenty-Six

"**M**ack? Please, please stay with me," she begged, holding his hand close to her. Her body was in agony. But her physical pain was nothing compared to the complete torment she felt seeing him so critically wounded—it was killing her.

He was still sitting upright but his breathing was labored. "I'm not going anywhere, my beautiful girl," he said, battling the pain.

The truck screeched to a halt at the doors of St. Michael the Archangel Church.

"Why are we here? Why not go right to the hospital?" she pleaded.

"Trust us, ma'am," they said, and assisted Quincy in getting Mack on to his feet. The men aided them to secure Mack inside the church. The EMTs were nowhere to be found.

"Shit! Miss Aurora, they left to help the injured undercover from the restaurant kitchen and they aren't back yet!" Quincy gasped. Aurora slumped to the floor with Mack in her arms at the base of a statue. Quincy quickly broke away to get help.

"Aurora, you're sitting on a church floor in your knickers. How many Hail Mary's and Our Father's do you think this will earn you?" Mack said with great difficulty, blood starting to ooze from his mouth

"I'll recite every one of them in Latin if you stay with me," she implored. "You promised me

Mack, you swore I wouldn't lose another thing! Remember? You and me, three straight days and forever on the other side of this," she cried. She held him close to her, kissing the side of his face. She sat with her back to the base of the statue, Mack lying in her arms. "Not you too, Mack, please…please… not you too," she pleaded. She couldn't even sob without pain searing through her sides. The silent scream was building up again in her broken body.

"I love…" he said, his consciousness slipping away. His body was now dead weight against her.

"Noooooo! Noooooo!" she screamed, at long last. Her body shook with the feral sound, her agony reverberating through the empty church. She didn't care how bad it physically hurt to do so. "Not again! Please not again!" she screeched.

"Aurora, cover your eyes." A strange voice instructed her. She looked up behind her and saw they were positioned against a magnificent statue of St. Michael the Archangel, resting atop a wide stone pedestal.

"St. Michael! I beg your intercession, I invoke your mercy," she implored, tears streaming from her swollen eyes. "I can't do this again! Take me! Take me this time, please, no more, no more," she sobbed. "I can't do this anymore," she ranted weakly, clutching Mack's beautiful, lifeless body. "Mack, you promised…" she howled, it came out like a wounded forest animal.

The church erupted into dazzling torrents of brilliant blue and gold illuminations. It flooded from the statue and out of the doors and windows, as if something inside had imploded.

"Aurora, cover your eyes," the voice appealed again. She did so and kept one bloody hand around Mack's limp torso on her lap and covered her eyes with her other hand.

Even with her eyes shielded she could see the dance of preternatural light as it flickered around the inside walls of the nave. The surge of multicolored cascades joined into a radiant ribbon of light that tunneled into Mack's chest. She heard the heavy shifting of marble behind her as the immense statue vanished from its base.

Mack's body flooded back up with life, strength, and new breath.

"Mack!" she cried out with joy and surprise.

"Not exactly," he answered. He shifted position to face her, sat up, and held her by her shoulders. "I'm going to borrow him for a short time, but he is here, and he will be returned to you unharmed."

Aurora was mesmerized. It was Mack, but it wasn't. His voice was different; there was no trace of his accent, and his eyes glowed with a strange, golden light. She recognized the light from her dreams. "It can't be," she whispered. She looked up to where the statue was just a minute ago and now the pedestal was empty.

"St. Michael?" she asked in complete disbelief and awe.

"Yes, Aurora." He examined her badly bruised face, beaten body, and the deep, bleeding knife cuts all over her. He held his palm out in front of her. Vivid beams streamed from his hand as he healed her broken nose, ribs, and closed all her bruises, gashes, and cuts. Her extensive injuries and internal bleeding were instantly repaired, the streaks of dried blood on her hands and skin vanished. Extending two fingers from his right hand, he reached toward her heart, but she stopped him. Her strength was completely restored.

"No!" She lifted her hand to block his. "He was the love of my life, he earned every tear I've shed. This grief belongs to me," she whispered fiercely. "I carry this wound with honor and will heal in my own time." The Archangel nodded his head in acknowledgment.

Dutch came running down the aisle, Quincy and the EMTs behind him, "Mack!" he yelled. "Aurora!" He got to his friend and pulled him to his feet, looking him over and not seeing the dire situation Quincy had described to him.

"Dutch," Aurora said weakly. "It's not Mack… it's… the statue." She pointed to indicate the empty pedestal.

"No, not possible," he grabbed the man who looked like Mack and said, "Who am I? What's my name?"

"Michael Edward Velarde. Your father named you to honor me," the man replied matter-of-factly. Dutch dropped his hands as if he touched flames. The Archangel held his hand out to help Aurora up from the floor.

Quincy dropped to his knees in supplication, and the medics, unsure who they were treating, backed away. Quincy stared at Aurora in utter disbelief—where she had been bloody and gravely wounded, she was now healed completely. Mack's blood was gone from her arms and legs, yet it stained the worn blanket around her.

"Who are you?" Dutch whispered suspiciously. He could see what Aurora saw—Mack's body—but his voice and eyes were celestial.

"I am Michael the Archangel, Commander of the Legions of Angels, and General of the Armies of God. I'm here to finish the work you have so valiantly progressed to this point. As history taught you, it's the point of my sword which crushes the snake."

Dutch fell back against the pews and took to his knees before the Archangel. "How? How is this possible?" Aurora knelt beside him wrapping the frayed blanket tighter to her body.

Dutch looked to her, instantly embracing her. Seeing for himself, not a mark on her; yet he knew she sustained terrible injury. The blanket she was covered in was saturated with blood.

"Tink, not a scratch on you?" he mumbled in astonishment. She nodded her head toward the being who had taken possession of Mack's body. "Where is Mack?" he whispered to his sister. They huddled together on their knees against the pews. She clung to his large frame.

"Dutch," she choked on the emotion. "He… he

was dead, in my arms, then there was all this light and it tunneled into his chest and… the statue moved. He sat up, healed me, and told me that Mack is in there, and he will be returned to us unharmed." She gasped into her brother's strong chest. He held her close, realizing he wasn't present for the beginning of this miracle.

"Shhhh, Aurora, he's fine. I can't believe I'm saying these words, but look at him, he has an archangel wearing him like a suit. He'll come back to you, honey. Just breathe." Dutch comforted his sister, still not trusting what he was seeing. She composed herself and turned to look at St. Michael. He was watching her, and she felt him drape warmth around her and assure her that Mack hadn't gone anywhere that she couldn't reach him.

Entering the church were the group of veterans she had intermittently seen throughout the night, led by the familiar black man in a wheelchair.

"We have him, General, caught him climbing out of the back of the building behind a dumpster," Roscoe reported proudly, glancing quickly over to Aurora.

"Bring him to me," the Archangel ordered. "Well done, Gunny." He then turned to Aurora and Dutch. "You two, on your feet. You've worked your whole lives to bear witness to this moment."

They scrambled upright and stood beside the empty base of the statue. Aurora eyed the veteran in the wheelchair again. And then she saw it—the figure who protected her in her dreams, the man watching her in the cathedral in Albany. Roscoe was her guardian. Tears sprung to her eyes. As if he heard her thoughts, the older man glanced in her direction with a bright smile and winked.

"Michael, or do you prefer Dutch?" the Archangel asked her brother.

"Dutch is fine, Your Grace, or—I'm sorry I'm not sure how to address you, sir."

"Dutch, you may call me Michael. Do you still carry the pocketknife that once belonged to your Uncle Jack?"

Dutch gasped, no one alive knew he possessed the treasured object from his childhood. He removed it from his pocket and handed it to him. Suddenly, into the church came the commotion of men dragging someone inside.

St. Michael held the knife in his open palm, and it erupted with brilliant bursts of gold and blue sparks. In its place appeared a magnificent ancient sword. Positioned in his right hand, it gleamed and shimmered with ethereal opulence. Blue and silver flashes of lightning arced from its shining blade and danced up onto Mack's muscled forearm.

Dutch looked at Aurora and they whispered together in bewilderment, "The sword of St. Michael."

Twelve men escorted Alejandro Vasquez to the feet of the archangel. He stood up, incensed, "Who are you? Didn't I just kill you an hour ago?"

he bellowed, seeing before him only the man who had rescued Aurora.

The archangel stood before Alejandro, gleaming with power and brilliance. His stance was solid and intimidating. "Alejandro Vasquez, as the time of your death approaches, you are presented one final opportunity of redemption before your fate is decided. I am the Archangel Michael, who calls men from their life on Earth to their heavenly judgment. Make your choice," he thundered.

Alejandro looked over at Aurora and Dutch with hate and disgust, and spit on the floor of the church. "Never! I will never die! I signed I made a deal," he said arrogantly. He stared with loathing at Aurora when it unexpectedly dawned on him that she showed no signs of the injuries he had personally inflicted on her. "I wasn't finished with you yet, puta." He snarled in Aurora's direction.

Aurora glared back at Alejandro, assuring that her face would be the last thing he saw on Earth as she promised. Without hesitation, St. Michael raised his sword and with a rapid slash, and the fury of God's own thunder, separated Alejandro's head from his body—killing him instantly. The air around them smelled of the vestiges of an electrical storm. He lowered the sword to his side and murmured, "Now you are finished with her, Alejandro."

Dutch and Aurora gulped, covering their mouths with their hands. Quincy made the sign of the cross from his position on his knees.

"Reveal yourself, Lucius," the archangel demanded as he removed a dark cloth from inside Mack's belt and tenderly wiped the blade of his sword. The chains of sparking arcs seemed to hum and align in a pattern.

From the center of Alejandro's falling, headless body, a black mist started circling up into the air and formed another unearthly being in the aisle. The older man was attractive, dark-haired, and hypnotic. He stepped over Alejandro's crumpled corpse, impeccably dressed in a black Armani suit with a crisp white shirt, expensive Italian shoes, and silk tie.

"What a waste," he said, shaking his head. He looked up at the archangel as if he were a petulant teenager. A sly grin spread on his face. "Michael, you have no authority here. Father gave them free will. The freedom to be as deliciously evil as I can persuade them. You are forbidden to tamper with the choices of men." His voice mocked and taunted the archangel.

"Dear God," Aurora whispered. "Dutch, we truly have been battling the devil himself." Her brother nodded in agreement, never taking his eyes off Lucius.

"Ahhhh, of course, the unrelenting Velarde siblings; how lovely to finally have a good long look at you both," the older man jeered in their direction. Dutch held Aurora tighter to himself. The appearance of Lucius brought Quincy up from his knees to join the siblings, bordering Aurora's other side.

"I must say, sugar, you're tougher than you look," Lucius's voice dripped with irony, sizing Aurora up with his malevolent gaze.

She felt the rush of realization deep inside her gut. Rick Shearing, her old college flame, had been the only person to ever use the nickname. She had felt something off about him the night she met with him in Bangor. Temptation—this is what Rick tried to deflect her from: Alejandro's destruction and Mack. Lucius didn't want her to join forces with Mack. Aurora caught the glance of the archangel—he stared down at her and slightly nodded his head to acknowledge her conclusions.

Visions flooded her mind quickly; she and Mack together in multiple former lifetimes, side-by-side in countless battles between good and evil. They flashed past her too fast and there were too many to clearly process. She was inundated with the understanding that they had always been together, all roads led to them finding each other for battle and those on the side of darkness tried what they could to keep them apart.

The archangel positioned himself between the trio and his feckless thug of a fallen brother.

He addressed Lucius in a voice worn of patience. The brothers had obviously been here before as well.

"Lucius, as always, you distort the rules to your whim. They have free will to abuse and defile themselves in the face of their Creator, but the innocents have always been off limits. You have forgotten your place. It's time for you take a leave and give humanity a chance to recover from your recklessness. As we speak, around the globe my armies are taking down your kingpins and rescuing thousands of children. I'm mindful that we cannot eradicate this degradation you have caused to mankind, but the scales will balance, and justice will rain down tonight. Now, I order you to return to your dungeon." He stood firm to his spot, all the majesty he held as Commander of God's armies blazing around him. The sword danced in his hand, anxious to be swung again.

Chains of lightning chased themselves around the blade as he held it down at his side.

Lucius laughed in the face of the brilliant archangel.

"Are these vagrants part of your army? Pathetic." He pointed to Dutch and Aurora, laughing. "You can't put me in a time-out. You can't order me anywhere, little brother," he sneered.

St. Michael effortlessly spun his sword, and bolts of light crackled across the blade as he split Lucius across his chest and the older man cried out in anguish. There was a deafening boom of thunder over the church as he whirled into a massive funnel cloud of thick black smoke. The column of smoke rose to the vaulted ceiling of the church and then quickly plunged through the floor of the nave, taking Alejandro's remains with him.

"So, Tinker Bell," Dutch broke the ominous silence. "Did he die good enough for you?"

She nodded her head, speechless with wonder. St. Michael returned to where they were standing. Dutch and Quincy joined Aurora like bookends to protect her.

The archangel placed his hand on Quincy's strong shoulder, his voice low. Quincy was mesmerized by the golden light shining from his eyes. He knew this man stood in the presence of Almighty God.

"I'm going to withdraw from Mack's body in a few minutes. I will retake the human form of the pastor here at the church, Father Micah. When I do, you will need to get Mack somewhere private to rest. His injuries are completely healed, and he will suffer no residual physical effect from my temporary residence. He will require a period of stasis, about twenty-four hours of sleep to recover. He will remember everything that has transpired here tonight—he has witnessed it along with all of you. Quincy, would you take him out of the church to begin the journey to your next destination? I have a few more things to speak with Dutch and Aurora about and I would like to wrap up this mission with those men," he said, indicating the veterans standing in formation across the back of the church.

"All of you, cover your eyes," he ordered.

They obeyed and from under their lids could see the blast of brilliant light illuminate the church once again. Mack's unconscious body slumped against Quincy, and two members of the NYPD SWAT team quickly joined him to carry Mack out of the church. Before they moved him,

Father Micah touched the medal bearing his likeness around Mack's neck. Tucking it back into his shirt, he then signaled to the men that they could safely remove him.

Father Micah, a young priest with shoulder length hair the color of wheat fields, stood before them. His golden eyes shone as he motioned for Aurora and Dutch to sit in the pew in front of where he was standing.

"There are a few things I want to leave with you both. Over two hundred children are imprisoned in the maze underneath Alejandro's corporate headquarters. Your teams are rescuing them as we speak. Those children are alive, but there exists a secret chamber with documented remains of his victims. If you could ensure that those are recovered and returned to their families, the final obligation for you both to this endeavor will be fulfilled."

He reached behind his back for a long wooden box, which he handed to the siblings.

"These are Tieghan's remains. You can now inter her and close this book in your life. Your service as soldiers in the army of God, has been and continues to be most respected. However, your work here on Earth is not finished."

He placed his hands on their heads, "I release you of your duty in her name, and all guilt and remorse you have harbored for Tieghan." He removed his hands from their heads and smiled, glancing to Aurora's right side as though acknowledging someone sitting beside her.

"She entered paradise as a five-year-old girl and chose to remain this age through eternity. She wants you to know how much she loves you both. Every instance you found inspiration on the path to save or protect a child, it was her soft voice in your ears that guided you."

Aurora and Dutch could not hold back their tears.

"She is insisting that I tell you—she has accomplished her dream to be an eternal mermaid. It is heaven, after all," he laughed softly. The siblings laughed through their tears.

"Dutch, she's here," Aurora whispered to her brother. This time it wasn't the scent of pool chlorine but the sweet, briny fragrance of the ocean that bloomed around Aurora. "Dutch, can you smell it? The ocean?" He squeezed her hand and nodded in agreement. She whispered quietly, "I love you too, baby sister."

"Aurora, I eliminated the pictures from your mind that you were forced to endure earlier. There is no justification for you to keep them in your memory. You have given enough to this cause. I also would like to apologize for the nightmares. I sent the dreams to you. I needed to fortify your faith, without interfering with it. It is the better medium for me to communicate with you. I'd like to promise there won't be nocturnal terrors in your future, but I cannot. Read between the lines as you always have, you'll know what to do."

Father Micah handed Dutch the pocketknife back. "I assured your uncle I would use this; in his opinion, you both turned out to be decent detectives. His words. I left my mark on the knife for you to always remember this night."

Dutch examined the handle and saw a new engraving, their Trident wrapped around the signature letter T. Aurora was so caught up in the surrealness of everything that she didn't want to leave his presence without asking him hundreds of questions.

"As I said, the two of you along with the small, trusted team you have assembled, have more work to do here. There will be new challenges on the horizon as you seek to right some of the world's wrongs. Together you are immeasurably powerful and serve on the side of righteousness. Keep your faith, we will always guide you. Ask for help, we cannot intercede otherwise. You won't need to seek out your purposes, they will find you."

"How?" Aurora asked, her voice hoarse. "How did this all happen?"

The archangel gazed into her eyes, "You Aurora, you summoned the fury of God's own thunder, and well, that's me." He smiled with a delicate humility.

Aurora exchanged glances with her brother in disbelief. "I swear Dutch, I had no idea this was even possible."

St. Michael watched her trying to process the miracles they had witnessed. He answered her with a tone of great respect in his voice.

"Aurora, you are an ancient warrior. Nowhere

in your current memory will you appreciate this—it's obscured for your protection. Battles such as this one have gone on for centuries and in some instances you call upon me to—how do you all say it? oh yes—you call me in for backup."

"I....me? I do? Really?" she gushed. "And Mack?"

Father Micah nodded, "Yes, him as well. An ancient guardian. He'll explain it all to you when he wakes up, but you both won't remember those facts in a few days, it won't serve this lifetime to carry with you all past information. What you must remember is to ask for help, anytime."

Dutch looked his sister over proudly, she never ceased to amaze him.

"Thank you," Aurora whispered. "For returning Tieghan to us, for saving Mack's life, and for answering my prayers. St. Michael, my children—every one of them is a first responder. My sons, their wives, I'm so grateful for your constant protection," she whispered, humbly.

Father Micah nodded in recognition of her gratitude and smiled at her. "Aurora, I know what you most desire to ask me. Ben is in our Father's paradise, resting in eternal peace; your love and light perpetually surround him. He prays daily for your strength. Your devotion for each other will sustain throughout eternity. You will see him again, for now look for signs from him among the children."

She fought the urge to hug the young priest.

"I did make a pledge to Mack as a condition

of replacing him this time in battle and taking control of his body to finish the work." He took Aurora's chin in his hand, and whispered solemnly, "You have my word, he will remain on this Earth one day longer than you. His love for you is infinite."

This time she did stand to wrap her arms around the younger man, surprising him as he warmly returned the embrace.

Dutch asked with bewilderment, "How can we ever thank you?"

Father Micah smiled again. "You both have frequently honored me and our Almighty Father. You have made unimaginable sacrifices and dedicated your lives to fight against those who seek the ruin of souls. The children you have rescued, or detoured from a horrendous fate, their parents, their grandparents, have all prayed with gratitude for your intervention and courage. Your faith has been all the thanks our Father has ever needed. Whatsoever you do for the least of my brothers, you do for him."

Father Micah mustered the veterans lining the back of the church to him.

"General?" asked Roscoe, wheeling himself forward, the self-appointed leader of the group.

"Soldiers, thank you for your service tonight and throughout your lives to God and country. Your assistance was crucial to the desired outcome of this battle. You are welcome to return to our father's paradise this day if you so desire."

Roscoe stood from his rickety old wheelchair; his legs completely restored. "We always said we would go down together, sir. We would very much like to rise as one unit as well. Thank you, General."

Aurora proceeded to hug every one of them and tenderly kissed each bashful veteran on their cheek.

Dutch went down their line and shook their hands. There was a great exclamation of "Ooh Rah!" among the Marines. The men joined hands in a long chain and with a tilt of his chin, St. Michael sent them to their final reward.

Aurora wanted to ask one thing more, "Father Micah?... St. Michael? Why Mack when you had already taken human form as this priest?"

The Archangel grinned proudly. "The line of his ancestors prepared him for this purpose. He is pure of heart, and his devotion immeasurable. Love, Aurora, it is by far the most effective weapon against evil. Understand that every one of you were chosen an exceptionally long time ago to be here, together as one on this very night. You all consented to this path. Yes, you have the gift of free will, but your purposes under heaven are also pre-ordained. You have only begun to awaken to the glory of Our Father."

He placed his hands on their heads, "Go now and always, go with God."

With that, he disappeared.

Aurora turned as the sound of the great

marble likeness of the archangel returned to its pedestal. Dutch took her under his arm, and with the remains of his other sister tucked against him, they walked out of the church.

Chapter Twenty-Seven

The car turned into the driveway of the Echo Lake cabin as the sun began to peek above the horizon. Aurora got out of the SUV, amazed at how in just twenty-four hours, from dawn to dawn, her entire life had pivoted, again.

Ken met them at the garage and helped Dutch and Quincy as they carried Mack, still in a deep sleep, to the great room and placed him comfortably on the long sofa. Aurora covered him with blankets and removed his shoes and socks. She kissed his forehead tenderly and adjusted the pillow under his head.

Cat raced from the bedroom and jumped into Dutch's arms. "Thank God you are all alive!" He kissed her roughly as if he thought he would never see her again.

"Put the coffee on, honey," he told her. "You're never going to believe this story."

"I'm way ahead of you," she replied, reaching for Aurora. She was still wrapped in a homeless vet's bloodstained blanket, but Cat hugged her tight anyway.

"Nice haircut. Did you force your brother to stop at Damien's Salon on the way back to match your fashionable new outfit?" She laughed with relief.

Aurora hugged her close and laughed with her. "Damien is going to have a seizure when he sees this chop job," she replied. Aurora stopped to greet her frenzied dogs, who jumped over each other to greet her.

"I'm heading upstairs, Dutch," she said. "I need three showers and when I come back down, it's my turn to stand guard over him," she pointed to Mack's prone, comfortable form on the sofa.

Once showered and dressed, she returned to the great room to check on Mack. She touched his handsome face and adjusted the blankets around him. She leaned down to kiss his soft mouth. Dutch and Quincy were also showered and changed.

Cat prepared and served fresh coffee and a delicious ham, egg, and cheese frittata.

"Sit, eat something," she ordered. "Don't leave out one detail."

They looked at each other, still in stunned disbelief at the events.

Ken broke the silence. "Dutch, we have it all. Aurora's hidden mic recorded everything. I saved it to our encrypted server. If I didn't hear it for myself, I don't think you could have convinced me." He continued, "While you were finishing with NYPD, I called Delta team back and returned all family members from protective custody. I spoke to your sons, Aurora, they know you are safe, and the danger has been neutralized."

"Thank you, Ken," she said wearily. She was going to have to call them soon. Aurora picked at her breakfast lazily.

Cat looked at them, "So, really... St. Michael?" she asked, her eyes bright with wonder. They faced her wide-eyed with bewildered stares.

"Aurora, did the devil call you 'Sugar'? 'cause I'm sure I almost peed my pants when I heard it," Cat whispered with horror.

Aurora nodded her head and reached for her friend's hand. "I knew something was wrong with Rick, he was a distraction or was attempting to be. I wonder if he even knew what he was doing," she speculated aloud to Cat.

Her friend stood to hug her again, "Rory your scream—it was... Ken and I both couldn't imagine the pain you were in and then we knew... Mack. Dear God, honey, are you okay?" she whispered.

She squeezed Cat close to her, "It was fucking awful, I felt him slip away." Aurora's tears came on suddenly again. "Cat, I could never live without him, and I realized it when I felt him go limp against me..." The tears gushed from her eyes. Cat held her close and handed her a napkin for her tears. "I still can't believe what happened, he was gone..." her voice trailed off in disbelief.

She then glanced anxiously over at Mack. "How long has it been?" she asked Dutch, wiping her eyes, attempting to control her tears.

"Not even twelve hours; give him time, 'ancient warrior' he will be back. There will be no living this down... can you imagine, Quincy? He'll pull the 'archangel possessed me' card for the rest of our lives." They chuckled in response.

"Do you believe it, Dutch? Me? An ancient warrior? I'm not sure how to sort out any of this," Aurora mumbled.

Dutch sat back, running his hand over his bald head. "I've been thinking about it Tink, so much of it makes sense. In our youth you were always protective of me, your friends, and then Tieghan. It was always you, Aurora, you knew she was in danger from the beginning, you convinced me."

Aurora was lost in a fog, she was curious to know the whole history, when her brother finished his thoughts.

"It won't matter in a few days anyway, Tink; according to him, we're all going to forget. At least the parts of our history too dangerous for you to remember. I'm curious to hear Mack's view of last night." Dutch and Quincy exchanged knowing looks.

She sat up in her chair and directed her next question to Quincy.

"Quincy, you have been so quiet all night, are you okay?" Aurora asked, using her motherly tone of voice.

He sighed and replied, "I'm dumbfounded. I've seen the atrocities men are capable of in my line of work and still my faith in God has always remained steadfast. But not until last night have I truly comprehended the glory of the Almighty. I've never questioned my purpose on this planet, but after standing in the shadow of the Commander of the Legions of Angels, I finally know why I'm here. It's a lot to process."

He shook his head and took a long sip from his cup of coffee. "You know, it's the craziest thing—he touched me on the shoulder. My knees, they don't hurt anymore. Not one creak from my ancient football injuries." He shook his head in amazement.

The group snickered. The miracles they witnessed were still coming to light for them.

"It's going to take a long time for all of us to process this," she agreed. "Not sure how I'm ever going to sleep now that the devil knows my name." She sighed. "Dutch, we can hold a proper funeral for Tieghan. I have my Tinker Bell wand stored in the bank safety deposit box and want it placed in the coffin with her."

There was no more sadness, no more tears or guilt, shame, or remorse. Just love and adoration for their departed sister. Justice was served and they had been relieved of their burden by the archangel.

Dutch nodded his head in agreement.

"Tink, we could all use a few hours of shut eye. Ken, Quincy, and I are going to tackle the mountain of paperwork at some point today to close out this operation. I spoke to the New York medical examiner last night about the remains of the other victims. Once she finishes making the identifications, they will be released to Trident for us to make contact, and we can return them to their families. The District Attorney wants our statements and the rest of the evidence we collected to finish off Jovencita Enterprises. There were 232 children rescued last night just in New York. Reports are coming in from all over the world of additional raids and the numbers are in the thousands of missing children rescued. News and social media are reporting it already. Alejandro is listed as unaccounted for, gone with the wind."

Dutch stood to refill his cup of coffee, still addressing Aurora. "I also received the fire marshal's report from Gull Cove and the insurance adjusters want to meet with you this week. We can stay here in Echo Lake as long as you wish. Rest today, sleep beside him if you want, but you need to sleep. Cat will keep watch over you both and if it proves too boring, I'm stealing her to help with the paperwork."

Aurora agreed in silence and left the table to step outside to smoke. She let the dogs run around the backyard; they were happy to have her back. They brought her their ball, and she indulged them with a game of fetch in return for a few minutes of peace and quiet.

Inside, she pushed the two oversized ottomans against the sofa to make a space for herself beside Mack. He was undisturbed by her presence, as well as the two rowdy Cavs in need of a snuggle.

Her head barely hit the pillow when she fell into a sleep as deep as her couch mate.

Much later, long after sunset, Mack woke slowly, gathering his bearings. He felt the control of his body immediately. He realized where he was... the cabin... *Echo Lake*, he thought to himself.

Mack heard the fireplace crackling and spitting, smelled delicious scents wafting from the kitchen, but most remarkable of all was the scent of the woman lying beside him. "Mimosa," he sighed happily. She was curled up in a blanket, both dogs at her feet, her back to him. He reached out to bring her close and nestled his face in her soft, fragrant neck. "Wake up—my warm, cozy, kitten." he whispered.

She stirred slightly, unable to break away from her slumber. She sighed in her sleep as she felt his arms encircle her. She turned over, nestled into his chest, and began to wake up.

"Good morning, my sexy kitten, do you remember your promises?" He raised her chin to look at her, her drowsy eyes blinking. He wanted this view every time he awoke for the rest of his life. His very own sleeping beauty beside him.

"Thank God you came back." She exhaled heavily. "My knight-in-shining-armor. As for promises I made, you might have to rattle my memory." She smiled dreamily, gazing up into his cornflower blue eyes. He was alive and it was the greatest of all the miracles they had witnessed. The image of life leaving his body while cradled in her lap burned her eyes with stinging tears.

"I came back for you, I let them know, loudly— they shouldn't even call it heaven if you're not there. I will never leave you, ever again," he vowed. He suddenly noticed the influx of her tears, "Hey, hey no tears, I'm fine." He tried to soothe her, and his thumb instantly went to her cheeks to brush them away. The sound of his voice, his accent, filled her with relief. "I'm gonna rattle more than your memory, beautiful girl," he chuckled into her ear. The feel of his beard brushing against her neck made her sigh with happiness.

"Mack, you scared me." Her voice cracked with emotion. "You were gone, dead in my arms—it was horrendous. I would have never survived it... it almost killed me. I didn't realize it, but I can't live without you," Tears now streamed from her eyes. She clung to his muscled arms tightly. "I'm so sorry I didn't know all this sooner..." She buried her head in his shoulder and sobbed.

Mack held her and kissed her forehead and cheek softly. "Shhhh, no baby, no more tears. This was inevitable. We've been doing this for centuries the both of us; we don't remember, we're not meant to." He yawned quietly and cupped her face with his hand. "You saw it briefly in the church, didn't you? We consented to this path, all of us. You and I have always been together. I was born in infinite lifetimes to love you exclusively and to battle beside you. I love you and only you, Aurora, and always will until they call us back for good. So, can you stop crying and let me kiss you?" he teased, wiping another tear, and bringing his face closer to hers. "We can start making up for lost time any minute now." He teased.

She sighed and looked up at him, "Please kiss me, and don't ever stop."

"Stop kissing you? Pfft, never again. I want three straight days to start with, Aurora, so tell me when the clock starts." He sighed, astounded that she had slept beside him. He lifted the blanket over both of their heads and covered her mouth with his own. The kiss was so powerful and passionate that she felt her blood rush to the corners of her body. This time, Aurora was the one to moan with desire into his kiss.

"Woman, if I can't come inside you soon, I'm turning around and going back," he whispered hungrily. "Please don't make me wait any longer," he pleaded, his mouth at her ear.

Aurora snickered modestly, "Mr. Egan, you have such swagger, you sweep a girl right off her feet."

Mack ran his hand down the front of her slowly, "Your feet won't touch the floor for at least a week if I have my way." He chuckled. "Sneak upstairs, I need a shower and this time you're getting in with me." He kissed her and she took his chin to gently bite his lower lip.

"Quite a dangerous move—you know what it does to me." He teased, gently placing his hand over one of her breasts. "I want these in my mouth," he groaned, cupping his hand around it, his confidence fueled by her reaction to his touch. Through her thin bra he felt the nipple harden and lowered his head to bite at it through the fabric. She purred softly, ran her hand down his back and rested it on his backside. He kissed her neck down to the V-line of her sweater.

"Aurora, meet me upstairs?" He stared into her luminous brown eyes. She smiled slowly and ran her hand over his muscled arm. "No dinner, no dates?" she teased. "Right to it?"

"Baby, I will give you the world—every single thing your heart desires. Starting tomorrow. Tonight, though, I'm taking you for a trip around it first." He laughed and sucked her bottom lip into his soft mouth. "Naked, Aurora. I want to see you, touch you, and taste you. I walked through hell to get back here, and you're my paradise, let me in," he whispered between soft, sweet kisses on her face and neck.

She ran her fingernails through his goatee. "I will give you every single thing your heart desires, my hero." Her honeyed voice flowed over him; she was a siren, and he could feel himself swoon.

All of his blood rushed to his groin. He would have consummated their union right there if it wasn't for the sound of Dutch clearing his throat. "I forgot we're not alone," Mack laughed, pulling the blankets off them.

Dutch saw and heard them start to wake but hesitated before disturbing them.

"Okay you two, it's obvious you're both awake. Dinner will be ready in fifteen so shake the sand out of your shoes," Dutch announced.

Aurora reluctantly rose from the ottomans and Dutch helped her pull them away from the sofa to give Mack egress. Dutch held his hand out to help him up from his position.

"How are you feeling, Son?" Dutch asked, pulling Mack to his feet. He examined him quickly, looking into his eyes and reaching around his torso to feel his ribs. Dutch could see the slashes in his shirt from Alejandro's knives and large patches of dried blood around them. "Mack, when I suggested a dramatic gesture for Aurora to notice you, I meant flowers or something. This was all a touch sensational." Dutch laughed softly with the younger man, great relief in his tone.

"You know me, boss. Go big or go home." Mack laughed. "I feel quite good considering, though I'm desperate for a shower. Give me a few minutes and I'll be down to join you."

Mack eyed Aurora conspiratorially and nodded his head toward the stairs. Dutch returned to the kitchen to help Cat set the table for dinner. Aurora hesitated, but then slipped upstairs to join Mack.

The water was running at perfect temperature when Mack began to peel off his ruined shirt. She tapped on his door and quietly entered. She felt inelegant and awkward, not sure if she was prepared. Aurora was cognizant there would be no going back from what would happen next. Alejandro's abrasive humiliation suddenly rushed in to plague her, leaving her feeling unattractive and unappealing. She unexpectedly lost all her bravado.

Mack was almost ten years younger than her and in phenomenal physical shape. What did he see in her and how could she satisfy a man like him?

He was overjoyed she'd followed him into his room but immediately saw her hesitation and shame. "Aurora, what is it? Oh no, you are not replaying the venom of a degenerate in your head, are you? Get into the shower with me, let's wash him off each other." He removed his watch and put it on the dresser.

She nodded sadly, eyes averted; ashamed that Mack had heard every vile thing Alejandro had said to her. She stood frozen to the spot and wouldn't look at him. He undid his pants and slowly stepped out of them. He slipped off his close-fitting boxer briefs and let her see him, completely aroused in her presence.

"Aurora, you're the most extraordinary woman I have ever laid eyes on. Everything about you turns me on—your sense of humor, your mythical beauty, that sexy as hell voice. Even your adorable pajama combinations. I can't keep my hands off you. Your body… dear God… it was custom made for me—a starving fucking wolf. Honest to God, if I don't get to burrow myself inside you like a coal miner on a Monday morning, I will lose my bloody mind." He was eager to have her, his entire way of life stood at a crossroads.

She gulped aloud, looking him over. *Why would he want her?* His body was a renaissance statue. A carved-from-Carrara marble masterpiece. The vision of him standing there should have been accompanied by slow motion soundtrack music and backlighting—he was spectacular.

"Look at me," he ordered as he walked slowly toward her, every muscle large and clearly defined. "I'm a big, bad, scary motherfucker. Nothing has ever frightened me. I have patrolled the worst spots on Earth with one hand on my ass and the other on my rifle. The possibility of living without you brought me to my fucking knees. I pledged to spend my life beside you. I bargained with an archangel to do this very thing and I would have signed with the devil if he hadn't agreed."

Still sensing her self-condemnation, he closed the distance between them, backing her up against the closed door. He took her hand and held it against his considerable erection.

His voice was scorching in her ear, "Touch me, Aurora. Can you feel this? You do this to me, baby. Just the sound of your voice makes me so hard. I'm in this condition constantly when I'm near you. You own me, and I'm taking you as mine." He kissed her roughly, pressing his naked body against her.

He was taking her breath away. His strong, remarkable physique, his yearning and need, were pulling her forward from an infinite period of denial.

She interrupted him, "Are you okay? What happened to you last night? Tell me what you saw."

"Not yet. I can't. Take me inside you, Aurora," he pleaded.

She lifted her head and held his face in her hands, assessing him carefully. "Mack, it's all you, right?" she asked, "Because I can't imagine the hours I'd have to spend in confession if I willingly had my way with an archangel."

"It's all me, kitten." He grinned slyly, looking down at himself. "Well, he might have left me his sword," he joked, returning her hand to his groin, and stroking it over his throbbing shaft.

They both laughed and he began to remove her clothes, tossing the items to the floor. Mack felt like a kid on Christmas morning, unwrapping his most coveted gift. He unclipped her bra with one hand and sighed with delight.

"Fucking flawless," he whispered with joy. He held her breasts in his large hands and gently kissed them, swirling his tongue around her nipples, causing them to stiffen from attention. He paused reverently to kiss the thin, red scar remaining from her heart surgery. She was filling with warm pools of longing, which settled in her abdomen and below. He trailed soft kisses down her lower body, removing her pretty underwear as he knelt before her. He lifted one of her legs onto his shoulder and languidly tasted her between them. She cried out quietly with pleasure. "Precisely how I like mine, juicy and sweet." He smiled to himself; she was ready for him.

Standing again before her, he lifted her arms above her head, locking her wrists in his strong hands, and pressing his body against hers, he kissed her hard. "You are mine, now and forever, surrender to me Aurora," he whispered into her soft mouth. "And you will absolutely require confession when we're done." He stepped toward the bathroom, reaching for her hand to bring her with him. When she paused, he looked back to see what stopped her.

Aurora glanced down at her left hand. Cat had returned her wedding rings when they arrived in the morning. They were now back on her ring finger. Mack stood waiting for her, watching her, and time seemed to freeze. She removed the three rings Ben gave her for their engagement, wedding, and ten-year anniversary. This time, she knew deep in her heart it was for the last time. Setting them on the dresser, she swallowed back her tears and took his hand.

Mack felt the magnitude of what she did. He helped her into the shower, and she stood under the running water. He stepped in behind her and ran his strong hands slowly down the front of her, whispering into her ear, "Aurora, give yourself to me now." She melted into his touch.

She lathered up a washcloth and slowly washed his back and shoulders, examining him everywhere for traces of his wounds. Not one welt, scar, or proof of injury anywhere. Even the lacerations he'd suffered in Syracuse were gone. He turned around to face her, grinning, "This side needs extra attention, please," he said with a clear agenda sparkling in his eyes.

Soaping his steel chest and rock-hard stomach, she paused to respectfully touch the medal still around his neck. Aurora kept searching for any sign that he had been mortally wounded just hours earlier. His skin was undamaged and perfect. She touched his arousal slowly, soap sliding between her fingers. "Mack, you take my breath away," she whispered. He moaned happily at the feel of her delicate touch around him.

He smiled lazily at her, "It's about time, Aurora, you've been robbing me of oxygen since the moment I met you. Let me show you what I can really do to you." He leaned down to kiss her again, the water falling around them. He roamed his soapy hands easily across her back and over her perfect ass. He lifted her leg and positioned her foot onto the shower bench, his hand holding the back of her thigh.`

"I'm sorry, this is not the way I planned our first time. I have dreamed of a slow, long, all night initiation. But I'm a powder keg right now; I almost died—I almost lost you. I can't explain it. I don't know a nicer way to say it. This is going to be rough and fast... please, let me fuck you?" he beseeched her. "Bring me back to life, baby." His sentiments were delicious in her ear.

"What took you so long to ask me?" she whispered, teasing and flirty. Mack laughed aloud. He gently shifted her into position and sank his entire erection inside her in one slow thrust. Remaining still for a moment, he savored her softness wrapped around him. "Damn, I knew this was where I truly belonged." He sighed low, his words thickened with lust.

Her laughter quickly turned into a yelp of surprise, "Holy shit... Mack!" She was shocked by how he fit and filled her entirely. He began to move slowly, relishing the feel of her around him, wishing his whole being might crawl in to live there. He braced her up against the wall of the shower, lifting her off her feet with his driving movement.

"Ahhhh goddamn, you're so tight and wet, I didn't think you could be more fucking perfect." He was overtaken with ecstasy, craving her with such an intensity that the animal inclinations inside him took over.

Entering her repeatedly, he nestled his face into her neck, her arms circled tight around him. Mack grasped that he was breathing an uninhibited, mythical goddess back to life. Aurora was responding to him with outbursts of guttural enjoyment.

"Is this how you like it, kitten?" His voice gravelly, "Tell me every way to please you," he whispered, submerging himself inside her.

"God yes, Mack... it's so good." She smiled to herself, the wants he'd listed to her over a week ago reverberated in her head. She whispered into his ear with her whiskey baritone, giving him exactly what he craved, "More, Mack... please give me more... come inside me," she begged between his thrusts.

He chuckled breathlessly at her words. "I feel good in there, don't I? You're all mine." He bit down on her delicate shoulder, the desire to mark her as his own raging through him. She was home, to a man who never knew a place to define it. This was no routine encounter for him, he couldn't remember ever being this crazy in love and lust simultaneously. Aurora was no schoolgirl, she knew how to satisfy him. The sex kitten was waking up all over her and he couldn't get enough of it.

He felt his orgasm hurtling toward him; breathless into her neck he cried, "Shit, I won't last, I'm gonna lose it, Aurora, I can't stop. Finish with me," His body was shuddering like a runaway train. He bit down on her tender neck, sucking the skin directly under her ear. It was her weak spot and she felt herself ready to collide into him.

"Don't stop… let go… give yourself to me now," she cried out, delirious with satisfaction, reaching back to grab his wet, muscled bottom to enhance his depth.

His stride quickened, allowing his thundering orgasm to ram into hers, her fingernails dug into his back, and she felt the last of her pleasure seize through her and wash over him. His deep voice rumbled out in a low roar as he emptied himself in her rushing surge. They almost fell to the floor of the shower with their release. Mack felt his strength drain from his body into hers.

"My beautiful Aurora," he exhaled, holding tight to balance her footing. "I'm so fucking in love with you." He backed her up against the shower wall again, kissing her softly. He felt tears rush to his eyes, all his stifled emotions surfacing. He had been stone-hearted, cold, and unfeeling before. Now she was inside of him, and it altered and tempered him.

Mack sensed that his former existence, as he

previously lived it, was circling the shower drain. Aurora was his life now and he'd clearly been waiting for her in order for it to truly begin.

"Three days and the rest of our lives," he whispered, staring into her kaleidoscope-like eyes of shifting brown, gold, and green.

She kissed him again, running her hands down his strong back. She whispered happily, "I'm quite content with that." And with that, she gave up any last thoughts of holding out on the depth of emotion this man awakened in her. Whatever this was with him; when she least wanted, needed, or expected it, here he was, and she wasn't going to take this gift for granted.

They finished the shower by washing each other's hair, continuing to kiss and touch each other sweetly. "I hate how it happened, but I like your new haircut." He kissed the tattoo on her left shoulder that matched his. She turned to look up at him. He held her face in his hands.

"Thank you, Aurora. I've never taken a shower with anyone. As luck would have it my first was with the only girl I will ever love. Sex has never been like this for me—you are phenomenal." He smiled happily.

She kissed him again, deep, and loving. "I'm sorry I'm out of practice, kind of rusty. You woke a jungle cat from its coma. Thank you for bringing me back. It only gets better from here," she promised.

Mack laughed happily, "Out of practice? Shit,

I better start taking my vitamins. Woman, if this was only half your game, I'm going back to boot camp." He shut the water and helped her out of the shower.

They returned to Mack's room wrapped in towels; they were like naughty teenagers, drying each other off till Aurora tiptoed over to her bedroom for clothes. She took her rings from the dresser and packed them with her medicine boxes. She changed into black wool pants and a soft gray cashmere sweater.

He met her in the hallway as they readied to go down to dinner.

"Aurora, are you okay? No guilt, no regrets, no shame?" he asked, his voice concerned. He was dressed comfortably in worn jeans and a blue pullover hoodie with US Navy emblazoned on it.

She smiled, "A little of everything, but I'll be okay," she assured.

He reached inside his sweatshirt for the medal, and she stopped him, "Do not ever take it off," she said. "I will feel better knowing it is protecting you."

"You don't have to worry your pretty head over me; nothing will happen to me while you are alive. I exacted a sacred vow." He kissed her, soft and tender.

"Mack, he touched it before you were carried out of the church," she told him. She reached for the medal and turned it over, shocked when she saw the same engraving he'd left on the pocketknife.

"Look, it's our logo. The Trident," she said with awe. He looked down to see it, just as surprised as she was. She tucked it back inside his hoodie.

"Never take this off," she said with a low, reverent voice. He nodded his head in agreement.

Chapter Twenty-Eight

They arrived hand in hand to dinner together, as the rest of the team were taking their seats. Even if most of the group assembled were not highly trained operatives, they could tell what took Mack and Aurora longer to get to the table from merely looking at them.

"Something smells amazing," Aurora said, her cheeks pink with embarrassment. Her hair, like Mack's, was still damp from the shower. Cat laughed knowingly as Dutch assessed them both and smirked, "Neither one of you has a good poker face. Sit down and eat something. With any luck the rest of us will have hot water in the morning." He rolled his eyes dramatically.

Quincy and Ken were occupied delivering the team's personal vehicles to the cabin when Mack had finally woken up. This was the first time they were seeing him. Both men were silently evaluating him for subtle physical changes. They saw none, other than his serenity and bright smile.

Quincy stood to hug Mack. "You terrified the ever-loving fuck out of me last night, brother," he said quietly. Releasing him from his massive arms, he ran his hands around Mack's torso the way Dutch had. "You all good?" he asked, worried.

"Better than ever, my brother." His smile was cheerful. "Thank you, Quince, for everything last night, and for always having my six," Mack replied humbly. Quincy smiled over at Aurora with gratitude.

Mack embraced Ken as he stood to welcome him back. "I'm glad you're okay, boss. I was afraid I'd never see you again," Ken whispered; his voice emotional as he slapped him on the back.

"Thank you, Ken, for tracking us and keeping us safe," Mack whispered in return.

Mack went to hold Aurora's chair for her while she sat and waved over at Cat in greeting.

Cat almost choked on stifling her laugh as she witnessed Aurora wince slightly with discomfort as she sat down. Mack caught it and winked at Aurora, "I warned you," he whispered proudly, taking his seat.

"You look terrific Mack, as if more than one divine being took possession of your body recently," Cat teased. It was hard to miss the afterglow surrounding them.

The group laughed at her double meaning. Cat whispered into Aurora's ear. "You have a sizable love bite on your neck. You might want to dig out your turtlenecks again before you go home," she laughed. Aurora flushed pink again and laughed with her best friend. She touched the spot on her neck where Mack had bit her. She smiled to herself, replaying the last incredible half hour in her mind.

Cat praised Quincy for the dinner preparation—slow-braised beef short ribs and creamy, cheesy polenta. They were all famished and ate as if they were headed for the electric chair.

Mack and Aurora kept stealing hooded glances at each other— snickering and whispering under their breath while they ate. He slid a hand over her knee, resting it on her thigh. They were even playing footsie under the table. Mack needed to touch her in any way. He couldn't stop looking at her, her presence was more incandescent than ever before. She pilfered a sautéed button mushroom off his plate and a smile bloomed all over his face. Still chewing the contraband, she blew him a kiss.

Quincy and Dutch exchanged looks. "We're in big trouble, boss. He's about fourteen years old right now. I don't think his driver's license is valid," Quincy murmured.

Dutch laughed with him, shaking his head in disbelief. "Christ, I hope he remembers how to swim," Dutch joked back.

They were praising Quincy's culinary proficiency and finishing up when Cat gently broached the subject. She topped off Aurora's glass of cabernet before she spoke.

"Mack, Ken, and I heard everything as it happened in the church last night, Aurora's second hidden mic recorded it. Can you share with us what it was like for you?" The rest of them quieted, waiting for his take.

Quincy stood to fix Mack a drink. Knowing his boss better than anyone, he traded him off "messy mission" bourbon. He prepared a Jack Daniels on the rocks for him and placed it before him. Mack sighed with appreciation; the familiar scent of Tennessee whiskey told his body—mission completed.

Wiping his mouth on his napkin, he leaned back in his chair. He glanced over at Aurora, her face etched with concern. "It's okay, kitten, I'm ready," he assured her. Taking her hand in his, he took a deep breath. The pictures came back to him clearly. His accent was thick—his voice heavy with emotion.

"I knew I was dying; I was furious. Not hours earlier, I promised Aurora she wouldn't suffer another loss and there I was reneging. I saw the end coming, the lights surrounding me were vivid, unearthly, and comforting. I tried to hold on, but I felt myself slipping away..." He squeezed Aurora's hand; the prospect of it crushed him.

The tears came immediately to Aurora's eyes. The reality that she could have lost him forever swept over her like a wave. He was a legitimate miracle sitting beside her.

Mack continued, "Then he appeared before me. I'd never seen anything like him. An ancient warrior, the commander of armies battling evil for centuries. He was brilliant, and unexplainable. I knew who he was and saw him with Aurora and I, throughout history, a movie that flashed across my mind. I was humbled and amazed. He asked me if he could step inside so he could heal me instantly but needed me to relinquish control to him. When I did, I was suddenly overloaded with a flood of indescribable power. I saw what he saw, and my brain couldn't keep up with the influx of so much information. It was as if I was trying to pedal a motorcycle. I actually viewed souls as they transversed the bodies of everyone in the church," he paused suddenly, looking up at the ceiling, searching for the words.

"I'm trying to think of the best way to describe it. Your soul floats fluidly around you, proclaiming who you truly are. It exposes your marked path and direction, the predestination and power. First, Aurora, her poor face and body so battered and bruised, looked at me/him."

Mack turned and brought her hand to his lips in reverence. His accent was literal music to her ears. "You are not going to believe this; I'm still trying to. Aurora, you, and I—we are 'looking glass light bearers'—mirrored souls. I'm sure this was the name he called us, as so much data sprinted past me."

The expression on his face was one of complete awe and wonder. "Baby, you, and me began as one soul; they split us into two. It's up to us in each incarnation to find one another and then we will know what to do… somehow." He realized the images were beginning to fade from his memory.

The archangel had cautioned him not to hold on to the information for his and Aurora's safety. He held her hand up to his heart. Her gaze was transfixed on his, it was ringing true deep inside her.

"Though you were mortally wounded, your soul is formidable; lit up like a sky filled with bursting fireworks, every color I could imagine. It sparkles and dances with a million tiny diamonds. Your strength and benevolence are unmatched. I will *never* unsee this part of you. You really are fucking amazing. Only moments before you begged to change places with me, you asked him to take you instead. Your tears, your scream...." Mack stopped suddenly, attempting to talk around the rock in his throat.

Cat and Dutch were holding their breath, tears filling their eyes. Neither Dutch nor Quincy had witnessed this part of the night. Cat heard it and it still echoed in her head.

"That sound, the agony... I tried..." His voice cracked with emotion. "I tried to get to you, I scratched at him to get back to you... I... I am not..." He exhaled heavily. "Aurora, there is no me without you... he held me back... and then I felt him heal you. Light from my hands spilled out to restore your broken, badly bleeding body. But you declined the chance to have your heartbreak minimized."

He bowed his head in admiration. Tears filled his gray-blue eyes. His love for her was immeasurable and beyond anything he had ever known. Aurora was spellbound by what he was telling her, and from a place in the corner of her memory she understood it all to be true.

Mack continued, "You wanted to keep your sorrow, and he let you. He was profoundly moved and felt such great respect for your request. He revealed the truth to me—you are a fearless, ancient warrior. You carry the Holy Spirit within you. Aurora, it was you—your prayer that mustered the fury of God's own thunder down on Alejandro's empire. They were not idle words. You possess the fierce, protective intuition of a mother, regardless of who the children belong to. I am here to guard and protect you, it's been my vocation for a millennia." He kissed her hand again, holding it up to his mouth and then his cheek.

He paused to take a sip from his glass. The group were mesmerized by his story.

Dutch was startled listening to the description of their conditions before he arrived inside the church. It made him sick inside that Aurora had been fatally wounded. Quincy warned him they were both in bad shape when he summoned Dutch and the paramedics. He was still not convinced that Alejandro's death was sufficient punishment.

Tears were slipping down Aurora's face, and she handed Mack a tissue as well. He held it to the corners of his eyes. He cleared his throat and began again, turning his attention to the rest of the table.

"Next, Dutch and Quincy came rushing toward me. Your souls were ablaze in blue and steel armor; you were chosen from your birth as soldiers of God. He let me see your purity of intention and golden hearts of strength and courage. You are both marked for the path of rectitude." Mack paused, taking a deep breath, running his free hand through his hair.

"This is the part I still can't wrap my head around, though. Maybe once I hear it out loud it'll make sense. Bear with me, this is really gonna sound crazy. I saw all of us." His focus went from person to person, shaking his head in wonder.

"We gathered before we were born, prior to coming here. Aurora and I are bound for eternity, and only if we can find each other—the rest of us chose each other. I witnessed it very quickly—we were in a large, round room where this entire plan was discussed and together we agreed to be a part of it." He sat up close to the table, still holding onto Aurora's hand.

"There were guides—a council of elders who described it to us and walked us through it. We signed on as one team for this life cycle. Including Alejandro and Tieghan. There were others, none I recognized but I understood that we will meet them along the way. I'm not exactly clear on all the reasons, but it has something to do with strengthening faith...work to be accomplished on personal karma and the evolution of souls. He called it star seeds or light walkers. It's all starting to fade away from me. It's about helping other souls, raising their vibration." He looked at Aurora again, understanding that he waited his whole life for her.

"Before we are born to this life, we're embedded with a spark of recognition for each other and those specific experiences in our lives are crucial to our path's integrity. We don't remember after we are born, or as we grow into adults, because we also have free will. We can always make other choices and veer away from the predestined direction. If and when we meet each other, something triggers inside us, a familiarity to the other person. I know it happened when I met Dutch. The same feeling occurred with Quincy and Ken when we met in boot camp. And it finally explained why I reacted so strongly the day I first laid eyes on Aurora." He stopped and looked over at Dutch.

"I told you this the other day; when it came to your sister, I felt my whole life had led me to this point in time. I knew in my gut that I wasn't just some lovesick sailor chasing after a sad widow. For everything to happen last night, it was essential for Aurora and me to reconnect; we were the catalyst, the final piece. Aurora needed all of us to be in place for her as she called down the final battle with Alejandro."

Aurora excitedly interrupted him, "Mack, he told us this right before he disappeared. He told Dutch and me, and we agreed that we were chosen long ago to be there last night as one. He said we consented to the path." She was amazed that their stories matched.

Quincy chuckled, "It has to be true. Mack and I have always said—a black kid from Mississippi and a white kid who grew up in South Africa during apartheid, why did we unite so naturally? We've been true brothers from day one."

Mack smiled and nodded at Quincy. "Makes

more sense now, but we never questioned it, we instantly bonded. And none of it works without Ken, he's our ground wire." He turned his attention back to Aurora, hoping she would understand his next recollection.

"There was a conversation about the 'threes,' the teams of three. Shit, it's going out of focus. Moving within the trinities… it's a key." He looked up to the ceiling again, but it slipped away from his mind's eye. She recognized the tenant, but like Mack, felt that it was just outside her mental grasp.

He turned back to Aurora, his face beaming with pride, "You were forged, Aurora. In the white flames of heaven, you are a fucking soldier in the army of the Almighty. I'm honored to know you." He kissed her hand. "Did you guess yet? Have you figured out what your spark of recognition was? We find our way to each other every time with instinct and raw courage," he said, giving her the pieces missing from the puzzle.

"Mack! The baby sea turtle!" she gasped. He smiled with joy. "Yes baby, the sea turtle. Tieghan handpicked it for you and implanted it in your memory. I never could understand why I bought or wear this bracelet. I told you as much."

Cat gushed, "Rore, you knew she was trying to tell you something! She never let go of the stuffed turtle as a baby. Of course, she chose it for you."

"The dreams, Aurora, do you remember the messages? He sent the allegories to you specifically," Mack asked.

She leaned closer to him, "He told me why, Mack, it was to fortify my faith. Lucius was brandishing temptation to try to separate us. Using Rick and Eve. You and I, we were the final connection as you've said. My grief was preventing me from putting the fragments together. He also told us the line of your ancestors prepared you for this mission. We serve in the same regiment, Mack. I'm honored to know you too." She brought his hand up to her lips this time, kissing it sweetly.

"Aurora, I've physically seen your faith, nothing can weaken it not even your sorrow." Mack whispered with amazement.

Cat then chimed in, "Mack, what you're saying is nothing is random? We can't remember consciously what our purpose is, but when we happen upon it, something internal knows?"

"Yes, exactly. Aurora, believe it or not, you even consented to marry and lose Ben early, for your soul and his to reach a heightened state. You both made the sacrifice for a greater good. It was all to purify your strength. Tieghan agreed to the atrocious path she would walk in life for her own part in saving the lives of numerous children. It's bizarre I know, but somehow it all fits," he whispered with awe.

Aurora sat back; the wind knocked out of her. She never heard this reason to lose Ben, but it resonated. She couldn't imagine why she would ever agree to it. In the grand scheme of things, she would have done almost anything to avenge her sister. Aurora knew when she married Ben that he wasn't in great health; he had a chronic heart condition, and she was always worried about him. Knowing what she knew, she would have done it all over again. Any amount of time with him was a gift she would have never refused, despite the anguish his loss caused.

"Take us back to the church, Mack." Aurora asked. "What happened next?"

Mack took a sip of his drink and sat up in his chair.

"Alejandro was then dragged into the church. He was so dark, a man made of rivers of thick-shifting road tar. Though he was offered salvation, he had no remorse. As for me, I felt confined in a control tower. I had no physical feeling of my body. I kept all my senses still, but no muscle memory. I wanted to wrap my hands around the fucking weasel's neck, but my arms were wet noodles until he touched the sword. The sword..." he paused, searching for words again.

"The sword... it's... unreal... alive. I don't think my limited vocabulary could ever explain it. It's an extension of him. Once he held it, my arm was mine and his, he let me feel the slice of the blade across Alejandro's neck. The magnitude of evil that oozed out of Alejandro's dead body was shocking. We've all had nightmare assignments, think we've seen the devil, but nothing—nothing—prepared me for standing in the presence from which all evil originates. I could see his horrendous thoughts, hints of his future plans.

And when we cut Lucius across his chest, it was the greatest sense of justice I've ever known in its purest form."

Mack stopped again, taking a breath, and rattling the ice in his glass. His audience was breathless, waiting for him to finish.

"Before Michael separated from me, I witnessed two things. I saw Tieghan." His smile was bashful and sweet.

"I've never seen a photo of her, but I knew beyond a doubt who she was. She walked into the church and sat close to Aurora and Dutch, waiting to be heard. A happy, beautiful little girl with adoration and worship on her face that was directed at her big brother and sister. She wanted to witness your discharge from duty in her name."

"I felt her," Aurora's eyes teared again. "She sat beside me; the smell of the ocean was everywhere." She glanced over at her brother. His eyes were filled with tears.

"Me too, Tink. It was so strong, no doubt it was her." He confirmed and squeezed Cat's hand under the table.

Mack continued, "The second were the invocations from the men who served; they were silently muttering for my safety and recovery, and the prayers were tangible—ribbons of light and love that wrapped around my body. As he began to shift I snatched on to him before he disappeared and asked him for one thing in exchange for his use of me. I humbly thanked him for saving my life. Then... I begged him to never let Aurora know a day on this earth without me beside her. To permit me to love her, protect her, and do whatever I could to comfort her. And then, everything went dark."

There was not a dry eye around the table, and even Ken found himself holding a napkin up to his face.

"Oh Mack!" Aurora gasped. Rising from her chair, she sat on his lap to embrace him. He held her close, his head on her chest. She raised his face to kiss him. "Thank you for coming back to me," she whispered.

He met her gaze with genuine reverence. Tightening his arms around her he said, "Since time began, you are my heart...and I am your armor," he whispered back, his voice sincere. He kissed her tenderly again. Aurora could feel her soul rising from its extensive hibernation. Now she finally comprehended why she was drawn out of misery toward him. Deep down she knew, she had always recognized him. He was her other half. Ben might have been the love of her life, but it was dawning on Aurora that Mack was the love of her infinite lifetimes.

"Wow, just wow," Cat whispered, tears falling from her eyes. She held tight to Dutch's hand under the table. He took it and raised it to his lips. Dutch was utterly speechless, he had yet to go back and listen to the recordings. He was still working through the reality of the implausible events they experienced. "This means you and I agreed to all of this, losing our spouses so early and finding ourselves together," she whispered.

"Thanks for signing on," Dutch whispered back, kissing her sweetly.

"Aurora," Mack whispered. "Your neck. I'm so sorry." He gushed awkwardly, looking over the mark he left on her soft skin. He was doubting how old he really was; everything about her turned him into a clumsy teenager.

She laughed quietly, touching her forehead to his, "Is this how a hungry wolf marks his territory?" Mack nodded enthusiastically.

Aurora returned to her seat and dried her eyes. She caught Quincy looking at her in wonder and went to embrace him as well. "Thank you for saving my life," she kissed his sturdy cheek.

"It was my honor, Miss Aurora," he said humbly, hugging her back.

On her way back to her seat, she reached around Ken's shoulders and embraced him, "You too, tech genius, thank you for guarding us." Ken blushed, and touched her hands clasped around his shoulders. "Just another day working for Dutch," he laughed gently.

"Dutch, I do have a question for you," Mack asked, breaking the reverie of the group.

"What's that, son?" he asked quietly.

"Do I have permission to date your sister?" He looked over at Dutch, slightly serious.

The whole room broke out in peals of laughter.

Cat chuckled and responded for him, "Well,

we were holding out for a god, but we'll settle for a former archangel." Dutch laughed along with them. He returned Mack's glance and nodded proudly with approval.

Ken spoke softly from his spot at the table. "Aurora, you may not believe this but just the other day, on our drive here, Mack told me he could die and still find a way back to you. I was shocked then when he spoke those words, but I'm not surprised he kept his promise."

Aurora looked at Mack, her eyes glowing with admiration. Her love for him was blooming inside her. Quincy, who was introspective for most of the encounter, suddenly spoke. "Dutch, this is highly classified, right? How much did NYPD, SWAT, and emergency services know about the circumstances in the church?"

Dutch thought about it. "No one asked. It was just us in there with the military vets. Most were at the building rescuing the kids. Two SWAT guys came in just as you readied to carry Mack out. Only Ken was monitoring Aurora's communications. No one else saw anything or heard anything to my knowledge."

Ken sat up in his seat, "Is anyone going to answer the why? Why St. Michael? If all of us are part of this purpose and we established our roles before we were born, why did we need divine intervention? Or was it part of the plan?"

Aurora replied to him, she could not explain where the answer came from. The sound of her voice held them in a trance as if she were speaking from one. "There was a covenant, centuries ago. Our ancestors pledged their alliance to the archangels, and each generation completes a sworn duty; some carry out several, as we will. I don't know the details, and I'm positive they won't let me see them. Mack, your father, he carried the holy card of St. Michael, remember? We form the Trinities. They are the key to something. The teams of 'three.' It's almost on the tip of my tongue, but I'm getting blocked," she said, exasperated.

Mack nodded. "I know Aurora, there's a reason we can't access everything. We cannot bring in past history to present circumstances. It affects our decisions. I do know whatever comes at us next, the answers accompany those challenges."

Ken sat back in his chair, completely overwhelmed with the conversation, and itching to research all of it. They sat quietly for a moment. Quincy stood to refill Mack's drink and make one for himself.

"So, what's next Dutch?" asked Ken, "We still have days of paperwork ahead, but what do you think comes after this?" He signaled to Quincy with his empty glass for another as well, and his friend happily obliged.

"Well, first you guys deserve a long vacation" Dutch said. "St. Michael all but guaranteed that there would be challenges on the horizon. He also promised they would find us. I'm not sure what they will look like yet. Do you guys have any ideas for R&R?" he asked.

Mack sipped at his whiskey and spoke, "I have a crazy idea. I was wondering, if Aurora didn't mind, of course, I'd like to take a shot at starting the restorations to Gull Cove. Oh, by the way, I live in Autumn Lake as well. Bonita Beach." He smirked like a reporter who had buried the lead story.

Aurora was speechless. She hadn't given it any serious consideration yet as she had been too distracted by Alejandro. She briefly thought she might relinquish the shore house. Where was home now for her? Did Mack say he lived in Autumn Lake? She had yet to regroup with her publisher about the remaining appearances, then there were the rewrites for her new book, and the kids, what was she going to tell them? Her brain was ready to short circuit.

Mack was done with the pretense of suppressing his feelings. He reached again for her hand and brought it up to his lips. "I'm not going anywhere, Aurora. You can always decide where, but I will not sleep another night without you beside me."

"You won't get much done with the weather getting colder; holidays are coming, and it slows down everything," Dutch replied. "But if you don't mind the company, I always carry my tools in the back of my truck. I'll be spending more time closer to home now. What say you, Tink?"

Tears again slipped down Aurora's face as she nodded her head in acceptance. She hadn't known a life without the shadows of Tieghan and the monsters in the dark. The idea of having her brother home again filled her with joy. She had no idea what was next, but she was anxious to find out.

With new plans emerging among them, they agreed to leave Echo Lake in the morning. Everyone was exhausted and left the table to retire for the evening. They all knew that it might be the first good night sleep for all of them in a long time.

Chapter Twenty-Nine

Aurora and Mack volunteered to do the after-dinner cleanup. The process was slowed by his inability to keep his hands off her once the room was cleared of their friends. Aurora was handwashing dishes with a starving man at her back, kissing her neck and running his hands all over her. She was weakening from his touch and the delicious insinuations whispered into her ear of the things he intended to do with her.

"You're delaying this entire production, Mack." She laughed as she turned off the sink water and reached for the dish towel he perched on his shoulder.

"Can you imagine? You and I have been doing this dance for generations? People talk about soulmates, twin flames; but us, we're the real thing. 'Looking glass light bearers,' I'm not even sure what it means but I like the way it sounds," he whispered. He backed her up against the counter, his hard body pressed against hers.

"We're going to forget again, right? Not all of it, but we aren't allowed to remember?" she asked sadly.

He ran his fingers through her hair, "Pretty much—he warned me that would happen. Encouraged us to not hold on to everything we saw, it's too dangerous. We can only live a life with the memories we make here, walk one path at a time or it causes a rift in the time/space continuum. Other souls are involved, they need to enter into our lives without preconceived judgment. Tonight, you and I remember. We have always belonged to each other—it explains so much, doesn't it? Finally, the hollowness inside me is gone," he whispered, kissing her face sweetly.

"Mack, I saw it—it flashed by me in snapshots. I know what you mean—there was always an emptiness I couldn't explain in me, it's not there anymore." She snuggled into his embrace.

"My God, you're radiant," he said to her with awe, touching her face gently. Her face, her eyes, her smile, all glowed and she appeared years younger. He was amazed by her transformation. Aurora's beauty had never been hidden from him, but now she was more stunning than ever.

"You did this to me, beautiful man. You dragged me out of darkness, isolation, and despair. I don't know how to thank you," she said softly.

"If I could make a suggestion?" He chuckled, running his hands over her back.

"Mack, what was your spark of recognition? You never told me; did you figure it out?" she asked, excited. He laughed and rubbed his nose with hers, a sweet Eskimo kiss. "Mimosa...from the second I was in your airspace. Immediately, I responded to you and your scent."

She ran her hands over his muscled back, staring into his stormy gray eyes. "You really are a wolf, aren't you?" she joked. "Okay, back to work—the sooner we finish here, the quicker we can go back upstairs."

"How about this? We finish what we've started on the sofa in front of the fireplace, and then we can clean up the kitchen?" he offered, sliding his hands under her sweater to caress her breasts.

She was melting; he was so strong and sexy she couldn't resist him anymore. But the thought of everyone else sleeping in quarters on the same floor helped to rein in her desire.

"They are all in bedrooms right behind the kitchen. Don't you want to do this in a place I can moan your name loudly?" she countered, letting her hands wander over his rugged body.

Motivated by her argument, Mack helped her to get the kitchen back in order, quickly. Soon, he followed her into her bedroom. Closing the door behind him, he took her into his arms. "I'm not dreaming, you will sleep with me tonight?" he asked cautiously. She kissed him, dissolving into his embrace.

"You slept for twenty-four hours, my hero. You won't get much rest tonight. But when you do, it will be beside me." She smiled and backed away from him. She shooed the dogs off the bed, and they found spots on the small love seat in the room.

She directed Mack to have a seat on the edge of the bed. She removed his hoodie and began to take off her clothes, much to his mouthwatering appreciation.

"About all those 'propositions' you muttered to me while I was washing dishes, time to make good on your promises." She smiled as she approached him.

Completely bare, she straddled his lap and anchored herself against his pants where his straining hard-on was trying to be let free. He pulled her closer, his hands fluidly moving down to cradle her ass as he buried his face between her breasts. "Dear God, how much I love you," he murmured. She kissed him softly, lingering her lips on his. "I will not live without you, ever again," she whispered between kisses.

Running her fingers into his hair, placing sweet pecks on his face, his neck, his mouth, she said, "Listen to me carefully. I have something that belongs to you, and these are my demands." Her sexy voice was at full power. "You want me filthy and unbridled? Buckle up," she taunted, tilting her head to run her tongue along his jaw line.

"Touch me—let me feel your strong, beautiful hands all over my body. Taste me—chase your caresses with your clever tongue everywhere, do not neglect an inch. Do you want to claim me as your own, have me crave only you going forward? Lose yourself deep inside me—slow, fast, hard, gentle, rough, however you'd prefer to drive. I recall mention of a winch and hoist being required to pull you out. Mark your territory, anywhere I can cover with clothes. Tonight, would you bring me back to life, and be so kind as to fuck me so effectively I can't remember my own name?" she whispered, her tongue tracing his ear.

Mack's jaw dropped with shock. Aurora was right, a jungle cat had been awakened from its long hibernation. He ran his fingers through her hair and made a fist. He brought her face close and paused before kissing her.

"You may not remember your name, kitten, but you'll never forget mine," he murmured. His kiss was greedy and hot. His tongue circled hers and they moaned in unison with yearning into each other's mouths.

He lay her back onto the bed, stood up, and quickly shed the rest of his clothes. His eyes raked over her staggering curves. She was moving her hands over her breasts, her nipples dark and hard, waiting for his attention. Her long, shapely legs were splayed out before her. She eyed him with expectation, he was the handsomest man she had ever seen. How did he manage to avoid being a cover model?

As she requested, he touched, kissed, and tasted every inch of her body, with certain veneration. His powerful hands traveled over her, as his mind had fantasized for weeks. He held her breasts one after another to his tender mouth. He traced her hard nipples with his tongue and teeth. He peppered kisses under her breasts and down the front of her body.

The feel of his whiskers against her skin and sensitive nipples made her squirm and squeal until she couldn't take it anymore. His head was buried between her thighs, his mouth affixed around her flushed sex, every surface of his tongue danced inside of her. Firing off one orgasm after another, she swore at one point that she lost feeling in her toes. She cried out his name, low and lustful as her body quaked and trembling under his mouth and hands. He knew without direction how to please her.

He climbed up into her arms and kissed her, "Taste yourself Aurora, you're delicious, like honey wine," he said, kissing her slowly. "You taste like *mine*."

She licked her essence from his upper lip and mustache and reflected his content visage. Quivering beneath him, she whispered back, "You're *very* good at that."

He snorted proudly, "Highly decorated Navy diver, ma'am. I can hold my breath under water longer than a killer whale, and you go down much sweeter than the Pacific Ocean," he crooned reverently. "I'm never getting out of a bed you're in," he assured, sliding two fingers inside of her and using his thumb to caress circles onto her clit.

"Mack," she hissed from the new sensation, "Stop stalling, I want to feel you inside me," she begged. He continued the gentle stroking, causing her to shudder and seize again.

Biting down on her earlobe he teased her, "Baby, I'm taking my sweet, fucking time. I promised I'd drain every drop from you, and I keep my promises." He sucked his breath through his teeth, "Mmmm…so wet, my sexy kitten, see what I can do to you? Do it baby, come again for me," he urged, curling his fingers inside her. He locked onto the spot, the one that dissolved any restraint to which she was clinging.

Arching her back, she cried out with the multiple spasms moving through her. "Mack, oh my God!" He cooed with delight, feeling her orgasm wash over his fingers. "Good girl, now I'll fuck you," he murmured, licking her off his digits and kissing her roughly, biting her lips and tongue.

His words, his actions, everything was turning her on so intensely that her body was an inferno; she was breathless, spent, and flushed. He took her legs and wrapped them around his waist. Sliding his cock inside an inch at a time, he held her close to him as he gradually moved in and out. Her fragrance filled his head, the feel of her soft skin against his, as he ached to consume her. She gasped when she felt him fill her up; he was so big and reached places she never knew she harbored.

He gently moved her hair out of her eyes and smiled down at her, crooning between soft, warm kisses. "Is this what you wanted, my love? I've been looking forward to this, claiming you slowly and deliberately." His rumbling carnal growls increased with his inching, upshifting rhythm. He felt her internal muscles squeeze around him. At the same moment she whispered in his ear, her voice heavy with desire, "Yes… it's all I want… this belongs to you now, take it."

Mack felt his entire body combust with her statement. The room and the world fell away from his peripheral vision; all he could see was her and the rest of his days interwoven with a profound love and the most soul-altering physical intimacy he had ever experienced.

"Who does this belong to?" he asked smug and swaggering, purposefully driving hard inside her.

"You… oh God… Mack, only you." Her breaths gusted rough in his ear, as he filled her over and over again. His frame was so strong and bespoke to hers, he was genuinely carved to adorn her. She ran her hands down his back and over the tensed muscles of his ass, as he pushed faster and harder in building acceleration. Aurora was delirious with pleasure; he flooded the void of her misery and desolation. He evaporated the walls of frost she had been living within with firestorms of desire.

"Aurora, fuck, you're so tight, who made you for me?" His jaw locked and teeth clenched as he felt every inch of her milk him from inside. He dropped his knees onto the bed and took her by the waist to grind into her and steer her body. Placing one hand above her pelvis and the floor of her abdomen he pressed softly. The penetration changed trajectory and with the pressure on her lower body, Aurora shrieked with surprise.

"Jesus, Mack!" she gushed unrestrained, finding his mouth, and kissing him as if she suddenly was released from heavy chains. She ran her fingers through his hair, urged him to move quicker; her escalating, deep, internal ache pleading to be released. "More, give me more, don't you dare stop," she beseeched him.

"Sounds like my jungle cat is awake and hungry?" he whispered with pride. "Don't you worry baby, I'm gonna keep feeding you... fuck, you feel so good..." His voice was deep and brusque.

The friction she made against him, her cries of enjoyment, and writhing underneath, gathered his racing orgasm like a summer storm. He lowered her on to her back and clutched her hips, spreading her open, thrusting himself deep inside again and again.

"*Ek is verlief op jou. Jy is nou my hele wêreld,*" he whispered solemnly in his native tongue of Afrikaans. Though she didn't know the translation, she felt his sentiment.

She wrapped her legs around his waist, tighter, rising to meet him, matching his tempo. He couldn't hold back any longer, she was driving him out of his mind.
"Aurora, I'm gonna come like it's my very first time doing this," he grunted, kissing her madly again. "Baby, come with me..." His breath was short, and perspiration beaded along his forehead and chest.

"I am... I will... please don't stop..." she implored, running her tongue up his neck, catching a bead of his sweat. Chills raced down his spine with the feel of her mouth. He raised her feet onto his shoulders, bracing one hand against the headrest. He reached out to hold her hand with his free one and plunged into her until he shattered— releasing inside her with searing pulses of lava. She met him there with her own teeming cascade of pent-up ecstasy. She cried out his name with her shuddering ending. He moaned her name with each throbbing beat of his finish.

They crashed onto their backs, breathless, damp, and depleted.

"Aurora… holy fuck! It has never been like this for me," he declared, his mind blown. He'd lost count of the women over the years he had randomly hooked up with—none of them had ever brought him where she did. Empty, wasted nights with nameless, faceless encounters, thankfully steered his path to this woman's arms and the rapture within.

Aurora was struggling with the words, "Mack, it was… holy fuck is right, it might have been supernatural. It's never been like this for me either. I lost count and I think my consciousness a few times," she snickered. She nestled under his muscled arm, her head resting over his heart.

"I'm madly in love with you Aurora," he whispered, his lips on her forehead. "Will you marry me?" Her heart caught in her throat. She couldn't answer him.

He took her silence elegantly. It was too soon but he was incapable of holding back the question. She flayed him wide open. He lifted her face to kiss her and smiled down into her doe-eyed expression. "No rush, baby, I'll ask you again tomorrow." He laughed and kissed the tip of her nose and forehead.

It took them a few minutes to catch their breath. Aurora's heart took longer to decelerate.

It was a new experience for her, having sex since her heart surgery. She never thought she'd need to consider this variable again in her lifetime. A groundswell of guilt and sadness washed over her and then swiftly withdrew. They lay entangled, listening to each other's breath return to normal. Wordlessly, they touched and kissed in relaxed devotion. Mack circled his fingers around her wrist, checking her pulse. Aurora smiled in the dimly lit room. He was worried about her arrythmia.

"You make it race, Mack, but it's a normal rhythm." He raised her hand to his lips. "Good," he said with relief.

"What did you whisper in Afrikaans?" Her voice was raspy and sexy. He smiled, "I hardly ever use it aloud anymore. I said, 'I'm in love with you— you're my whole world now.'"

"It sounded so beautiful, like a prayer," she whispered, humbled.

"It was, it has been. Those words have echoed in my head since I met you. God must have heard them," She kissed him again. She was perplexed by the realization that she had completely missed his growing affection for her all this time.

Mack, not one to have ever indulged in pillow talk, was incredibly vulnerable yet secure with Aurora in his arms. He was habitually already dressed and out the door by this point.

"I've never loved this passionately in my entire life. I had no idea it could even be like this.

I have nothing to compare it to. I'm not sure I'm doing any of it right, Aurora," he admitted, his tone humble.

She laughed low. "Oh Mack, you're doing it right. Granted, it's been a long time since I've done any of this; but trust me, you're doing it exceptionally well."

"I don't mean the sex. We definitely knocked the rust off you. It's the feelings. I've repressed all mine for so long, I didn't think I had them anymore. But you. You've pulled me out of the deep water. I still have my sea legs. I want to get this—us—right. I know your heart is broken, and this all might seem so sudden. Emotionally, I'm lurching around like a newborn colt. I'm way out of my league," he whispered with concern.

"Mack, my whole life has been a whirlwind; nothing happens slowly. You're not out of your league, we're in this together," she assured him. "We were made for each other, literally. I was clueless that something like this was possible, and even if we don't remember after tonight, our bodies can't forget."

He kissed her again, his heart so full he couldn't remember who he was before meeting her.

"I meant what I said tonight, kitten. I will not live another day or sleep another night without you beside me. Of all the things we have been through together, indescribable as they may be, waking up next to you was the most extraordinary of them all. I won't survive without it ever again."

She paused to consider what he was asking. Her heart, though still broken, was overflowing with a passionate love for him. Aurora looked into his gleaming, azure eyes.

"Mack, you're my home now. My life before you was burned to the ground. I could go back to live with my kids for a while, but I'm not the same person I was last year. If it's me you truly want I'd like to stay with you. You died and found a way back to me. For this alone I will deny you nothing. Yes, I'll sleep next to you, unless you find someone you like better." She smiled up at him.

He wrapped her in his arms and kissed her deeply. "Truly want? Aurora, you're all I have *ever* wanted. You'll live with me on Bonita Beach. I'm close enough to Gull Cove for you to decide whether you'd like to go back after it's restored. As for discovering someone I like better, impossible. I've traveled the world, you're one of a kind." He lay on his back again, holding her close to him.

"Mack, how did we get here?" she whispered with awe.

He laughed quietly, "Aurora, it seems we find each other every lifetime. Our lovemaking proves we've done this before. I know your body instinctively; when I touch and kiss you, something internal hums, I can't explain it." She sat up slightly to look at him.

"Mack, it happened the first time you kissed me. I was shocked and scared, but I felt 'it' at the base of my sternum. I didn't know then that it was recognition."

"I'm sorry Mack, that I made you wait so long. I didn't know, really. My grief can be a blindfold; I never wanted any harm to ever come to you." Her voice caught in her throat.

"Shhhh, don't get upset, baby, we don't remember." He brought her back into his arms. "We arrive here with the sealed orders, and we have free will. If we can find each other—it's only then that the mission commences. You can't control it, none of us can."

He kissed her soft and slow, never happier in his life than at this moment. "There is still so much I don't know about you. Tell me what it is you desire, Aurora?"

"This," she answered softly. "You. I was sure it would never be possible for me again. Who would want me?" Tears started to well in her eyes. "You're this man for me—your strength, your devotion, these things are my armor. Mack, you saved me. My life, my heart, and brought me back from darkness."

She kissed him back, captivated by the perfection of his soft mouth conjoined with hers. She bit his bottom lip playfully and he sighed with joy. He shifted in the bed to hold her face and gaze deep into her eyes, "Aurora, I know I will never be your first love, but I'd be honored if you let me be your last."

She sat up quickly to look at him, his

handsome face so sweet and adoring. "How?" she asked, "How did you know?"

"Know what, kitten?" He attempted to be blasé.

She was riveted by the irony. *How in the world?* No one alive ever heard her utter those words. She looked at him closely, surprised. It came to her quickly. She knew it could be the only explanation. "You saw him, didn't you?" she whispered, her heart skipping beats. "You didn't tell us everything tonight at dinner. You saw him?" she asked hoarsely. She held the bedsheet around her naked body.

Mack grinned, knowing he could never keep the secret from her. "I did. How did you guess?" he asked, intrigued.

"You amazing miracle of a man. Once upon a time, I asked Ben precisely the same thing. I asked him to honor me by being his last love." She looked at him with anticipation.

"It was brief, kitten, you were close to death. He was there to take you with him but knew it wasn't your time. Nor was it mine." He ran his hand down her back.

Tears rushed to Aurora's eyes. "My God, he was there?" she cried. Her tears of joy and sadness mixed together.

"Yes, he was, and he will be there when it's your time to leave me. Until then, I gave him my word that I'd guard your precious heart." She fell back into his arms, humbled by everything this man had endured for her.

"What else do you know now that you didn't before this encounter?" she asked.

Mack sighed. "Something I never thought about—that the devil hears our prayers too."

Aurora locked eyes with him and nodded her head in grave understanding. They didn't need to speak, the road before them would reveal the trials they'd battle together, shoulder to shoulder, as they had since the dawn of time.

Rejoined and consummated, their divided souls fused back into one. It seemed like an audible click of a lock passed between them. The hidden knowledge and images diminished, settling far into the recesses of their memory, leaving in the forefront only those recollections needed for the purposes of this lifetime.

"Mack? Please say it again to me, your prayer," she asked quietly.

"*Ek is verlief op jou. Jy is nou my hele wêreld.* I'm in love with you—you're my whole world now," he whispered happily, spooning up behind her as he closed his eyes.

Chapter Thirty

"**S**pecial Friend?" She offered, and they both made expressions of distaste. Aurora and Mack were driving back together with the dogs to Autumn Lake. The night before he surprised her with the news that he was her neighbor. Knowing she had nowhere to live presently, she agreed to stay with him, until she could sort out her home in Gull Cove.

Currently, they were trying on titles for Mack. Aurora was meeting the family at her fire-damaged house, and she was expected to introduce him to her grandchildren. She wasn't sure if they were ready for this. Any of them.

"Handyman," he offered. "Or Shower Toy. I've got it, how about Special Angel?" he laughed at his own joke.

"You're not helping the matter," she sighed, a slight grin escaping from her lips.

"Relax. I'm sure when they have a gander at you and you're not plodding about regularly like Eeyore the sad donkey, the lightbulbs will switch on. You do know you can't hide it, right? Your whole being smolders and glows now. Brilliantly shagged looks great on you." He smiled proudly. He slid his hand onto her thigh and held it there while he drove, flushing Aurora with arousal.

"Modest much?" She shook her head. "You, too, seem less angry resting recon face, Sailor," she declared, also gratified.

"Kitten, I'm quite wildly in love. I'm sure I have a billboard plastered across my forehead announcing it. If I don't, I'll be stopping at Staples this afternoon to have one made," he replied.

Aurora laughed again and leaned over the console to kiss his cheek. "Order one to cover your splendid ass as well, with the word 'Taken' in big block letters," she teased.

She sat back in her seat and returned to brainstorming nicknames. "What do you want me to call you?" she asked. "Can we give it a name?"

"You can call me whatever you like, as long as you call me to your bed." He smiled.

"Well, 'humble' is obviously out as an option. Okay, it's going to have to be 'boyfriend.' No, ugh, I hate the way it sounds. Are you sure you're ready for this? The Delsea vortex of loud, crazy, and one million questions?" She ran her fingers through her shortened waves of hair. Panic started to wash over her.

"I want you, and everything that comes with you. I told you yesterday, I'm a bad motherfucker, nothing scares me. In the past three days, I have faced death and the devil. The grilling from five children will not be the thing to suddenly spook me." He squeezed her thigh gently.

"What would you like to call me? You'll have the opportunity to introduce me at some point," she asked.

"My beautiful wife," he answered quickly. He glanced over at her for a reaction.

"Well okay, that's very ambitious." She laughed nervously, not returning his glance.

"Until then I'm sticking with love of my fucking life," he assured her. Mack wouldn't push her, but he also wouldn't rest until she agreed to marry him.

"Oh, these kids are going to eat you alive," she dropped her chin to her chest knowingly.

"Completely fine with me, as long as I get to reciprocate the specific encounter on their delicious grandmother," he whispered hungrily, licking his lips.

She snickered, shifting in her seat.

"What's wrong? Did my suggestion cause a tasty reaction?" he asked cleverly.

She didn't have a chance to worry the issue another second as they pulled into the drive at Gull Cove, and the entire brood rushed the truck with happy screeches of "YiaYia!" The dogs were instantly awake and anxious to run out to be with them.

Sam and Robbie approached behind their children to welcome her home.

Mack came around to open her door when Sam directed the kids, "Say hello to Mr. Egan, he's the man who saved Yia Yia's life."

Sam and Robert were given an abridged version of the events in New York. Dutch and his team kept the paranormal aspects of the mission top secret though. The boys knew Mack and Aurora were injured, but as far as her sons were aware, nothing substantial. Dutch did credit Mack for saving Aurora's life.

Sam held out his hand to shake Mack's. "We don't know how to thank you," he said in a low voice. Robert came up from behind his brother to reintroduce himself to Mack. They briefly met the day the tour bus had boarded. The children were gathered wildly around Aurora for hugs and kisses, not yet paying attention to the man who brought her home. Tim and Sydney were yapping around their feet, begging for their own attention.

"Sam, Robert, good to see you both again," he shook their hands warmly.

"Is there anything we can do to thank you?" Robert asked genuinely.

"Well," Mack began, "since you've asked, I was hoping you would both give me your blessing to date your stepmother. If you are ready for that."

The men exchanged glances and smiled. "You saved her life, aren't you stuck with her now?" Sam asked jokingly. "Of course, we're ready— if she is."

"You may change your mind after this throng is done with you," Robbie added, indicating the huddle of children and dogs around his stepmother.

Aurora finally made her way from the crush of grandkids to her sons. She blushed with a bit of shame and wasn't sure how to face them. Sam saw the change in her quickly. Sadness shadowed her eyes, but the rest of her walked tall with confidence and grace. Her dark hair was shorter, and she looked much younger to him than the day she left. No hunched shoulders or thick layers of clothes. Something else happened in New York, or thereabouts, and he hoped it wasn't just an enemy takedown.

"Nice haircut, not a bad job for a switchblade," Sammy teased, as he hugged her close. "You, okay?" he whispered in her ear.

"I am," she replied, kissing his bearded cheek. She touched his sides gently. "How are you healing?" she asked, concerned.

"You know me Rore, I never had a bad day someone couldn't make worse. I'm good, I go back to full duty in a week." He confirmed the end of his sabbatical to her.

Robert grabbed her in a bear hug, "Jesus, Aurora, you had us scared to death. You look different," he smiled innocently. She blushed again and kissed his cheek.

She lined them up in age order. "Okay, everybody, straight line. Mack, I would like to officially introduce you to the loves of my life— The Titans of Chaos. From oldest to youngest: Benjamin, thirteen; Madeline, eleven; Liam, eight; Misha, Sam's bonus daughter, six; and this is Ryder, four, the youngest and Robert's little girl."

"Kids, this is Mack Egan," she said, leaving out any bio or titles. She knew her grandchildren would come up with their own questions as well as their own conclusions.

Mack went down the line to formally shake each of the children's hands. He towered over them, and they were assessing him very closely. Except for Ryder, who held her arms out to be picked up. Mack hoisted her up and onto his shoulders to her complete delight.

"YiaYia, I can see the ocean from up here!" she sang with glee, clapping her hands.

Something powerful shifted inside Aurora, to see her youngest granddaughter seated on Mack's shoulders, her small hands wrapped in his waves of auburn hair. He was tremendous. It was also only the second time she witnessed him dressed in something other than operative attire. In worn jeans, a white thermal, long-sleeved shirt, his red and black flannel jacket, and broken-in Timberland boots on his feet.

Mack was the embodiment of a lumberjack in those calendars. Sexy and strong. She was falling for him and though she had sworn she *never* would again, she wasn't entirely sure she hated the idea.

The older children began their blitzkrieg of questions for Mack as they prepared to launch into their session. The inquiries fired like a pinball shot into play.

"Are you Yia Yia's boyfriend? Are you dating her? Did you kiss her? Are you going to live with her now? Are you Kris Kringle? You look like him. Where are you from? Your accent is on fleek. What are we supposed to call you? Are you going to marry her?"

Sam and Robbie burst into laughter and raised their hands in surrender. Aurora covered her face with her hands, blushing wildly.

"Welcome, Mack," laughed Sammy. "Have you met our squad of detectives?"

Mack laughed with them, relaxed and still with Ryder saddled on his shoulders, "I was waterboarded for days in Iraq, this crowd might be tougher."

Mack squatted to face them, as they were braced in a protective stance between him and their beloved grandmother.

"Yes, I'm her boyfriend. Yes, I'm dating her. Yes, I've kissed her. She is coming to live with me while we fix this house, after that she can live wherever she wants, and I will go with her. You will all visit my house as well. YiaYia is so happy the tour ended early and would like to celebrate Thanksgiving down here. I'm not Kris Kringle, but I know him very well and can reach him on the phone at any time. Me and my 'on fleek' accent are from South Africa. You can all call me Mack, and I don't think YiaYia is ever getting married again, but I will never stop asking her, was that everything?" he asked gently. The kids exchanged looks as if ready to reload.

The oldest, Benjamin, took his responsibilities seriously. He silenced his siblings and stepped forward to approach Mack, "Do you love her?" he asked curiously.

Mack stood again and faced him. "She is the

great love of my life," he replied tenderly. His eyes lifted over the teenager's head to gaze adoringly at Aurora.

Benjie nodded his head with approval and shook the older man's hand. "Never, ever hurt her," he warned. Sam and Robert watched the interaction with bittersweet appreciation. They knew he was a good man and a nice match for their stepmother. Their father had looked at her the same way when he was alive, and they were grateful for the years of happiness she had given him.

They stepped in to shoo the kids away, ordering them to take the dogs down to the beach while they inspected the damage to the house with her. Robert relieved Mack of his horseback duty and grabbed Ryder into his arms.

It was physically painful for Aurora, navigating through the remnants of her dream house. Mack walked around alone to assess the destruction. She managed to reach the kitchen and saw one piece of the Italian tile from the backsplash unharmed and left on the ruins of her countertop. She took it and put it in her handbag.

"One piece," she sighed, shaking her head. All the furniture was destroyed; she almost threw up when she saw Ben's recliner in charred pieces. Sam and Robbie were upset as well with the devastation—it was some of their father's greatest woodworking. Aurora and her sons were discussing what, if anything, could be salvaged.

"Aurora?" Mack called from the back of the

house. She went out to see what he was looking at.

Sam and Robbie casually followed her. Mack stood next to a pile of wooden debris stacked against the back of the house. It might have previously been her small garden shed.

Positioned at the top of the pile sat a long piece of a scorched two by four. At its center, secured by a shining switchblade was her missing ponytail.

The men froze to their spots.

"Is it mine?" she asked Mack. He was busy dialing Trident but lifted the corner of the wood to bring his nose near the ponytail. It smelled like the beach, no trace of her perfume.

Her sons were instantly agitated. "How could this be? Isn't he dead? Wouldn't they have secured it as evidence from the restaurant?"

Aurora faced them, "You two sound exactly like your kids right now. Yes, he is dead, I watched his head separate from his body. Dutch will be here shortly."

Mack held the wood close for her to examine the knife and she could see the blade was not Damascus steel. Someone without enough information was having fun at her expense.

She touched her sons on their shoulders. "I've spent the better part of my life searching for monsters in the dark. You couldn't fathom what I've seen in the last few days. Please trust me. Whatever this is, it's a new game, not the old one. This knife, it's not from his collection. He was strictly Damascus steel. This is a pawnshop switchblade."

Sam was startled by her quick evaluation of the situation. *Who was she really?* He had never witnessed her in this mode, making a cool assessment like she did in under five minutes. It made some sense, if she had been studying her mark for twenty years, she knew enough about him.

"He cut you didn't he, Aurora, not just your hair?" Sam whispered.

She nodded with affirmation. "It's not bad, Sam, they're already healing. Mack and Quincy got there in plenty of time," she assured him. He hugged her again. He was sorry he wasn't there to protect her.

"I'm okay sweetheart, really I am," she said. "Don't make the kids see you like this, they are convinced you don't like me, and I don't want to dash their hopes and dreams," she laughed. Sam laughed with her and affectionately tousled her shortened hair.

Robbie sighed and said "This is going to take some time to get used to, Aurora. Life was simpler when you were a cookie-baking, storytelling grandma."

Sammy was still trying to assimilate to this version of Aurora, "Rory, you are home now, don't forget the resources we can provide. We know how to find and fight monsters ourselves. We want to be a part of it."

"Thank you, Sam," she said happily. "The hardest part is over; these are the aftershocks, but

I accept your applications to the team."

Sam and Robbie waited for the insurance adjusters to leave before loading their kids in the cars to head back to their homes. The boys stood outside with her, saying their goodbyes.

"You're going to be okay alone?" Sam asked. "Oh right, you have a permanent bodyguard now," he taunted.

"I'll be fine. The dumpsters come this week, so I'll have plenty of work to do crying over my ruined things," Robert went to hug her goodbye and while she had them both alone, she asked. "Are you guys okay with Mack helping Dutch to restore it?"

"Aurora, it's your house. Whatever keeps a smile on your face works for us," Robbie replied sweetly.

Sammy interjected in a low voice, "He's done a great job putting you back together so far, Aurora; time will tell if he knows how to swing a legit hammer." The three of them broke up laughing and Aurora blushed, shaking her head. Sam and Robbie took her into their arms at the same time and hugged her affectionately.

Sam started his car, still smirking at her. "Let us know what you want us to bring for Thanksgiving," he said from his open window. The kids yelled over him, "Bye, we love you, YiaYia!" from their windows. Aurora blew them kisses and waved.

Minutes later, Dutch pulled into the driveway

in his vintage pickup truck.

"What the hell, Tink? Can I get a minute?" he said, his voice changing when he caught a glimpse of the house.

Cat jumped out of the passenger seat to survey the area.

"So, are you two a legit thing right now?" Aurora asked, sounding like her son and even her eleven-year-old granddaughter on Snapchat. Cat laughed and her brother snickered.

"By the way," Dutch responded. "You need a new assistant. Cat's coming to work for Trident."

"Oh, thanks Dutch, could I at least have gotten two weeks' notice?" she asked, grabbing her friend, and hugging her dearly.

"Mother of God," Dutch mumbled. "This is a shit show." He looked over the annihilation of her beautiful home. "Thank God Ben didn't live to see this," he said shaking his head sadly.

Mack came out carrying both dogs. "I didn't want them walking through the broken glass," he said, loading them both into his truck. Aurora smiled at him in gratitude. He winked at her as he led her brother to the back of the house. Dutch snapped on a pair of gloves and opened a large evidence bag. "Did you find anything else?" he asked Mack, following him out to the debris pile. "Tink, before I leave, I need your hairbrush to send to the lab with this," Dutch mentioned as he made his way to the back of the house.

Cat and Aurora went inside to see if there were

any salvageable clothes that Aurora could bring with her to Mack's. Cat could not hold her tears as she gently sifted through the burned remains of most of Aurora's bedroom.

"How'd it go with the kids?" Cat asked carefully, composing herself again.

Aurora laughed, "A million questions, but his accent is 'on fleek' according to them."

"Where do these kids come up with these sayings?" Cat laughed. "So, Mack made it through the Delsea inspection?"

Aurora nodded her head happily, "Like a champion." She was searching for something on the shelves of her destroyed closet.

"Cat, I'm not crazy right? This isn't all too fast and intense? He isn't a rebound?" she asked abruptly.

"Rory, the first day on the bus I could see it. He was madly in love with you and was from then on. Where is the rule book on being a widow? No one has ever written it. With everything you have been through, why would you question the timing of happiness? And don't let other people pass judgment on you, fuck them and their perceived timelines. People like to keep widows in their place. Guess they're afraid we'll go after their husbands," Cat snorted.

Aurora laughed, "If I didn't want their husband while mine was alive, what would make theirs more interesting to me now?" she asked.

"Because women suck, for the most part. With

the exception of losing a child, losing a spouse has a colossal impact. No one understands it unless they have suffered it themselves. Take your joy back with both of your hands, you know how priceless it is," she ordered.

Aurora nodded quietly, sifting through the rest of the clothes in her way. Nothing looked wearable.

"Rory, don't you see Ben's hand in all of this?" Cat continued.

Aurora looked carefully at her friend, "Do you think?"

"Ben used to tell everyone his first wife sent you to him, so why wouldn't Ben do the same?" Cat countered. "Rory, you know Ben's sense of humor, right? Who was hovering around him on her broom when you met him? The one you teased him about constantly? You called her 'The Competition.'"

Aurora started to shriek with laughter, "Oh my God, Cat!!! That bastard! He *would* send me a redhead." They were stifling their giggles in the closet.

"Well, he sent a genuine ginger to you, not like 'The Cherry Bomb,' with her fake-ass dye job and everything else," Cat grunted. "Ben did good; Mack is so handsome it hurts, and only has eyes for you." Cat wrapped her arms around her friend.

Aurora hugged her close. "Thank you, my sister. I worship you."

"I don't think anything made it," Cat said

sadly returning to rummaging through the mess formerly known as Aurora's closet. "Good news, shopping trip!" she attempted. The small, fireproof box on the bottom shelf was intact. Cat handed it to her with a quizzical look. "Cash or Ben?" she asked gently.

"Ben, thank God," Aurora whispered. It contained her husband's last bit of remains, the ones to be scattered with her own one day. Her boys had personal urns in their homes with the combination of their parents.

Aurora had to leave the bedroom, seeing her bed in cinders drove home the certitude that not one location remained where she had slept beside Ben. She was overcome with tears. All of his clothes were burned, nothing in the house smelled like him anymore. Aurora struggled to fight back the terrible anguish reaching for her again.

She moved on to her office, holding the box of Ben's ashes close to her. Her desktop computer was torched, but luckily everything was on the cloud. She searched through bookshelves and the closet, but everything was burned or damaged by water.

All her first edition books that Ben had collected for her over the years. The classic art prints she put together from their travels. The entire shelf of her Murano glass collection, shattered. She was devastated over and over again.

Her wedding album was destroyed, but fortunately, most of her photos were stored on hard drives and uploaded. Mack walked in behind her as she was lost in her thoughts.

"Kitten how are you faring?" he asked gently, enveloping her in his strong arms. She surrendered to his embrace, her mind exhausted by all that she had to absorb. Everything she owned was destroyed. It was soul crushing.

"This is bloody awful," she whispered in agony.

"I will spend our life replacing whatever I can, Aurora. I promise you," he whispered solemnly.

She sighed heavily, "Mack, it's just things. They can't torch my memories, and together we will spend our lives collecting new ones. This I promise you," she said with determination.

Mack saw her death grip on the small, fireproof box, "Is this coming with us?" he asked.

She nodded her head, tears filling her eyes. He guessed instantly.

"Of course. I understand," he said, gently. "I would say very nice to meet you, but I actually did not long ago," he whispered. She smiled into his solid chest.

He lifted her chin to kiss her. "Let me get you home. We can have something to eat, lay by the fireplace. Three straight days, my beautiful girl. Not one minute less. Agreed?'

"Agreed," she sighed.

Aurora was astounded by the simple beauty and comfort of Mack's ranch-style house. The vista from his floor-to-ceiling windows was breathtaking; viewing the ocean jetty from three sides could captivate her for hours. Furnished with large, plush sofas and chairs and a matching farmhouse-style throw rug, the slate, pewter, and warm blues wove serenity throughout the first floor. Natural light flooded the space as the sheer and darkening curtains pulled back to the walls.

She toured the house slowly, soaking in the quiet and soft, rustic touches. The stone fireplace in his sunken living room was enormous, it took up half the wall. There was a modern, open concept kitchen, along with the living room and a cozy seating area to watch TV.

Tim and Sydney were doing recon as well, running from room to room, exploring.

While he was away, Mack's part-time housekeeper was sent to clean and stock the house, the kitchen, change out all the bedding, and empty half the walk-in closet and its drawers for Aurora. He even thought of Tim & Sydney, with dog bowls and unopened bags of the correct brand of food available on the kitchen counter. Mack had invested time and money on the slight chance he could convince her to stay there, down to new pillows when he had only ever owned two in his life.

Mack arranged the largest of the spare bedrooms to be painted in a soft lilac and furnished it as an office for Aurora. Its focal point was a vast view of the private Bonita Beach from the windows, a new cherrywood desk, matching office furniture, and a brand-new desktop computer. Two dozen, long stemmed amnesia roses were arranged in a vase atop her desk, with an unopened bag of Reese's Pieces propped up against it. Aurora entered the room and watched Mack complete the setup of her new computer. She opened the closet in the office and placed the small, fireproof box on the top shelf.

"How did you know about the roses? Mack, they are so beautiful, thank you. When did you do all of this?" she asked in disbelief. Her laptop and briefcase were resting on the desk beside the vase of gorgeous flowers and chocolate.

He smiled leisurely at her, "Kitten, when you spend your life as a committed bachelor, you plan for the possibility that the universe might send you the woman of your dreams. I deployed a great deal of help and put it all into motion after I met you. It was a gut reaction. Cat told me about the roses. Especially when 'college heartbreak' couldn't get it right. My next-door neighbor, 'Coast Guard' Joe grows different varieties, and your favorite is one of them. The rest I guessed," he said humbly.

He handed her a book he'd hidden behind the vase. She touched it, awestruck. A first edition of Jane Austen's *Pride & Prejudice*.

"Oh Mack!" she gasped. "When? How?"

"I ordered it weeks ago, after the night in Boston. I was sure you already had one, I never could have known your collection would be destroyed. I wanted you to have this one, from me. I promise I will replace the others you've lost." He gazed up at her, knowing she was touched deeply.

"Oh, one more thing." He crooked his finger, summoning her closer. He took her left hand and wrapped a blue cord bracelet around it, the clasp a sterling silver baby sea turtle.

"Mack! When did you get this?" she gushed with joy, standing still as he attached it to her wrist.

"Again, weeks ago. I ordered it after our first night on the bus. When you admired mine and told me how much you vibe with them. I had forgotten about it till today. Wait, you haven't seen the best part." He held his bracelet close to hers, and the two turtles magnetically attached to each other. "So, when I'm holding your hand, our bracelets connect." He grinned like a teenager. "It's all you baby, instinct and raw courage, and now you are safe, close to the water."

She leaned down and kissed him, soft and tender. "I adore you," she murmured. "Thank you, for all these beautiful gifts and welcoming me into your home." He pulled her onto his lap, running his hands over her. He brought her face close to his, rubbing her nose with his own.

"Aurora, up until today it was merely a house; you being here makes it a home. It is who you are for me—my home, my rest, my sanctuary. Please stay forever." His voice was tinged with the uncertainty of making the request aloud.

Her life had taken so many drastic turns, in a short time, that she wasn't sure how to steer through another. She stood and looked him over. He was slouched in the new desk chair, long legs splayed out in front of him, staring up at her like a puppy waiting for a reward. She felt butterflies bursting to life inside her. She placed the book on a shelf of one of the empty bookcases.

Aurora walked toward the door. Glancing at her watch, her voice glided over him as if it were her hands sliding up his thighs, "I'm starting the clock, Sailor. Are you ready? Three straight days and nights, hope you took your vitamins." She arched one eyebrow and grinned wickedly, biting down on her lower lip.

His breath caught with her indecent expression and his whole body prickled. Mack couldn't remember a time a woman ever made him feel this way: alive, ardent, virile, and truly seen. Like a panther, he was out of the chair, and she was over his shoulder. She giggled and squealed, "Mack! I was kidding, feed me first!"

He slid her into the center of his brand new, pillow top, king-sized bed, and slowly crawled on top of her. Removing her sweater to kiss her quivering abdomen, undoing her bra to bite at a stiff nipple. He reached her mouth and kissed her tenderly, his lips touching the heart-shaped birthmark under her ear when he whispered, "Here at the castle, the king feasts first before he feeds his queen." His hand slid down inside the front of her pants to caress her wetness and indicate his intended target.

Chapter Thirty-One

Aurora's stomach was growling, they were well into the second half of the second day of their mutually-agreed-upon lovemaking, nap-date, dirty pillow talking marathon. It was half past noon when she tried to slide out from the hold of the slumbering king. He awoke abruptly and murmured, "Five more minutes," he yawned and adjusted his position to look at her. His crooked smile made her tremble inside.

She kissed his drowsy mouth and whispered, "I'm making us lunch because you are sapping my strength, baby." She eyed him up and down with appreciation; he was naked but cleverly draped in their crumpled white sheets. Right now, he was a *GQ* cover—his lengthy, muscled body was stunning and effortless. *Who wakes up looking like this?* she thought to herself. "Dear God, you're a work of art, what are you doing with me?" she uttered, her tone heavy with lingering self-doubt.

He chuckled with modesty and nuzzled her hair. "I'm doing whatever I want with you, my queen and good luck trying to stop me." He took a deep breath of her. "Fuck, you smell so good, like sex and wildflowers. You taste the way you smell, too amazing. Lay here a few more minutes." He wrapped his arms tighter around her. "When you get up the bed is cold, and I'm finished with that life. Just order food—stay with me." He sighed into her neck. Aurora stroked his rugged face, planting soft kisses on his scruffy cheeks.

"Not again Mack, we ate takeout all day yesterday. It's time for me to cook. Let me spoil you, we can have a picnic in front of the fireplace." She bargained. Mack ran his hand down her back and caressed her bare bottom. "I quite enjoyed the picnic this morning," he grunted, smacking his lips with contentment. "You gonna be okay to walk? Legs done trembling?" he asked proudly. Aurora laughed and kissed the tip of his nose.

"I fully recognize you're a gifted, highly skilled deep-water diver. I do think I'm dehydrated though, so could you let a girl get a glass of water and a piece of bread? You're insatiable." She stroked his goatee lightly. His smile was brilliant as he gazed up at her. The slight space between his straight white teeth was so sexy. She was astounded at how beautiful he was for a man. His hair was tousled and wavy, his eyes heavy, and their color was currently deep blue. She was convinced God took extra time and carved him from marble.

"I'm not dreaming, right? You're here, you're mine?" he asked with disbelief. Her heart melted with the adoration in his voice and his sweet questions. They were the same ones running through her own mind.

Aurora leaned down to kiss him. "You're awake, it's me who is dreaming. I can't look at you without my belly doing backflips." He took her face in his hands and kissed her softly. "I'm out of my mind in love with you. He sighed with genuine contentment.

She ran her hand down his six-pack into

the toga wrap of sheets around his waist. "So, I received some intel that your favorite dish is cacio e Pepe from a tucked away restaurant in Rome. I'm making it for lunch, so your highness needs to release me in order for me to prepare it." Mack took her hand and slid it the final inches to rest onto his thick erection. She shook her head in disbelief at his ability to be ready again.

Mack grinned wickedly, "Her highness is my new favorite dish, and Quincy gives secrets up too easily for the smile of a pretty girl." Begrudgingly, he let her out of bed and watched as she slipped clothes on. "You're gonna leave me like this?" he teased, freeing himself from the sheets. His completely naked and aroused body made her gasp slightly as if she were just seeing it for the first time. "I wonder if you didn't originate from a building in Rome," she said with awe.

He ran his hand down over his granite erection, "Get back up in the saddle baby, take a quick ride," he taunted, his voice lazy and deep. He smiled, openly biting his tongue at her. Aurora felt her blood rush in the direction of her panties.

She blushed slightly and laughed, "Let me feed the stallion first before I ride him; for the record, that tongue biting thing almost got you what you want," she teased back as she headed toward the kitchen. He took her pillow and breathed it in. At last, his bed smelled of Aurora, and was still warm from her body. He lay back and stretched, wondering if he was in a dream he couldn't wake from.

It took minutes for the bloom of scents to waft through the house from her cooking. Aurora was in the zone and singing along to the slow country music Mack had playing through the first-floor speakers. She didn't notice him leaning against the doorway arch, admiring her as she cooked, and quietly duetting a Morgan Wallen song.

She wore one of his red bandannas, tying back her shortened tresses, and one of his Navy T-shirts, which covered her exceptional ass. He was hypnotized by her presence in his house, barefoot in his kitchen and completely in his life. He idly toyed with the medal around his neck. "Thank you," he whispered to the saint it venerated.

Aurora bent over to open a cabinet, pink underwear peeking out under the shirt. Mack pounced on her once again. She hit him playfully with a wooden spoon, "Back, you greedy wolf; I'm starving, go light a fire."

"I'm trying to light a fire, I'm hungry too," he growled, palming her ass cheeks in his hands, and pulling her against him. He lifted her face and kissed her with a longing he would never satisfy. All the years of deprivation he had endured; he could forage off her for eternity and never be satiated. Kissing her repeatedly, he knew she'd been worth the lifelong wait.

She smiled up at him, "I really like the way you kiss me."

"I'm relieved to hear it. I fought the urge for so long—you can't stop me now. I'm kissing you every single chance I get. I'm never letting you change your mind," he vowed, touching her lips with his again.

"Go, fire, build," she ordered, slapping his ass playfully with her spoon. Mack did as the queen demanded. Once the fire caught, he rolled out a thick comforter and covered it with the oversized pillows from the sofa and two of the fluffy blankets.

They sat cushioned atop the lunch love nest, across from each other. "Aurora, this is better than the place in Rome. You're incredible." He chewed happily, taking another forkful. "There's something I've wanted to do with you since the first day on the bus."

"We haven't done it yet?" she asked in disbelief. He rolled a forkful of the cacio e pepe and reached out to slip it between her waiting lips.

"You wanted to feed me?" she asked quizzically, after she finished chewing.

"Kitten, your mouth. It's a work of art. The day we had lunch at Havana's when you announced your lack of shame with sharing food, I wanted to hand feed you everything in front of me. I imagined it as a hot scene in a great soft porn movie," he laughed, partially embarrassed for disclosing his early feelings.

"I know that movie," she laughed. "We'll have to save the 9½ *Weeks* theme night for when we have strawberries and whipped cream. The only movie we're going to emulate right now is *Lady and the*

Tramp and I'm game if you are." She twirled pasta on her fork and held it to his mouth, caught a long, errant strand of spaghetti in her mouth and slurped it in until she reached his warm lips.

"I'm very jealous of that spaghetti right now," he said cleverly, finishing his bite.

"Oh, does the king now request that the queen feast upon him—return the favor so to speak?" She laughed, finishing her lunch, and carrying both of their empty plates back into the kitchen.

"Well, I'm sure I've never requested it. I'm not used to getting it, either. As a matter of fact, I can't remember the last time I've had it. But since you brought it up… literally… I'm open to negotiations." She returned to the oversized pillowtop by the fireplace and sat down across from him.

"Ask me," she said in a throaty voice. He looked at her with uncertainty. Her eyes were glowing and filled with mischief.

"Ask me—for it," she clarified.

His face flushed and he squirmed, "No, Aurora, I'd sound like a drunk squid on leave asking for it." She inched closer to him, so that he was pushed against the arm of the sofa with his legs stretched out in front of him. His loose-fitting sweatpants were swelling at their apex.

"Mack," she said again in a low rasp, her finger tracing the rigid silhouette in his lap.

"Ask me for it, convince me in the most erotic terms you can muster, what act you'd like me to perform on you right now?"

He looked at her through a dreamy haze. She was his every imagined fantasy. "You want me to ask you—for it?" He wanted to be very sure. She slid his pants down and off him and starting from his ankle, kissed her way slowly up his left leg.

"Ask me," she demanded. "You only get it if you ask for it."

"Aurora, would you... I can't do it, I'll sound like a rake," he murmured. His body was on fire as he felt her tongue behind his knee.

"Do you want it?" She toyed with him. "Do you want to feel yourself in my mouth? Do you want my tongue to perform wonders you haven't yet dreamed about?" she mocked, kissing the inside of his tensed thigh softly between her questions.

"Oh, kitten, I've dreamed about it." He laughed impishly. "I've dreamed of nothing but it for a good stretch of time." He writhed under mouth, her range to target was close as her kisses climbed the inside of his thigh.

"Mack, surrender and ask me," she purred, her lovely gaze staring from every man's daydreamed focal point.

"Aurora, please..." He covered his eyes with his hand.

"Really? That's all you got?" she teased him. She climbed into his lap, kissing him sweetly. "Bad motherfucker, right? Fierce, strong, scary, Navy SEAL can't ask for this? I'm sure I can report you to the Judge Advocate General on this issue, Sailor." He laughed out loud and tried to kiss her.

She held his face in her hands, her voice smoky like a cabaret lounge singer, "Here is how this is going to happen. I'm going to feast upon you, Your Royal Highness. When I'm finished, you will eagerly hand over your crown, passport, and request a change to your citizenship. Because if you think I enjoy food, you ain't seen nothing yet," she assured, dramatically licking her lips to drive her point home.

He grabbed her hair in his hands and sucked her bottom lip gently into his mouth. "You can't be real. I'm fucking dreaming this and I'm going to wake up tomorrow in a Turkish prison, right?" he asked, mystified.

She slid down between his legs, kissing along the deep vee of his hip to his treasure trail on her way to his magnificent erection.

"Mack is there anything you'd like me to do right now?" she asked, batting her eyelashes up at him.

His voice changed into a husky, breathless growl, "Blow me, you randy little tiger, I want you to suck my dick like it's your job. Don't neglect an inch and do not stop until I forget where I live."

"I serve at the pleasure of the King. At last, the neighbors will learn my name," she laughed into his lap. She wrapped her hand around his splendid cock and owned him quickly. Her tongue soft around the head, alternating between swirling light circles and quick, tight sucks between her lips. She ran her tongue down his shaft, not missing an inch. Slowly, she took him into her warm, wet mouth. She did something with the back of her throat that Mack had only heard rumors about in Thailand. There was no way he was going to be able to hold back to extend his pleasure or give her any at all.

Mack was beguiled watching Aurora's focus as she performed the act of oral gratification. She was sexy, confident, and summoning sounds of bliss and ecstasy from him he had never heard himself make. He hadn't invoked those noises even in his daydreams.

"Bloody hell, Aurora," he snarled with pleasure. "I knew it... I knew you would be... this... fucking good." His jaw clenched as he plummeted into where she was taking him.

She reached for her glass of warm seltzer water on the hearth of the fireplace, lifted her head quickly and took a mouthful, then plunged it over him, forcing the effervescent warmth around his erection. She took his scrotum into her hand and switched her mouth from the head of his cock to take each ball, one after another, between her lips. First, licking and once inside her mouth, hummed, causing a low vibration against the base that radiated to his tip. He moaned with pleasure beneath her control.

"Baby, look up at me, let me watch you—take it, take it all... Ahhhh, so fucking good," he whispered, feverish with the feel of her soft mouth containing him. He ran his hands roughly into her hair. She looked up at him, letting him see her eyes and watch her mouth as she brought him to the threshold of his longest running Aurora fantasy. She slowly covered him completely with her lips again, felt it building inside him, and picked up her pace. Her wet hand was sliding in tandem with her soft mouth and milking him like a sought-after expert in the art. Never breaking eye contact with him.

"There's the money shot," he murmured with worship and his eyes locked with hers. He felt his body tremble with impending release. "Aurora... fuck... I'm almost there—can I...?" he growled. She nodded her head in agreement to his implied request, not disturbing her rhythm.

He grabbed her hair and held her head steady while he plunged deep into her mouth, his orgasm screaming out of him and erupting across the inside of her hot throat. Mack threw his head back and shouted her name with his finish, his voice cracking as it thundered through the room. He saw stars exploding behind his eyes, his body wrung out like a wet towel. She softly kissed his now relaxing manhood.

Aurora stood up, took a bow, and headed to the kitchen to retrieve two cold beers from his fridge. She opened them and returned to the fireplace. She handed him a beer and sat back down on the raised hearth of the fireplace, taking a sip.

"You have effectively ruined me for other women. Please marry me," he begged, spent and breathless.

Aurora started to laugh, "You know why it's funny? My last proposal was presented in those exact words."

Mack laughed with her. "Smart guy, that one." He paused to catch his breath, taking a long sip of the cold beer. She had genuinely blown his mind along with everything else. "I can guarantee you what you did has never been done to me before. Not like that." He sighed, shaking his head. "I'm keeping you, kitten." He stood and put his pants back on before returning to his seat.

She smiled up at him arrogantly, confident she had marked her territory permanently.

Leaning back against the arm of the sofa, he smiled slowly and crooked his finger with his best come hither glance. Aurora laughed and looked around as if he couldn't mean for it to be her. "Me?" she asked with feigned disbelief.

"You. Only you. Forever you. Come here," he whispered, sexy and scorching.

She slid onto his lap, and he laid her back against the soft pillows and started to kiss her. "I'm not anywhere close to started with you, Aurora Delsea. It's only been two days. I still have twenty-four hours of this orientation, and then forever. I mean to make our uninterrupted time count."

"Mack, I really did think that I forgot how to do all this." She laughed happily.

"You seem to have gotten your memory back, and I must say, you're gifted," he professed smugly, biting under her ear. She moaned with delight, "I enjoy turning you on."

"Tell me what you like, my sexy kitten. What

truly turns you on? I enjoy you breathless and begging me for more." He removed the T-shirt and ran his hands over her bare skin, lowering his head to her breasts.

"Pretty much every single thing you have done so far," she snickered. He raised his head and kissed her mouth. "Tell me the truth, I want to be so deep inside of you and not only in the way you think. Tell me who you really are." She stared into his eyes, the light from the fireplace glowed from his indigo gaze. His striking face was framed by his dazzling smile and sleepy eyes that made his lashes longer than should be legal. Aurora touched his cheek softly.

"Who am I? I'm a woman falling in love, over the broken shards of her life. The way you look at me, the things you say, when you reach to hold my hand at the moment you climax. I… it's never felt this way. I don't even know what day it is today, and I couldn't care less. I want to be deep inside of you too—you breathe, I breathe. You're every romance author's fantasy come to life. The guy on the cover. A champion, a smart, sexy, strong, beautiful man who sees me. How can you be real?" She sighed. She touched his bearded chin gently and reached up to bite his lower lip, causing him to groan happily.

Mack responded, "I felt it the first time I saw you. I knew you were different. I'm not built for an average lover; I need a fucking storm. A whirlwind that can rattle my bones, a love so extraordinary even God stills in his heaven to admire it. It's the reason I joined the Navy, the force of the ocean and what she can do to a man. Quiet him, challenge him, and remind him every day that it's she who brings the swells that can lift him up or destroy him. You, Aurora—you're my ocean, my storm, and my calm. No one else has ever moved me like this." He pulled a blanket up to them and tucked them together. She was cuddled beside him, touching him gently.

"Marry me, Aurora, be my wife, take those vows with me before God," he pleaded.

She held him close to her, wrapping her arms around him, lacing her legs between his, kissing his shoulder and neck. "Mack, I need time. Not time for me to have the depth of feelings you have—I'm getting there, it's... I'm still too close to the grief. I need distance from the heartache. Does that make sense?" Tears came quickly to her.

He stared down into her glistening eyes. "I will give you anything within my power. I will ask you every day for the rest of my life. I will ask you every day even after you agree and when you wear my rings and take my name, still I will ask you. You belong to me and I'm yours." He kissed her tenderly, holding her close.

She whispered quietly in his ear, "I'm falling in love with you, and it's scaring the shit out of me."

Mack chuckled softly, "My beautiful warrior goddess, I know nothing scares you, least of all me. Fall in love, fall crazy hard in love with me, you will never cry again. This I swear to you." He snuggled her close to him and closed his eyes.

Chapter Thirty-Two

They were asleep for almost three hours. Aurora was naked from the waist up, the blanket draped over her hips, covering her legs and her breasts molded into Mack's chest. One of her hands were tucked inside the waistband of his gray sweatpants.

A man appeared from the direction of the garage and cleared his throat, waking them both as well as the sleeping dogs. "Is it finally intermission? Brought yourself back a mermaid, 'eh squid?" the older gentleman asked, assessing the two strategically covered bodies entangled together in the glow of the fireplace. Tim and Syd raced to him, barking to check him out.

Mack started to laugh but didn't move to keep Aurora sheltered. She hid her head in the crook of his arm. "Who let you in here you old bastard? Didn't I lock that door?" Mack joked, "Kitten, this is my neighbor, Coastie Joe." He slid the blanket up her back to shield her. "Joe, this is Aurora, the love of my fucking life. Turn around, Puddle Pirate, let the lady sneak away to get decent," Mack joked. Aurora peeked out from Mack's embrace and waved to Joe.

"Ahhhh, amnesia roses—nice to meet you finally, Aurora. I'm going to use the head. Find your clothes," Joe laughed happily as he walked toward their powder room. After dressing, Aurora began to prepare dinner for the three of them as she got to know Coastie Joe.

"I saw the truck on Saturday, but then all the windows were fogged, so I wanted to give you time. But you two were going for some kind of Guinness World Record. Somebody had to give this girl a minute to catch her breath," Joe teased, reaching down to pet the happy dogs. "So, which one is Tim, and which one is Sydney?" he asked the couple. Mack made the distinctions for him as Joe played with the two pups. Joe and Mack caught up on the last two months, giving him a closely held version of the incidents that had transpired.

The room was coming alive with the scents of garlic and rosemary-scented pork chops cooking. Aurora was a ballet dancer in the kitchen, graceful to watch as she juggled the pans and moved between chopping, stirring, and mashing potatoes. Joe measured Mack carefully.

"She's the one, isn't she, Swabby?" he whispered. "Christ, you were right—she's beautiful, though I can't imagine you ever finding an ugly one. It's more than pretty with her, though," Joe said quietly, watching Aurora perform her culinary dance. She was older than Mack, but it barely showed. She shone like a woman in love, even as her eyes still reflected the losses she had endured.

Mack was watching her, her hair retied in his bandanna, wearing one of his hoodie sweatshirts and soft yoga pants. She was radiant and hypnotic to him, as if she walked within a web of spun sugar. He nodded his head happily as he answered Joe. "It's indescribable, but the moment I saw her,

Joe, I saw eternity," he said. Joe nodded his head knowingly.

"Same thing happened to me when I first met Adrienne, that woman hit me like a thunderbolt. Never saw another one after her. Good job, squid, about time you found a partner. And she can cook? Lucky for both of us—I thought we would starve to death," Joe teased.

Aurora handed the men cold beers and started to put out plates and silverware.

"Let me help you, baby," Mack stood up and went around the counter to bring the platters to the table.

"Thank you, Aurora, you didn't have to make dinner for me, too," Joe said with humility.

Aurora knew Joe's story. His beloved wife had recently been diagnosed with dementia and moved to a permanent care facility about an hour away. Joe and Mack took care of each other, and she was personally and painfully aware of the loneliness that came with eating alone. She never wanted anyone within her reach to suffer it.

"It's my pleasure Joe, and it won't be the last time. I love to cook, so since you've already seen my naked back, feel free to come over anytime." She blushed modestly.

"My dear, anyone who can make this old granite face smile the way he is now has my vote. Thank you, Aurora, for bringing joy to Bonita Beach." He held his bottle up to toast her as they began eating.

Living together was not as awkward as they imagined. From cohabitating in such proximity over the past few months they had developed a comfort level with each other's routine and rituals.

Aurora easily made herself at home, washing their combined laundry from the trip and finishing the folding and putting everything away. She smiled to herself as she matched Mack's socks. She stripped the bed and changed out the sheets before joining Mack in the shower.

He set up her ICD monitor next to the bed and handed her the box of her evening heart medicine with a cold bottle of water. She took them quickly and kissed his cheek before heading into the bathroom. He prepared and set a hot cup of chamomile tea on the bedside table for her and placed a long stem rose on her pillow with a box of imported truffles from Spain.

Tim and Sydney were attempting to establish their own spots as they wandered around the bed, spinning in circles, scratching at blankets, and building their own nests. She smiled when she returned to the room and saw the rose and chocolate staged on her pillow. "Mack! Truffles from Andalusia?? How did you find these? When?... I don't deserve you," she sighed.

"I know." He tried to repress his smirk. She laughed at his recall.

"I told you baby, I'm in love with you. I wasn't letting 'Pretty Ricky' use all the intel on you. I want to see you exactly as you are right now, happy. I'd have walked to Spain to buy that chocolate." He beamed as she crawled across the bed to kiss him sweetly.

"I'm keeping you and the truffles," she whispered to him, kissing him softly again.

Mack relaxed back against the pillows, dressed comfortably in soft pajama pants and white T-shirt, reading on his iPad when it began to ring.

"Ahh the Chadwick's of California. Hey, Mum, how are you?" He smiled and waved into the FaceTime screen to his mother.

"Mackenzie, my pet, are you back at home now from your dangerous mission?" Aurora slipped back to her side of the bed, out of camera view, listening. She took a sip of the tea and found her spot against the headboard. Mack reached out to hold her hand, and she laced her fingers between his and sighed.

"Yes, I am luv, sorry for all the madness. Did you enjoy your time as stars of a *Dragnet* episode?"

"It was quite exhilarating, pet. Pop and I were overcome by all those men who came to squirrel us to safety with their impressive firepower and fancy night goggles. We were about to confess to something, but you know Mummy, my worst is using expired coupons at the Costco these days!"

Aurora was captivated by her thick accent and grinned at the images she was invoking.

"Are you back at home, luv, or have you returned to the interstate, exploring in the mighty trailer?" Mack asked.

"We're back on the road, pet," she said. "Just recently we made camp for the night, thought I'd give you a jingle. We are heading up to San Francisco on this go, we're hoping to catch up to the Billings couple. You might remember they were talking about splitting up last year, but they started a honey farm instead. Not sure what one has to do with the other, but they have real bees and all now and seem inseparable again," she said happily.

"You know we love to play rummy with them, even though Pop loses his drawers most of the time. You know what Mummy always says, 'every hill has its tombstones and every valley its shadows, you don't ever know,'" She looked at Mack carefully from her side of the camera.

"Mackenzie, you seem different, my boy, got the glimmer of the naughty about you, what's it about?" she asked.

Aurora stifled a laugh and whispered, "Tell her I'm shagging a cougar." Mack laughed aloud and was caught dead by his mother.

"Pet, do you have company? I'm so sorry, Mummy's not used to you picking up when you are clearly up to your neck in scamps," she said coyly. Mack brought Aurora under his arm and into the camera to introduce her.

"Mum, meet my Aurora. She is the love of my fucking life," he said with a stunning smile. He kissed her hand ceremonially in view of his mother. "Kitten, I'd like you to meet my mother, Janet Chadwick."

Aurora waved into the camera, "Hello Janet, very nice to meet you." Aurora greeted the older woman and saw where his dark auburn hair originated from.

"My, aren't you a pretty little thing?" Janet exclaimed. "I don't know what spell you've cast on him, but I've never seen him this happy. Unless you count the time the Spice Girls came to Johannesburg. Anyway, keep it up, luv. He looks quite well-bedded. Arthur, Arthur..." Janet called her husband to the screen. "Mack's got himself a real live girlfriend! Come darling, meet her."

Aurora buried her head on Mack's shoulder to stifle her laughter. She whispered to him, "How many dead ones did you introduce to her?" Mack burst out laughing, the two of them with tears streaming from their eyes. Their attempt to suppress their mirth made it worse, to the point where they couldn't control their hysterics.

"Hang on to a branch, woman, I'm coming. Mackenzie?" Arthur appeared in the picture now, adjusting his glasses on his face, "Hello, son. What's this? You capture yourself a lovely bird then?" he asked, skeptically.

Mack held up the iPad for Aurora to meet his stepdad. "Pop, this is Aurora, isn't she fetching?" he smiled adoringly at her. Aurora managed to pull herself together for a second, wave, and say hello.

"Hello lovely girl." Arthur waved back. "My, you are quite charming now, aren't you then? Listen here, blink if you're being held against your will, pretty one. Hmmm, well now, it seems you've got her tangled up, good on you, son," he said. "I'd say it's about time, Mackenzie. We were starting to wonder if you hadn't gone and switched cricket teams as it were and didn't have the sack to tell us."

Aurora and Mack lost it all over again, giggling uncontrollably. Aurora was shaking her head, "Blink if you are being held against your will," she repeated, falling back against the pillows, snorting with mad laughter.

"You know, it would make no mind to us, pet," Janet explained. "We are Californians after all; of course, neither of us care for the taste of kale you understand, but who a bloke pokes is of no concern to us at all. If you find happiness, Mummy wouldn't care if you shacked up with goats."

Aurora ran to the bathroom before she peed her pants.

"I've tried it, Mum, but those pesky goats just chew on the furniture. They aren't much for a nibble on the ball sack." Mack was laughing at Aurora's attempt to get to the bathroom in time.

Aurora was relieved she was on the toilet because the goat thing could have resulted in an accident. She cried out with laughter.

"Oh Mack! Naughty boy!" Janet chuckled. "It seems as if you finally found a keeper, isn't that lekker? Luv, no tequila this time, right? You weren't walking two lines when you nabbed her up then?"

Mack shook his head, "On my name, Mum, no

tequila. I answered a job query for this one. They doled out extra hazard pay for her, and it was well earned. She's a right handful, leaves me good and knackered after she's had her naughty way with me."

"Darling, you are funning with Mummy now, stop you bad boy. I'm tickled to see you this way. I'd love to see you in person, you know, whenever you think you can manage it," she added, trying to lay guilt on her only child.

"I think we could make it happen, maybe after the holidays. I'll drag my captive little minx out there to meet you. I'll chat you up before then, luv, so good to see you both."

Aurora came back into the room to say goodbye. Mack turned the iPad toward her, "Goodbye Janet, Arthur so nice to meet you," she waved.

"You as well, pet, keep up the good work then," Janet waved and disconnected the call.

Mack started to laugh again, "Did you wet your knicks, little girl?" he asked, his eyes roaming over her.

"Almost," she chuckled. "I don't know what came over me, they are such characters." She laughed again. "Well-bedded, I can't even—so funny! Translate the idioms for me, 'hang on to a branch'?" she asked.

"Wait a second," Mack interpreted.

"'Walking two lines'? You've said it to me before."

"Drunk," he replied.

"'Isn't that lekker'?"

"Nice or great news," he answered.

She laughed again, reliving the conversation. "Switched cricket teams, they are fantastic," she sighed.

"It does my heart good to see you laugh, Aurora. Your whole face lights up." He patted the bed next to him. She was wearing a pair of his shorts, a long pink T-shirt printed with cartoons of sleeping puppies all over it, and fluffy pink ankle socks.

"I enjoy these sleepwear combinations," he smiled. "Not a frilly, see-through, wasted thing in the repertoire, eh?" Aurora did a catwalk stroll across the front of the bed and drawled like a Southern debutante, "Try to control yourself, Sailor, I'm singlehandedly bringing sexy back."

He laughed and looked her over admiringly, "Kitten, sexy never left."

She slid into the bed beside him, tucking herself into his solid arms, "I'll find something more enticing to wear to bed, I just don't own anything currently," she said sadly, knowing she'd thrown every piece of lingerie she possessed in the trash days after Ben died.

Mack kissed her succulent mouth, neck, and whispered in her ear, "I have no use for frilly, lacy anything—the only thing I want you to wear to bed is me. You're all the enticement I will ever need… ah, but your tack outfit from New York, shame that," he teased.

She laughed again into his chest. She leaned up to kiss him goodnight and snuggled beside him to sleep. "So, tomorrow is day three, have a big dismount planned?" she snickered.

Mack sighed with contentment. "Let's sleep late. I'll take you to breakfast near the Sea Cove pavilion. We should probably get out of here for a few hours, so let's go shopping and start replacing some of the things you lost in the fire. We do need to pick up strawberries and whipped cream."

Aurora laughed aloud, "You're impossible to satisfy."

He lifted her chin to look at her, his tone more serious. "Not true, you're all I need in the whole fucking world, I'm more than satisfied. I have the image of feeding you cream-dipped strawberries stuck in my head now and I want it. Big difference. And tomorrow I'm taking you on a real date, with expensive food and live music. We can walk on the beach, and then I'm fixing a fire, undressing you slowly, and performing lewd and lascivious acts with you, after I lock the garage door. Unless you have a better idea." He shared with delighted anticipation. Aurora sighed into his chest, "I don't think a better idea exists," she whispered.

"This is the best part of the day," Mack sighed, holding her close to him as he closed his eyes.

Chapter Thirty-Three

The holidays were Aurora's favorite time of year. She loved to cook for a crowd, loved ones gathered around a table happily eating, drinking, and enjoying each other's company.

This would be the second round of holidays without Ben. Nothing was the same without him, yet his absence seemed more noticeable during this time of year. She was worried about the dynamic of the new setting, different circumstances, and new people.

Her late husband loved nothing better than a full house, congregated in celebration. It gave her incredible joy to see him at the head of the table— the gray-haired lion, chief of his pride, observing the family around him. He would sit back with a look of genuine contentment, a glass of scotch in his hand, watching her flutter around, making sure every detail was perfect. He would sneak a sexy glance in her direction, wink, and mouth, "I love you." She knew she would miss him for the rest of her life.

Aurora and Mack worked for days to ready his house for the crowd. He turned a small storage room at the rear of the house into a video game room for her grandsons with new flat screens, Xbox, and gamer chairs along with new controllers.

He cleaned all his guns and rifles and organized them in his locked firearm room.

Aurora had assured him that this would excite Sam. Once he saw the shiny hardware, wood cabinets, work bench, and reloading station, he might ask to move in with them.

She encouraged Mack to discover that one rifle had suddenly developed a problem. Sammy was a military small arms and precision rifle armorer and would take great pride in the ability to identify the problem and know how to repair it. Robbie would be easier, he would enjoy the gun display, but Mack's restored, cherry red '66 Mustang coupe in the garage would inspire an equal reaction. Robert would know every part Mack had searched for to bring the car to its original glory.

They rearranged the living room to hold a long, wide table for the crowd of fifteen.

Aurora covered it with beautiful, fall-colored linens and flowers but saved the place settings for her older granddaughters, as they enjoyed setting the table.

` She was in her head, adjusting cooking times for the menu items, when Mack appeared showered and dressed from the bedroom. He cleared her thoughts immediately with the handsome figure he cut, dressed in jeans and a black turtleneck sweater. He reminded her of the romantic sea captains who starred in the novels she read as a teenager. With a striking mane of dark red hair, matching goatee, and his tall, muscular body—all he needed was a black peacoat and a pipe. She practically purred aloud when she looked at him.

"The house smells incredible, kitten; how are you doing? Anything I can help with?" he asked. Seeing her appreciation of his attire, he leaned in to kiss her sweetly, while admiring her flour-dusted apron with "World's Greatest YiaYia" embroidered across it.

She was worried and anxious. "Mack, how are you holding up? This is such upheaval to your life. You took on my vortex, this holiday, the dogs, and now children in your pristine, quiet house. Were you not content, set in your ways? No dog hair on your expensive furniture, no toddlers near cranberry sauce in your living room in a few hours…"

"….and no goddess in my arms, in my bed, or in my life. No, my beautiful girl, I was not happy without you, and I knew it the second I laid eyes on you," he interrupted. "My life was the first half hour of *The Wizard of Oz*—all black and white. You, Aurora, you are the color and the magic. There is no life without you in it." He kissed her again.

"Would you fancy a dance with me?" he asked like a shy teenager.

He reached on the top of the fridge for a tiny remote and turned on the wireless speakers. Scrolling on his phone, he found what he wanted and hit a button and the entire three rooms filled with the doo wop sounds of The Duprees harmonizing "My Own True Love." He reached out his hand and led her from behind the counter and held her in his arms to dance.

"The Duprees?" she questioned, astonished. "How do you do it?"

"What? Know what you like? I had a dossier on you before I met you," he laughed.

"Swindler." She smiled.

Slow dancing was a way more intimate act to Aurora than sex. At its core, sex was sweaty, primal, and dirty in all the right ways. She wasn't complaining. Yet, slow dancing was erotic, sensual, a paced seduction. Bodies and faces close, arms holding each other, slow movement to the right music was vertical lovemaking.

When she began dating Ben, he asked her not to accept any offers from other men to dance at a wedding or a function they attended together. Her stepsons and her brother were the only exceptions. He told her she was his partner to dance with and others could find their own. She understood completely and though she teased him for being old school, she knew he was right. A couple could convey the nuances in each other's arms to music that words might never express. It was the first thing she missed as a new widow— the idea that she'd never slow dance with the man she loved again.

In this moment, wrapped in Mack's arms in his living room, dancing to her parent's favorite music, was where she fell the rest of the way in love with him. A place she never imagined she would be again. The way he held her close was so protective and loving. How he looked down into her eyes while he led her around the room with infinite adoration and bottomless desire. She had an innate awareness of his body and where it would move next, together in sync, like two raindrops on a window. He sang low into her ear, the perfect words from the song, "No arms but yours… will ever lead me… to heaven's doors."

For Mack, it had been decades since he'd slow danced with a girl, maybe since his high school graduation dance? He couldn't recall. It wasn't something he considered missing in his life. Until now. The idea of holding Aurora in his arms to music, stealing soft kisses from her, had been excruciatingly absent for Mack. Another amazing new experience she brought to his life.

He held her through one more Duprees song, "You Belong to Me," which was one of her favorites. She lifted her face to kiss him. "I'm madly in love with you… I surrender," she sighed. He spun her around, dipped her in his arms, and kissed her passionately. "Welcome to the party, Aurora. I'll give you the clubhouse password tonight." He chuckled. They held each other close, kissing and swaying to the end of the song.

Dutch and Cat quietly entered through the foyer, but they didn't have the heart to interrupt their dance. Cat motioned to advance toward the kitchen, but he held his arm out to hold her back, shaking his head. She looked up at him, puzzled. "Look at her, look how happy she is right now, let her finish," he coaxed.

The song ended and Mack and Aurora emerged from their daze. She brushed the flour dust from his shirt, which had transferred from her apron. Dutch and Cat then entered the room. "Duprees, eh?" Dutch smirked. "This is why you are my number one operative; you use all the intel against the target, don't you, son?"

Aurora laughed and grabbed her brother into a giant hug. He looked her over carefully.

"Less sleepless nights, less tears... you on the turnaround, Tink?" he asked quietly. She nodded in the affirmative. "Benny would be relieved to see you like this—you made him so happy after his sorrow, now it's your turn." He hugged her tight.

Mack reached for his hand to shake, but Dutch surprised him by bringing him in for a hug. "Thank you," he said as he slapped Mack on the back, "she looks wonderful."

Pandemonium descended with the immediate arrival of all their guests. Mack and Aurora made all the introductions. Ken, sadly, would not be joining them as he was traveling with his father; but Quincy and his fiancée, Tara, arrived bearing an assortment of desserts. She was a small, beautiful Asian woman who looked at Quincy like he had invented toasted bread. Aurora greeted her happily, glad to finally meet her. Aurora then unabashedly jumped into Quincy's arms; she had missed the chance to see him off from Echo Lake and was overjoyed to see him again.

"You look fantastic, Miss Aurora, sleeping better?" he asked with a sweet smile.

"Quincy, you big bear, you can drop the

formality, it's just Rory and I'm sleeping quite comfortably, thanks for asking," she kissed his rugged cheek.

"I cannot do it, Miss Aurora, my grandmother would tan my hide if she heard me address a lady any other way."

Aurora introduced them to her family. The last of them to meet Mack were her lovely daughters-in-law. Rhianna, Sam's second wife and mother of Misha, was a tall, long-haired, brown-eyed beauty built like a sleek gazelle. Rhianna was also a police officer, in a smaller town in the suburbs of Philly.

And Natalia, or Tally, Robert's wife, and Ryder's mom. Tally was shorter in stature, sweet like a doll with straight, dark hair and bright hazel eyes. Tally was an ER nurse in their local hospital. All four of them were first responders. Aurora spent many restless nights when something specific had them all working an overnight shift. No wonder she had a heart condition.

Mack, ever the gentleman, greeted them bashfully and handed them both a chilled glass of chardonnay. He then took charge of the men and boys as Aurora and Cat took the girls with them for final preparations. Her grandsons whooped with joy when they saw the gamer room set up for them. They instantly donned headsets and were lost until dinner. Her older granddaughters went to work setting the table, debating loudly which side of the dish YiaYia told them the fork was traditionally placed.

It didn't take long for her son's wives to corner

her in the kitchen. Rhianna and Tally were the daughters she had dreamed of—she often quietly credited and thanked Ben's late wife for sending them to her. They were gifts from heaven. Each of them had warm and loving personalities and the ability to soothe the tumultuous personalities of Ben's sons.

"Aurora!" They besieged her. "That man, my goodness, how do you do it?" Tally asked. "You are two for two on Ralph Lauren models. Right off a magazine cover from a day on the farm photo shoot."

Aurora started to laugh; it was true. Once she stopped to think about it, Ben was in his way a similar type—strong, serious, ranch hand handsome, and incredibly sexy. He had been blessed with thick waves of silver hair, gray mustache and goatee, and eyes of the purest sapphire. It was all in his smirk, his swagger. Back then, she cut to the chase and just handed him her bra the first time he kissed her.

"We are so happy for you, Rory; the boys feel the same as we do. You're too young to spend the rest of your life alone," added Rhianna. Aurora blushed and demurred, she was getting there at her own speed.

Tally and Rhianna had toured the house earlier with Aurora, impressed with the beauty of it. They exchanged knowing looks between them, sure that their mother-in-law would eventually make the living arrangement permanent.

Cat laughed and whispered, "She's all bashful

and coy now, you just wait until she sees him in his uniform at Tieghan's funeral, in those navy dress whites. We should have a cardiologist on call. I was there in the eighties when she saw *An Officer and a Gentleman* the first of ten times. This is going to be classic. She might toss her underwear at him in public." The girls laughed together.

Dutch and Quincy were in front of the television looking for college bowl games and placing friendly bets on their favorites. Tara was teaching Aurora's granddaughters how to make lotus flower napkin folds for the place settings to their wide-eyed fascination.

Mack escorted Sam and Robert to his man cave and watched for their reactions. Robbie shook his head, "My wife is never letting me have a room like this, why God?" he jokingly whimpered. He was openly jealous of the display of assorted weaponry, examining the collection closely. Sam, who never let anyone see him impressed, mostly because nothing ever did, could not hold back a bit of envy when he saw Mack's custom GA Precision Gladius, bolt action 308 sniper rifle, complete with the Nightforce ATACR F1 Scope with Digillum.

"What's the spec on the scope?" Sam asked casually.

"5-25x, 56 millimeter" Mack replied, equally as nonchalant, handing the rifle over to him.

Mack then went in for the kill. "My jewel trigger must be out of alignment, the firing pin is dropping when the bolt closes, scared the fuck out of me on the range. I just closed the bolt on a round, and it fired off about four feet in front of me in the dirt."

Sam smiled knowingly, "Ah, it's nothing but a trigger malfunction, I can stop back next time I'm here and pull the jewel trigger and replace it with a Triggertech 700 diamond two stage, no problem."

Mack perked up, "Really? You wouldn't mind? Figures a HOG would know exactly what was wrong with it," he smiled.

Aurora made it to the doorway for the last remark and tilted her head. "Did you just call my kid a pork product?" she asked.

Sam turned and laughed, "No, HOG stands for Hunter of Gunmen, it's the term for a sniper who kills an enemy sniper in combat. He then has to remove the round from the enemy sniper's chamber—the one meant for him, you know, the one with his name on it."

Mack reiterated, "It's a military superstition. Ultimately, there's one round to end the life of each person, the one with your name on it. Until the round is fired, the person is invincible."

"Exactly," added Sammy, "the sniper carries the round with him at all times, the round can never be fired and therefore leaves the sniper untouchable. I'm gonna stop back next week, Aurora, to fix this for Mack, if it's okay with you?"

"Of course it's okay with me, why wouldn't it be? You know the rules, bring me Dunkin Donuts coffee." she smiled. "Great room, right guys?" she asked.

"Robbie has been crying like a girl because Tally won't let him have one like this, but I'm going to start bringing my luggage here in the morning to live with both of you." Sam laughed. "Aurora, all I want for Christmas is in here, so if you are looking for ideas, just putting it out there," Sam went back to examining the rifle, as Aurora looked up at Mack and winked, job well done.

"Let me know when you show them the garage." She grinned mysteriously.

Sam and Robbie looked at each other as if to say, "More toys?"

The Titans of Chaos warmed up to Mack as well, asking less questions in rapid fire and more inquires of a holiday-themed nature. She recognized the "Christmas-is-coming" marketing campaign. They competed to show him on their phones the latest exciting holiday gift ideas for grandchildren on YouTube. Ryder attached herself to him from the very start; she set up her toy tea set on the plush ottoman and had Mack sit beside her, sipping imaginary tea from little pink cups. Aurora thought she would melt to the spot.

She caught his eye a few times and he smiled up at her proudly. Currently, he was looking more like Kris Kringle than before.

Mack was happier than he had ever been seated at the holiday dinner table. Other than the recent meals he'd shared with his team, he couldn't recall the last time he'd been present around a table with an entire family. The room was filled with laughter and the sounds of conversation, dishes being passed, and the delight of everyone at the smells and tastes of the meal.

Everyone gathered the newbies to each other so quickly. Sam and Robbie, seated down at one end of the table eagerly coaxed combat stories out of Quincy. Dutch and Cat were taunting the children into fits of giggles. Rhianna and Tally discussed wedding details with Tara.

One by one, the grandchildren took turns sitting on Aurora's lap to steal a bite from her dish, kiss her cheek, and complain about their siblings to her. Most began their lament with, "Don't tell my dad." Even her thirteen-year-old grandson changed seats to chat with her and Mack, swapping the name of his secret new girlfriend for the last homemade buttermilk biscuit from her plate.

Mack enjoyed watching her interactions with them. She was patient, attentive, took their complaints very seriously, and offered brief guidance. She loved them unconditionally.

Ryder was the last to approach them and she asked to sit on Mack's lap, instead. Aurora was astounded. Of course, the youngest of them still wanted to eat from Yia Yia's plate but would rather sit with him. He flushed with pride as Aurora gazed at him with sheer amazement.

She had outdone herself. Everything on the menu was amazing. Besides the traditional oven-roasted turkey, Aurora also prepared a beef tenderloin with her signature drunken onion gravy. It was Mack's newest favorite thing, ever. She also cooked many sides: macaroni &

cheese, sweet potato soufflé, cornbread stuffing, homemade cranberry sauce, and a grilled vegetable lasagna.

He moved her into his house, but she instantly made it a home for them both. He sat beside her as she looked out over the room with pride, the ghosts of holidays past floating around her occasionally. Mack ate off her dish as well and she happily picked off his. Occasionally, he held his fork full of something delicious to her mouth and looked lovingly into her eyes as he fed it to her. It was as natural as breathing. Everything did taste better from her plate.

Dinner went off without a hitch, her sons and older grandchildren took on clean up duty as Aurora sat at the counter packing up leftovers for everyone to take home—she had it down to military precision. Sammy fixed her a dirty martini with three olives and put it in front of her, while he and his brother loaded the dishwasher. She made them both a Dewar's on the rocks, and they held a private toast to Ben.

Mack observed their comfortable banter and was amazed. They teased her incessantly and she made them laugh with her quick comebacks. He could see their expressions change as memories of her husband were warmly recalled. The kids all cleared the table and helped to bring out dessert, anxious to get to the pies and cookies. Aurora packed to-go bags for her sons to bring home and prepared two additional ones for Dutch and Quincy.

"Mack, pick a number between thirteen and four," she asked as he approached her at the counter. Not knowing the game, he noticed all the grandchildren were suddenly assembled near her.

"Eight," he replied, wrapping his arms around her waist, and kissing her neck.

"Liam, that's you, Boo Bear." Aurora held up the wishbone from the turkey to her delighted youngest grandson. He twisted the bone in Aurora's hand and Mack could see her rigging the action in Liam's favor. The rest of them groaned and left the kitchen in defeat.

"I did it, YiaYia!" he shouted with glee.

"Make a wish, Boo." She kissed his cheek with delight. Liam squeezed his eyes closed and mouthed something quietly. When he was finished, he threw himself into Aurora's embrace.

Mack tousled his blond hair. "Well done, little man," he exclaimed. Her crew had to leave shortly after dessert to comply with their shared custody schedules. Robbie and Tally wanted to get Ryder home to bed since she had run herself ragged with her cousins. Her boys and the grandkids picked up to leave. Lots of hugs and kisses and promises to get together soon were exchanged as they headed out. Robbie was still shaking his head over the cherry red Mustang.

Dutch, Quincy, and Mack broke down the table and stored it with the extra chairs back in the garage. The couples seemed to sink with contentment into the plush furniture by the fire to enjoy the rest of the day.

"Miss Aurora, this meal, girl, you do not play. I haven't had mac and cheese that perfect in years," Quincy sighed with genuine happiness.

Tara nodded her head in agreement. "Aurora, the drunken onion gravy for the filet, my goodness, it was incredible," she gushed.

"Thank you, both." She smiled. "Lots of leftovers, I packed you a bag."

Aurora was tucked under Mack's arm on the loveseat, nursing her cup of coffee and taking a breath; she had been so worried all day. Now she was happy it went well, and it was over. Mack was glad to feel her body rest against him.

"Kitten, you do make it on days other than Thanksgiving, right? The drunken onion gravy? I'm going to want it on my pancakes in the morning," he joked.

Dutch and Cat came into the room with an open bottle of champagne and six flute glasses from the bar. Aurora looked up and quickly assessed the situation, "No! You did it?" she asked, squealing.

"You know, you are no fun," Dutch feigned a whine, while pouring champagne into the glasses. "Can't put a goddamn thing past you," he complained in jest. The rest of the group were mystified.

"Well, tell the rest of the class," she ordered. Mack took her coffee cup from her as she stood to hug her friend. Shrieking and jumping up and down.

"I asked Cat to marry me, and the crazy ass agreed," Dutch announced. The group erupted in merriment and stood to hug and congratulate them.

"You're really gonna be my sister now," Aurora sighed, holding Cat close to her.

Aurora got to her brother and squeezed him in a hug. "I can't believe this, you swore."

"I know Tink, you swear lots of things when your world drops out from under your feet. You of all people understand this. When Lily died, I never saw myself fifteen years down the road wanting to be with someone else. But time, time does its thing. Besides, fifteen years is a long time doing your own laundry."

Aurora snickered with delight, "You are so bad."

"Little sister, the important thing is, I realized how much time I've wasted being alone, not having a partner, a confidant, and a voice of strength to whisper in my ear when I lay my head down at night. Don't make the same mistake. You've got a really good one here, don't make him wait too long."

"I'm not going anywhere, Dutch, I'm in love with him. I don't need the jewelry, just him."

"You know what I'm telling you. When you're ready, give the man his dignity as he stands beside you. He isn't a prom date. Don't wait fifteen years," Dutch explained. She eyed him with suspicion. Her breath caught as she started to see the picture clearly.

Chapter Thirty-Three

"Dutch? You did this didn't you? It was you...
you put us together," she gasped.

Chapter Thirty-Four

In the early afternoon of New Year's Eve, Aurora hit the send button on the final edit of her new book, *Oceans of Time*. Jen Patterson was waiting on the other end at Haas & Mendelsohn patiently. Together, they rescheduled her remaining appearances for the spring to coincide with the release of the new novel.

Mack had surprised her earlier with his culinary debut by preparing dreamy lemon ricotta pancakes, which he insisted on feeding to her, one sexy mouthful at a time. She hadn't seen him since; he was occupied making a crazy racket in the kitchen after they finished breakfast.

She sat back in her chair and sighed; so much activity had transpired since the afternoon of Tieghan's burial. Christmas in all its frenzy had spun past them as did the amount of work they accomplished in a short time. The renovations at Gull Cove were complete—it was now time to pick paint colors and new furniture.

She looked out on to the private beach, amazed that this was her view now. All the whirling changes in her lifetime, the ocean had always been a constant. Beautiful and powerful. It brought her so much peace to watch the waves rush to the shore.

She heard laughing men heading toward her airy office refuge. Mack entered with her stepson Sam, who carried with him the obligatory cup of Dunkin Donuts coffee to her. He was also balancing a cardboard file box on his hip and placed it on her desk.

"Hey sweetheart, what a nice surprise." She stood to hug him. Back on active duty, his face was completely shaved again, like his head. He looked ten years younger and more and more like a brief glimpse of his father.

"I came to visit Mack's gun, to be sure it didn't miss me." He laughed, hugging her tight and kissing her cheek.

"While I was here, I thought I'd drop off the paint samples for you to start choosing. It looks great over there, at Gull Cove, Aurora. Mack and Dutch did an amazing job and so fast, my head is spinning," Sammy replied.

"Mack, I saw the new gun closet. Nice touch, thanks, man," he said appreciatively.

Aurora looked up at Mack as he sat down next to Sam in front of her desk. He nodded in silent encouragement.

She took a deep breath, "I'm not going to pick out paint colors, sweetheart," she said sadly. "You and your brother, your wives, you will decide on them. I transferred the rest of the insurance money to your checking account to go toward paint, furniture, the rest of the appliances, and this is the deed." She handed him an envelope. "It still requires yours and Robert's signatures, but the house belongs to you both now."

"Wait, what? Why?" he gasped.

"I can't go back, sweetheart; I can't live there again. It was all about your father and me and the dream will always live in my memories. Our plan was to leave it to you boys when we were both gone, and without him, there is no place for me there permanently." Her eyes misted with a flash of melancholy.

"It gives you the luxury to be down here all summer with the children, and they can walk or ride their bikes here to visit with us or have sleepovers with YiaYia. I'm staying with Mack; I know it's crazy and might be too soon and..."

"Aurora." He held his hand up to silence her. "You being here with Mack is fine, but you don't have to give up your house."

"I'm not giving it up, I'm going to see it pass to you and Robbie's hands. Your dad and I both wanted this, and I'm honored to pass the torch on his behalf. It belongs to you and your brother now. If you want to sell it, flip it—anything—you can. I'd be happy if you kept it and spent your summers, maybe even all the holidays, down here. That would be amazing." She paused and smiled at him, "Sam, I know you resist it, but occasionally let me be a mother?"

Sam sat silently holding the envelope, not knowing what to say to her.

"What's in the box?" Mack asked, to break up the quiet.

Sammy stood to open it. "Aurora, I brought you a cold case. I inherited it from the last sergeant to retire who had it passed to him by another one. I'm the fourth supervisor to have possession of it. It is currently assigned to two county-wide detectives. I brought it to you since it's been shuffled around since the early nineties in my police department.

"I'm not sure I'm completely on board that this is what you're best at or not, but it can't hurt for you to look at it," he said seriously. "You are out of the closet now right? No more secret criminal investigations? But not completely a full-time author?" he half smiled. "It could use a fresh set of eyes." He sat back in the chair to give them the summary.

"St. Ignatius Seminary in Wynnewood has had years of disturbing calls and incidents. Young priests have mysteriously gone missing. There are investigative reports, statements, autopsy reports, persons of interest, detective's notes, photos, and collected evidence logs. No one has been able to put the pieces together, and a string of the best detectives I know have worked this case. Recently, the land has been sold to a developer and bizarre things are being unearthed. Signs of dark rituals, possibly human sacrifice. What do you think? You want in?" he asked.

"Sammy, this is fantastic! Of course, I want in. I'll read through it. I'm not sure what I can do, but I'd love the opportunity. Thank you for trusting me." She smiled proudly.

They were interrupted by the sounds of her not-so-graceful brother entering the house. "Tink?

Chapter Thirty-Four

You home?" he bellowed.

"Back here, boss," Mack yelled back.

The dogs went spastic, running and barking at his arrival. Mack pulled up another chair in front of Aurora's desk for Dutch. He hugged and kissed her quickly and shook the hands of the men in front of her. He sat down and took a pause.

"You have the look, Dutch," she said warily. "What did you bring?"

He handed her a confidential folder, perking up the interest of all of them in the room. She looked up in silent inquiry.

"DNA results," he hesitated. "When we got Tieghan's remains returned to us, I had the lab run the DNA anyway against the records I tested on her skull. To be sure it was her. They came back positive as a match to her, that's not our issue. I got a hit on her results for a familial match to us."

"Right, because we are her siblings." She eyed him curiously.

"No Tink, the familial match is to another person. Apparently, we have a half-brother, twenty-eight years old from California."

"What!? How the hell is this possible? Dad had another child after Tieghan died?" she asked in disbelief.

"The hell do I know? It would be around '92, I already graduated out of Parris Island by then and was probably headed to Bosnia. I wasn't around, you were still with them. I haven't confirmed his birthdate yet, but it must have been just a few months before Mom died and then Dad wasn't gone long after her. We need to tighten the timeline. My guess is he never knew about this child."

Mack and Sammy sat silent, stunned with the newest development.

"Dutch, what the hell? How did we not find this?" she asked, putting her glasses back on her face to review the report.

"That's not the fun part. The DNA came back on the ponytail. It's not yours."

"Okay, well that is great news," she interrupted him.

"Is it though? I ran the DNA nationwide, and it came back with a hit. It belongs to Deanna Watkins, also briefly known as, Deanna Egan."

Mack and Aurora froze. Sam shook his head with confusion. "Who is Deanna Egan?" he asked innocently.

Mack stared at Dutch, bewildered. "My ex-wife?" his voice dipped down.

Dutch nodded, "Believe me buddy, I made them run it again, because it couldn't be true, but it is."

"How? Where? Jesus, Dutch, I haven't seen her since I signed the papers, twenty-five years ago. It was days before I even left for boot camp at Great Lakes. She couldn't possibly know where I am or who Aurora is. She had a serious alcohol and drug problem; I'm surprised she's still alive."

"I'm relatively sure she didn't remove her own ponytail and nail it to the remains of Aurora's shed on her own. Where she fits in is the puzzle. I have Kai digging. Her last known address was in Nevada, so we are going to find her and try to figure out what play is afoot here," Dutch said with confidence.

They all sat in quiet contemplation for a moment.

"Well, Happy Fucking New Year," Sammy laughed. "Seems like you guys can fire up the Scooby Doo Mystery Machine again after the ball drops tonight."

"No shit," Aurora sighed. She smiled up at her stepson and saw the intrigue and lingering disbelief he had about Aurora's involvement in non-grandmotherly pursuits. She caught his eye and bit her bottom lip, "You want in?" she asked her son on the sly.

Standing next to her behind the desk he returned her gaze, "I'm not sure I can handle the fun you people get caught up in," he laughed.

Dutch took a breath and asked Mack, "What's the kitchen project you started?"

"It's actually finished, let's show Aurora."

They made their way from the office, down the corridor to the open kitchen, where she saw it immediately. Mack had removed the entire backsplash behind the stove and re-tiled it. The expensive Italian ceramic was exquisite. The tiles fit together to create a hand-painted picture. In the center were a bouquet of blue cornflowers, bordered by vines of lush, green leaves bearing clusters of lemons. At the very top of the rectangle, settled in the center was the surviving piece of tile from her Gull Cove kitchen, restored and placed at the keystone.

"Mack!" she gasped. "What did you do?" she beamed up at him.

Dutch and Sammy exchanged looks and declared in unison, "What a suck up!" as they laughed together. She approached the area to inspect it closely. It was so beautiful she started to cry. Her old piece of tile sat perfectly at the pinnacle and accented the rest of the display.

"My God, how did you find this?" she whispered in awe.

Dutch and Sammy made moves to leave. They made plans for more consultations together to unravel the things both men had left on her desk. Hugs, handshakes, and salutations left them alone in the kitchen.

"Thank you for this, it's stunning," she said as she rushed into his arms. He held her close and kissed her. "This is your home, Aurora, I want you to have what your heart desires in every way. You are everything my heart desires," he said lovingly.

She kissed him again. "I love you," she sighed.

He led her to sit with him before the fireplace. "I have something else for you." He handed her a small velvet box. She took it and looked into his eyes nervously.

"Don't worry, it's not what you think," he assured.

She opened it to find a brilliant two carat diamond pendant in the shape of a perfect teardrop, attached to a white gold chain. He quickly fastened it around her neck. It sat flawlessly just below the base of her throat.

"Aurora, I couldn't make wine from your tears, so I turned one into a gemstone. I'm going to ask you to marry me every day for the rest of my life. Whatever you decide, would you do me the honor of wearing my diamond here?" he asked, kissing the spot below where the pendant sat.

"I am yours; you are mine, forever," he whispered. She kissed him back and nodded in agreement. "Mack, it's magnificent. Thank you. Yes, my beautiful man, I will proudly wear it. You are mine; I am yours, forever," she vowed.

Epilogue

Laying Tieghan to rest...

Mack left early to pick up his men, so Aurora, accompanied by Dutch and Cat, drove into the cemetery following the hearse. Courtesy of Sam, twelve members of the elite highway patrol team escorted them.

The officers wore crisp dress blues, poised above their motorcycles, with the roar of their engines and lights flashing, driving slowly, led the hearse to its destination. As they exited their cars and made their way up the path to the gravesite, Madeline, Aurora's oldest granddaughter, grabbed her hand. "YiaYia watch this," she whispered. Aurora turned to watch the motorcade park. They reversed and backed up to the curb in a forty-five-degree angle, in alignment. Once parked, the entire unit dismounted from their chariots and stood at attention.

Aurora was awestruck with the pageantry and detail. Madeline whispered, "Isn't it sexy?" she laughed quietly and hugged her. "About as sexy as it gets, cupcake."

Madeline joined the row of seats with her father and his wife, also dressed in their police dress uniforms, and the rest of her siblings. Robert, wearing his fire department dress uniform, arrived with wife Tally and little Ryder and they all sat behind Aurora.

Though the mood was solemn, there were no more tears for Tieghan Rose Velarde. It was a ritual of closure for the living that had been a long, hard time coming. Before the casket was closed, Aurora tucked her authentic Tinker Bell wand and a brand new, stuffed baby sea turtle into the casket with her remains. Dutch had her skull exhumed and placed it with the box that was returned to them by the Archangel Michael. Her earthly body was reunited to be interred in peace.

They sat in the first row of chairs across from the tiny white casket. Aurora dressed in a new black dress, imprinted with tiny sunflowers. Dutch had donned his Marine dress uniform which, he proudly noted, still fit.

Filing into the row with Aurora, Dutch, and Cat, came Mack, Quincy, and Ken. Scattered throughout the remaining rows were most of the Trident team and military vets from the area.

Though in traditional funeral protocol the Navy SEALS would wear their service dress blues, for this off-book ceremony the men of Trident wore their summer dress whites.

The priest arrived to begin the short service. At any funeral, Aurora tended to get lost in her thoughts of Ben. Her mind far away, she suddenly recalled the words of St. Michael. He assured her she would see signs from Ben among the children.

"YiaYia," Ryder whispered loudly behind her. "Mack has wadybugs!" she gushed with joy.

Aurora turned to look at the excited, adorable

toddler as she was pointing to Mack's right shoulder. Ryder discovered there were a pair of ladybugs perched atop his shoulder epaulets.

"He sure does, sweet pea." she whispered back.

"YiaYia, you wuv wadybugs," she reminded her.

"I do, very much. Thank you for finding them for me." Aurora smiled, leaning back to kiss her sweet, chubby hand that rested on Mack's back.

"Aurora," Tally whispered. "It's November, where would they have come from?"

"Poppy sent them," Ryder whispered loudly again. Aurora and Tally exchanged looks.

"He did, sweet pea?" Aurora asked in awe.

"He's happy, you smile now," Ryder explained, her little face alight, Aurora touched her cheeks sweetly.

Her heart filled to overflowing. She closed her eyes to hide the tears and silently thanked her amazing husband for his approval.

She opened her eyes to look up into Mack's splendid face. He turned to look at her, assessing her reaction after checking on his two tiny stowaways. The uniform made him glow—a glorious champion in a dark universe. His hat was perched atop his head, with curls of red hair peaking from the back rim.

The ribbons and medals affixed on each side of his chest in straight rows reminded her of the dangerous chances he took for her freedom. It all made her weak to be in the proximity of his power.

She murmured into his ear, "Who carved you? Michelangelo?" He reached for her hand and brought it to his lips gently to kiss.

The priest read prayers over Tieghan's small coffin, and a Marine bugler played "Taps" in the distance.

By far the most dramatic sight, the one that did bring tears to everyone's eyes, was when each SEAL member in attendance removed their gold Budweiser or Trident pin and tacked them into the top of her tiny casket. Ten in all stepped up individually to her coffin and performed this act. By doing so, they acknowledged that she was one of them, and the pins would go with her until they would all be gathered together again.

The living would now mourn with the primary symbol of their brotherhood gone until the dead was buried. It was the highest honor the service team performed for the fallen. Mack was the last, thumping his pin at the head of her casket. He gently bent to kiss the coffin and whispered, "Rest now, little mermaid."

Aurora could hear Sam and Robert behind her, in hushed voices, explaining the tradition to their children. Their voices were heavy with respect and emotion. Her sons each reached to touch her on the shoulder in silent support. Aurora almost burst with pride and gratitude.

Dutch clasped Aurora's hand in his. "It's done, Tink." They wrapped their pinkies together and then released them in a ceremonial finality. It was full circle from the day they locked pinkies in a vow at their parents' grave to bring Tieghan justice and peace.

After the casket was lowered into the ground they walked away together toward their cars to head to a luncheon in Tieghan's honor.

Dutch and Cat were the first to go along with the rest of their team. Her kids and grandkids had to return home for work and school, and so she showered them with hugs, kisses, and appreciation for their attendance.

Aurora's hand in Mack's, they walked to his truck as she eyed his uniform.

"Mack?" she whispered when they were alone. Her eyes raked over him, like a hungry animal.

"Kitten?" he whispered back.

"Don't take this the wrong way or anything but try not to mess up the uniform at lunch. I have a whole Navy SEAL/bad girl scenario pictured for later," she smiled, half her bottom lip between her teeth.

"What is it with you bad girls and the dress whites?" he asked, turning on to the highway. "I could not get pissed on if I was on fire wearing the blues but put the ice cream man uniform on and you girls are soaking your denims."

"Navy dress whites," she sighed in ecstasy, the hem of her dress riding up her smooth legs and her hands gripping her full breasts.

"Woman, I will wear them every night if you react this way." He could barely keep his eyes on the road. Suddenly, she was blooming like a ripe, juicy peach beside him. The neckline of her dress revealed the slightest glimpse of her delicious cleavage, suddenly flushed pink.

"Baby, pull over somewhere, we can be late for lunch," she purred provocatively, sliding her hand between his legs to compel her request.

"Are you yanking my choke?!" he asked, shocked. But she used the magic word. Mack's entire body reacted to her lusty voice and how she used it when she called him "baby."

"Precisely what I'm suggesting. I'm not kidding, pull in somewhere private," she urged, removing her seatbelt, and kicking off her shoes.

Mack quickly found a deserted industrial park and screeched around the back to position the truck so that it was unseen from the road. He shut the engine, tore off his seatbelt, and reached for his zipper. Aurora swiftly removed her underwear from beneath her dress and climbed over the console to straddle his lap. She started to kiss him roughly as she kept her legs above his so that he could undo his fly.

"You sexy lunatic," he roared, freeing himself from his pants and grabbing her ass to assist in the maneuvering.

"Permission to come aboard?" she asked, staring into his bewitched expression.

"You randy little tiger, you want me to fuck you? You got it," he growled, finding the right position, and nailing the target. His hands gripped her hips as he supported her in the saddle. He buried his face between her tits and grunted like a mad boar lumbering uphill. It didn't take them long to accomplish the objective, her ass only pressing the horn on the steering wheel one or two times.

In a flash, the voice of the old Roman gypsy fortune teller repeated in his head. Aurora was his strength and by far his only weakness. He could not get his fill of her and currently, he was balls deep. She rode atop him, hot and hungry.

Her voice, low and husky, taunted him, "Is this what you like? Does this turn you on? C'mon sailor… more… harder… come inside me and take me with you," she blew hot in his ear. He couldn't speak, consumed by her intensity and wanting to continue to thrust inside her until he lost consciousness. He was so turned on by how aroused she was and the way she used her voice to bring him home.

"Aurora," he huffed, "I'm taking you with me." His body was a raging volcano ready to blow.

"Let go, Mack. Lose yourself inside me," she groaned.

Together they experienced their accelerated lust and great love with such force that they imagined the truck would melt from the inferno.

Out of breath and sapped, he gasped, "Bloody hell, Aurora!" He looked her over proudly, admiring her breathless, satisfied body. He reached up to touch the wet tendrils of her hair stuck to her flushed cheeks. "Who knew all it took was the uniform?" he laughed. "This information would have saved some time, I'm just saying," he teased.

"Anchors aweigh, my friend." She kissed him again before she climbed off. She fell back against the seat, wasted. "Next time you're in town, Sailor, give me a jingle," she laughed. They did the best they could to straighten their appearance before they entered the restaurant, using napkins and hand sanitizer.

"Well, there's another first," he said quietly, zipping up his pants.

He opened her door and helped her out of the truck, then leaned her against the vehicle and kissed her deeply. She slid her hand between his legs and whispered, "Ready to cast off again?"

"I am so fucking in love with you," he sighed, touching his forehead to hers.

She straightened his jacket, buttoning his top button for him. "All the worse for you, my beautiful man; I feel the very same way about you," she exhaled with contentment.

Naturally, it was Cat who was near the entrance and the first to greet them as they arrived behind the rest of the guests. She stood inside the doorway of the restaurant shaking her head.

"Seriously?!" she smirked. "Where are your panties? Tell me right now!" she demanded under her breath.

"In my handbag," Aurora grinned wickedly.

"Navy fucking dress whites," they laughed together as Mack ducked into the men's room to clean up.

A sneak peek at Book Two...

THE CORIOLIS EFFECT

Dana G. Devine

BOOK TWO
OF THE TRIDENT TEAM TRILOGY

A sneak peek at Book Two...

Preface

The Coriolis Effect

The Coriolis effect is an "apparent" effect, an illusion produced by a rotating frame of reference. This type of effect is also known as a fictitious force or an inertial force. The Coriolis effect occurs when an object moving along a straight path is viewed from a non-fixed frame of reference. Typically, this moving frame of reference is the Earth, which rotates at a fixed speed. When you view an object in the air that is following a straight path, the object will appear to lose its course because of the rotation of the Earth. The object is not actually moving off its course. It only appears to be doing so because the Earth is turning beneath it.

Coriolis effect affects everything not firmly attached to the Earth's surface. It affects fluids, like air and water as well as floating and flying objects like ships, airplanes, and bullets.

Military snipers sometimes have to consider the Coriolis effect. Although the trajectory of bullets is too short to be greatly impacted by Earth's rotation, sniper targeting is so precise that a deflection of several centimeters could injure innocent people or damage civilian infrastructure.

A sneak peek at Book Two...

Prologue

Lenore *First to Dance* Sandoval-Tobin was a patient woman. She learned from very young, raised among the thinned herd of her native tribe, to wait was to know sure conquest.

She was stalking her prey. A ridiculous little East Coast girl who turned her son's head, took apart Lenore's life and her beautiful family. Lenore blamed Aurora for every storm cloud which filled her sky. The silly girl was directly responsible for Lenore's only love to die violently and among strangers. Her beautiful only child to languish in a rotten prison. To steal their livelihood and call it a crime. Lenore would wait until the time was right to take Aurora's happiness away with her own hands. Dying was too painless a retribution. Lenore wanted her to witness what she loved die in front of her eyes. This would be worth the wait for Lenore.

She herself would not succumb to her own journey to the other side until her revenge was realized. The spirits of those who had gone before her, lingered in her doorways. Her body was wracked with cancer and disease, but the idea of finishing off that cheap little tease, kept life on this side of the veil for Lenore.

Lenore's ancestors had suffered for years from their native lands and homes being stolen over and over again by governments. By the time Lenore was old enough to understand there was an entire world outside her community, her society was forced to move again. To wear strange clothes and speak strange words.

She met her husband, William Tobin at her first English speaking school. Descended from the Norse men of Europe, he was tall, light-eyed and mesmerizing in all the differences he was to her. Lenore was short and rounded, long flowing black hair, darkest brown eyes. Lenore broke her family's hearts.

Her father, Chief *Morning Light* Sandoval was the leader of their tribe and the council of their elders. He forbade Lenore to associate with Bill Tobin, much less run off and marry him. Lenore defied her upbringing and left everything she had ever known behind to be with Bill.

Lenore knew where Aurora was, she followed her quietly like the shadow of a crow. Slowly she gathered information about her. She knew there was a predisposition for bits of Aurora's life to be concealed, but Lenore had the vision of her ancestors wrapped around her and would strike when all the stars positioned, and the right moon was waxing in the sky. The arms of her sundial were creeping up on Aurora, and it gave Lenore great pleasure. Her long wait was coming to an end.

Chapter One

Case #PA-107902809-St. Ignatius Seminary-Wynnewood, PA.

The dusty cardboard box containing over three decades of cold case investigative notes and files had been haunting Aurora for weeks as it sat next to her desk. The ghosts inside were restless to be heard.

Her stepson, Sam, had brought it to her requesting her insight. Insight he was still undecided in his belief she could provide. Aurora was his father's second wife--his widow, and the grandmother to his and his brothers children. His image of her was difficult to alter.

Aurora had finally confessed to him, though her master's degree was in English Literature and put her publicly on the path to teach high school students, and ultimately become a bestselling author. Her secondary master's was in Criminal Justice and Forensic Psychology. It was not something she advertised or divulged on resumes during her career. It had been acquired to bring justice to her baby sister, who died after suffering years of heinous torture and sexual abuse. Convinced finally with this information, Sam agreed to introduce her to the two detectives who were currently assigned to the thirty-year-old cold case. They were scheduled to meet for lunch in a few weeks and it was time for Aurora to do her homework.

The house was empty, Mack and her boys were spending the day at the gun range, and she had enough time on her hands to begin.

For close now to almost thirty years, she worked with her brother in secret. Dutch Jenson was a former Marine, former CIA trained special operative and also a forensic profiler. After her master's degree Aurora learned quickly and developed an instinct for it. Her concentration had been primarily on child predators, immersed in their psyches, patterns and routines.

The incidents at St. Ignatius Seminary were proving to take her down a new dark path. As she disappeared into the mystery, she was finding the shades of ancient religious practices and the instruments of dark rituals. A world most normal policemen and women didn't typically look for or recognize in their daily investigative work. A world Aurora saw clearly.

About the Author

Dana Giovinetti-Devine by her own admission is a 'late bloomer'. Married for the first time at age forty-three and instantaneously gifted with stepsons and grandchildren she lived happily with her family in Delaware County, Pennsylvania.

After suffering the agonizing loss of her husband, she packed her things and her two spoiled Cavalier King Charles Spaniels; Dash & Chima and moved to the southernmost point in New Jersey with this manuscript under her arm.

Just like a baby sea turtle herself, she fled to the shelter of the ocean's proximity.

Dana has been a corporate meeting and event planner for almost thirty years and has returned to writing after toying idly with it for ages.

She loves her cozy home at the Jersey shore, good books, iconic movies, legendary music, the occasional glass of whiskey and cooking for her friends and family.